MY DADDY WAS
A BANK ROBBER

Eddie Warke

Michael Terence
Publishing

First published in paperback by
Michael Terence Publishing in 2022
www.mtp.agency

Copyright © 2022 Eddie Warke

Eddie Warke has asserted the right to be identified as
the author of this work in accordance with the
Copyright, Designs and Patents Act 1988

ISBN 9781800943087

No part of this publication may be reproduced, stored
in a retrieval system, or transmitted, in any form or
by any means, electronic, mechanical, photocopying,
recording or otherwise, without the prior
permission of the publisher

Cover images
Copyright © VectoraA, TopVectors
www.123rf.com

Cover design
Copyright © 2022 Michael Terence Publishing

This book is dedicated to
Miranda
My wife & best friend.

Part One

Bank Robber

"My Daddy was a bank robber,
And he never hurt nobody,
He just loved to live that way,
And he loved to steal your money."

The Clash

Prologue One

Belfast, Northern Ireland
Sunday 6th October 1968

"Where's my boots?" shouted Jimmy.

He waited at the top of the stairwell, swaying rhythmically to the sound of the Beatles Hey Jude booming at almost full volume from his radio. Almost full volume was as good as it went without getting distortion and crackling through the transistors single speaker. Jimmy loved the song, in fact he liked most music no matter what the style, and in 1968 there were many new sounds and even more new styles. He wasn't singing "Hey Jude" though, but was adlibbing his own version of "Hey Jules in anticipation of his first date tonight with Julie Bennett.

"Hey Jules, don't make me sad, just take me out and make me glad." Jimmy didn't know as he sang that Paul McCartney had originally written the song as "Hey Juls" in an effort to console John Lennon's five-year-old son Julian following the separation of Lennon from his then wife Cynthia when he left her for Yoko Ono. McCartney later changed it to "Hey Jude" when he thought it sounded better.

Jimmy also didn't know that at that same moment Julie was listening to the same radio station and singing along to the same song, correct words though, as she too got ready for their first date. She had been dreaming of this night for months, which was yet another fact that Jimmy wasn't aware of. He had spent the last two months since starting work at the Co-op as a trainee manager, where they both worked, and making excuse after excuse and purchase after purchase so that he could go through the checkout where Julie sat for four hours every day. One morning she had commented that she liked his shoes,

"They're pointed toe Beatle boots," Jimmy said as he looked down at his feet. Julie followed his gaze. "They've got Cuban heels just like Paul McCartney's," he added.

"Brown's lovely," said Julie.

"Tan," Jimmy corrected quickly, "the brown ones are darker. I liked these ones as they go better with my suit." Jimmy stalled then and looked up at Julie, blushing slightly and hoping that she liked his trousers with his boots. His younger brother Billy constantly ridiculed Jimmy's fashion and his mod image, calling him a "faggott", which was a derogatory word for a gay man, used then, but frowned upon today.

Julie smiled and then said, "Yes, I love your trousers too," then added with a sparkle in her brilliant blue eyes, "tight aren't they!"

Jimmy's blush deepened, but thankfully he was then rescued by the customer behind him in the queue when she said.

"You moving along there love? Some of us don't have all day you know."

Jimmy took his change and moved on. Later that morning he waited on Julie finishing her shift on her checkout and caught up with her when she was getting her things from her locker.

"Hello again," he said. She smiled but said nothing. After a few seconds of silence, Jimmy said, "These boots like to dance. Do you?"

It didn't take long for Jimmy's nerves to settle, even though at first Julie didn't answer, but her widening smile gave her response away and told Jimmy all he wanted to know before she spoke a word.

Julie glanced to the door of the staff room to check if anyone else was there, her Dad in particular as he was the store manager. Satisfied they were alone she eventually answered "I love dancing." Then with a giggle she added "just don't stand on my toes with those boots."

Their first date was arranged. The only issue for now though was that Jimmy couldn't find those beloved Chelsea "Beatle" boots.

"Mum," Jimmy shouted. No response again. Hey Jude was fading on the radio and the DJ then announced it was time now for the six o'clock news.

Jimmy listened for noise downstairs in the small terrace house in east Belfast and hearing nothing decided to give up on his mother and called for his younger brother, "Billy. Billy are you there?"

As he waited for a response, really not wanting to go downstairs as he had no shirt on, the presenter on the radio began to announce the news.

"Police have condemned the rioting that took place in Londonderry last night following trouble at a civil rights demonstration in Duke Street in the city. Several Police Officers were injured, along with several of the protestors and Police say they have made several arrests. Local politicians and leading figures have appealed for calm. We will cross over to our reporter on the ground, Eamonn Lynch in a moment. In other headlines a security guard is critically ill in hospital following an armed robbery at the Northern Bank's city centre branch at Donegal Square in Belfast. It is reported that 4 armed and masked men fired several shots before making away with an undisclosed sum. Two people were also injured when the bank robber's getaway car collided with their car. Their injuries are reported as minor and both are receiving treatment in hospital. We will cross over to our reporter David Dyke, who is at the scene, later in this bulletin."

With no response Jimmy sighed and started downstairs. He found both his mother and Billy in their kitchen where they too had the radio on and the presenter was continuing on with the news. Jimmy's Mum was feeding clothes through the mangle and collecting the subsequent water being squeezed from them in a bucket. Billy was sitting at their fold-away table with his elbows resting on the one half opened table top and his head resting in his hands, which nervously ruffled his hair. Jimmy sensed that their conversation had stopped abruptly with his entrance to the room.

"What's up?" he asked.

His Mum continued rotating the handle of the mangle and seemed happy to remain facing backwards to him. Billy just glared his eyes almost wild and his pale face expressing guilt or nervousness, or maybe both. He seemed agitated and fidgety, his demeanour coiled like a tight spring about to explode.

"What's up," Jimmy repeated, then looking at his brother he said "you look like you're going to shit yourself!"

"Fuck off," Billy spat back lowering his head, which Jimmy thought was quite submissive and unusual for his younger brother who wasn't slow or backward at being aggressive towards Jimmy. He didn't know though that Billy was trying to hold back tears that he didn't want his older brother to see.

Jimmy heard a tut from his mother, probably in protest of the swearing, but she never spoke to chastise as she normally would. Just wanting to get ready to go out with Julie he gave up all interest as to what was going on between his brother and his mother and asked, "Do you know where my boots are?" As he asked he glanced below the table at his brother's feet to establish if that solved his quest, but even though it wasn't unusual for his kid brother to borrow his boots, or clothes for that matter, despite the fact that he slagged them off when it suited him, but he was innocent on this occasion as Billy was in his bare feet.

"They're upstairs," his mother said. "I left them on the landing yesterday."

"Well they're not there now, Will," Jimmy replied as he turned to leave. Back upstairs and in his room he bent down to search under his bed. The news had finished on the radio and the new song from Jimmy James and the Vagabonds, "Red Red Wine" was now playing. I'll have some red wine myself tonight if I can ever get ready and out the door Jimmy thought as he pulled out his guitar case in search of his illusive boots. Dust bunnies and half of his old broken drum stick were all that he found. Getting back to his feet he went in to his brother's room, which despite being the younger brother he had the larger of the two bedrooms, which actually highlighted a lot about the dynamics in this small terrace house where the three of them lived. Being larger it gave room for more of a mess and Billy took full advantage of this. The floor was littered with magazines and clothes, two shirts Jimmy noticed belonged to him. Alas though despite being a mess it was clear to see that the boots weren't there. He bent down to look under his bed and bingo spotted his beloved boots just under the opposite side of the bed. Jimmy started to move stuff aside so that he could get at his boots when his hand hit something hard and heavy, which was wrapped up in what seemed like an old sweater. Jimmy pulled the object out from under the bed to examine it further but even before he unwrapped it he knew what it was. The black barrel of a gun was protruding from the neck of the jumper. Jimmy's heart beat quickened. He removed the weapon from its covering and held it in his hand, careful and nervous to ensure he handled it properly. Jimmy had never held a gun before and even though it was smaller than he would have imagined it still sat big and awkward in his hand and he totally respected how deadly this small black thing could be.

"What the fuck is this doing here?" he whispered to himself almost in a sigh. Other questions began to flood his mind. He knew his younger brother fancied himself as a bit of a lad, but a gun? He knew the group his brother hung around with imagined themselves as being in some sort of a gang. The Woodstock Tartan or something like that they called themselves. Careful to keep his fingers well away from the trigger he opened the barrel. The slick mechanism opened smoothly on its hinges to reveal a cylinder with some empty holes and some full ones. Rotating the barrel he counted 3 bullets. He closed the barrel again and lifted the gun to his nose. He didn't actually know what smell he was looking for but what he smelt was Smokey. Did this mean that the gun had been fired recently, or was this just how guns smelt. Only one way to find out.

Holding the gun in his hand by the handle, but again careful to keep his fingers all away from the trigger he stood up and headed downstairs to see his little brother once more. He'd forgotten all about the music on the radio, and for now about his pending date with Julie. As he descended the stairs the front door knocked with a purposeful knock. Assuming it was one of Billy's eejit gang; Jimmy continued up the short hallway and opened the door. Two uniformed policemen stood at the threshold, which took Jimmy somewhat by surprise. Before he recovered himself he noticed the nearest policeman to him glance down to Jimmy's right hand, which was holding the gun.

Shouts filled the small hallway. Jimmy was rocked back violently as one of the policemen grabbed his right arm, twisting it away and behind Jimmy while the second policeman bulldozed him to the floor.

The next few seconds were a total blur

The next few days were a total nightmare.

The next few weeks would present Jimmy the biggest challenge of his life.

The next few years were going to be a total waste of a good man's life.

Prologue Two

Belfast, Northern Ireland
Tuesday 15th October 1968

Nine days later Jimmy sat in a smokey visitor's room waiting on a visit from his mother. The room was dark and cold and miserable. Two armed guards stood abreast at each of the two doors. One door leading to the outside world where the visitors entered and the other door leading back in to hell.

Every other prisoner, apart from Jimmy, was smoking at their tables. This was a good time to smoke as your visitor was duty bound to top up your cigarette supply and therefore it was the one day when you didn't need to consider rationing. Jimmy sat slumped in his seat, his tired bones almost unable to support his weight. He hadn't slept properly since his arrest and his frayed nerves constantly buzzed in his ears. His pale complexion framed by his unusually untidy hair along with his sunken cheeks totally transformed his looks as good as a Halloween disguise. In almost every way, and in only nine days, he had changed from the good looking confident young man that had eventually asked Julie out on a date. He doubted she would go out with him now.

Not that he had the freedom to actually go anywhere.

His arrest had been swift and following a search of his house, which found a large part of the stash stolen from the Northern Bank the previous day hidden in his guitar case, the charges issued against him soon followed. His protests of innocence were ignored and his alibi was non existent as he had spent the most of that day as his day off work, listening to music in his room.

He had asked to see his brother, but that hadn't happened. He hadn't asked to see his mother as he hadn't wanted to bring her to this place and even though he knew of his own innocence he still felt ashamed to be here and didn't want to share that shame with her. When the guard had told him this morning that his mother was visiting it almost made him physically sick. Now he was nervous and dreading to see the woman he adored walk through the door just ten feet in front of him.

Almost as he thought it though she was there. She too looked nervous and almost diminished in size. The guard showed her to the seat across the table from Jimmy and as she sat down he said, "You've got twenty minutes left of visiting time love," then walked back to his station beside his colleague at the door.

For some time neither Jimmy nor his mother spoke, then Jimmy spoke quietly.

"You OK Mum?"

She continued to look down at the table refusing to meet his pleading eyes. This reminded him of a scene in their living room that had taken place many, many years before.

Jimmy's father, Clarence Ruddock, although Jimmy wasn't certain if that actually was his real name, was a drunk, a gambler, a woman beater and a cheat. He had deserted from the army and would eventually desert them also. Clarence had the good looks of the gods, but the soul of the devil. Most women couldn't resist his charm and handsome face and some also liked his devilish behaviour. Maybe they thought they could tame his fiendish ways?

Six weeks following his conscription in to the army in early 1940 he deserted and fled to Scotland. Here he lived for six years, four with his first wife Nelly to whom he had two children, Charlie and Bonnie and two years to his second wife Catherine to whom he had one child Kenneth. Both relationships ended when his money and credit ran out, his debts caught up and his affairs discovered. His love of Scotland now depleted the Bigamist fled again and this time across the sea to Northern Ireland.

With new lines of credit now available it wasn't long before Clarence found himself in the arms, and house as luck would have it as his new love Margaret's parents had both passed away and left their house to her.

Margaret fell pregnant and so wedding bells soon chimed for Clarence again. But the ringing had barely stopped before he embarked on his first affair. Once again the unpaid debts mounted and the dark side of Clarence became the norm. Heavy drinking, reckless gambling in an effort to chase his losses and various scams in the hope of scheming up some money, as he most definitely didn't want to work for it. When

Jimmy was two years old along came his younger brother Billy. Board of the mundane tasks of once again raising and supporting a family Clarence took to bouts of disappearing for months on end. This was followed by an emotional return where forgiveness was given for free. The drinking and gambling continued and the debts mounted. Jimmy's mother would borrow on the house and pay Clarence's debts, much to his appreciation, but then Margaret began to innocently enquire what he was doing with all this money, much to Clarence's annoyance. This was when the beating started.

At first it was controlled to the point that Clarence was careful not to hit Margaret anywhere that anyone else would notice, but it didn't take long before this also, like most other of Clarence's traits became reckless and out of control. Even at the tender young age of six Jimmy could see what was going on, but when he spoke to his mother about it he was the one that got scolded. He couldn't understand why he was the one who was scolded, that was until he was much older, when it was too late, and he understood fully why his mother had taken her frustrations out on him.

One terrible night Jimmy awoke to shouting and screaming coming from downstairs. He quickly arrived at their living room door to find his mother lying on the floor, her face covered with blood. Her left arm was twisted at an awful angle and it looked to Jimmy as if it had came away from her shoulder. It almost made Jimmy sick. His father, unaware that his oldest son was there, was swearing and rambling on an incessant rant, "Nosey bitch, bitch, nosey fucking bitch," As Clarence staggered around his wife's inert body Jimmy realised suddenly that his father was steadying himself to kick her. Jimmy ran to the fireplace, grabbed the poker in both hands and swung it towards his father with all of his strength. It landed on his shoulder and glanced off to his head. Clarence went down. Jimmy feared for several seconds that he had killed him. It was then that he saw that his mother was indeed conscious and staring straight at him, but it wasn't a look of gratitude, it was a look of total disgust.

Several curses informed Jimmy that his father was still alive. Some time later, how long Jimmy wasn't sure his father forced himself to his feet where he stood staring at his son.

"You little bastard," he slurred. "Is this the respect I get?"

Jimmy still held the poker, although he didn't intend to do anything else

My Daddy Was a Bank Robber

with it as his madness was over for one night. As he stood there watching his father he noticed the cowardice in him through his eyes. Even though he was spitting out angry, nasty words, there was actually fear there. Why wouldn't there be, Jimmy thought. A man afraid of work, only willing to hit a woman, and now standing here showing fear towards a six-year-old boy.

"You're pathetic!" Jimmy said strength in his voice.

For some time the room remained in silence and during this time Jimmy could see his father before him wither. His mother must have noticed it as well as she began to sob and cry, "No, don't go. No don't leave me."

Jimmy watched as she tried to turn to face her husband despite her many injuries, but before she could turn to see him Clarence left without a word. When Jimmy looked back at his mother she was looking at him, and the look broke his heart.

Sitting here now in this visiting room Jimmy knew that when his mother eventually looked up at him she would hold that same look in her eye.

Several minutes later she raised her gaze from the table and her look devastated him.

In an effort to reflect from her glare, he said, "I didn't do it. I didn't do it Mum." His voice almost wavered and gave away how close he was to tears but he knew he couldn't allow that to happen here. Not here he would be destroyed for it.

As he focused on controlling himself he almost didn't hear when his mother said softly.

"I know."

He did notice though that after she had said it she nervously looked around to make sure that no one else had heard her.

Jimmy was confused. In one way he was delighted to hear her agree with his innocence, but in another way she didn't seem to share his delight. He didn't know if it was his thoughts of the past dredging up old emotions that were blurring his senses.

Her next words though cut through his confusion like a hot knife through butter, or his heart.

"Billy can't do this." She nodded to their surroundings. "He wouldn't survive." She looked away then unable to hold Jimmy's eye any longer.

"But Mum," Jimmy began to say then lost his words. After some time he asked, "You expect me to take the rap?"

His mother never answered but her silence was all the answer he needed. He sat in shock.

The room came back to him. The smoke, the other people, their voices and conversations. The odd laugh here and there. Jimmy couldn't laugh, this was a nightmare. He couldn't speak either. What was he supposed to say? "Oh Yeh, sure no problem, sure I'll go to jail for that prick of a brother of mine whose never done a good thing for me in his entire life." He shook his head to take the thoughts away.

Interpreting his shaking head as a refusal, Margaret pushed on.

"You're stronger," his Mother then said. She still wouldn't look at him.

"Stronger?" Jimmy asked, almost pleading. He wanted to say more. He wanted to scream. He was almost going to break down. His Mother spoke again and the words she uttered ended it there and then.

"You owe me."

So there it was.

After thirteen years and those unspoken words. All those secret meanings hidden in her eyes, well she tried to hide them, or maybe she didn't, but Jimmy could see them. The accusations, "Why couldn't you just leave him alone?" "I could take it. I could put up with it." "Why couldn't you?

And the killer one was, "It's your fault he's gone."

These words were never spoken but Jimmy read them all as if they had been carved in stone to last for all time. He couldn't understand them though. How could anyone love someone so much who did all these terrible things to them? He hated his father and even from the tender age of only six he knew exactly what his father was. It shaped his life in one way that he was determine he would never become what his father was. It shaped his life in another way by the fact that he absolutely adored his mother and all he wanted was to please her and for her to love him. But the barrier in all of this was she blamed him for his father leaving.

"You owe me." Those three words summed it up and confirmed everything that had gone unsaid for years.

Jimmy shrank in to himself so deeply that he didn't notice the guard coming over to tell his mother that her time was up. He didn't see her leave through the doorway to freedom. He walked back to his cell in a daze, not even aware if anyone or no one had spoken to him.

That night he gave his cell mate his dinner and he lay in his bunk seeing every second of every minute that passed until the dark cell started to fill with light from the tiny barred window at the top of the wall.

Two days later Jimmy pleaded guilty in the hope of receiving a reduced sentence.

One week after that the security guard that was injured during the bank robbery died.

Jimmy got twenty years.

Chapter One

Tenerife, Canary Islands
Thursday 21st October 2021

As Tommy was quickly making his way to his newly configured skate board circuit, he was reflecting that this was the best holiday he had ever had. Being twelve years old had brought a level of independence he had never known before and his Mum seemed cooler and more chilled, even in this thirty plus heat of Tenerife, than she ever was at their home in Manchester. He did consider that it wasn't at all to do with his age, but maybe down to the fact she wanted him out of the way so that she could spend more time with Paul from the apartment next door. Either way he didn't care. Fact was he relished the freedom.

The skate board also represented something different. On his previous holidays, of which there were quite a few, he usually only bought crap. But then most holiday shops only sold crap. The skateboard though was no piece of rubbish. He had bought it in an authentic sports shop on the second night of their holiday and he had used up almost all of his holiday funds to buy it. And it was worth every euro!

His circuit was also a find.

Before this holiday Tommy hadn't owned a skateboard and had relied on borrow boarding time from friends, which was limited at best. His skateboarding skills therefore reflected this and the ramps, pipes, bowls and other obstacles on the new skate park near his home were beyond his ability, and he had the bumps and bruises to remind him of this. But that was before this holiday!

On the day they had arrived Tommy's mum had to visit the local bank to sort out some issues with her bank cards. While waiting outside Tommy noticed that the shops and other premises including the bank were elevated from the street and new ramps had been installed adjacent to each set of steps, which he assumed was to create access for wheel chairs. Each ramp was just longer than the length of a car and a perfect gradient to skateboard on.

Tommy then noticed that these ramps were built with one running down and the next running up and this ran along each side of the street. The street itself had road access at one end and then became a pedestrian walkway at the other. The effect was a perfect U shaped circuit with alternating ramps. The footpaths were also wide and the street itself was quiet. Perfect!

He had seen loads of skaters weaving around holiday makers on the main promenade, but although the surface was good for skating, it was mainly flat and boring and crazy busy with people. Here, on the side street where the bank was, it was a novice skaters dream.

Well it had been for almost two weeks but not today. Some prick had parked his car outside the bank, but had ignored the spaces provided. This moron had not only parked the wrong way across the parking spaces, but had left his car at such an angle that he cut off most of the access to the down ramp. Tommy had tried to take the ramp as normal and navigate the car at the bottom but the angle was too severe and not only did it kill his entire speed momentum he nearly flipped over the car's bonnet.

He figured, and hoped, the driver wouldn't be long, but that was more than twenty minutes ago.

As he waited impatiently beside the car, skateboard tucked under his arm, almost in protest, a man stopped nearby to let his dog have a crap. The dog, a beautiful golden Labrador, the man a weird skinny bloke with scuffed trainers and knee length white socks. His eyes seemed too small for his face, but Tommy wasn't sure if this was due to his baseball cap and face mask that everyone was wearing, due to the virus, making his eyes seem almost beady like peering out from between the gap from his cap peak and the top of his face mask. He reminded him of his Mum's older brother Eamonn who not only wore knee socks with his shorts, but wore sandals with them. Weirdo! And he wondered why he couldn't get a girlfriend?

The man nodded to Tommy then bent down and expertly retrieved the fresh crap in to a poop bag with one hand. He then sealed the bag, placed it in the nearby bin and wandered on down the street, the dog's long tail wagging behind him almost like he was waving good-bye.

Tommy looked at the moron's car, then the bin and had an idea.

He retrieved the poop bag from the bin, careful to lift it by one end of the tie as the bag was still warm from the freshly deposited contents and returned to the car. The windows were all open slightly, but not just enough to allow Tommy to squeeze the bag of shit inside. He considered forcing it through the gap but thought better of that in case the bag burst and the shit went all over him. He tried each of the doors but all were locked. As he was considering the best resting place for his gift to the moron driver an explosion of noise from a gunshot almost made Tommy shit his own shorts. Shouts then followed as two men emerged from the bank, both wearing masks and carrying shot guns. The masks though weren't the ones that everyone was wearing for the virus; these were full ski masks and looked like something you'd see at Halloween. And there were plenty of Halloween costumes in the shops as it was only just over a week away.

Tommy was about to throw the bag of poop on to the ground and get out of there when he noticed the silver exhaust pipe protruding from the back of the car. He bent quickly, deposited the poop bag in to the pipe, flipped his skateboard, jumped on board and began pumping his right leg to pick up speed down the street and away from the bank. As he moved there was more shouting and another gun shot. He looked over his shoulder to see the taller of the two men facing the bank and whilst shouting, pumping his shot gun and shooting in to the air. The other man was at the car boot stuffing in what looked to Tommy like two large heavy bags.

Tommy kicked on and shortly ducked left and out of sight of the two bank robbers, his heart pounding in his chest and his mind buzzing as he couldn't wait to tell his mum his story.

Unknown to Tommy, if he only had waited for 10 more seconds, his story to his mother might have included these further few snippets.

As the two men finished loading the bags in to the boot of their car, the smaller robber distracted the bigger robber just enough to enable him to crack his partner on the back of his head with the butt of his shot gun. The big man went down like a puppet with no strings.

The smaller robber then got in his car and started the engine, but just as the car began to move, it back fired with an almighty explosion almost louder than the previous gun shots, which created a shit storm in a cloudy brown mist that hung over the prone robber on the ground like a dark shadow of shite.

Sniff. Sniff. Sniff

Montgomery Davis-Spence opened his eyes and stared bewildered at a bright blue cloudless sky. He blinked several times, and then opened his eyes wide until the brightness of the daylight made him close them tight again.

He thought he could hear a Cliff Richard song, but he couldn't place it as the Boom, Boom Boom beat in his head didn't seem to match the songs he knew so well.

Sniff. Sniff. Sniff.

"What is that bloody smell?"

He sniffed again, this time drawing deeper pockets of air through his nostrils. "Fuck! Smells like shite!"

With his eyes still closed he moved his head to the side to try to investigate the smell further, but that was when his head exploded in a tidal wash of excruciating pain that flowed over his entire head from the base of his neck. He froze his movement and screwed his eyes tight shut to try to stem off the rush of pressure and noise across his head and in his ears and eyes. As he lay still the pain slowly subsided like the end of the tide dissolving in to the sand. For some time he lay still afraid to move and detonate the dynamite again. The smell of shite now forgotten, and the Cliff Richard song gone, Montgomery, or Monty as he was called, realised that although the explosion of pain had faded, a throbbing beat of dull pain was pulsing at the back of his head.

Boom, Boom, Boom.

He loved Cliff Richard and knew all of his songs, but the beat just didn't fit?

He remembered. "That fucker Jazz!"

He saw Jazz point to something behind on the ground; Monty thought he'd dropped a brick of cash, but as he turned away from Jazz and bent to look, that was when, bang, and the lights went out.

He sat up. Back came the pain, this time accompanied with dizziness that made Monty sway like a buoy bobbing at sea. Just as he thought the swaying and nausea were going to ease, he threw up. With no thought or regard for what was happening he made no attempt to direct the projectile away from himself and instead vomited all over his trousers, with the final drabs dripping over his shirt and mixing with the speckles of shit that were already there.

Steadying himself, he raised his right hand and nervously felt the back of his head. It was wet and sticky through the torn flap of his ski mask. His hand came away sticky with blood which he quickly tried to wipe away across the front of his shirt. In fairness to Monty it wasn't a bad attempt but unfortunately while he did manage to wipe away most of the blood his hand came away covered in puke and shit. He then gripped the torn flap of his mask and pulled it off his head and flung it to the ground.

Twenty yards away, he saw two women nervously staring at him. Both women were dressed the same and he had a flicker of recognition that he either knew them or had seen them before. As well as wearing the same clothes, they both had the same expression on each of their faces. Like the women, the expression was also familiar to him, but unlike the fact that he couldn't place the women, he knew what the expression was. It was the look of fear, and it made him feel sad.

He then noticed a shot-gun lying on the ground several feet away from where the ski mask had landed, which caused his face to crease in a question. Ignoring the gun and the two women, he pushed himself up on to his feet. No mean task in normal circumstances as Monty was six foot and seven inches tall and weighed just over two hundred and sixty pounds, but the dizziness increased as he struggled to steady himself upright. With some effort and several stutters, first to his right then to his left, he stood straight and began to take in his surroundings. With the ringing in his ears reducing he then heard the sirens. The police were on their way!

At the same time as hearing the scream of the police car sirens announcing their imminent arrival, he noticed that one of the restaurants, or bar or whatever it was, had one of the outdoor freezers that enabled parents to choose an ice cream or lollypop for their child with a wave to the waiter to let him or her know to add it to their bill. Monty walked towards the freezer, sheepishly at first and eventually with slow deliberate strides. Once at the freezer he raised the lid and surveyed its contents. He smiled, almost a child like grin, and his freckles of shit followed the contours of the creases on his face. So many colours and so much choice. His favourite was the orange squeeze ups, but they only had the lemon ones and the lemon ones made his eyes go funny. The Fruit Pastilles looked inviting but then he saw the Chocolate Magnums and the Cornettos. Both mint and strawberry ones. His favourite!

The police sirens got louder.

He couldn't decide which one he wanted. There was so much choice.

The sirens wailed.

Eenie! The strawberry cornetto?

Meenie! The mint cornetto?

The sirens got closer by the second.

Miney! The Magnum?

The sirens were so loud now the police must be only a couple of seconds away, but Monty ignored them.

MO! The strawberry cornetto!

He removed the cone from the freezer, tore off the lid and wrapper, letting both fall back in to the freezer unit before gently closing the lid.

With his face angled to one side and slightly facing skyward, he continued walking slowly and steadily down the street, smiling and licking his Cornetto as he went, the bright sun warming his face.

"What was that Cliff Richard song?" He couldn't get it so he give up and started to hum the tune of Summer Holiday. It was his favourite Cliff Richard song, and his favourite Cliff Richard movie. As he walked happily down the street, the strawberry cornetto already beginning to melt in his large hands, he tried to remember if he had packed his DVD of Summer Holiday. He hoped so as he really wanted to go back to his room and watch it. This made his smile widen further, but then a dark thought came back to him which tuned out everything about his beloved Cliff Richard.

"He was going to kill that fucker Jazz. Yes, he was going to kill that fucker Jazz."

The two female bank tellers standing outside the bank looked on as if they were watching this on their televisions at home and slightly detached from the reality that it was. The owner of the bar continued to stand at the back of his premises with the phone still held to his ear, his wife still saying something that he had stopped listening to. He had phoned her straight after he had called the police and now he was watching in almost amazement as one of the bank robbers, a monster of a man, his clothes a dirty mess, walk down the street eating one of his strawberry Cornettos. The man was looking up to the sun, a child like smile on his face, and his head was bobbing as if he was listening to some music. Tenerife never ceased to amaze Pierre and every season you saw something stranger than you had the season before. But the owner of Café Submarine didn't know yet that this summer season in the very sunny and very hot Tenerife might just turn out to be the strangest ever.

Jimmy Ruddock, or Jimmy Jazz as he was affectionately known by his fellow inmates, or ex fellow inmates to be more exact, was also feeling the heat of Tenerife and sweating buckets. The car didn't have air conditioning and although the windows were open the flow of warm air wasn't doing anything to cool him down, in fact the opposite. Another factor was that Jimmy's adrenalin was pumping and his heart was pounding like a big old bass drum.

He was also straining to concentrate as he just couldn't afford to get lost and he had never driven this route before, just walked it to scope it out. A wrong turn or any kind of delay could be disastrous. He could hear the police sirens but thankfully as he had hoped in his planning, they were coming from the opposite direction than he was travelling. He had ditched the ski mask, changed his shirt to his fake Tommy Bahama Hawaiian shirt and now wore sunglasses just like all the other tourists. So keep it cool, if that was the right word to use in this thirty plus degrees temperature, and disappear amongst the other tourists just doing the same as them, then he would be fine. He'd also got rid of the shotgun, down a flood drain, where he hoped it was never found again. It hadn't been loaded; he never had used a loaded weapon. It was only for effect and it had also came in handy to knock out Monty.

There wasn't a mass of CCTV; very few in fact compared to the UK so no reason to worry about appearing on film somewhere. Blend in and get to his destination with the least amount of fuss.

A thought struck him and he smiled. He was now a bank robber. After all these years and those failed attempts, he had eventually done it. He wasn't proud of it. Not one bit. A bank robber wasn't what he had set out in life to be. He had joked about himself in prison that the proper definition of a bank robber was someone who stole money, or jewels or whatever, from a bank. But you had to actually get outside the bank with the loot to truly classify as stealing it and in Jimmy's case that hadn't happened until now. He hadn't even been at the first robbery, and the next two they had been caught before they even crossed the front door. Snitched on Jimmy's partner Roger claimed. Okay, he had a bit of help on this one, but now at his age who cared. This relaxed him somewhat, but the heat in the car was still stifling and difficult to endure.

He thought about Monty and shook his head. He was glad to be on his own now as that mad eejit was likely to kill someone, and that someone could be Jimmy. Considering that Jimmy had just double crossed him and left him out cold in front of the bank they had just robbed he was certain to be at the top of Monty's hit list. Hopefully the police would get there before he regained consciousness and put him in some Spanish prison cell and throw away the key. Jimmy wasn't worried about Monty informing the police of his identity as in his opinion it wouldn't take the police long to come to that conclusion them selves anyway. And besides, where Jimmy was going and how he was travelling there had already taken that in to account. His plans now were simple. Stash the cash, see his son Ray, and then split.

He thought of the cash. Four Hundred Thousand Euros, plus whatever cash happened to be on deposit at the bank, maybe another fifty or sixty thousand euros. The truth was that Jimmy had no idea what level of actual cash a bank had on hand at any given time, and the fact was he didn't care. The robbery wasn't about the bank's cash, although they did take that while they were there. Why wouldn't they? They were bank robbers after all, so it would have been a failure of their duty not to. The robbery was targeted at four safety deposit boxes which held the profits of one of Ulster's paramilitary organisations who pretended they had a cause but they were really just thugs with a cover story. This money started as drug profits on the streets of the towns and cities of Northern Ireland and had then made its way around Europe through many various channels to end up as some groups or individuals savings pot or retirement fund. Well thanks to Jimmy, and of course the people who had brought this job to him, the pension fund was now bust. Although, not for Jimmy, his pension fund had just received a pretty big cash injection. They do say that someone's loss is someone else's gain, and today for once in his life the gainer was Jimmy. And it would soon be Julie too. He thought of the old Beatles song, this time no adlibbing on the words, apart from the name.

"Hey Jules, don't make it bad, take a sad song and make it better."

And he was now on his way to make Julie better. It was his pay back, not only to Julie, but he hoped maybe to his son Ray as well. Jimmy really had some healing to do. Another song came to his mind, a great Abba number. "All the things I could do if I had a little money."

Heal old wounds, he thought, heal old wounds.

Chapter Two

Tenerife, Canary Islands
Thursday 21st October 2021

"Keep left, keep left.

Ray Ruddock kept his steady walking pace, but veered left as instructed, trying to look natural and confident.

"That's you, straight from there."

"How far now?" Ray asked.

"Past the next two bars and then it's the entrance on the left. Once you get to the entrance stall and wait until I get set up. I'll let you know when you're there."

Ray walked on and Joe watched him carefully. Once Ray had reached their next reference point Joe spoke through their Bluetooth link again, "That's you, now give me a couple of seconds as I need to get where I can see in to the entrance as we don't have the camera on." Sometimes they used a small camera attached to Ray's sunglasses but today they thought they could be too far apart for the signal to work. Anyway outdoors keeping in visual contact was a lot easier than inside were walls, stairwells for example made it difficult and the risk of loosing visual contact was high.

"OK," replied Ray and then bent down to pretend to tie the lace on one of his trainers, which was one of his many stalling techniques. A few seconds later Joe's voice came back through his earpiece.

"Good to go. It looks just like it was when I scoped it yesterday. Turn left almost exactly forty-five degrees and head straight in."

Ray began the move he'd been instructed to do when almost immediately Joe spoke again.

"Wait, someone is going to walk across you. No hold on I think he's coming over to you. He's on your right, turn right slightly and you'll be facing him. A bit more. He's holding his hand out he must know you. Hold out your right hand and slow down."

Ray again did as instructed, easing to the right and holding out his hand. He smiled, which he considered was a natural thing to do if someone he knew was approaching, but he forgot that he was wearing a mask, as everybody was due to covid, and so his smile went unnoticed.

"Two more steps and you should be there, maybe slow down a bit let him make the move with his hand."

Again Ray complied. In a couple of seconds he felt the other extended hand and he adjusted his wrist to take the grip that was being offered to him. At the same time the voice said.

"Ray," he said it like there were ten A's and four Y's. "How's my man?"

Ray answered not recognising the voice, "Good man, Good."

"Its Bruno man," then he repeated, "Bruno. You know I was at the gig Friday in Hard Rock. Fucking ace man, best band we've ever seen on holiday. And Cece loves the Clash man, always did. She screamed when you did that Lovers Rock, fucking ace man, fucking ace."

Ray thought now he remembered him and the request for Cece as she had been the first person ever to request Lovers Rock as it was quite an obscure Clash song.

"Great," said Ray, "glad you both liked it. We've got the Friday night in Hard Rock for the entire season and it's a great spot. Really busy there last Friday. How long you here for?"

"We're not home til next Friday," answered Bruno, "Don't you remember I told you as Cece was givin' me shit man 'cause we won't be here to watch you next Friday, and we're on a trip tomorrow. You not performing nowhere else Ray?"

Ray didn't remember that part of their conversation as the truth was you spoke to so many of the tourists and most of the conversations were the same, as were most of the requests.

"Ray nodded towards the complex he was about to enter, "Meeting the owner in here, Pepe from Hard Rock knows him and gave me an intro, so hoping to get a few more gigs. Things are tight since this whole covid bollocks, but hopefully they'll start to pick up."

"Dad," Joe's impatient voice muttered in his earpiece. The one word and tone told him what he needed to know.

"I've gotta go Bruno, good to see you again and enjoy the rest of the holiday."

Bruno slapped Ray on his back and said, "Sure Ray, good luck with the gig. If the guy wants a recommendation you tell him to come ask my Cece." As he started to walk away he added, "Ray you get a gig there before we're going home you be sure and let me know. If Cece sees you playing there without me telling her she'll have my fucking balls in a sling man." Bruno chuckled as he walked away giving Ray the peace sign as he did so, totally unaware that this visual gesture was a waste of time.

Joe then seen the Bruno guy look at him with a look of recognition also, but Joe glanced down to his phone anxious to avoid any further chat and get back to another adventure with his father. Some kids had remote control cars, or maybe even a drone. Joe he just had remote control of his blind dad, helping him on his quest to act like he wasn't blind at all. For the record it wasn't that his Dad had a chip on his shoulder about being blind, or was ashamed of it or anything like that. He just liked to pretend that he's got twenty twenty vision. Sometimes for fun and sometimes to see how far he could push the boundaries. Today's play though was because he was meeting about work and the last thing in the world that his Dad wanted was the sympathy vote. He strived to win on merit alone, and he hated all the bullshit like, "It's amazing what you do being blind!" Not that he didn't like praise, or even enjoy it, but for singing or playing his guitar was OK, the blind thing just confused it, so much better to keep that hidden. Unknown to Ray, Pepe in Hard Rock had sussed it as he had came to Joe one day suspecting that Ray and his other band members, who were also visually impaired to varying degrees, were drunk due to their clumsiness. Joe had to level with Pepe who thankfully had accepted this without fuss and had also agreed to respect the secret and say nothing to Ray. The truth was that Pepe was relieved as Ray's band, "Us 4" and their Clash tribute routine was bringing in the punters in numbers that he hadn't seen for years. As it was a great cash cow, he didn't want it to be a drunken cow, holiday makers don't like that and he had seen it so many times with bands or singers that drank too much.

Joe surveyed his Dad's position and then relayed his next instructions, "There's an empty table at the end of the bar just about eight to ten paces from where you are now." He watched as his Dad started moving.

"I'll let you know when you're coming up to the seat."

Joe's phone then beeped to announce an incoming text message... He glanced down to his screen and read, "Is your dad therapy." It took him a few seconds to realise what his Mum had meant to say, which had been scrambled most likely due to predictive text and the fact she was pist. "Is your Dad there?" he assumed, but at that same moment he heard a "Umph!!" over his earpiece and looked up to see that his Dad had walked in to the table. "Sorry Dad, got distracted there. Put your right hand down and that seat is the one." He watched as his Dad found the back of the seat, pulling it out and orientating himself to sit down in line with the table. "Didn't Pepe say to phone the guy once you were sitting at the pool bar?" Joe asked, although he already knew this, he was just trying to move on from his fuck up.

Ray took off his mask and removed his phone from his pocket and plugged in his earpiece to enable him to use the Apple "voiceover" screen reader to navigate the screen. The first thing he noticed was the reason why his phone had been constantly vibrating as there were five missed calls from his ex-wife Liz. He hit the home button to clear the screen and opened the phone and scrolled under contacts to find the number Pepe had given him for Stu, the hotel's owner. Finding it he double tapped to make the call and within a few seconds the call was answered.

"Stu."

"Stu, its Ray. Pepe from Hard Rock gave me your number to meet."

"Ray yes mate, you at the pool bar?"

Ray could hear the scraping noise that suggested that Stu was holding the phone to his ear by his shoulder, but he still managed to make out what he had said. "Yes I'm at one of the tables at the back."

"Get yourself a drink there and I'll be out with you in a few minutes," Stu said quickly, and then hung up.

Ray unplugged his earpiece, wrapped it in a ball and put it and the phone back in his pocket. As he did it began to buzz again with another incoming call. He ignored it and checked his other ear to ensure his earpiece connecting him to Joe was still firmly in place. While he waited he discreetly surveyed the table to check if there was anything sitting on it. Empty glasses, or even worse full ones, were a potential missile for him to launch flying while maybe shaking Stu's hand. A gentle sweep found that the table was clear. Just the usual umbrella pole holding up a much appreciated open umbrella shading him from the strong midday sun. He also listened as he sat periscoping as he called it in an audible way to listen to what was going on around him. This was mainly an additional part of his awareness of his surroundings, but from time to time it did also serve to entertain as you couldn't believe the conversations some people had between themselves in public. The bar seemed quiet; it was just the beginning of lunch time. It seemed to Ray that there was only one family several tables away discussing lunch options and asking a toddler what it was that he or she wanted for lunch, so unless some tables were occupied by loners like himself the bar was almost empty. The music was also not too loud, which for a performer who pumped up the volume when he was on stage seemed a bit hypocritical that he preferred it to be low. It is a misconception that anyone with a sensory disability makes up for it as their other senses improve. The part truth is that you can learn to use you're other senses better or more focused, just like Ray was doing with his hearing and taking in his surroundings. But on the flip side, even he thought his hearing was pretty good, since his sight loss he did find it harder to hear people when having a conversation if there was a lot of background noise. Ray's theory here was that we all do a bit of sub conscious lip reading, obviously having sight that is, and now with his sight loss he found he struggled hearing in certain circumstances. So good that it was quiet enough here.

As he waited, one of those entertaining moments did start to play out from the table with the family choosing lunch. Ray's periscoping homed in on the conversation when the mother said to one of her children, "Your Daddy is an asshole!"

The father then said, "Fuck sake Kelly you can't say that to the child." She responded quickly, "And it's OK for you to swear in front of her? That would be about right, one rule for us but big man Johnny can say what he wants!"

A Childs voice said, "Can I have nuggets?"

"What's that big man all about; you're the one called me an asshole?"

"Sorry I should have said a big fat asshole!"

"Fuck off Kelly, just cause you're in one of your moods. What's up your hole anyway?"

"Can I have nuggets?" a young girl's voice whimpered and then added "Please?" The please was drawn out as if it was spelt with ten e's, but again she was ignored as the supposed adults continued with their supposed adult conversation.

"I'm not in a bad mood. You're the one mentioned my tits."

"Lack of them you mean," Johnny said chuckling to himself, but really only making his wife's anger worse.

"You're a fucking asshole," Kelly spat this time, her anger rising, "And with a tweeny dick like yours my tits should be the last of your worries."

"Dad," Joe said over Ray's earpiece, "I think that's your man coming over now. He's coming on your left side."

Joe's prompt caused Ray to miss Johnny's response, but he needed to concentrate now and forget what was going on several tables away. A few seconds later he heard a strong cockney accent ask, "Ray?"

Ray looked up and smiled and said, "Yes, Stu?" He began to stand and held out his right hand, which almost immediately Stu took and shook.

"Did you not get a drink?" Stu asked. "I'm going to get a beer; it's a hot one today. You want a beer or something?"

Truth was Ray could have murdered a beer, but it just gave him something to have to worry about knocking over, so he declined. Once this meeting was over he'd get a pint in one of the bars along the front.

"Give me a second," said Stu, "I'll just grab a lager."

When he came back he asked as he sat down, "Pepe tells me you've got the Friday night slot for the season."

"Yes, it's a great gig. We had it last year as well," added Ray proudly.

"A Clash tribute?" asked Stu, but before Ray answered, he added, "Don't think that would work here Ray."

"NO, no," replied Ray, "The Clash thing is just for Hard Rock. We did U2 there last year but it's the same old songs over Andover that people want and it got a bit boring. Pepe wanted something different this year. We do lots of stuff, covering rock, pop, and middle of the road." Ray pulled an envelope from his pocket and handed it across to Stu. "That's pretty much our entire song list, so you can pick the set yourself if you want to, or we can play requests."

The conversation had went straight in to the business part of the meeting, which Ray was happy with. He didn't like all the pass the time talk and preferred to get to the point. He heard Stu open the envelope and knew he was reading the list of songs and artists and also taking large gulps out of his beer.

"Some great songs here Ray, Ed Sheran, he's really popular, Paul Weller, The Changing Man that's one of my favourite songs. You're a band Ray yes?"

"Yes four piece." Ray didn't think it was worth telling him that his son Joe was playing guitar also while over on half term, making it a five piece.

"We don't have a whole pile of room here, might be tight to get a drum kit in," added Stu,

"No problem at all," answered Ray, hearing the moans of Terry the drummer already when he wouldn't be able to set up his complete kit, "Our drummer likes to set up a minimalist kit," Ray lied. He also thought he might need to tell Joe he had to sit out on this one and that would lead to more complaints.

"Stu," a woman's voice said, "Sorry to bother you but Housekeeping have been on screaming that the laundry isn't here yet."

"I've phoned those fuckers three times already," said Stu and then as if to explain, "We've two busloads on their way from the airport and half the rooms aren't ready, people gonna give me some shit." Then after pausing, he said, "Listen Ray, we're starting a barbecue night on Thursday's and I was thinking of putting on some entertainment to try to up the numbers cause we can make good on the food. If you're up to give it a go with the first night free. I'll feed you and the boys and whatever yous drink. Then we'll take it from there."

"Starting tonight?" Ray asked, not minding the short notice as the sooner they got started the sooner they got paid.

"No, sorry Ray, next week's the first one."

Sensing that Stu needed to go and sort out his laundry issue and Ray was happy with the deal anyway, he agreed. It was exactly what he had hoped for, apart from the first free night as that didn't sort out his immediate cash flow issues, but unfortunately this was the state of play since bloody covid and the power was with the bars and hotels as there were too many singers and bands and not enough gigs.

Joe watched as the girl came over to his Dad's table and sensed that the meeting was coming to an end as the owner looked under some pressure as you could tell by his frustrated expression. Joe sucked down hard on his fag, two long draws, before crushing it out under his trainer. While he was waiting on his dad he had wandered over to the outside tables of the two bars next door in search of cigarettes. He was amazed at just how many people left their fags and usually their lighter also behind them. He wasn't disappointed as he found two such generous tourists, one a half packet of Marlboro Gold and the other Lucky Strike with four left in the packet. He had tried the Lucky Strike, which were a bit rough but at his tender age of fourteen, beggars couldn't be choosers.

While waiting he had also answered two texts and one phone call from his mum, which had confirmed his earlier suspicions that she was pist. Nothing new there. Her news though was new and also alarming. She was coming out to Tenerife, arriving on Sunday, and wanted his dad to arrange Colin, the driver he used as a roadie for the band, to pick her up at the airport. His dad was going to have a kitten. Joe was also pissed off. This half term was supposed to be his time with his dad. Plus, his mum could see, which did somewhat curtail Joe's freedom.

He now sat in a bit of a frump with a feeling of dread swelling in his gut. His mum was coming, which was just shit. He knew that his dad was going to feel the same, most likely worse. His parents had only been married for six months when he'd been a baby and that had been a disaster. It hadn't been much better before their divorce, but it had been a lot worse since, and he had been there to bear witness to that. After Sunday his holiday was fucked and the peace and tranquillity of this sunny canary island was going to be shattered by the Ruddock Wars.

And most important of all as far as Joe was concerned, she wouldn't let him play guitar in his dad's band!

He sighed deeply and decided to have another fag. A Marlboro this time, they were his favourite after all.

Thirty minutes later he would have loved another fag, but he couldn't as he was sitting with his dad, who had just had a difficult call with his mother and was now trying to call Joe's grandmother.

"Hello Rosemary?" said Ray, recognising her voice when she had answered his mother Julie's phone.

"Ah hi Ray," Rosemary said warmly, her voice soft in Ray's earpiece. He could also hear the familiar "glug, glug, glug" of his mum's dialysis machine in the background. Rosemary, his mum's nurse, continued, "she's sleeping," she was going to add that Julie was almost sleeping round the clock now, but stopped herself as she knew that Ray would immediately read from this, albeit correctly, that his mum's condition was getting much worse. The chronic condition of her only remaining kidney, end-stage renal disease did cause extreme fatigue, but Rosemary knew that there were other factors affecting Julie's physical and mental state. There had been tears and phone calls that then caused more tears. Rosemary was also aware of the divide between Julie's husband Jimmy and her son Ray, but she didn't know how much Ray knew about what Jimmy was doing now and she didn't want to give anything away that could lead to questions she didn't want to answer. She didn't think it was her place to answer. So she just said, "your luck's out again Ray."

Ray too was cautious about what he said as he didn't know if his father was there and the last thing he wanted was for Rosemary to say, "hey your Dad's here, do you want a word?" His luck was out indeed. The last three times he had called his mum had been asleep; he maybe needed to call at a different time. "Seems to be, is there a better time to call maybe?"

"It's hard to say Ray, it's hit and miss," Rosemary answered, "Listen I'll get Julie to give you a call when she's up and about."

"Great thanks," he was thinking maybe to add a best time to suggest to Rosemary, but then she said, "OK Ray, I'll do that, you look after yourself now, bye."

"Bye Rose," then not sure if he should call her that he nervously added, "Rosemary," then cut the call.

Joe didn't need to ask and Ray didn't need to say anything either. They both sensed that things with their Mother and Grandmother weren't good, weren't good at all.

Changing the subject of their thoughts Ray said, "here, I heard one of the tour bus companies are looking for sight seeing announcers for their open top tours. You could help me on the interview, pretend to be a tourist?"

"Dad!" sighed Joe shaking his head, "you're mad. Why do you want to go for all these stupid jobs?"

"Maybe I could apply to drive the bus?"

"I'm not going with you for that interview," Joe quickly said, then went on, "why can't you just get a dog or use a white stick, like Terry or Trace? Stop all this charade crap?"

"Ah! Think how boring that would be." Then laughing Ray added, "Plus a white stick wouldn't go with my super cool image." He spread his arms wide in a gesture to say, "Look at me!"

"Super?" Joe was going to swear but then stopped. They both laughed.

"C'mon," said Ray, "we'd better get back. Trace will want you to do your poop duty."

Joe sighed, "And poor Bumper's stomach hasn't been the best." Translated this meant that Trace's guide dog Bumper had the shits.

"You see," countered Ray, "that's why I don't have a guide dog. They can shit for Belfast. And besides, you're not here all the time so who would shovel all the shit when your not here?"

"Good to know I have my uses," answered Joe.

"And be thankful for small mercies," said Ray, "I was reading that they were training some ponies as guide horses, so you'd have some shit to deal with there."

"Nah dad, that wouldn't work," replied Joe, "a guide horse? Say you came up to a fence, the horse wouldn't take you around it, it would most likely jump over it, thinking it was in the Grand National."

They both laughed. "Can you imagine that, you'd have blind people flying all over the place over fences and hedges."

Ray enjoyed the banter and he cherished these moments with his son. It was a pity that his ex wife was coming over on Sunday to ruin it.

Chapter Three

Tenerife, Canary Islands
Thursday 21st October 2021

Jimmy Jazz Ruddock sat in the shade sipping a zero alcohol Heineken. It wasn't bad, almost like the real thing, but it was cold and it was very hot today and so he was grateful for it. He had put a call in to the clinic in the hope of speaking to Julie, but she was sleeping and Rosemary, her nurse, promised she would call back when she was awake and able to, although she did say that it could be tomorrow. Jimmy was killing time now, listening to music on his phone, waiting in the hope that Julie would wake up and be fit enough to make the call.

The music was from a random radio station he'd picked up as his own play list of over five thousand songs, which his grandson Joe had downloaded for him over many years was gone now along with his old phone, his old passport and his old identity.

He was for now Gerry Mulligan from Dublin and he had an Irish passport to prove it, thanks to his old cellmate Lenny Harris, whose nickname had been Rolfy after Rolf Harris due to his artistic skills. Lenny had quite liked the nickname due to Harris's celebrity status, but once it had came out that he had been a paedophile Lenny ditched the nickname with vigorous and sometimes brutal energy. The last thing that you wanted to be associated with in prison was anything to do with child crimes and in particular ones of a sexual nature. Jimmy helped Lenny by inventing another nickname, "The Cat," referring to "Copy Cat," and relating to Lenny's skills as an artist which were now utilised mainly for forging documents such as driving licences, passports, birth certificates and basically anything useful to his audience, and customers who were lodging at the same Majesties pleasure as himself. Not the best of nicknames, Jimmy admitted, but it stuck, which was mainly due to the fact that Lenny had a tendency to slink around just like a cat. It didn't matter; the main thing was the reference to Rolf Harris was forgotten.

Lenny had also been one of Jimmy's pupils during his time inside and by the time of Lenny's release in 2020 he could play the guitar, the banjo and his favourite, the double bass. Jimmy himself was a self taught musician, expert in a wide range of instruments and better still, the skill and patience, along with the time afforded by imprisonment, to pass these skills on to his many inmates. This made Jimmy a very popular inmate, and as I have mentioned before, earned him the nickname of Jimmy Jazz.

Another of Jimmy's inmates, although not one that he would consider a friend, was Charlie Bassett. In Jimmy's opinion never had a man been better named as Charlie, like the liquorice sweets, was a bit of an allsorts. Quite simply he was all things to all men, and this mainly included those inmates that were the hierarchy of their paramilitary organisations, on either side of the political divide, which was unusual but not unknown, especially for leaches like Charlie. This made Charlie more dangerous than the men he sucked up to because you never knew were you stood or what the play could be, as there was always a play with Charlie.

Prison just like society had its classes and groups, some majorities and some minorities. It had places you shouldn't go and people you should avoid. All criminals of various degrees and many crimes, some political, some motivated by hatred and violence, most through greed, and the worst group driven by sex, but with all these groups they were what they were and as long as you were careful you could be safe, even though you were locked up night and day with them. Charlie was like a chameleon being whatever he needed to be, doing whatever he needed to do to seek favour, no matter who he needed to stand on to get there.

Jimmy was fortunate though that his association with Charlie while on the inside had been thankfully minimal. It was when he had been released that Charlie had become a bigger player in his life.

Jimmy's final release from prison, his third in his unwanted career labelled a criminal, was in November 2020 just as the UK and Ireland headed in to their second lockdown due to covid. It was almost as bleak, but not quite, as Jimmy's first release back in 1982.

After pleading guilty for a crime he hadn't committed in October 1968 he had hoped he might receive a lenient sentence. This hope was shattered following the death of the bank's security guard and as a result the maximum sentence was handed down to Jimmy. He was able to resign himself to his fate and focused relentlessly to try his best to put his head down and serve his time. One dark night awake in his cold prison cell he had silently agreed to his mother's wishes and his single hope was that someday she would love him for his sacrifice. This was the source of his strength in his early days of imprisonment. The terrible thing was the shame he carried as people now would see him as a murderer. This constant grief was devastating. The face of the security guard, who he now knew was called George Wilson, haunted Jimmy's dreams each and every night. He also later learned that George had just become a father two weeks before the bank robbery to a baby girl he had named Mary-Jane. This knowledge broke Jimmy's heart and almost shattered his resolve and sanity.

His rescue came four weeks in to his sentence when his name appeared on the list of inmates to have a visitor that afternoon.

Chapter Four

Tenerife, Canary Islands
Thursday 21st October 2021

Charlie Bassett's rage had subsided, for now.

Anger was a feeling he was very familiar with as he had spent most of his life feeling that way. He wasn't very clever so he wasn't sure if it was due to Biology, Geography, Physics or Genetics. A large source of his anger was down to his height. He was one centimetre over five foot tall. Was this because of biology? Had he been born too soon? Did he still have some cooking to do in his mother's womb? Was it geography that located his arse far too close to the ground? Or was it physics and the pull of gravity that had stunted his growth?

Maybe it was genetics? He had learned that his grandfather on his mother's side had also been a small man. This knowledge caused him to wish that the man wasn't long dead at all as Charlie would sure love to have had the pleasure of killing the little bastard for passing on his shitty shorty genes.

His grandfather on his father's side could also do with a visit too as that prick had been bald and therefore responsible for Charlie's current need for his comb-over, which no matter how much hair lacquer he used still turned out to be an unruly fuck up at the slightest little breeze giving the impression that his head had a fucking trap door.

And now that we're on the subject of grandparents that bitch of a grandmother on his father's side had a nose bigger than fucking Concorde with a hook on it that most eagles would be proud of. And yes, he had that also.

So looks weren't going to win him any prizes or get him very far. For that matter neither was his brains or stature. His first career teacher had told him to join the circus. That cheeky bastard had paid for that remark when Charlie had poured sand in to his petrol tank of his beloved mark two Ford Escort. The engine had been well and truly fucked. When the car was being towed away, Charlie commented to him, "Maybe you should join the AA?" Then much quieter he muttered, "Up yours you fucking prick."

So anger had been manifested from a very young age, along with many of the other poor traits that Charlie portrayed on a daily basis. His outlook on life though was quite simple. "Fuck everybody and fuck everybody else as well!"

His potential for violence and cruelty frightened others, and those others were actually violent men them selves.

When in his early twenties in 1983 he was part of a crew of three despatched by the north Belfast division of the Ulster Defence Association, (UDA), which was one of Belfast's leading paramilitary organisations, to carry out a punishment beating. The target was located in east Belfast and the hit had been sanctioned by the eastern division. Charlie was the junior member of the squad, which meant he did look out and that sort of thing. Intelligence had advised them that the target would be home alone, but when they arrived on scene the team found a young woman was also in the house, which they wrongly assumed was the targets girlfriend. The two senior squad members instructed Charlie to take the girl in to another room while they saw to their key task. Recognising that the girl was frightened and in some shock Charlie took advantage of her passive and fearsome state to quickly overcome her, then proceed to rape and beat her. The violence and raw anger of the assault on this young woman shocked Charlie's two comrades when they entered the room to see what was going on. These two men, who were no strangers to violence themselves and had just blown out the kneecaps of their target in the next room, were stunned speechless and motionless at the brutal savageness being inflicted on another human being, never mind a woman. It was animal like. One of these two young soldiers, which were as they saw themselves, almost cried. Even men accustomed to violence had a threshold, but Charlie was in that very small group were boundaries just didn't exist. Knowing that this man was prepared to go to much further lengths of violence than they were was scary. Very scary indeed.

Later it was reported that the young woman had actually been a junior Nun from a nearby convent who had been just visiting the targets house.

Even though this caused a shit storm in the media, and across the wings of the UDA Charlie was never reprimanded about this clear breach of the organisation's code of conduct. His reputation for violence spread along with the knowledge of his many affiliations with important people across various loyalist organisations. These two powerful auras served to protect Charlie in one way, but prevented his ambitions of scaling the heights towards leadership in another.

His lack of respect for women continued and because of his lack of actual relationships with them also, his anger towards them grew.

A few months before he was about to turn thirty he met a young woman that showed surprising promise of becoming a relationship. Up to this his sexual encounters had mainly been with prostitutes along with the very odd one night stand. This woman was kind and gentle, which he found disarming.

Their dates continued, meals out, the cinema and out for drinks but without progressing to sex. As the weeks went on this was driving Charlie mad as he wasn't used to being patient. Finally on their eighth date she, Maria, agreed to come back to Charlie's house.

Nerves and anticipation of what was to come pushed Charlie to the booze, Maria on the other hand had declined. As their evening progressed and the whisky, which Maria had brought for him, fuelled his confidence, he said, thinking it would turn her on.

"I've been having wet dreams about you all week!" He looked at Maria smirking as he said it. Charlie thought the smirk was sexy, Maria though had seen it before and it disgusted her, almost costing her to lose her nerve. Steadying herself she answered, "I have wet dreams about you all the time." Charles eyes almost popped out of his head as his testosterone surged through him like an electric current. But then his fuse box overloaded when she continued.

"I wake up pissing myself laughing about you!"

The silence in the room was like a vacuum, but it was soon filled with the explosion of Charlie's anger and rage as he was on her, pummelling her with punch after punch after punch. He soon became exhausted, his breaths coming in long deep gasps. Even though she was being beaten, and being beaten quite badly, Maria was smiling inside as she knew the drug in his drink would soon have him. She needed his efforts to make the drug work. And soon it did. Some moments later his arms stopped swinging, his gasping slowed and he slumped unconscious half on top of her.

The next morning Charlie awoke. His head was throbbing, his throat parched and he had a severe need to piss. As he stumbled towards his bathroom he hadn't even started to recall the events of the night before as his desperate need to piss was overwhelming. Reaching the toilet he grabbed and pulled to lift the toilet seat. The piss was bursting so much that he almost didn't notice that the seat hadn't moved. "What the fuck!" his mind scrambled out. He yanked harder to raise the seat but it wouldn't budge. "Fuck sake," he blew out, not knowing what the hell was happening. His balls were screaming in pain to release the piss. He looked over at the sink, but being only five feet tall there was no way he could raise himself up to it, so he jumped on top of the toilet seat and facing the sink grabbed at his shorts to relieve himself. Sheer panic then followed when he realised that his throbbing morning pea hard was stuck fast to his thigh. Worse still the end of his cock was glued shut in a mess of hardened glue. He screamed and jumped off the toilet seat in agony thinking his balls were going to burst, tears flooding down his face.

He didn't see it then, but he would find it there much later. A note left weighed down on the top of his toilet's cistern by a used tube of Superglue read, "Goodbye Sticky Dicky" and signed "Sister Maria".

"Sister Maria? Who the fuck? Sister Maria?" Then he saw through the blonde hair and make up and he suddenly knew. "That fucking penguin fucking Nun bitch." "Fucking penguin bitch mangled my fucking cock!"

He would also later discover that she had stuck down the toilet seat as well.

The ambulance crew were able to relieve Charlie, but alarmed by his hysterics and screaming, and fearing his bladder could burst, they did a fairly rushed job. The result was, in Charlie's words, "You'd think I'd been fucking circumcised with a jig-saw by a fucking blind man!"

This episode didn't much improve Charlie's respect of women, but it did make him avoid Nun's at all costs. The sheer site of one sent a surge of pins and needles through his lower regions that was crippling.

Today, thirty years later, he still bore the scars and he still was ultra sensitive in his manly parts and his screaming rage and kicking fit that had followed Monty's return had set his groin on fire.

Monty had watched him as he had kicked the side of the bed sofa screaming, "You fucker Jazz! You fucker Jazz!" Then stamping on the floor shouting, "I'm gonna fucking kill you Jazz, gonna fucking kill you!"

Monty slipped past him unnoticed and went in to his own room in the two bedroom apartment, closing the door tightly behind him to help shut out the noise. He was going to watch Summer Holiday and didn't want Charlie's shouting to spoil it for him. Before he'd even found the DVD he was already humming the song and it helped to soothe all the bad things from his day. Even Charlie's rage when he had told him what had happened at the bank.

"No more worries for me and you." Cliff's words brought hope to Monty, but his peaceful feeling wouldn't last long. When Charlie realised that Monty had lay down on his bed covered in shit and puke there was sure to be another tantrum.

Chapter Five

Tenerife, Canary Islands
Thursday 21st October 2021

Dozing in his chair, the phone still by his side awaiting Julie's call and the beer half finished, but now warm, he was dreaming of that day when Julie came to visit him in prison. Her beautiful face framed with her golden blonde hair cut in that sixties style of a bob, that Jimmy loved, was crystal clear to him just waiting for him to reach out and touch it. He also longed to touch her tender cheek.

He couldn't touch her now just as he couldn't do that all those years ago as prisoners and visitors were not allowed any contact.

The sight of her did touch his heart though, just like it had done when she walked through the door of the visiting room all those years before. He had thought his visitor might have been his mother. In a way he was glad it wasn't, but the same fact also made him sad. Seeing Julie there didn't take the sadness totally away, but it did help suppress it to where the pain was bearable. Before she had even sat down he was a bundle of nerves. He had to fight to hold her eye and when she was sitting down he got his reward for his perseverance. Her eyes, so deep and so beautifully blue, smiled warmly at him. It was those same eyes were he had read all those weeks before that she had liked him and they made him feel safe. He wanted to feel loved, but safe was good for now, as loved might just be hoping for too much.

"Hi," he said, the nerves fluttering back to the surface.

"Hi," she replied softly, her cheeks flaming red. Jimmy wasn't sure if she was blushing or if it was the heat in the room compared to the harsh cold day outside. He was about to thank her for coming, the only thing he could think to say, when she spoke again.

"You don't mind me coming?"

He heard the fear in her voice and he thought, no he hoped, that it was there in case he hadn't wanted her to come here. He managed to smile, a soft smile.

"Thanks, it's good to see you." He was going to say great, but great would have been their date that had never happened. Meeting here in this awful place could never be great, but he admitted to himself that it was good. And good was a rare commodity inside these walls.

"They won't let me wear my Beatle boots," he said, trying to say something, anything to ease his nervousness. He saw her start to bite her lip and he could see that she was nervous too. He rambled on. "Did you get a lift up? Or did you get the bus?"

She didn't answer him, or pay any attention to whatever he was saying. When she spoke, her words stunned him.

"I know you didn't do this."

He had to swallow down his shock. He hadn't even thought if he was going to try to tell her of his innocence. He hadn't had time to think of anything he was, or wasn't going to say as he hadn't known who his visitor was. But he definitely hadn't expected her to say this.

Sensing his surprise she added, "It's not in you." She paused then went on, "these things, not you. You're no robber," she was going to say "killer" but pushed that awful word away for now.

He felt an inner warmth take over him. A warmth from the inside. From the heart or deep down in the soul. It smothered him and as it grew and mushroomed inside him, all the sadness he had felt, all the misery and shame, melted away and seeped slowly out from his pours. It must have been pushing out from his eyes as well as they began to swell and puff with tears. He forced them back.

Here she was. A girl he barely knew and who barely knew him, at least he thought she barely knew him, but it seemed that she did indeed. In that moment the only thing he could do was to nod in agreement and acknowledgement of what she said was true. To speak would have been to open the valves holding in the warmth and he just didn't want to let that go. It was beautiful. Just like Julie. And the beauty was more than skin deep, much, much deeper.

From that day, Julie visited Jimmy every fortnight without failure. She listened to him when he needed her too, then talked to him when he had exhausted his conversations. She kept him up to date with the outside world which cushioned the harshness of his inside one. That was until six months in to their remote relationship when she reluctantly had to break the awful news that his brother Billy had been killed.

Like the actual known facts, her story of Billy's death was sketchy. But unlike the news reports, she did have some additional street knowledge. It seemed that Billy had gotten two girls pregnant almost at the same time. His father status for one had been confirmed, the second hadn't been as yet. The first girl was the sister of a member of a rival gang, or paramilitary organisation as they were now becoming known as. Reports were that the second girl was underage at only fifteen years old.

The street knowledge that Julie had heard was that there had been in fighting within the group that Billy belonged to, the Woodstock Tartan, and this was due to some stolen money and some other things, but Julie wasn't sure what these were.

She then came to the difficult part to tel.

"The younger girl tried to commit suicide." She saw Jimmy drop his head in shame, and she hadn't told him the worst part yet.

"She took some drugs and alcohol." Continued Julie, and after pausing she added, "When she recovered she claimed that she hadn't taken drugs, and that she had only had alcohol when drinking with Billy."

All Jimmy could do was shake his head in disgust. He thought he knew the rest of the story before hearing it. He asked,

"How's my mum?"

Knowing she couldn't lie to him she answered sadly, "broken." Then quickly added, "I'll help her Jimmy, I promise, I'll make sure she's all right. I promise."

Even though he had asked, he knew both of these things. Billy's death would crush his mother, she adored him. He took some solace knowing that Julie would keep her promise.

"Was it street justice," meaning for Billy Jimmy asked.

Julie just nodded. She wanted nothing more but to reach out and hug Jimmy. Kiss him, console him and even though she was free and in a few minutes she would be outside, she felt every bit of the prisoner that Jimmy was.

Jimmy felt numb. He wasn't sure how much of this was down to the death of his brother or for feeling that his pact with his mother had been a total waste of time, worse in fact. Truth was that Billy would have been safer in here.

He looked at Julie and he too longed to hold her. That longing though would last for several years yet, just over fourteen in fact until his release for good behaviour in 1982. For all that time he had to watch this girl become a woman as she carried out her promise to look after his mother and she continued her unspoken promise to Jimmy, visiting him every two weeks. He owed her everything and he swore that he would make it up to her when he got out, but unfortunately it was a promise that Jimmy couldn't live up to.

He awoke then from his doze in his chair. The sun had moved on and the chill of the shade had acted as his alarm clock. He checked the time, but didn't need to check for phone calls as he knew there hadn't been any as he would have surely awoke for that.

He was aware of his thoughts of the past, almost like an old film constantly playing in the back of his mind and he didn't need to doze deep for the film reels to start running and all the good and all the bad of his life was there on display.

Thankfully there was good as well as the bad. But the good carried a weight with it, which was sometimes as heavy if not heavier than the bad. Good like his mother, Julie, his son Raymond, his grandson Joseph, Mary-Jane Wilson, George Wilson's baby girl, who was now a woman, his brother's two children Matthew and Billie. He owed them all so, so much and it was what this entire caper was all about.

Pay back, his only salvation.

His release from prison in November 1982 wasn't as easy as Jimmy had thought. Quite the opposite. It was great to eventually fulfil all those dreams he'd had for years and eventually take his relationship with Julie on to another level. That level meant she was soon pregnant, which inspired their marriage.

Despite Julie's care as promised over the years, Jimmy's mother was still broken. Even the reunion with her eldest son hadn't impacted much on her bewildered state. It did impact on Jimmy though. And quite badly.

He had devoted his life and giving up his freedom and his life of sorts to please her and it seemed it had all been for nothing. He had resolved himself in prison to live with his decision, but now he was out the bitterness and resentment began to gnaw at him.

Employment too was proving impossible. Unemployment was high and no one wanted to employ an ex con. Truth was they didn't need to as honest labour was in ample supply. Being a husband and a father then began to weigh on Jimmy. And it was a weight that hurt. His only friends now were also ex cons. His boyhood friends had all moved on, got married, had careers and in their eyes he had let them down. He was not only a bank robber but a killer and that stain wouldn't dissolve. And almost two years later the stain deepened.

Margaret Ruddock passed away in her sleep, peacefully they had said. It was the thirtieth anniversary from when her husband Clarence Ruddock had left them on the first of March nineteen fifty-five.

Jimmy knew they were wrong. She may have seemed peaceful, docile in fact, on the outside, but Jimmy knew that deep down inside she was tormented. Broken hearted since his father had left them all those years ago, and a shattered soul since the day his brother Billy had been killed. He carried the heavy burden of guilt for both, even though in his dark hours of reflection his rational part of his mind tried to tell him he wasn't to blame. But the guilt continued to grow and swell inside him like a balloon. It was a demon, fed also by his guilt of not providing for his wife and son Raymond.

Six weeks later Jimmy attempted another bank robbery, which failed miserably. Two minutes in to the attempted robbery and the police were already on the scene. Jimmy and his colleagues walked out from the bank with their hands on their heads and their pockets empty. The only saving grace this time that no shots were fired and therefore no one was hurt, never mind killed.

Jimmy got another fifteen years and ended up serving twelve.

Julie's devotion continued. His son Raymond grew up absent from his father, creating a void that Jimmy was later never able to fill.

The only difference from his release from prison in 1982 was that it only took him six months this time to get involved in another attempted bank robbery. Sadly once again his second attempt didn't prove any more successful than his first. His reward was worse though, he was sentenced to twenty years as a repeated offence, which this time he served.

And now here he was in October 2021 having mastered that craft that he had been associated with for the majority of his life and now could claim to be, a bank robber.

He felt a pang in his chest. The guilt for all those weak and wasted years. If only he had Julie's strength. He owed so much too so many people and now maybe he had the means to repair some of the damage he had caused, or helped to cause.

The pang in his chest became a twinge. Indigestion from the beer he thought, but then he noticed that the beer wasn't even half finished.

The pain increased, as did the tightness between his shoulders, and he was suddenly overcome by fear and anxiety. He reached out for the phone, but clumsy with his clouded vision he knocked it to the floor. Grasping for it in desperation he knocked the beer over as well, but by the time it smashed to the ground Jimmy was slipping in to unconsciousness and he never heard a sound.

Chapter Six

Tenerife, Canary Islands
Friday 22nd October 2021

Ray was tuning his guitar; the guitar was a 1969 Fender Custom Shop Telecaster Thinline Journeyman Relic. It had been tuned for sometime now but Ray was stalling as his next task was attempting to balance the books on their finances, which he knew unlike his beautiful guitar, were seriously out of tune. Joe Strummer from the Clash had also favoured the Fender Telecaster, but his was the 1966 model. The link to Strummer was a coincidence as Ray had been given the guitar by a friend as a thank you for not only teaching his son on guitar, but more importantly helping the boy accept his sight loss.

His friend's son, Aurimas, had lost his sight following an accident at a bonfire. While attending one of Northern Ireland's many bonfires as part of the eleventh night's celebrations in July something thrown on to the fire caused a small explosion that blew back at Aurimas. He suffered facial burns, hair and eyebrow loss and severe damage to his eyes. The burns eventually healed, his hair grew back, but his eyesight never recovered. Fifteen years old and with a promising career in football most likely in front of him, Aurimas suffered severe depression. His father Terrick lived next door to Ray's mother and he sometimes accompanied Ray's band to gigs as he was an accomplished drummer.

At first Ray resisted the request to help. He didn't see himself qualified, neither professionally or even by his blindness. Ray's sight loss had been a more gradual loss, which had also been diagnosed when he was seven years old, so considering he was twenty when they said all the sight he had left was light perception, Ray was happy that he had been given fair warning. Aurimas sight loss was like someone had just flicked a switch, and that was really tough to handle.

At seven the toughest thing that Ray had to handle about his condition, Retinitis Pigmentosa, was how to spell the bloody thing. He and his mum just nicknamed it Piggy. It was a hereditary eye disorder, but Julie and Jimmy had no idea who he had inherited it from as visually impairment hadn't shown up in any of their ancestors that they knew off.

Typically as parents, Julie and Jimmy were devastated by the prognosis curtly delivered to them by the consultant at Belfast's Royal Victoria hospital, "He'll go blind, most likely in his teens." And that was that. No treatment, no help, no hope. They researched and found that there actually was treatment, although it was pioneering at the time, in Russia and in Switzerland. A false hope though as both were very expensive, and considering that Jimmy was five years in to his second prison term at the time and Julie was struggling to afford Raymond's school uniform, private treatment abroad was painfully out of their reach.

Ray wasn't as fazed though. Given the choice of course he would prefer not to be losing his sight, but the consultant hadn't offered any choices. In one way Piggy became a big part of his life growing up. Every bump, trip or fall triggered the question, "Was this Piggy and was his sight failing?" Whereas the loss was very gradual and like most sensory deterioration he had lost about sixty percent of his sight before he even noticed as we don't actually ever use one hundred percent of it. He was sixteen then, and it seemed that the process accelerated over the next four years to the point when he was twenty that all his useful sight had gone.

It wasn't "lights out," and suddenly all was black or anything like that. He was left with what's called "light perception," which basically means he could tell the difference between dark and light, or see shadows moving across light, albeit as a blur.

What also helped Ray, unlike Aurimas and his dreams and ambitions to become a professional footballer, Ray at seven years old hadn't thought that far ahead. So his life beyond the age of seven hadn't taken a different path that he hadn't wanted it to take. For the next nine years he led a fairly normal childhood, developing his love for music and his natural talent with whatever instrument he had taken his hands to. When the sight loss kicked in, he actually thought that this helped his focus and drive for music. He loved his career in music, which he often thought he wouldn't have without his loss of sight as he would have been forced down more normal paths of having a proper job and career. Admittedly the income could be irregular and the hours unsociable, but what other job allowed you to spend six months in Tenerife every year.

Their season in Tenerife through the winter of 2019 had been fabulous and rewarding and he had almost earned enough to see him through the winter until the next season, but covid then changed everything. Thankfully they were back trying to duplicate the rewards of that year, but that was proving very difficult indeed. Gigs were harder to secure and the session rates had plummeted. Cash flow issues aside and Ray still loved every minute of it, especially the time now he was spending with his son Joe.

Joe had been the real reason that they had been able to help Aurimas. Even though he had only been ten years old at the time. Knowing that Aurimas loved the band Biffy Clyro, Joe was also a fan, he suggested to his dad that they learn a couple of their songs so that Joe could play them to him. This quickly took legs and before long Ray was teaching both Joe and Aurimas to play the guitar and they used the Biffy Clyro album "Ellipsis" as their source of material to learn and practice with. Both boys were quick to learn and quick to demonstrate their natural talent for music. Aurimas was now nineteen and played lead guitar in Ray's band, "Us 4" and would be accompanied by Joe at their gig at Hard Rock tonight were Ray and Joe would rotate on bass and rhythm guitars. In their other gigs they still included two songs from the Biffy Clyro Ellipsis album, "Wolves of Winter" and "Howl" were Aurimas sang lead on both.

Ray was taken from his reverie when Joe entered his room, "Dad Trace," which was short for Tracy the bands keyboard player who also mainly took charge of the cooking in their villa, "is complaining there's nothing to cook except for pasta with Heinz tomato soup for a sauce." Without waiting for a response Joe continued as if reciting a list, "Mum's phoned twice about her lift from the airport on Sunday. Aurimas wants to know can he play your Telecaster tonight. The electric box is beeping and needs topped up. And Mr Garcia is here to see you."

There it all was, laid bare for all to see. His entire worries all included in Joe's opening remarks. No food. His ex-wife's arrival pending and Mr Garcia was here to collect the rent, which he didn't have. And the lights were about to go out.

He answered, "Tell Trace I love pasta and tomato soup. Tell mother I'll arrange the lift with Colin, and do me a favour, text Colin and tell him to make sure he's on time tonight as I want to get to Hard Rock before Pepe leaves so that I can get some cash. Tell Aurimas I've the Teleblaster all tuned for him, you can play a number on it yourself, that's if you can get it back from Aurimas once he gets his hands on it."

Ray heard the smile in Joe's voice when he responded, "Yeah, you serious? We can both have it? Aurimas was sure you'd say no way."

He could tell that Joe was already turning to now leave the room, busting to give the good news to Aurimas. Truth was Ray was going to suggest they played it anyway, as they were much better than him on it.

"Tell Mr Garcia to come on in," Ray shouted hoping that Joe heard him before he left. He was also going to tell him to tell Trace that he'd have money later and they could go shopping tomorrow, but he didn't bother as he guessed Joe was long gone by now. A few seconds later he heard Mr Garcia say as he entered the room.

"Raymonde, Raymonde my friend," his voice somewhere between talking and singing.

"Mr Garcia," said Ray, "good to see you, how you keeping?"

"Antonio," sang Mr Garcia, "call me Antonio. I tell you all the time no Mr Garcia."

"Sorry Antonio, come in sit down." He assumed the seats in the room were free, or at least one or two of them he hoped. This was the room they used to store their music stuff and it could get a bit messy.

"I'm cool," answered Antonio "just here for one memento," he went on, then starting shaking his forefinger at Ray, "you killing me with the rent Raymond. I never need to chase you before but this year you make me always come to you." He then spread his arms wide in a gesture to say, "look at your surroundings" and then said, "I give you my villa this year, more room for your guys and you make me chase for rent."

It was a fact. The villa had been part of the deal this year, and the part that Ray was struggling to keep up with. The deal was half price rent on the villa plus one free gig each week on Monday nights at Antonio Garcia's complex, The Sol Antonio.

The five bedroom villa was superb and was much better than their previous accommodation arrangement in separate studios, but since arriving at the start of September the gigs this year were proving difficult, almost impossible to get.

"Sorry Antonio, I'm really sorry, but you know gigs this year are slow, the tourists are only coming in numbers now," pleaded Ray. I can pay you half on my credit card," he added, although he was hoping this wouldn't be a runner as it would max out his card and he wanted to keep something as back up as he was responsible for the two lads, Joe and Aurimas. Although it seemed sometimes that he was responsible for the entire band.

"No, no," Antonio came back quickly, "credit card charge me big percentage, and ah," he paused, "you know, cash is much better."

"I've got another gig lined up," offered Ray. "You know Stu," Ray didn't know his second name; "Stu from the Compo Stella Golf booked us for Thursday's." "First gigs free, but he'll pay after that and then I can get up to date with your rent," he went to say Mr Garcia but then corrected, "Antonio." And then to try and strike a deal he added, "all cash!"

"I tell you what," said Antonio, "Halloween is coming up, it's on a Sunday and then the next Saturday my new hotel is opening in Barcelona, it's called the Gabrielle Sol for my wife, oh it's so beautiful Raymond." He paused reflecting on his new addition to his property portfolio then continued. "You play me a gig both nights and we forget two months rent. Gabrielle wants you to play there, you know how much she loves you Raymond?"

Before Ray could answer Antonio added, "Oh expenses of course, I will pay for the flights and everything so no need to worry about that."

Ray liked the sound of both the deal and the trip to Barcelona. "I'll have to run it past the others, but it sounds OK to me Antonio."

"Great, great," said Antonio, sort of closing out the deal, but then asked, "Can you do some Sting for Gabrielle?"

"Not a whole set, but we can do a few."

"OK, Raymonde, OK," answered Antonio cheerfully, knowing indeed that this would please his wife, especially if he told her that he had insisted that Ray play these songs for her. "We'll discuss the details on Monday night at our gig."

Chapter Seven

Tenerife, Canary Islands
Friday 22nd October 2021

Sasha Moreno had been appointed as the leading investigating officer for the bank robbery. He was currently serving as Deputy Police Inspector of the Policia Canaria and located in Tenerife, and had taken his role when this police force had been formed back in 2010. Prior to this Sasha had served fifteen years as a Detective in one of Spain's four police forces, the Cuerpo Nacional de Policia located in Barcelona, the city of his birth.

Sasha had two loves in his life, his job as a policeman and his passion for fishing. This fact was the main reason why his marriage hadn't worked and so following what ended up being a messy divorce, the transfer to Tenerife was his perfect escape.

From Monday to Friday he proudly wore his starched sky blue uniform and carried out his duties with diligence. This mainly consisted of dealing with crimes against tourists, pick pockets, theft, scams, fights, or crimes carried out by tourists on tourists, pick pockets, theft, scams and fights. At weekends he went out on his boat fishing.

Bank robberies were a rare occurrence in the Canary Islands and he was delighted to have been given the case. Already he had interviewed the bank staff, the owner of the café-bar beside the bank and from what he had observed to date the only other witness was a young boy on a skateboard, but he had concluded he was a tourist who had already returned home.

Sitting at his favourite beach front restaurant enjoying his ice tea which had followed his lunch, he reviewed the three key things that interested him.

Firstly the banks CCTV had been carrying out a reboot just at the time when the robbery took place. Sasha naturally thought this suspicious, but the truth was that the system had been faulty for some time and being down during the day was quite a frequent occurrence.

A fact that the bank didn't want to advertise. Secondly, apart from the cashier's tills and the back up cash for the telebank machine, the only other thing that had been touched and taken were four safety deposit boxes. And finally, the smaller of the two robbers had knocked out the larger robber and left him behind unconscious at the scene. It appeared simply only a fluke that the second robber had regained consciousness in time to get away, although the witness reports seemed to suggest that he had hardly rushed his escape.

No other useful facts or points, or clues were available to him as yet. He didn't even have any lead or description on the car the robbers had used.

One conclusion though he had already reached was that this was, either in part or in full, an inside job. He would need to interview the bank staff again.

As he sat at his usual table, watching the waves foam as the tide came in he was sipping his ice tea and subconsciously smoothing down his moustache, thinking about the interviews of the bank staff when he became aware that a Looky Looky man had popped up, making his way around the tables, which were full mainly of tourists. Sasha had removed his police shirt and swapped it for a tee shirt before his lunch, mainly in case of any lunchtime spillages but also so as not to put off any tourists by sitting beside a policeman. It also let him be more invisible, hence the oncoming scholar of the never ending school of looky looky men.

If on duty, and if not assigned to the robbery, it would be Sasha's remit to move on the illegal trader and even confiscate his goods. Thankfully he was off the hook on this occasion, as it was a service that wasn't very popular with the tourists.

What amazed Sasha though was where did all these guys come from and where did they learn their patter. No matter where you went, any town, any resort in Spain, Portugal, the Balearics, the Canaries, Turkey, Greece etc.etc.etc. They were all there and they all were selling the same crap and gibbering the same babble. Was there a factory somewhere that produced all this stuff for them? If so what was it called? Del boy and the Looky Looky factory? Was there a school or college group who taught them all the slick talk and the patter? Did Professor Looky Looky provide seminars, trade shows, teams or zoom meetings, online classes? And did they have various levels? "Hey there I'm a junior Looky Looky but can't wait to become Big Boy Charlie and get me own patch!"

No sooner had these thoughts, as they did many many times, run riot through Sasha's head, when the looky, looky man was upon him.

"Del Boy My Man!" he sang cheerfully, "looking good man, looking good." Then proceeding to set sunglasses on the table he continued, "Designer glasses, I give you best price, how much you pay?" "You like these ones?" holding up a pair of fake Ray-Bans. "Go on Dell Boy My Man," thrusting them forward for Sasha to try on, "You try," then excitedly, "Lovely Jubbly, hey man, Lovely Jubly eh?"

Then suddenly three watches appeared on the table, all lined up perfectly. "You want a Rolex?" Then with a grin that would possibly break a mere mortals jaw, he smiled and added with sincerity and honesty that would have gotten most criminals let off whatever they had been charged for, "They're not fake man, no the real thing." Holding one up he asked, "You give me thirty euros?" "Go on Dell Boy, its Lovely Jubbly."

A girl from the next table then leaned across looking at one of the watches and asked, in what Sasha thought might be an Irish accent, "Hey mate, are those Rolex's really real?"

Sensing a sale like a shark senses blood; the fully qualified Looky Looky Man collected up his wares and swiftly transferred his display to the adjacent table. As Sasha finished his ice tea, he witnessed two Irish girls haggling for ten minutes for what they believed was a genuine Rolex watch, eventually settling for twenty euros. The girl's friend decided she also wanted to partake of this bargain of a lifetime and so also bought one for the same price, which they thought was awful generous of this man of enterprise. Finally the first girl also decided to buy a pair of Rayban's, which she bought for what she considered a bargain fifteen euros. Settling up the cash, the girls then tipped Mr Looky Looky a ten spot to say thank you for his generosity, and as they admired their newly acquired range of designer accessories, our fully qualified king of Looky Looky Men hustled on down the beach front thinking it was Christmas and rushing to report his newest experience with that strange specie called tourists to the evening edition of the Looky Looky Newsletter.

Sasha decided to take the rest of the afternoon off, it was Friday after all and he suddenly felt the need for a drink. A large one!

Chapter Eight

Belfast, Northern Ireland
Friday 22nd October 2021

At the same time when the two Irish girls debated whether or not their Rolex's were real, just under two thousand miles north, a Jet 2 flight bound for Tenerife had been loaded up and ready to taxi for take off when a passenger who had filled himself too full of the holiday spirits they were selling in the departure lounges bar made a complete arse of himself when he refused to sit down when instructed to do so by the stewardess, and loudly insisting that he needed an urgent visit to the toilet. In a further display of drunkenness and aided by both the planes momentum and his wobbly legs he went head over tit and landed face first on another passengers lap. To add to the pandemonium the passenger, a middle aged woman, screamed. Several more women, startled by the scream of the first woman, then joined in. Frightened beyond their wits at all the screaming on a moving plane, the children on board all started to cry.

Thirty minutes later and following the subsequent arrest of the drunken man and his swift removal from the plane, the passengers were still waiting on the man's luggage being removed so that the flight could continue. Back in row twenty five the passenger in the window seat, Dennis Crawford was trying to get the attention of his travelling companion, Jeffrey Byrne in an effort to have him look out for the stewardess as he now needed to top up his hip flask with Johnny Walkers Black Label, which he had purchased in duty free. His last refill was now gone thanks to the delay departing. At that time, just like Sasha Moreno, Dennis needed a drink, not to get intoxicated like the pratt that had been taken off the flight but to ease his anxiety when flying.

Unlike the two Irish girls purchases from the Looky Looky Man though, Dennis was sporting a real Rolex, a Rolex Yacht-Master 37Oyster, Steel and Platinum and sticking out from the pocket of his shirt, was a pair of genuine Ray-Ban Aviators. Also unlike the two Irish girls who were enjoying the final week of their holiday in Tenerife, Dennis Crawford, no middle name or nickname, and his colleague who had both a middle name and a nickname, Jeffrey Cuthbert Byrne, nicknamed "The Digger," were heading to Tenerife to try to establish who had stolen the contents of their four safety deposit boxes from the Blanco Santander Los Cristianos, and to remove the similar contents from the remainder of their safety deposit boxes from two other banks, before the robbers decided to steal these also.

Dennis and Jeffrey had both worked bloody hard at their legitimate haulage business, which had earned them very little returns in terms of profit, and they had also worked, maybe not just so hard, at their not so legitimate business of smuggling. Their bounty was mostly cigarettes, but sometimes drugs and sometimes people, and the mark up and profit margins here were great. Hence the euros stashed in banks, not only in Tenerife, but across the canary islands. Heading closer to retirement they had also recently began to filter some of their hidden profits in to property, two villas in Playa de Blanca Lanzerote, a small cruiser currently moored at the Los Cristianos marina and other luxury items, the Rolex being one of these examples.

But someone else knew where there profits were stashed and they needed to find out who that was.

Before that though, Dennis needed a drink and it seemed that Jeff the digger was fast asleep.

"Jeff," he whispered loudly. No response. The guy in the middle seat had his headset on and was watching something on his tablet and Dennis thought that he may have fallen asleep as well.

"Jeff," he tried again, slightly louder, which did the trick this time as Jeff stirred and slowly turned his head towards Dennis. Dennis flashed his hip flask, which was acknowledged by a slight nod from Jeff, who then gave the aisle a quick scan in both directions. With no stewards in sight Jeff nodded again and Dennis then lost no time filling up his hip flask, which he hoped Would be enough to get him up in the air, provided that this Jet 2 crew got a move on. Jeffrey Cuthbert Byrne, the Digger, settled back in his seat, rolling the stiffness out of his neck, and tried to get back to sleep. He wanted to get some R&R as he had an idea that the next few days could be draining.

Dennis also leaned back in his seat, sipping his Johnny Walkers. A few minutes later the Captain announced that they were good to go. He

My Daddy Was a Bank Robber

apologised for the delay, gave them the usual bumph about the flight time and weather and promised to try to make up some time on their way down to Tenerife south so that they could all get on with their holidays as soon as possible.

"Holiday?" thought Dennis, "If only!" This was a search and rescue mission. To rescue the rest of their pension funds, and search out whoever had stolen a chunk of it already. And if they did happen to find these bank robbers, then old Jeff might have some digging to do, Dennis chuckled to himself.

Jeffrey wasn't chuckling, quite the opposite in fact. He was struggling to keep the lid on his bad mood. This trip could blow back on him big time and he could end up requiring a digger for himself, or wearing a concrete overcoat while being thrown off their fishing boat far out in the deep Mediterranean sea. The key source of his concern was that he didn't need to ponder who had broken in to their safety deposit boxes. He knew who it was, because it was him who had told him, well boasted might be more accurate. And that little midget Charlie Bassett had fucked him over and if Dennis found out Jeffrey was a dead man,

Although partners, Jeffrey was the junior of the two, much junior actually. The word partner translated for him as lackey or gofer, or as we've mentioned, the digger. The digger though had been Jeffrey's nickname long before he had even met Dennis and long before he had fulfilled that role to get rid of people, cleaning up for Dennis's many messes. The name also bore no reference to Jeffrey's love of gardening and growing his own vegetables on his grandfather's allotment. It was simply from his initials. Jeffrey Cuthbert Byrne, JCB.

At school it was difficult to hide your middle name as it was there on the register for all to see on the role call that the teacher marked off every morning, and once kids learned something like that it stuck. And once they nicknamed you that stuck even more. So very early in his life Jeffrey was known as Digger. Later in his life, when thankfully for Jeffrey, it was much easier to hide his middle name Cuthbert, and therefore it was impossible for anyone to link his nickname to his initials. Instead it took on a much darker meaning, which suited within the circles in which he moved.

Jeffrey knew only too well, and Charlie Bassett suspected, that the profits they had made over the past years and stashed away belonged to Denis. Jeffrey's share was a mere ten percent. Okay, he would have maybe a couple of hundred thousand euros, but this was nothing compared to Dennis, and not much when it had to do him for the next thirty, maybe forty years.

Charlie, being the little weasel he was and making it his business to know things, had over the years gleaned the top line of Dennis and Jeffery's business activities and relationship and with this knowledge he had sensed unease and jealousy from Jeffrey. You didn't need to be a brain surgeon to notice that Dennis wore a Rolex and drove a Mercedes S Class, while Jeffrey sported an Enoksen Dive watch that cost less than a monkey, and drove a Skoda.

Charlie had, like the skilled leach he was, slowly extracted this information from Jeffrey and then twisted and manipulated his jealousy that eventually had Jeffrey boasting about their stash, which in his boasts he had a much bigger share than his measly ten percent. Then damningly, drunk one night, he told Charlie were their cash was stashed. Every bank and every name they had used. Now sitting in the plane on his way to Tenerife and that prick Dennis clicking his fingers for him to do lookout so that he could have more of his Johnny Walkers, Jeffrey knew deep deep down that Charlie Bassett had played him like a fiddle and if he didn't get to Charlie before Dennis did he'd be hearing that fiddle play his last lament as he sunk to the bottom of the Mediterranean sea. At least his divers watch would tell him how deep he was!

He decided to join Dennis on the Johnny Walkers Black Label. Fuck the rental car they could get a taxi from the airport. Jet 2 had the Black Label on two for a tenner; he'd have twenty quids worth there as he was sure there was no way that Dennis would be sharing his.

Chapter Nine

Tenerife, Canary Islands
Friday 22nd October 2021

Colin had been late as usual. He had tried to squeeze in a pick up from the airport before collecting them for the gig, but the job took longer than expected as the two men just in off the Belfast Jet 2 flight, and both pist it seemed on Johnny Walkers, had wanted to swing by their boat, which was moored in Los Cristianos marina, before going to their hotel. It not only meant that the band were rushed getting set up, but Ray had missed Pepe and so hadn't got paid. Elaine, Pepe's partner did say that there was a chance that Pepe would be back later, but Ray knew that it was rare for him to return as he had already most likely put in a twelve hour shift that day. He would just have to see him tomorrow, or failing that use his back up credit card to buy some well needed groceries for their villa.

He was feeling pressure. Even despite making a part deal earlier that afternoon with Mr Garcia on their rent, having to use his back up credit card already, only two months in to their six month stint, was a real concern. Another concern was the pending arrival of his ex-wife. And on top of this he was hungry as the pasta hadn't stretched far. He told himself that he needed to shake off his funk and concentrate on helping the band set up for their gig.

While the familiarity of Hard Rock's stage area and general layout was great, having Joe here for his couple of weeks of half term was priceless. Even though each band member pretty much set them selves up it was having that ability to move around when the place was so busy. Even though they all knew the layout, the constant unknown and erratic movement of the customers confined Ray and the band to their stage area. That was except for Joe. And having Joe there meant that he responded to the bands hunger by going in to Hard Rock's kitchen and bringing them all out amazing burgers and drinks. It was a part of their deal that they could have food and drink, but they normally had to wait until the gig was over as before this the staff were too busy to provide waiter service, but later the selection of food could be limited, or if busy like tonight, non existent.

So with their hunger now abated, the band got down to finalising their set up.

Terry Bell was really fussy about setting up his own drums. His set was a mix of brands and colours all bought on the internet and all set up in perfect alignment as Terry was totally blind, and had been from birth. Although impossible to be certain the doctors thought that his mother had been in contact with Rubella or Measles during her pregnancy and when born just over 6 weeks premature Terry's eyes had not properly developed, and never would. Learning of other mother's and babies who it was presumed had also been in contact with Rubella or Measles which sadly had resulted in much more serious disabilities and birth defects, his parents were grateful that their son was healthy and perfect in every other way. Terry knew no better and went about his life in his own way, and that included his drumming.

Ray thought he had too much clutter on his kit and personally preferred a more basic arrangement on the occasion when he picked up the sticks. Terry though was proud of his array of percussion options, even though visually due to the various colours they wouldn't please most drummers, but all drummers would definitely nod enthusiastically at the skill, structure, timing and overall feel and understanding that Terry exhibited in spades when he played. What was also important was that he played, not over played.

Terry had heard Ray and Trace play at a gig over six years ago, when they were just a duo. After the gig was over he had asked to be introduced to Ray and after a couple of minutes of idle chit chat about the gig he had asked if he could join up with them to play percussion. Ray had noted at the time that Terry hadn't said drums. They arranged to meet a few days later and the three have played together ever since.

Tracy was the sister that Ray never had. She was born in Burundi in 1993 around the time when civil war had broken out between the Tutsi army and Hutu Rebels. Orphaned and living in terrible squalid conditions she developed Trachoma, an eye disease caused by infection, which untreated leads to blindness. Although this was a very painful condition it wasn't the worst disease or infliction that babies like Tracy endured. She was one of the lucky ones that managed to survive until eventually she was adopted by an Irish aid worker and brought to Ireland in 1995.

Her adopted mother, Maryanne Dooley christened her Tracy Adamma Dooley. Adamma was African for "child of beauty" and it was thought was her name, either by birth or given to her by the aid workers as they didn't know who her parents were and any sort of paperwork simply didn't exist. Tracy was after Maryanne's mother, a gesture that Marieanne hoped would bring her mother closer to the child as she had severe reservations about the adoption. The gesture worked, but it was the child herself that drew her grandmother in regardless of having the same name.

Tracy surely was a child of beauty. Her smile lit up the room, even though her own eyes kept the room in darkness for her, but she never allowed that shadow to fall across her path. The opposite in fact as she shone like a beacon on most of what she did and on most of whoever she met in her life.

Educated firstly in St Joseph's Primary school for children, a specialist school in Dublin for visually impaired children, but then progressed to a main stream secondary school where, with some assistance, she was able to cope and excel throughout her studies. Her two areas of excellence were in languages and music and it was while studying both at Dublin University she first met Ray.

Arthur's Day, on Thursday Twenty sixth September 2013, was an event to showcase the best of Ireland's creativity and talent from the world of music and culture taking place at over five hundred pubs and venues across Ireland. It was at the hub of this event, at the Arthur Guinness store house at St James Gate Brewery in Dublin, where Ray and Tracy had been introduced by another spectator who for some unknown reason assumed they both knew each other just because they were both blind. It was something they both laughed at. Maybe if they had sight, they discussed later while enjoying one of Arthur's creamy pints, they too on seeing two people standing close together sporting white sticks, might also assume they knew each other.

It wasn't only Tracy and Ray that became friends as their entire two groups they were with that day struck up a bond. Two of whom, Valerie and Davitt got married four years later. Tracy and Ray provided the music that night. Two other musicians from the group, Steff and Simone both played from time to time with Ray, Steff played Saxophone and Simone played guitar. Simone was also an IT expert and a lover of gadgets, and it was thanks to him that Ray, Tracy and the other's all wore head set microphones that not only got rid of the need for the stand alone ones that were a disaster as they were easy to bump in to and knock over, but the head sets also allowed the band members to talk to each other at the flick of a switch. The profitable season of 2019 had also helped with the upgrade on technology.

Another of Simone's great ideas was the rubber mats. A simple issue, but a band without sight had the tendency to stand totally still, which didn't look great, or to move and then run the risk of bumping in to each other, their equipment, or even worse end up disorientated and not facing the audience. The mats solved this. Each tactile mat, placed carefully, not only told them what direction they were facing, but provided them with their boundary that they were safe to move around in without causing chaos.

With the mats now in place they were good to go. To finalise their set up and as a last sound check Ray agreed they could play Biffy Clyro's song "Rearrange", which was one of Aurimas and Joe's favourite songs. The two boys doubled up on the guitar, Ray played bass and Trace took on lead vocals. The song had a beautiful melodic rift and soft vocals that suited Trace's voice. Ray had hoped that one of the boys, who could both hold a note, would have sang on lead, but although their confidence on guitar playing was good enough for public consumption, their desire to sing had still some growing to do. Ray was pleased though as he could hear Aurimas quietly singing along in his headset, but being careful that Trace's volume drowned his out. When the song had ended Aurimas said, "Cheers Ray, loved that, and your guitar is just sweet mate."

Ray flicked the switch on his own headset to move off his main mike so he could speak on their "group chat" line, "You made it sweet Aurimas, so no problem." Then to them all he said, "Sounded good to me so we're good to go, so we'll kick off in about twenty minutes."

"If anyone needs the bog, I'm going," Joe added when Ray had finished. Terry was the only one who took Joe up on his offer. Unlike Ray, Terry didn't go in for all the incognito stuff, he headed to the toilet like most blind people and took hold of Joes right elbow in his left hand. Joe was an expert and guided Terry to the men's with ease, even navigating a couple of blokes that had certainly taken full advantage of the happy hour and were swaying somewhat. Joe lined up Terry at one of the urinals and then took the one beside for himself.

"You're Mum coming over on Sunday then," Terry asked. He was just making casual chat as men do when urinating.

"Yeah," answered Joe, "should be fun."

Terry laughed, "It'll be that all right."

Joe finished first then headed over to the sinks to wash and dry his hands. To let Terry know were he was he spoke again, "Sinks are over here Terry and you're OK there's no one else here." This enabled Terry to finish up and head over in Joe's direction using his voice as the guiding reference this time rather than his elbow.

"Soaps up on the right," Joe said and then pulled several paper hand towels free and waited until Terry had finished washing before pressing them in to his hand.

"Cheers," said Terry and dried his hands. "Were's the bin?"

"Just here," answered Joe, tapping the bin with his foot to enable Terry to follow the sound. Once the waste paper had been successfully deposited in the bin, Joe asked, "Good to go?"

"Sure thing," answered Terry and then added, "cheers kid."

Joe turned to enable Terry to take up position on his right hand side again and once Terry's hand had found his elbow, Joe retraced their steps back out to their stage area.

"You want to get a drink or anything Terry?"

"No, I'm good; just stick me back on my stool. I've a bet running on the West Brom match so want to check it for a cash out before we get started."

Joe did as asked and then took a curious look around the crowd. The bar area was jammed and the seating area too was almost full, only a couple of free tables left. His eye caught two men being led to a free table by one of the waitresses. A tiny man who looked like he was smaller than five feet tall, although Joe wasn't sure as the size of the second man in comparison, who must be loads over six feet, maybe close to seven, might have made the small man look smaller. Or maybe it was the other way around and the smaller made the taller look taller. Whatever, they were an odd couple.

The tiny man had a scowling face and was giving off to the waitress about something. The waitress almost looked frightened. Joe knew the girl, Nicky, and she was well seasoned with difficult tourists but she clearly looked nervous. He glanced around to check were the doorman was but he couldn't see him.

The big man was wearing a large sun hat, which looked like a woman's, and underneath and hanging down at his back was what looked like a bandage. He didn't seem to be involved, or aware, of whatever was being said by his mate, he was just following behind with a smile on his face that made him look like a little boy. A giant little boy.

"Why can't we have proper menus?" Charlie Bassett moaned. He was going to swear, wanted to in fact to highlight to this bimbo that he wasn't to be messed with. All he wanted was a menu. He thought if he sweared though she might have cause to ask him to leave, or go get the bouncer, and he needed to stay here. Besides, he was hungry.

"Its Covid rules Sir," Nicky answered. "No menus log in and order through the tablet there," she pointed to the smart tablet she had placed on the table. "Your table number is 41 so just log in; user name is hardrock, all one word and lower case. You also need to register your card to pay, no cash. Sorry." Once the instructions were relayed, Nicky hurried off.

Charlie looked at the tablet as if it was a turd sitting there in the middle of his table. He swore under his breath, and then quickly looked around to make sure no one had heard him. A small boy with his face covered in ketchup was smiling at him from the next table, his toothy grin showing the half chewed contents of his mouth. Charlie tried to slide across his bench to sit on the outer seat away from this little brat, just in case there was a food explosion when he realised that Monty had sat beside him rather than on the opposite bench. Digging him with his elbow Charlie said. "Why are you sitting there? Sit over there," pointing to the opposite side of their table.

"I want to see the music," puffed Monty.

Charlie then noticed the price tag and security tag hanging down from the back of Monty's hat.

"Where'd you get that hat?"

"In the shop."

"I know in the fuc.." sighing then corrected himself, "I know you got it in a shop brains of Britain, but what shop?"

Monty didn't answer. He hadn't done this on purpose, his attention had been taken up as he noticed the band starting to lift their guitars and get ready to play.

"There starting." He said.

Charlie looked closer at Monty's hat. It looked like a woman's hat. He exhaled then reached over and pulled hard at the price tag. It only came away partially leaving the string there but the label and price tag were gone. He threw them under the table. He then tried his best to tuck the security tag underneath the hat and was finally able to hide it by using part of the bandage. Sighing once again under his breath he said in disgust, "over here to get rich and you're gonna get us lifted for shop lifting or cross dressing!"

Monty was tuned out on the band so Charlie set to working how to use the stupid tablet, thinking to himself, "Covid rules my arse."

Chapter Ten

Tenerife, Canary Islands
Friday 22nd October 2021

Drowsy from the flight and heads buzzing from the Johnny Walkers Black Label, Dennis and Jeffrey were grumpy, tired and hungry. Jeffrey also sensed that Dennis was pissed that he had a drink and they now needed to wait for a taxi rather than take a hire car as they had planned. The queue for taxis was long as several flights had all landed together. When it was their turn a large mini bus type pulled up on the rank. Jeffrey was aware that the people next in the queue were a family of five or six and with their luggage and push chair would require a taxi like this, whereas he and Dennis only required a standard car. But just as Jeffrey had signalled to the family to go ahead before them, Dennis had slid the side door open and slumped in to one of the back seats. Fully aware that if asked Dennis might tell him where to get off, Jeffrey shrugged an apology and then slid in to the seat in front of Dennis.

Glancing to the other people just outside the taxi door Colin asked, "You not all together?"

Sliding the door closed Jeffrey answered, "No, just the two of us."

Slightly annoyed as this meant that Coline could only charge a standard fare and not the enhanced fare for his bus, he asked, "Where to lads?"

"We need to go to the marina in Los Cristianos first than to Playa de Las Americas; we have a private apartment rented there." Jeffrey reached forward with the card with the address of the private rental on it, which Colin took. Colin glanced at the clock on the dash and calculating quickly in his head thought he could just about make it on time to pick up the lads for their gig. Tight though so he'd have to get a move on.

"When you get to the marina I'll show you were to go," Jeffrey added.

At first Colin tried to chat, but it was soon clear that the lads weren't the chatting type. The only thing he learnt was that they had both had a few drinks on the plane, Johnny Walkers Black Label, which he could smell, and then pretty much where they were going, which they had already told him. So he gave up and concentrated on driving, quickly where he could as he knew Ray would be pissed if he was late again.

Colin had been taxiing in Tenerife for just over twelve years, pretty much since his parents had moved their from London to open their bar. But not wanting to work in a bar all day, Colin got his taxi licence as soon as he could and he hasn't looked back since. He loved taxiing and he had constantly upgraded his vehicle so that now he owned the Mercedes bus they were now in and also a 2016 Lexus he had for premium pick ups which paid great money and sometimes tipped even better. Like everyone else who relied on tourism the last eighteen months had been difficult but now you just had to chase the money and work the hours and that's all there was to it.

It took just under fifteen minutes to reach the marina in Los Cristianos and he had to almost shout to get his passengers attention as they had both fallen asleep. Once awake the one who had done the talking, well for what talking there had been, gave him directions and told him where to stop. The same man got out and disappeared down steps and on to one of the decks where the boats were moored.

Jeffrey found their boat, unzipped the tarpaulin enough to step on to the side and then jump down to the deck. With his keys he unlocked the cabin and headed down to the small bunk room on the starboard side. Removing the base of one of the beds he found another panel with a padlock, which he also unlocked. This revealed a small safe with a combination lock. Once he had keyed in the correct code three was a small click and the door opened slightly. He used the small handle to open the door fully and lifted out the one bag that was inside. The bag consisted of a large bundle of cash wrapped in plastic and aback shiny gun, which was also in a plastic bag. He put the gun in his jacket pocket and then removed the cash, counted two thousand euros, which he placed in his other jacket pocket and then returned the rest to the safe. Once locked up once more he retraced his steps back to the taxi to now head on to their rented apartment. They could have stayed on their boat as they had done before many times, but they'd come out here in such short notice they didn't have their usual time to instruct the company who looked after their boat to fuel and stock it up, as well as ensure all the batteries were fully charged. So a last minute rental would have to do, and despite all the talk of covid there wasn't a whole pile of choice left. It took another twenty minutes to reach their apartment due to a road accident and as soon as the two men had settled up, no tip, Colin hurried off knowing he was late again.

The apartment had a plus and a minus. It had one bedroom but the sitting room was set out like a studio, so the lads, who both snored, could sleep separately. The bathroom had a bath with an over shower that had a plastic curtain that had seen better days. No walk in shower. Dennis summed up the showering facilities when he said, "You could piss harder."

Once sort of showered, Dennis and Jeffrey headed out to find somewhere to eat. The plan was simple, as they couldn't go to their two banks until Monday morning. Eat, have a couple of drinks, then bed. They would use Saturday and Sunday to walk about to see if they could possibly notice some familiar face or faces here that might point to who had robbed their stash. They both knew that they would know who it was as soon as they saw them. There was no room for coincidence here. The right people here or maybe should say the wrong people, and bingo. Jeffrey knew this better than Dennis as he was certain that one glimpse of Charlie Bassett and Dennis would suss it all.

They were late for some places in terms of food but they soon came across Hard Rock Café, which seemed to be buzzing. They both agreed that a good burger or a steak would hit the spot. Also, Dennis saw the poster announcing that night's band, A Clash tribute band, and he loved The Clash, so they soon joined a small queue. But for the poster, either man might just have noticed a large man wearing a large hat and a tiny man wrestling with a smart tablet. They were still able to hear though and they heard the band announce they were about to start.

"Good evening ladies and gentlemen," Ray announced, "and welcome along to Hard Rock Café. I hope you are all enjoying your holiday and the fabulous weather here in Playa de lads Americas? I've just a couple of bits of housekeeping before we kick off with our tribute to the Clash tonight. Elaine, your manager for tonight, has asked me to remind you that masks do still need to be worn when you are walking about. Also, food and drinks can be ordered from your table using the smart pads, but the bar is open for service for drinks only. Your three bar staff tonight are the three imagos, Pat, Drew and Fredrico, and in charge of the tables the lovely trio Susan, Nicky and Karen. We're going to kick off here with one of the Clash's biggest hits, Rock the Casbah and if you want to request any Clash song please pass these on to the bar staff." He paused and then added, "As Joe Strummer once said, Welcome to the Casbah Club." This was Trace's cue to go with the piano intro.

"Now the King told the boogie man,

> You have to let that raga drop,
> The oil down the desert way,
> Has been shaken to the top,
> The Sheik, he drove his Cadillac
> He went a-cruisin' down the ville,
> The muezzin was a-standin',
> On the radiator grill.
> Sharif don't like it,
> Rockin' the Casbah,
> Rock the Casbah."

They worked their way through the first set songs, "Should I stay or Should I Go?" "White Riot," "I fought The Law," "Tommy Gun," "Career Opportunities," which Joe finally agreed to sing so they played the softer keyboard version from the Clash's fourth album Sandinista, which had been recorded with the vocals by the keyboard player, Mickey Gallagher's two young sons Ben and Luke. Joe, although nervous, soon settled down once he started to sing.

> "They offered me the office,
> Offered me the shop,
> They said I'd better take anything they'd got,
> Do you wanna make tea at the BBC,
> Do you wanna be,
> Do you really wanna be a cop?
> Career opportunities the ones that never knock,
> Career opportunities to keep you out the dock,
> Career opportunities the ones that never knock."

Joe got the best applause of the night when the song finished and it made his cheeks blush. On their internal mike Ray said, "I think we'll keep that one on the play list, well done Joe."

Joe's blush deepened and his embarrassment made him forget to answer his dad and instead in a momentary lapse he forgot the sight thing and smiled as his thanks for the praise.

Terry counted them in to their penultimate song of their first set and they launched in to "Police and Thieves." Shortly in to the song Joe noticed the giant with the stupid hat heading towards the stage. He was staring straight at his dad as he walked, or actually seemed to dander. He stopped just in front of Ray and Joe could see that he was speaking, asking his dad something. At first Joe waited hoping he would go away, but when he just stood there and knowing that his dad wouldn't know he was there, he flicked the switch on his head set to talk internally.

Ray was enjoying the song, Police and Thieves as well as there final song of this set, Julie's Been Working For The Drug Squad, were 2 of his favourite Clash songs. Just after the first verse he thought he could hear someone speaking in front of him. He also sensed that someone was there. Several seconds later Joe's voice came over his head set, "Dad, sorry, but there's a big guy standing in front of you and I think he's talking to you or something."

Ray sang on, but he felt awkward. He couldn't answer Joe and he couldn't talk to whoever it was.

Joe also felt awkward and didn't know what to do. Actually he did, there was nothing to do but carry on. He played on, but the song seemed to last forever and the time enhanced his tension.

Unaware of how Joe felt, Ray also felt tense and he also felt the song would never end. Eventually it did and straight away Ray turned off his mike and once the applause had died down he was then able to hear the man in front of him.

"Can you play a Cliff Richard song?"

Ray was taken back for a moment. The voice was that of a man but the way he spoke was almost child like. Before Ray answered him the man spoke again.

"A request for a Cliff Richard song?" he repeated, with a slight irritation in his voice this time.

"We're only playing Clash songs tonight," said Ray, "sorry."

"Oh," Monty replied, and then paused. After a few more seconds the next words surprised Ray.

"You Jazz's son?"

Jazz's son? Ray got it straight away. He knew who he was talking about, but that didn't mean it made any sense to him. A minute ago this man, who he didn't know from Adam, was asking him to play Cliff Richard songs and then in his next breath he asks him was he Jazz's son. Jimmy Jazz's son. Jimmy Jazz Ruddock's son. His father who he hadn't seen for years.

Then Monty spoke again, which brought Ray back to that moment, "Mr Bassett wants to see you."

Ray was asking who Mr Bassett was but Monty had already turned to go and was making his way back to his table.

"He's gone dad," Joe said over the head set.

Ray didn't speak. He had no idea who this man was, who Mr Bassett was but the reference to his father had left him with a feeling of dread. It sat like a huge lump in his throat and almost made it impossible for him to sing their final song of their first set, "Julie's Been Working For The Drug Squad."

As he struggled through the song, he couldn't help but realise the irony that he was singing a song about a girl called Julie, his mother's name at a time when he was thinking about his father and who these men were, and more importantly what they wanted with him.

Apart from her name, the song bore no other slight comparison to his mother that was unless you deemed the time she had spent working for Boots the chemist was what the Clash referred to as "the drug squad!"

Thankfully he got through the song and announced their break. Sometimes they shuffled music in their breaks and sometimes Trace played on alone. Tonight she was playing a few Adelle songs as well as trying out a couple of her own. As their first break was the longest, thirty minutes, which allowed the Hard Rock staff to make the transition from serving food to only serving drinks, Ray liked to relax at the bar enjoying a cold beer and maybe chat to some of the customers. Tonight he would have to find this Mr Bassett and see who he was, what he wanted and possibly what the next instalment would be in the life of his estranged father Jimmy Jazz Ruddock.

Chapter Eleven

Tenerife, Canary Islands
Friday 22nd October 2021

The wait for seats at Hard Rock was estimated at twenty minutes so Dennis and Jeffrey decided to move on with a view that they might come back later for a drink and listen to the music, provided they could get seats. But food was the priority for now. From Hard Rock they headed past the Cleopatra Hotel and towards the Safari Centre where they knew had loads of bars and restaurants that served late. Approaching the centre they could hear the end of Nessun Dorma booming and see the tall fountains rising and falling to the sound of the music. As they got closer Nessun Dorma finished and Bohemian Rhapsody started, the water rising and slapping in perfect timing. As usual a crowd had gathered to watch, young children amazed as the array of fountains dancing in harmony to the beat and tempo of the music. Fancy dress was on full display as most of the children and some of the adults were out partying in their Halloween costumes, even though Halloween was over a week away. The hotels, bars and restaurants were milking the Halloween theme for all it was worth by organising fancy dress events well before the actual Halloween weekend, and maybe they'd even do the same the week after. The shops too were cashing in, all full of costumes and themed merchandise. You couldn't blame them as tourism was only really starting to come back and so dressing up the October half term holiday fortnight as a Halloween cash cow was a marketers dream. Plus, the tourists loved the fancy dress and it was bringing them out in droves in party mood and very willing to part with their holiday funds.

Superheroes seemed to be the most popular costumes but there were also the traditional witches, skeletons and ghouls as well as a party of Monks and Nuns, who were currently dancing around the fountains like it was some form of religious ceremony.

Dennis grabbed Jeffrey's arm, "Look," he whispered and nodded towards the crowd standing on their right side of the fountains. "It's

Cherry."

As Jeffrey looked Dennis intensified his grip and started to pull him away to their left out of view.

"What's he doing here?" asked Dennis.

Jeffrey had seen who Dennis was talking about. A tall man, well built and in his early forties and he recognised him at once. Arnold Cherry, Arnie as he was known was a driver. He drove everything and anything; if it had wheels Arnie had a licence for it. From long distance haulage, which he had done for Dennis and Jeffrey, as a luxury chauffeur, or weddings and stuff like that, to speed driving, either at his hobby rallying or as a getaway driver, although the latter of these driving exploits didn't feature as part of his repertoire on his driving website.

Knowing that Arnie had nothing to do with their missing cash, Jeffrey wanted to state the obvious that he was most likely on holiday, but aware of Dennis's suspicions and not having any reason to waylay these, without coming clean about Charlie Bassett, Jeffrey was forced to play along.

"Yeah," he said conspiratorially, "and it looks like he's on his own."

"And that girl you spoke to at the bank," added Dennis, "said that one of the bank robbers had been tall. Look Cherry must be six two, six three maybe."

Bohemian Rhapsody finished and the fountains calmed their dance but still stood tall waiting on the cue to their next performance. Some of the crowd started to move away, including Arnie. Dennis nudged Jeffrey, nodding in the direction that Arnie had gone and confirming they were going to follow. He then leaned in close and asked, "You carrying?"

"No," answered Jeffrey, "I left it in the safe back in the apartment," then knowing that this would probably piss Dennis off he added as a further excuse, "I thought we were just coming out to eat, have a few drinks you know!"

This answer made Dennis feel a little unsure. Arnie was a big lad, looked fit, did he really want to pursue him to a possible confrontation without a clear advantage. He had committed now though and to back off would be a sign of weakness in front of Jeffrey. To keep face and also enforce his authority he said, "In future keep it on you at all times. We're not over here to fucking party." Then he thought of something that sounded sensible. "Let's stay back though. We wanna see who he's over here with if we can. That might tell us a lot."

Focusing on Arnie neither Dennis nor Jeffrey noticed a young man who was paying careful attention to them. Unlike the stand out costumes of the fancy dressed, this young man, or boy, was unremarkable, almost invisible from the way he blended in to the crowd and his features and dress had nothing that was remarkable, or memorable. Sitting just twenty feet behind this man was Sasha Moreno who was really unaware of most of his surroundings. The policeman who was trained to observe had, as he had intended to do, totally switched off from his Monday to Friday duties and had passed the afternoon drinking and smoking cigarillos. As he only smoked when he drank, he had stopped to enjoy his last one while listening to the music and watching the fountains dance. He was also feeling quite sad. The afternoon had drifted along in the sunshine, at first drinking sangria before moving on to Bloody Mary's, which did serve to achieve his key objective of relaxing and forgetting about work. However the solitude had led to a period of inward reflection and this had brought the feelings of loneliness back to the surface just like the bubbles in his sangria. The bars too were full of couples and families, which exaggerated his feeling of being alone, and this made him feel even more alone, which then fuelled the switch to Bloody Marys.

Alcohol affected everyone in a different way. Some became more extrovert, some more introvert, some fell asleep, some fell over and some just got downright nasty. This was Sasha's alcohol zone, he brooded for company, or to be more precise, female company. His various relationships, including his marriage or more accurately especially his marriage, just hadn't worked. And the reason for this was quite simple. In his usual day to day routine of work and home or fishing or whatever Sasha was doing he was quite content. Relationships needed time and attention and TLC during these parts of his life, but he had found that restraining and almost somewhat suffocating. Weekends too spent on his boat, where as a rule he didn't drink if out at sea, he found relaxing and fulfilling. Not always as sometimes too alcohol put him to sleep, but mostly alcohol fuelled his melancholy and stirred his need for company. And it was nothing to do with sex, he thought. This was a holiday resort where people came to have a good time. Sasha was an attractive enough man, deeply tanned and he kept himself fit and trim, so if he put his mind to it sex should be easy enough to come by. His mother, probably like most mothers, said she knew him best and would tell him often that he just hadn't found the right woman yet. She did also add that he should maybe get his finger out as time was ticking on. And as a further piece of motherly advice, she told him to ditch the horseshoe moustache as it made him look like Hulk Hogan's whipping boy.

He puffed on his cigarillo, enjoying the slight burning in his throat mixing with the Tabasco spice from the Bloody Mary's and thought he should get a move on and walk the final distance to his apartment. He would need to get up early in the morning to walk back and collect his police car so that he could take it back to the station. The first loud crack startled him from his thoughts. The following noises mixed in with the sounds from the crowd alerted a part of his brain that something wasn't right.

The crack of the first firework made most people jump, Dennis included. As it crackled in to a burst of amazing light and ballooned out in the shape of a perfect sphere, several more explosions followed as an array of fireworks went up. Screams and cheers of the crowd and surrounding pockets of tourists blended in to the cacophony of sounds. Clapping and drunken whoops could be heard in appreciation of the display. Then several other sounds that didn't quite fit joined in.

Sasha's attention from the light show in the sky was brought back to ground level when he heard what he knew was breaking glass. He saw the shop window explode in a shower almost as visually attractive as the fireworks. He also saw the large steel bar that had been used to whip across the glass, arc and spin to the ground. But the shop window was one of the cheap and tacky shops that sold tourist junk. Just next door was a brightly lit jewellery shop that had behind its reinforced glass windows thousands of euros worth of watches and jewellery. Then it hit him. A decoy.

Dennis and Jeffrey had moved forward to begin following Arnie. They had separated slightly with Jeffrey taking the lead. The first loud crack from the firework caused Dennis to miss his stride and he was quite startled. Once he heard the familiar fuzz of the firework as it burst to light high up in the sky he was slightly embarrassed. As he slowed and looked around to see if anyone had noticed his initial fear the gap between himself and Jeffrey widened. Several more explosions followed as the sky lit up, but then another explosion which was much louder and much closer to him erupted only a couple of feet from his left hand side. The crowd around him became aware of what was happening beside them rather than several feet above them and started to scream and shout. People started to move in many directions, these movements more irrational and less planned. The result caused several people to bump in to Dennis, first from his left and then from his right.

"Fuck sake," he spat, but no one seemed to take any notice. He used his weight and strength to push his way through the throng as glass showered over him. He closed his eyes for a second worried that the glass fragments would blind him. His hair quickly became full of glass. As he brushed at it he realised that the pieces weren't actually sharp, so he ruffled at his hair in an effort to clean them out. Clearing the main crowd he began to look around for Jeffrey and quickly noticed that he was already twenty or so feet in front of him in pursuit of Arnie, but as he settled down to catch up his right hand, by pure instinct, patted his pocket of his jeans where his wallet had been. The pocket was empty. He checked his other pocket but no wallet. He looked around him at the crowd which were all heading in their separate directions, but not sure what he was looking for he turned back to Jeffrey.

"Jeffrey," he shouted, but as he did he also became aware of his left wrist. No Rolex. His wrist was bare. At that moment Arnie turned to face him and Jeffrey. As their eyes met there was something else in Arnie's expression other than recognition. It read to Dennis as fear. Jeffrey noticed this as well. Arnie then turned and began to run and after passing several shops he ducked in to a dark walkway.

Dennis hesitated. He didn't know if he should follow Arnie and drive Jeffrey on to do the same, or if he should turn and go back to see if he could spy the little pick pocket fucker who had stolen his wallet and watch. To replace his watch would maybe cost around twenty thousand pounds and he had five hundred euros in his wallet that Jeffrey had given him earlier. The man currently running away from them could have stolen his four hundred thousand euros from his safety deposit boxes or be a part of the crew that had. Decision made he began to run.

Sasha saw the aftermath of what had happened as more fireworks cracked and whistled skyward. He saw several women looking for their handbags that had been over their shoulders just seconds before. Some men were also patting their pockets with bewildered expressions on their faces. He was also certain that some of the people walking away hadn't even realised yet that they had been victims of a well planned pick pocketing team raid.

He saw two people heading in one direction and three in another that he guessed were the pick pocketing team. He was in no state to pursue and so he tried his best to blend in to the crowd just in case some of his colleagues were around. He didn't want them to see him drunk and he didn't want them to see him walk away from what was a crime scene. Most tourists don't realise just how rife this sort of crime is and as a result they walk around with no perception of the danger whilst brandishing their expensive jewellery and having their wallets or purses full to the brim of their holiday cash. Sitting ducks make these people look static and easy prey. But that wasn't Sasha's problem tonight as from Monday to Friday he dealt with this ongoing purge, which unfortunately all tourist spots had to deal with. Now, he just wanted to get home and go to bed. Alone, unfortunately!

Chapter Twelve

Tenerife, Canary Islands
Friday 22nd October 2021

"Why are you still wearing your sunglasses, there's no fucking sun in here?" said Charlie Bassett as Ray sat down in the booth opposite. "Do you think you're a cool fucker like your dad Jazz?" Charlie was using his usual tactic of attack when he first met someone he wanted to have control over. Ray didn't answer and just removed his mask and stuck it in his shirt pocket. Joe had led him down to the booth using one of their stealth modes were they both walked casually side by side and once they reached were Ray needed to stop, Joe gently touched his left hand to Ray's right. Ray stopped and swung in to the booth with confidence having sat at them many times before. Joe continued on.

In a way Ray was glad that Charlie had began mouthing as soon as he had started to sit down as his voice helped Ray locate him and so he slid across the booth and followed the sound until he was looking at him face to face just like any sighted person. He was aware of another sound. A gurgling, sucking sound he knew was someone sucking on a straw that was struggling to find the remains of whatever was left. The sound of a spoon tinkling against glass and grunts and slurps were also present.

Going from acting tough to embarrassed Charlie then said, "Can you eat that a bit fucking quieter." There was meanness in his voice but the voice had a twang to it as if the person was holding their nose. The words were also lost as Monty was phased out and totally focused on eating the rest of his ice cream sundae that had come out with a sparkler on top which almost caused Charlie to hide under the table in total embarrassment. It was like being out with a five-year-old child. Monty was also trying his best to extract every last drop of his chocolate milk shake and in fairness he was doing a great job as if he sucked any harder the entire glass was going to disappear up the straw.

Shaking his head and trying to get back to business Charlie was about to speak when one of the waitresses stopped by the table and asked, "Any more drinks here?"

"I'm OK Nicky thanks," answered Ray recognising the voice.

Before Charlie spoke Nicky added, "Can I get you another glass of milk Sir?" Her enquiry was directed at Charlie, and there was a slight mocking to her tone. He'd been suffering from bad indigestion since arriving in Tenerife and he was now caught between telling this girl to fuck off or explaining to Ray why he was drinking milk. Yet again before he had the chance to speak Monty piped up, "Can I have another milk shake? Chocolate." His mouth was currently full and the words came out garbled, but Nicky seemed to fully understand them and so cheerfully she answered that that was no problem and again before Charlie spoke she left to fulfil Monty's order.

Ray sensed that the man in front of him was unsettled.

Charlie was puffing and blowing and struggling to suppress his frustration. He was trying to have a fucking meeting here and he was surrounded by sparklers and slurping and if Monty didn't grow up he'd be wearing the fucking milk shake as his pyjamas. In only a few seconds his control here was in disarray and he was trying to settle himself and get back to his train of thought.

"How do you know my father?" Ray asked.

"Jazz?" said Charlie as if he was asking Ray to confirm who his father was, but then he continued, "We served time together. We shared a cell for a while." Some people would be more cryptic or try to evade the fact that they had been in prison, but not Charlie. He wore it like a badge. He was proud of it. It made him feel tougher, and bigger.

"And so?" said Ray.

Charlie paused, he didn't understand the question.

"What do you mean? You trying to say that doing time is no big deal?" Charlie was getting his metal back. "You fucking try it man. Pretty boy like you would soon know his arse from his elbow." Then he sniggered, a twangy snigger from his nostrils as he laughed at his own unintentional joke. "Know your arse; yes some boys in there would want to get to know your arse OK." His sniggering continued.

"I meant," said Ray sternly, "and so what has this got to do with me?"

The sniggering stopped and Charlie's face darkened. He pointed to

Monty's head, "Do you see that?" he asked, his own voice now stern. "Your fucking dad did that to him. The double crossing bastard." Then he added, "As if poor Monty's head wasn't scrambled enough already?"

Ray guessed that he was talking about the other man at the table, the one who had first approached him at the stage, so he moved his head slightly as if he was looking and then turned back to Charlie.

Outside a firework display had started and people were still coming in to the bar looking for seats. Trace was just starting to play her new song that she had written for her partner Jess. They were getting married in a few months and Ray had helped her with some of the words. The song was called Just to Have You. "Trace sang the opening lines,

"I see you in my dreams,

And I dream to see you now,"

Ray was pissed off that he couldn't just sit here and listen and enjoy the song. It was a beautiful song, made more special because it was personal. It's beauty was marred though because he was sitting here with this idiot with a squeaky voice and bad breath, so he shut out the song. He would listen to it again when he was in better company.

"Look," said Ray now wanting to get rid of this man, "I haven't seen or spoke to my father in years, so I don't know about anything, and frankly I don't want to know."

"Your dad fucked me over and its either he pays or you pay. It's as simple as that."

"If it's money your looking for," Ray laughed, "you're looking in the wrong place mate."

"I'm not your fucking mate. Your dad came over here with me, working for me do you understand, and we had a deal. I know he took the job cause he needed money to help your mum." Charlie saw the expression in Ray's face when he mentioned his mother. "Yes your mother, Julie. You think I don't know? I've known your mum Julie for years." Charlie paused as he sensed he was starting to get at Ray. He could see he'd hit a nerve when he had mentioned his mum. "And do you know what else I know," boasted Charlie now. "Yes," sniggering again, "I know more than you think." Leaning forward and lowering his voice conspiratorially, "I know that one of the reasons your dad took the job over here was because he knew you were in Tenerife singing." Really feeling vibrant now he added, "If you could call that crap your doing singing? The fucking Clash, they were shit. Punk shit."

It was Ray's turn now to feel agitated. He had just been about to dismiss this man as a fool and not worth wasting his time with, but the mention of his mother and that his father had came to Tenerife because he was here, unsettled him. And there was something else gnawing at the back of his mind about all of this that he couldn't grasp because his head was a mess.

Joe was watching his dad. He had planned to go outside and have a quick fag while his dad was busy, but the small man had rattled him. What the man lacked in size he made up for with his face and in particular his eyes. There was something there. Something like a picture you didn't want to look at. A picture of something cruel or nasty, or evil, that you had to turn away from. Instead of going outside he had gone looking for the bouncer, but discovered that he had gone home sick and so the head barman Pat was doubling up on the role. The bar was jammed with customers and waiters serving tables so Joe didn't want to disturb Pat. He had done his toilet duty again for Terry and now Terry and Aurimas were sitting on one of the outside tables out the back. Terry was having a smoke break, his bet had come up so he was on his phone placing another one. Aurimas said he was going to phone home to

Check in with his mum. So all Joe could do was sit and watch. He had hooked up their blue tooth ear buds and he would give it a few more minutes and then check in to see if his dad was OK.

Ray's mind sorted itself out, a bit like a re-boot on a computer, and the nagging thought that evaded him came front and central and sat there like a neon sign flashing brightly on the cinema of his mind. It was like an advert for an upcoming film release, and the film was called, "The Bank Robbery."

Elaine had said something to him about Pepe wanting to get home early so that he could put their lodgement in their home safe as he didn't get to their bank as it was closed due to a robbery there yesterday. He hadn't really been paying that much attention to the details as she had been going on about being worried about having so much money on the premises and Pepe had wanted her to go to another branch and that was so far away, and she had a hairdressing appointment and after all she was working tonight. There was even more to the story, but Ray had just been disappointed that he had missed Pepe, and he certainly would have lightened his load by taking some of that cash from him had he been given the opportunity, and so the mention of the bank robbery, insignificant as it was at the time, had just filtered its way to the back of the filing cabinet that was his brain. But it wasn't insignificant any more.

"You's robbed that bank yesterday?" Ray asked, although it was probably more of a statement rather than a question.

Without any hesitation Charlie replied, "Yeah, Jazz and Monty did, but that's what I've been telling you," he said strained as if Ray was totally stupid and just wasn't keeping up here, "that's what Jazz fucked us with, he knocked him out with his fucking shotgun and fucked off with my money." He leaned in closer and continued. "I paid good money up front to fix this, I'm well out on this and Jazz is trying to shaft me." He thought Ray looked puzzled. "What? You don't believe me about Jazz; don't think your daddy'd do that?" Then the wheels in Charlie's mind spun. "Job?" he said. "You didn't know what I meant earlier about the job?" He sneered and blew out his cheeks. Ray edged back slightly in his seat as he was hit by a wave of sour breath. "What other sort of job would you want Jimmy fucking Jazz for? The only thing he's ever done is rob fucking banks."

He sat back in his seat and looked around. The music was covering their conversation so he continued. "Listen, I was doing your dad a favour. He treated me OK inside. Used to play music like you and it helped pass the time. Last time he got out and your mum was sick and all, Jazz hadn't got shit. I offered him a chance to get a good wedge and what's he do? Fuck me over that's what." Then he thought of something else. "He left him for dead back there." He was pointing again to Monty. "That's low man, you don't do that. Only that the police over here are a bunch of pussys Monty would have been nabbed."

Ray was finding this all a bit surreal. He had dealt with this for his entire life. Even from his very early childhood when he was five or six years old his friends would say, "What's your dad do?" Other boys would answer, "My dad's a plumber." "Mine's an ambulance driver." "My dad works in an office." "Oh yeah, my dad works in an office too. Do you think it's the same one?" Ray would say, "My dad's in the navy." "Oh yeah when's he coming home?" Or, "What's the name of his boat?" Unprepared for these follow ups he changed it later to, "My dad works on an oil rig." The questions then were much easier to deal with, "What's an oil rig?" And when he told them their response was, "Wow, sounds cool."

But covering up the fact that his daddy was a bank robber was one thing, it was still there as a back drop to their life. Now though it was here right in front of him. It didn't change anything really and so he came back to were he had started from.

"Look, I've told you I haven't seen my dad for years. I can't help you with any of this bullshit."

"What about your mum?" Charlie asked. "Jazz loved that woman, always went on about her, and she came to visit him no matter what. There's no way he is going to run out on her like he did on me." Then he lied, "I've got someone watching her house and that clinic she goes to." Charlie felt good. His play had worked. This lad in front of him should never play poker as he gave everything away in his face. The simple mention of his mum again and Charlie knew he had him.

"You think I'm gonna let Jazz walk away with my four hundred thousand euros, and not cover my arse?" The lie had worked and so he expanded on it. "We're watching your little mama and we're now watching you too. That fucker Jazz is going to come to one of you and when he does, well we'll leave that one to your imagination."

Charlie was feeling great. Tall and tough. He had this kid by the balls and he felt a foot taller, no two fucking feet taller. Now he just needed to nail him and get him to do what Charlie wanted him to do.

"Look kid," he offered, leaning closer again, "Maybe I believe you. Maybe Jazz shafted you like he shafted me. My old man was a waste of space as well and a fucking nobody. But I made something of myself; I didn't let that loser hold me back."

Ray said nothing. The references to his mother were like punches to his stomach. He could see the threat there, as to how real it was with this prick he didn't know, but couldn't risk finding out. Joe had spoken in his ear to ask if everything was all right. Ray had nodded subtly. Joe had also told him that they were back on in fifteen minutes. He sensed that Bassett was leading up to something and he just hoped he would get to it then go.

"I'm gonna offer you a deal," said Charlie, his sour breath continuing to cloud Ray. "The same deal I offered Jazz." And as an after thought he added, "Although I'll throw you in a bonus."

Charlie held out his hand and beckoned Ray to come in closer by waving his forefinger. Joe couldn't see the gesture as his dad blocked his view, so Ray didn't move. After a few seconds Charlie said impatiently, "Come here, in closer, we don't want the whole fucking bar to hear."

Ray moved in closer and immediately regretted it as the sour breath got worse.

"We didn't just have one job over here," Charlie said, an arrogance slant to his voice. "No, no kid. Those fuckers stashed their money in loads of banks over here, three on this island alone."

Ray had no idea who those fuckers were, but he could hear the smugness in Charlie's voice.

"I could only sort two of the banks here though, my man said the third had nobody he could bend, and you know what I mean. Although two is enough, two out of three is seventy five percent right, so good enough." Boasted Charlie.

Ray didn't bother to correct his maths.

"It's easy Ray," using Ray's name now, "real easy. I had the man in both banks in my pocket so all we had to do was turn up and strip out the four deposit boxes in each bank, then leg it. No fuss." He sniggered again, "Well that was until Jazz decided to go solo."

The bad breath was really starting to turn Ray now so he said, in an effort to quicken things up, "What is it you want from me?"

"Charlie answered, but it wasn't a request, it came out more like a directive, "The second job is on Monday morning and you're going to do it."

Ray was about to blurt out that he was blind, but stopped himself. Unlike all those times, now being one of them, when he had pretended and tried to fool people that he could see, he wished now that he had his white stick sitting on the table and Trace's big guide dog Bumper sitting at his feet with his full harness gear on. Two blatant signs that were not only walking guides but were things that said, "Hey look, I'm blind!" Having said that they didn't always work or have that effect. He remembered one particular occasion when he was standing outside their local medical centre waiting on Trace who was in having her covid vaccine. There he was standing with his white stick and Bumper all rigged out in his harness and reflective gear, when along came a woman coming out of the doctors. She stopped in front of Ray and asked, "I can't make out that Doctors writing, it's awful," and handing the paper to Ray she asked, "could you read that for me son?" Ray tapped his white stick and raised Bumper's harness in an effort to say, "Hello I'm blind!" But all went unnoticed, so as the woman stood there waiting for Ray to relieve her of her document he finally had to say, "Sorry love, but I'm blind." Her swift response wasn't what he had expected, "Oh my god son, do you want me to get you an ambulance?"

Nicky returned to their table and said cheerfully, "there's your milk shake love." He heard Monty grab for it and pull it in close to him and then begin sucking hard down on the straw. Charlie continued.

"I'll pay you ten percent of the four hundred thousand, that's fifty grand in euros. You'd need to go some gigs to make that."

Ray really did want to pull him up on his maths but let it slide again.

"And," said Charlie, "I'll leave your mum out of it. That's your bonus." Then he added quickly as an after thought, "But not Jazz. He owes me!" Charlie glanced over at the girl playing the keyboard and singing. Ray was most likely shagging her so he thought he might bring her in to it as an extra leverage. She was a tasty looking thing and he'd never done it with a black woman before. He'd had an Indian, she worked in the kebab shop around the corner from his house, but she'd been in to lighting loads of candles and they gave him a headache, so he'd knocked her on the head. And then there was the Chinese girl, but she was a bitch and had laughed at his cock saying it looked like an overdone duck spring roll. He'd slapped her for that one, but then the bitch had whip whooped him with all this kung fu ninja shit and ended up beating the shit out of him. So Chinese was off the menu and the thought of her had put him off women in general so he'd maybe just keep the piano player out of it for now.

"You owe me," he then said. "You know what they say about the sins of the father and all that? Well Jazz's sins pass on to you my friend."

Ray didn't like his use of the word friend, but he knew that was just splitting hairs as here was a guy trying to get him to rob a bank and all Ray was getting annoyed about was being called friend. Part of his mind was also processing the offer, the money, the promise to leave his mum alone, and the prospect of robbing a bank, whilst blind. The challenge had excited the stupid part of his psyche that got kicks from pretending he could see.

Charlie also pushed on. "I'll give you ten grand up front." He offered. "It'll be the easiest money you ever made. The man in the bank is greased, so all you have to do is turn up and collect." He thought of a joke, "It'll be like argos, click and collect." He laughed fully appreciating his humour, then once he had calmed he said. "I'll give you to tomorrow, I'll meet you here at lunch time," then he looked at Monty who now had chocolate milk shake running down his chin. This fucker ate like a drunk baboon. "No not lunch, after that, say three in the afternoon. If you agree then I'll take the squeeze off your mum for Jazz, although let me down and I'll tell the lads to squeeze much harder."

He pushed a bit of paper across the table. "There's my number." Then in a stern voice, "Here at three tomorrow and you'd better have the right answer." He nudged Monty and started to slide out of the booth, but Monty didn't move. Instead he looked at Ray and asked, "Can you play Cliff Richard?"

"Would you fuck up about Cliff fucking Richard and get the fuck up." Snarled Charlie. "Now get out you big fucking moron you."

Slowly Monty stood, but his eyes never left Ray. Ray wasn't looking at him and it made the anger in Monty rise. "You Jazz's son?" he asked again. Again, Ray stayed silent. Monty stared, looking mean now the little boy face had gone. He held his chocolate milk shake with one hand and reached to feel the back of his head with the other. He almost knocked his hat off when he touched the bandage were his wound was. It was still bleeding slightly as it most likely needed stitches, but Charlie didn't want to risk a doctor or hospital so it would just half to heel on its own.

"Jazz hit me," said Monty.

Pushing him Charlie said, "C'mon, forget that for now I told you. We need to go."

As they were leaving a party of fancy dressed tourists began to filter through the front doors. Two Monks led the way and then Ray heard Charlie say, "Oh holy mother of Jesus," he croaked, backing his way against the table. Ray felt the vibrations of the table as Charlie bumped it but it was in no danger of moving as it was anchored to the floor. He heard girls or women's voices giggling and then another plea from Charlie, "Jesus Harry Christ the night," he was blabbing, "get those fucking Nuns away from me. Get those fucking Penguins away from me!"

Ray hadn't a clue what was going on, but in truth didn't care. Eventually as the party of Monks and Nuns moved further in to Hard Rock Charlie and Monty headed outside. Charlie was sweating and it wasn't from the heat. Monty was still sucking his chocolate milk shake, the Hard Rock glass in one hand and his burnt out sparkler in the other.

Ray sat quietly at the table. Nicky came over. "Can I get you a drink Ray, you've still got a few minutes before you start again."

"Love one Nicky thanks. A Jameson's on ice please, plenty of ice, he said, and then added, "Maybe make it a double, please."

"My mum and dad are here tonight Ray. Can I maybe bring them over to meet you later? My dad's a big Clash fan, he seen them live at Shea Stadium in New York back in the eighties. He hasn't shut up about it all night. They're over on holiday."

"Sure Nicky, love to meet them."

She went then to collect his drink and he was left alone. He needed to get himself sorted for the next set. He laughed to himself. The fourth song on the second set was, "My Daddy Was a Bank Robber." He'd been singing it for years, but then the thoughts were of his dad. Maybe now he should let Joe sing lead vocals for this one. His final thought before Joe came was, "Fifty grand? Fifty Grand?"

"My Daddy was a bank robber,

And he never hurt nobody,

He just loved to live that way,

And he loved to steal your money."

Ray repeated the last line to himself.

"And he loved to steal your money."

The challenge had a lure to it that was dangerous, like a moth being lured by the flame.

Was he the moth? Or could he dodge the flame?

Part Two

Santa Clause Is Coming To Town

"You better watch out,
You better not cry,
You better not pout,
I'm telling you why,
Santa Clause is coming to town."

John Coots and Haven Gillespie

Chapter Thirteen

Tenerife, Canary Islands
Saturday 23rd October 2021

Bumper woke with a sniff and a fart. He could smell the sea air drifting in through the open window and he could hear the waves crashing their way on to the beach. It made him feel happy and that made his tail flick and thump a couple of times on the cool wooden floor. He loved the sea, and had loved swimming in it when the two lads, Joe and Aurimas, had taken him to the beach.

He was a dog, a guide dog, which he was very proud of, a dog feeling love this morning. He loved people and in particular his mistress Tracey, he was a people dog, although yes some of them were assholes, but in general people were lovely. He also loved this room as it was the coolest in the house, no that wasn't actually true. Other rooms were cooler but that was due to the air conditioning and Bumper didn't like that. It made him sneeze. This room was the bedroom at the top of the house and it was a room that wasn't being used, so each night, once Tracey had fallen asleep, he had softly and silently made his way upstairs. The night breeze had not only cooled the room and the floor, but it brought in the aroma of the sea, and he liked that. Although he had swallowed some sea water while swimming and he wondered if that's what had upset his stomach. It wasn't too bad yet, just a bit gurgly and a few cramps, but his farts were humming. That was confirmed as his most recent one now drifted up under his nose. Yuk. He blew out and rolled over in an effort to get away from the smell. He thought to himself that he better not drop one of those at the breakfast table or he'd be in the shit. He laughed to himself at his clever choice of words there, then stretched out on the floor and relaxed to enjoy his last few minutes of half sleep before his day as a first rate guide dog began.

Bumper, a short haired Golden Retriever, was a bloodline pedigree first honours fully qualified, top rate guide dog. Those were Bumpers words. His family had been proud guide dogs for many, many years, well that was apart from those you didn't talk about. He was the third puppy of a litter of seven and his siblings although it had been touch and go for a while, had all made it through guide dog school and training. Bully, Buddy, Bumper, Bella, Bomber, Bingle and Britvic were all now fully serving guide dogs. The litter all named with the traditional same first letter, it was used to relate to their age, and their youngest sibling Britvic, being the lucky recipient of a sponsorship deal with the worldwide leading consumer brand, which was all the fashion these days, and did also served as a great fund earner for the charity as raising and training guide dogs was an expensive business. "Well why wouldn't it be? They were superior dogs after all!"

His brother Bingle had nearly let them down though. He had almost gone to that place that was not supposed to be talked about, but for the sake of this book, and of course for educational purposes, Bumper set his family pride aside.

The truth was that two of his brothers had issues. One was either just one of those freaks of nature, and the other suffered by a simple human error, which maybe this little snippet of education might just prevent humans repeating in the future.

Bingle had the dog equivalent of the human behaviour disorder ADHD. Bumper wasn't sure what the actual doggy version was or how to spell it, but in laymen's terms he was just nuts. No discipline, no work ethic, no bloody brains. This was obvious from an early age, the greatest sign of all coming when he broke one of his legs running wildly in the park chasing a squirrel. The broken leg itself was a factor that could dismiss you from guide dog school and send you down the road that no dog likes to talk about, but thankfully the excellent health package provided to guide dogs mended his leg by fitting a steel plate. All fixed, and Bingle was passed once more to take up guide dog training. Unfortunately, the general opinion of Bumper's family was that they should have also put a plate in Bingle's brain, that was if they could find it. The sheer patience of the trainers, and to be totally honest, the severe shortage of guide dogs, had pushed Bingle through. The trainers did hope that he would settle down once he became a fully working guide dog.

Bumpers family just hoped that the threat of failure would in itself be enough pressure to sort Bingle out. Failure quite simply meant he'd be shipped to that place that any self respecting guide dog just didn't talk about, and most certainly didn't want to end up at. And that place was the bomb squad!

Yes, the bomb squad!

So instead of a life of guidance going shopping, just walking or to a lovely coffee morning where the humans drank coffee and had a chat while you got the chance for a mid morning nap. Instead of being able to wear that harness and sign that all guide dogs were so proud of. Instead of being praised and petted in the park at being so clever and so beautiful, maybe even given a small treat there. No, no, no.

Your job was to sniff out explosives or bombs

, it was as simple as that. And sniffing out meant that you had to find this bloody device and stick your snout right up to it. Devices that could blow your brains to the opposite side of the park before the rest of you even knew what was happening. No bloody thanks! No self respecting guide dog family could handle the shame as it just wasn't considered clever in the doggy world to sniff out something that blew your nose out your arse faster than a bullet from a gun with not even enough time to kiss your ass goodbye on the way past.

And just think how poor Bomber felt. Do you see now how human error affected him. From the little age when you're just coming off your mother's breast, poor Bomber thought his fate had already been decided. It took some time and some explaining until he eventually accepted that it was just a name. A stupid name for a guide dog granted, but just a name none the less. But even though Bomber did make it through guide dog school with flying colours, he still saw the fear in other dogs eyes when he told them his name. Fear probably still existed in his own eyes from the many nightmares he'd had.

"Let's go Bomber old chap! Left, right, left, right that's it get that snout of yours sniffing there old bean. It's a live one today, mighty big one they suspect back in command," which just happened to be forty miles away as they were making sure there was plenty of distance between them and this unexploded bomb.

"Sniff it out there Bomber old boy," their voices more muffled now as they too hunkered down behind their sand bags. "Watch the wires Bomber, Sergeant Major Bond said the last one was a flimsy little bugger. We're going to go to radio silence now just in case the old radio waves set off the damn thing." Then with a chuckle, "we don't want that old chap!"

Bomber was then left alone, shaking and terrified that he'd actually find the bloody thing. Radio silence, maybe just as well as his bones were shaking and rattling like a wind chime. He didn't want to let the chaps down, but he also didn't want his four paws spread to the four corners of the earth. Alone he steadied himself for Queen and Country, and being the good dog that he was he found it all right. It was there, and just like the cartoons it had a big sign on it saying, "BOMB!" After the sign, the last thing he saw was the second counter on the display tick down to zero, zero, one. Then boom!

He woke up sweating, but happy to be alive and happy that all four paws were in the same county. He promised himself that he would pass guide school with flying colours and then the only things that he would be seeking out would be curbs and zebra crossings, and maybe a friendly little coffee shop where he could have a nice afternoon nap below a table.

Bumper yawned, enjoying the beautiful morning and enjoying the memories, but then the cramps in his stomach tightened once again. He blamed it on all the talk about the bomb squad. It just showed you though, he was a fantastic guide dog, but he'd be useless in the bomb squad. Here he was just thinking about it and he wanted to shit himself, can you imagine what he'd be like on the job seeking out a live bomb.

He got up and headed down stairs hoping that someone would be up so that they could let him outside as he needed to get busy, busy, and quick.

He pushed around the door with his nose and immediately felt the heat coming from the other side of the house that got the sun in the morning. That bedroom belonged to Ray and as he passed the door Bumper saw Ray lying across the top of the bed, one of his arms across his eyes, which Bumper assumed was to block out the bright sun.

Ray was actually deep in thought. He hadn't slept even though unusually he'd had several drinks after their gig the night before. And several too many if his sore head was anything to go by. Although unfortunately it hadn't helped him sleep.

After his session with Charlie Bassett and his weird hulk of a partner, Ray had played through the second set of the gig on auto pilot. On their second break he'd had a couple more whiskeys. Nicky's parents, Henry and Pamela, had then bought the band a round of drinks as a thank you for playing two requests, "Train in Vain" and "Pressure Drop." Trace had sang lead on the first request and Terry sang lead on the second, as it was one of his favourite Clash songs that they didn't usually include in their set. Henry and Pamela also stuck ten euros in the bands tip bucket, which they used to collect donations to "Guide Dogs for the Blind." In 2019 they had collected just over nineteen hundred euros and this year their target was two and a half thousand. The bucket was sealed until after their last gig of their last night.

When the gig was over Ray had sat on with Aurimas and Joe. Colin had taken Terry and Trace home but Ray felt agitated and so stayed behind with the two boys. Joe was drinking shandies, too many Ray later thought and felt guilty that he was maybe trying too much to be a friend to Joe rather than a responsible parent. He was only fourteen after all.

Now Ray just felt shit. Tired from no sleep, hung over by the booze and dehydrated by a combination of the alcohol and the air conditioning. Maybe it was also due to the pressure in his head put there squarely by Charlie Bassett, and like the Clash song words had said last night, "You make the wrong move, now when it drops, drop, you gonna feel it, oh pressure, oh yeah, pressure's gonna drop on you."

And Ray felt as if it had dropped fairly and squarely on his head. Heavily!

It may well have been the sensible part of his brain pushing against the side more likely to take risks that was causing the pressure. There was definitely a war going on in there somewhere. He was no criminal. He had no desire to become one. He was happy and content doing what he was doing. Alright there was some pressure on cash flow, or lack of it, and he felt responsible for the other members of the band, although he knew this came more from him rather than from them. He did think that on the round, he was happy. He also thought that as Clint Eastwood had once said, "A man's gotta know his limitations," that he did quite know his own. But there was something there inside him, and it was growing. A want, a need, a curiosity, a challenge a desire to prove himself. He didn't know. But it was eating at him and feeding there and getting stronger as each dark hour had passed during the night. As soon as Charlie had said that he was going to do the job, the bank robbery, it had appeared. Been born and now it had grown and reached adolescence. His thoughts had moved to do I, to should I, to how could I, and he had already had some promising ideas. Also mixed in to his thoughts were ways to justify it by ways of doing good from it. These thoughts had festered in the early hours before dawn when he had a dawning of his own. These same thoughts must have gone through his father's mind.

Now and also all those years ago the thoughts must have been the same. So there it was, he was more like his father than he would ever have wanted to admit. He had taken the righteous stand many times and condemned his father's actions and here was, one visit from a thug with bad breath and off he was running down the same path and making the same reckless decisions. Yes of course there were different reasons, but they were all drivers that ended up going down the same roads. The same roads that led to the same old dead ends.

He knew that his father had taken the blame for his younger brother and that had led to his first stint in prison. His mother had told him this story many, many times and then reminded him of it many times more. It was an honourable act and one he wasn't sure he could do himself. But still he'd condemned his father for the decisions and acts he had taken later. Deep down Ray knew the answer, but it was an answer he'd tried to suppress and keep deep. He allowed it to surface now though, just for a moment. His anger and his disappointment directed at his father was more to do with what he had missed as a boy growing up rather than judging what his father had done. It was the consequence, not the act, and it was the consequences that Ray had felt alone with no dad there to help him.

"What's your dad do?" "Where's your daddy?" "My daddy is taking me to football, do you want to ask your daddy if you can come?" Daddy, daddy, daddy, the hole was there every minute of every day and every day of every week, year after year after year. And it hurt. So criticism and condemnation were his fight back.

But where was his father now? Charlie had said that he had come to Tenerife knowing that Ray was there. So why hadn't he contacted him? Could he not risk maybe being seen by Charlie? His mother might be the key. He didn't want to bring her in to all of this and he wasn't sure how much she knew already, but he had no other choice. Joe had given him his father's mobile number, but there was no answer and Ray guessed it was turned off. So he needed to speak to his mother, he would just need to be subtle to try to suss out what she knew. First though he needed coffee, some vitamin C, and some headache tablets. That's if there was any as the cupboards were bare. He really needed to get some cash.

As Ray headed downstairs for a cure Charlie Bassett was chewing on more antacid tablets, the previous four just hadn't worked. He chewed the dry tablets, which tasted like eating chalk, and helped them down with a glass of milk. The indigestion was killing him and burning in his throat. He hadn't slept good either as the heat in the apartment was stifling. Also, even though in the next room, that big fucking oaf Monty snored like something from a farm yard or zoo. Charlie had considered trying to smother the bastard in the middle of the night but did then worry that Monty might awake and not realise who it was and then break Charlie's little neck like a twig. He decided to use his pillow to cover his own head to muffle out the sound, but it just made him sweat some more.

So in terms of grumpiness Charlie's mood this fine and sunny morning in Tenerife was just shite. It was just past eight in the morning and already he had shattered the TV remote when he'd flung it at Monty, and missed, when the cloth eared moron just simply refused to stop singing Cliff Richard songs. Even though this mornings rendition had moved on from Summer Fucking Holiday and was now some garbled out of tune shit about some Devil Woman. Charlie certain that the song was about a Nun had told the prick several times to shut the fuck up, and now the remote was fucked. The only consolation was that Monty had buggered off in to his own room to watch DVDs, most likely some Cliff Richard bollucks, and Charlie had some time on his own to reflect.

He was quite worried. Worried that Ruddock junior wasn't going to go ahead with the bank job. Worried that he hadn't pushed him hard enough, threatened him or put the squeeze on his girlfriend. If junior looked like he wasn't playing ball when they met later, that's if the wee fucker turned up, Charlie would need to raise the stakes, or more to the point, the threats. He knew he didn't have much time. Both jobs were supposed to have been done on Thursday then Friday before any of the lads back in Belfast had time to react, but now that the schedule had moved over the weekend he knew it was very likely that Dennis and his henchman Jeffrey and maybe some of their crew had plenty of time to get a flight out to Tenerife. But what could he do. Jazz had disappeared and screwed him on the first job. All he could do about that now was stay close to the son and then when they got home put the squeeze on Jazz's wife to help find him. At least if the second job was done then he'd have the resources he needed to lie low and plan things at his pace.

Another worry he had was Monty. The big man hadn't been too clever or switched on before Jazz cracked his head open, now he was like a six foot seven, two hundred and sixty pound five-year-old child. And with the IQ of a budgie. When they were in the apartment all he wanted to do was listen to Cliff Richard or watch his movies, of which he only had two with him. When they went outside all he wanted was to eat ice cream. He was supposed to be Charlie's muscle and his protector. Fat use he'd be now though if things got sticky, not unless it was possible to beat someone to death with a fucking Cornetto! Maybe if Charlie told Monty that whoever it was had stolen his Cornetto, then he might beat the fucker to death. Or failing that maybe tell him that his assailant was a Cornetto and he'd then maybe lick him to death. Needless to say, none of these put Charlie's mind at rest. He might need to use that contact he'd got the shot-guns from and get himself some proper protection. He did have another shot-gun as the guy Stefan had made him buy three, but it wasn't the easiest thing to walk around with. The other issue here was that he'd never fired a gun before. Of course he had told people he had loads of times. Told them he'd riddled some fuckers on multiple occasions, but the truth was he'd never fired a round. He didn't even know what gun to ask for, and that little fact could even make him look stupid, and these people you dealt with for these things didn't take kindly to fools. He might have to take that risk though as he needed something. He needed that something that gave him cover to portray fear and if necessary commit violence, because at just five foot tall his victims needed to be chosen very carefully, unless he had the backing of someone like Monty or a weapon of sorts. As he didn't have the luxury of carefully choosing who he needed to deal with he would need to ensure he had the means to get what he wanted. He'd just have to risk a phone call and see how he could bluff it. He grabbed his phone and found the number.

After five rings the phone was answered, but no one spoke.

"Hello," said Charlie, "that you Stefan?"

The call went dead. Charlie cursed the shitty foreign network. He dialled again.

"That you Stefan?"

"No fucking names on this line fuck sake."

"Sorry," Charlie almost went to say his name again, "sorry," he coughed, "It's me, we met on Monday, and you sold me three shot-guns."

The line went dead again. Charlie cursed again. "Fucking phones over here." He dialled again.

"Sorry these fucking lines over here are shit." Silence. "Hello, Stefan, fuck sorry, sorry."

"You call back again, Jiminy fucking Cricket and we'll feed you to the fish. Fuckin' Leprechaun!" The line went dead.

The reference to Jiminy Cricket and Leprechaun enraged Charlie. Once he realised that the line was dead again he threw the phone with an over arm that would have impressed most cricket bowlers. The phone took almost the same flight path that the TV remote had taken some minutes before and crashed in to the wall, shattering and falling to the floor.

Hearing the noise Monty came in to the room to investigate. As he entered he immediately saw the phone on the floor broken in to a mixture of several big chunks and millions of bits of shredded glass.

"Your phone's broke," he said pointing.

Charlie glared back, "No shit Sherlock."

"Who's Sherlock," asked Monty. Not receiving any response he then asked, "Can I have another Cornetto?"

Charlie's indigestion burned in his throat like a fireball. He wanted to grab one of the shards of glass and stab Monty to death, twice. He then remembered that he had given the Ruddock kid his phone number and he might try to phone him. Monty didn't have a phone. Why would he? The dick head couldn't use a fucking abacus.

Charlie sighed, a great deep sigh. Translated to Belfast speak it said, "Sons of fucking Mary and Joseph give me fucking strength!"

Monty, not fluid in Belfast speak, or English for that matter ignored the sigh and said, "Can I?"

Charlie Bassett, just one centimetre over five feet and weighing just under ninety pounds, turned and glared at Monty.

Monty's eyes went to the floor and all six feet seven inches, two hundred and sixty pounds trudged back to his room, in a huff.

Charlie shook his head and said, quietly and calmly, "Why hadn't your dad used a fucking condom?" Then added, "Most probably he used a fucking Cornetto wrapper."

Chapter Fourteen

Tenerife, Canary Islands
Saturday 23rd October 2021

Ray struck out on both the headache tablets and the orange juice, but there was still coffee. He was the only one up, apart from Bumper who had been scraping at the patio doors to get out. Ray obliged and also give Bumper the go ahead to do his morning constitutionals, "Busy, busy," Ray said, although Bumper didn't need any encouragement this morning, it was as quick as he could get out the door, have a quick sniff to find a spot, then let go with some relief.

Ray left the door open so that Bumper could come back in and went to wait on the coffee filtering through. He'd used the last of the drinking water for the coffee, but they did have some ice, so he put some in a glass and while waiting for the coffee he shook it like a cocktail in an effort to hasten the melting process. Not having much success hurrying up the melting process he set the glass on the window ledge where he hoped the strong morning sunshine would eventually do the job. Thinking then of the others, he took out the remaining ice from the freezer and put it in a saucepan and left it to melt, which by the time they all got up would at least enable them to have more coffee. He hit the button on the side of his Iphone to check the time and the voiceover computer voice announced, "eight fifty two."

Bumper sauntered back from the patio and headed to his water bowl, his claws clicking along the tiled floor. Ray was relieved to hear that there was water in his bowl, plenty it seemed, although he was sure it would be warm after sitting out all night. He removed some of the ice from his glass and stepped over to drop them in to Bumper's bowl. As he did he gently patted the bristly fur around his shoulders and immediately felt the draft of the air as Bumper's tail swished slowly in appreciation.

"Where's your mummy? Eh Bumper? Is the lazy bones still in her bed?"

"Yeah I passed her room coming down and she's still snoring," Bumper thought as he continued to drink the water, now much cooler since Ray had added the ice.

Ray poured himself a mug of coffee and replaced the pot back on the machine. He used his finger to judge the fill and when the hot liquid touched the tip he stopped pouring, and once the pot was back securely on its hot plate, he washed his hands. He did use to have little gadgets that you hung over the side of the cup and once the liquid hit the sensor an alarm would beep. The problem was they didn't last long. He'd bought several batches from the Royal National Institute For The Blinds, RNIB, website but they were all the same. After a few uses they stopped beeping. They weren't expensive, but he complained anyway, more to flag that they didn't do what they were supposed to do, rather than looking for his money back. The response he got back wasn't the one he had expected. Only by the fact it had come back in an email he would have been certain that he had misheard. In a long winded email the crunch of it was basically that the products were not waterproof and therefore were not recommended to be used around water or other liquids.

Ray had emailed back, "But how do you make tea or coffee without using water? These products are designed for blind people to let them know when the water is at a certain level, so how else are you supposed to use them?" He never received a response and so now he just used his finger. The only problem here was that you needed to remember to wash afterwards and most likely wipe down the worktop due to drips. Anyway, at least this method worked, and his finger was waterproof!

He took his coffee black and without sugar, which was just as well as he wasn't sure there was any, so he took his mug and sat at the dining table in the centre of the kitchen area. He hit the button on the side of his phone again and the voice announced, "Eight fifty six." His first task was to get in touch with Pepe from Hard Rock, but even though he knew that he started most mornings early he thought a text might be better than a call just in case. So he scrolled through his contacts, found Pepe, double tapped to open the details and selected the message button, his fingers working fast and managing to stay ahead of the voiceover software. Once complete he hit send. The phone made its usual noise to signal the message was now winging its way to Pepe's phone. He thought about carrying out his second task while he was waiting on a response from Pepe, but before he had scrolled to his mother's mobile number in his contacts the phone beeped with an incoming text. It was from Pepe and it said, "Sorry Ray. Need to do a CV test. LF pos so need

PCR today."

"Shit," said Ray, blowing out a long sigh. Then after a while he felt bad for being selfish. Pepe could have the virus and get sick and maybe even Hard Rock would need to close. And all he was worried about was his money. He quickly text back, "Hope all OK mate. Keep me posted. No worries re doh."

He flipped back out of contacts and found the Ap on his phone for his bank, double tapped it and used his thumb on the home button to scan the finger print ID to pass security. The Ap opened to reveal both his current account and his credit card account. He didn't bother with the current account as he knew that was maxed so he tapped on the credit card and immediately the voiceover read out the account details, "Mastercard account ending four three three five, credit limit three thousand pounds, current balance two thousand five hundred and sixty pounds and fifty pence, available to spend four hundred and thirty nine pounds and fifty pence."

When he factored in Colin's bill, which would be due at the end of the week as it was the end of the month, he just had enough to stock up the villa for the week. He had direct debits due out the following week, but he'd have to deal with them later. If Pepe did test positive for corona then God knows when he would get paid. They had two gigs this week as well as their usual Friday spot at Hard Rock, but both of these were freebies. Charlie's offer came to the front of his mind, but he pushed that aside as best he could as he had already decided on his next step and he couldn't do that until everyone was up. He drained his coffee and got up for a refill. Before he moved he called Bumper to check were he was just in case he tripped over him as he hadn't been paying attention to where he had gone. At the mention of his name Bumper moved his head and Ray heard the tags on his collar jingle against the tiled floor at the other side of the room. Ray guessed he was lying in the most shaded part of the room. "It's OK Bumper, you stay, boy stay."

After refilling his coffee mug he checked his glass of ice and found that it had partly melted and so he gratefully drank what he could and then replaced the glass on the sill. Back at the dining table, he searched back through his phone and found his mother's mobile number, double clicking the digits to activate the call. Like the majority of his calls to his mother he was expecting it to go to voicemail but after only three rings she answered.

"Hello Ray love." He thought he could sense a smile in her voice.

"Hi Mum, you sound good. I hope I'm not calling too early?"

"No, not at all it's great to hear your voice. Sorry I've missed you the last couple of weeks but I've just been zonked out, but Rosemary's been giving me all your messages." She didn't want to linger on herself so she quickly moved on, "how is Joseph and how's it in Tenerife? I bet you two have some tans?"

"Joe's great mum and its brill just having him out here. The tans good too, much bronzer than you I bet." Even though he couldn't see it, and no one had told him, he knew for sure that he had a great tan. Even just on a two week holiday he would get a great tan. It had been a point of banter with him and his mum as they both took great tans and when on holiday when he was younger they would have a competition on who got browner.

"Maybe," his mother retorted, "but if I was out there I'd give you a run for your money." Then she asked, "you OK? you sound worried?"

There it was, a mother's instinct. The sudden question paused him but in a way he wasn't surprised, in fact, he should have foreseen that she could read him like an open book. He tried to stick as close as possible to the truth for now.

"I'm good mum, it's just a bit harder out here this year with the virus. I haven't got all the work fully set up yet, the place is still opening up somewhat. But, hey, that means I've more time to sun bathe."

Julie's mothering instincts took over and she passed on the sun bathing banter, instead saying, "you and Joseph be careful out there with that virus, it's still rife. Especially where you do them gigs with the crowds and all."

"We're OK mum, you don't need to worry, Joe got his jab before coming out and I've been double jabbed so we'll be fine. The tourists all need to be doubled jabbed to come here anyway, so probably safer over here than back at home."

"Well, still be careful," insisted Julie.

"We are," reassured Ray and then continued carefully in to the hard part of the call, first about his mums health and then about his father. He knew that there was really no point asking about an update on a donor kidney because he knew of course that would have been the first news she would have shared, but he did still need to ask.

"Anyway we're OK, but what about you? Any news on a donor?"

"I'm good," she lied, "just tired all the time, but that's normal with the dialysis."

Then she paused thinking how best to say the next bit so that it sounded right. Ray noticed the pause but stayed silent giving her the space. Eventually she said,

"I'm no spring chicken you know," another pause, "I'm not going to be at the top of their donor list." She thought back over her words. She wanted to say that she was old and there were younger people than her that deserved a kidney more as they had much more to lose. But she didn't want to sound like she was about to join the euthanasia club. Of course she wanted a new kidney, she didn't have much of a future without one, but her nature was her nature, and her nature was to think of other people before she thought of herself.

"Mum, you deserve a kidney just as much as anybody else. It doesn't matter about age, anyway you're not old."

She didn't want to sound like a moan, or as if she felt hard done by, but she thought, "Oh yeah, you want to sit here in this body, and you would feel old, old and weary," but she said, "you say all the right things son, but it's just like my doctor says we suffer from having too many birthdays."

"Yeah, but there's plenty of birthdays left in you yet. And you promised you would come out here and see Joe and me play, he's bloody good on the guitar now you should hear him."

"Yes, but would you play the Beatles?" she asked.

"For you mum," he laughed, "We'd play anything." Then he saw a way to move to his dad, hoping she wouldn't notice he'd done it on purpose. "Apart from all that jazz stuff of dad's that you used to listen to." Truth was he didn't mind it now himself, but when he was younger and still living with his mother he didn't get jazz at all and used to complain when she played it.

"Now that's not fair," she said, "you said you would play anything."

Her answer sounded like she hadn't noticed, so he pushed on.

"OK you win, although Joe might complain." Then as subtly as he could he said, "talking of dad, how is he?"

Julie was taken back for a moment. It wasn't like Ray to speak about his dad, never mind ask how he was. She tried her best to think back on how it had came up and she tried to read if there was more to the question than the words themselves. She struggled though because the emotions fogged her mind. Sensing she had paused for too long she said, "Em, he's fine son." Curious she continued, "it's not like you to ask about him."

"We were just talking about him," Ray said, "so I just thought I should ask, that's all."

"Talking about him?" she said quizzically, "you mentioned his jazz records, that's hardly talking about him."

"Well mentioned him then," Ray added, "and I just thought you might think I was rude, or didn't care, if I didn't ask. That's all." Ray was nervous he'd played it wrong and she had read it.

Julie detected that his defences were up and thought she then knew that he was trying to ask something. Or hide something. She was worried now. She did know that her husband had gone to Tenerife. Gone to Tenerife to do another job. Another bank. Of course she knew. They had argued about it, fought about it. That was one of the reasons she had been so exhausted as she had cried for days. But Jimmy wouldn't listen. This was the one, he had said. So what were the others then, she had retorted. And it went back and forth like that for days, but she couldn't change his mind. Nothing she said could change his mind, and so he had gone. The last she had heard was when he had left a message with Rosemary some time on Thursday, but when she had phoned him back he didn't answer. She had to think for a moment to be sure, but yes it was now Saturday. So why was Ray asking? Had Jimmy tried to contact him like he said he was going to? Or was it something else? But what?

The fatigue gripped her like a riptide and started to take her away. What little strength she had drained like a broken bottle. She was broken, broken and shattered. The emotion came next and she didn't have any power left to resist it. She asked, almost in a gasp, "Ray, what is it, what is it Ray?"

He heard the tremble in her voice and when she said his name for a second time it almost cracked. He also heard movement upstairs. Someone else was up and would most likely be down any second. Even though his mother was almost two thousand miles away the energy between them was as if she was sitting right in front of him. He felt her pain, her emotion, it was there like a force he could touch. He didn't try to touch it, didn't want to touch it, but it was outside his control. It touched him, and he cracked with the pressure.

He felt a tear bloom and bubble in his right eye first, then his left. He wasn't wearing his sunglasses and in that moment couldn't remember where he had left them. An air bubble began to swell in his throat and it threatened to choke him. And in one single moment all the stress and all the worry that had been building broke through his defences. He heard more movement upstairs and then a door opening. To gain some time he tried his best to steady his voice and said quickly in to the phone, "Hold on mum." Then he got up and headed quickly to the downstairs bathroom at the rear of the villa, Hurrying he caught one of the chairs on the opposite side of the table causing it to scrape noisily across the floor and then he shoulder charged the corner of the hallway to the bathroom letting out an "Umph" as he did so. He heard his mum say something on the phone but as he was moving through the bathroom door and swinging it closed behind him he hadn't heard what she had said. Locking the door and moving back to sit down on top of the closed toilet seat he said, "Sorry mum, I was just moving there." The quiver in his voice was clear to Julie.

"Ray what is it? Tell me? The last two words were pleading.

He had no choice. Even though his mind was scrambled it was still clear that he'd blew it. Either he'd blown it, or he never had a prayer of succeeding. Either way there was only one way out. Honesty. Or honesty of sorts.

"Mum, is dad over here in Tenerife?"

"Did he call you?" she asked, her mind assuming that this could be the only way he would know Jimmy was in Tenerife.

Seeing his chance Ray took a risk. "Yes, he left a message, but I didn't fully understand it. I've tried to call him back but haven't got talking to him yet."

"What did he say?" asked Julie, hopeful now.

"He just said he was here and wanted to meet, but it was a shock, no one had said he was coming out so I wasn't sure." He was surprised how quick he'd come up with the lie, but then he wrapped it in some truth. "The last person I expected to hear from was dad. You know best how we've been these last few years." He waited hoping he hadn't over done it.

"I know," Julie said, "I told him to let you know he was coming over." Julie too added to the lie, "he said he wanted to surprise you and Joseph. Said it might work best that way."

Ray began to settle down. As if as a reminder to still tread carefully as his emotions were still fragile, the tear in his left eye blossomed and trickled down his cheek and dripped on to the tiled bathroom floor with a tiny slap.

"Maybe," he said, "him and Joe are close that's for sure." Taking another chance he asked, "Do you know where he's staying?"

Julie then felt stupid as in all the rowing she hadn't wanted to know any of the details. "I can't remember, sorry. My heads been scrambled with this treatment."

"Is he on his own?"

She was getting deeper and deeper in the lies and it hurt. But she knew for sure that she couldn't tell Ray about the bank job. Absolutely not. "Yes," she said, "Don't tell him but I was glad to get him out of my hair for a few days."

Ray judged that he wasn't going to learn anything else. He had confirmed that he had indeed came to Tenerife, so most likely Charlie was telling the truth, and he had learned that his mum hadn't heard from him since Thursday. He was most likely lying low after the robbery.

"OK mum, I'll keep trying his phone. He's maybe let the battery die or something, but we'll get each other soon." His mum said nothing, he thought she was crying.

"I've gotta go mum. Are you OK?"

"Yes," she sniffled, "will you call me as soon as you get that old fool? And Joseph too, tell Joseph to phone me too?"

"I'll get him to send you pictures of my tan."

She laughed softly through the sniffles.

"Love you mum,"

"I love you too son," the sniffles increased, "love you to the moon and back."

That made him smile. It was a phrase she had used for as long as he could remember, but she hadn't said it to him in a while.

"To the moon and back mum."

They said their goodbyes and he killed the call on his phone. He sat for several minutes to settle his emotions and thought over the call. He was sure that his mother knew exactly what his father was up to and why he had came to Tenerife, but he didn't blame her for not telling him. How could she? After all the criticism he had heaped on his father over the years. He was hardly an ear she could confide in on that front. So he had now to believe that what Charlie Bassett had told him was the truth, or a version of the truth, but why had his father gone solo and screwed Charlie? Did he not trust the little shit, Joe had told him after their meeting that Charlie was about five foot tall and Monty was almost seven foot tall, so now Ray pictured the little shit in his mind and did his father not trust him to come through on his share, or fee, whatever it was. Charlie had offered Ray fifty thousand to do the same job that his father had done. And they were supposed to do two robberies. So was his father then set to get paid one hundred thousand euros? According to Charlie they had inside help on both robberies. He had said he had greased insiders. So why wasn't his father content with the one hundred grand? He felt that he was missing something. Not trusting Charlie didn't totally fit. Yes Ray was certain that he was an untrustworthy little shit, but his father had shown no fear in dealing with Monty and he would have had possession of the money before Charlie got near it and so could have easily sorted out his own share. No, there was something else. Another motive.

He got up and headed to the sink to wash his face when a thought struck him. He stood for a moment and then sat back down and took out his phone. He opened up Safari and google and began to type. He typed, "Kidney transplant" but the deleted it and typed "buy a kidney transplant" and hit search.

In a couple of seconds the voiceover screen reader began to read, but he hit the screen to stop it. Screen reading software was fantastic and visually impaired people like Ray couldn't use phones or computers, and a lot more gadgets, without them. But one disadvantage they did have was that they read something from the start and then worked their way to the very end. With the results of a typical google search that might take it a fortnight. Sighted people scrolled and on his laptop he did this by the tab key or the up and down arrow keys, but with the phone he had developed a habit he called "hopping." And that is simply what it was. He scrolled the phone's screen down and randomly tapped the screen, hopping as he went, his finger selecting random items in the search which the screenreader would then start to read. If of interest he stopped, if not he hopped on. The first few hits on the search results were adverts, he skipped these, and then he hit "The kidney transplant waiting list, what you need to know." He let the screenreader read on here and when it announced, "People also ask," he tapped on the next line which read, "Is it legal to buy a kidney from someone," and then the next line?" Where can I buy a kidney?"

He opened both and read and hopped for a few minutes, and in a few minutes, like with most things on google, he discovered a wealth of knowledge, and it was information that told him clearly what his father's motive was.

He had thought he had worked it out when he was reading about kidney transplants in America. The article had claimed that the cost of a kidney transplant in the USA was four hundred thousand dollars and it was the coincidence of the sum of money, even though one was euros and one was dollars, between this cost and the sum that Charlie said they should have stolen from the first bank, that lit up flashlights in his head. Doubts then began to set in around the travelling there for his mum and also that his father, as a convicted criminal, wouldn't be able to set a foot there. But then he read an article about Spain and the lights came back on and stayed on this time.

Spain was one of the very few countries in the world that had an "Opt Out" rather than an "Opt In" system in relation to organ donor ship. This meant that people had to actually declare that they didn't want to be an organ donor, instead of the system that was in place in the UK and Ireland were the various organ donor charities spent millions advertising in an effort to encourage people to come forward and register. The web article claimed that the difference in terms of numbers for the two systems was that in Spain eighty percent of it citizens were organ donors, whereas in the UK and Ireland the figure was only around thirty percent. The benefit to the Spanish in terms of waiting times for organs was incredible. And this quite simply saved peoples lives in their droves. But the key factor for Ray was when he read that non Spanish nationals could, provided they had the money, come to Spain and pay for a kidney transplant. The article estimated the average cost at one hundred thousand euros.

At first the cost caused him to pause. He pondered again, why had his father double crossed Charlie Bassett? He was in line to earn one hundred thousand euros for his part. But then he thought of his mother back in Belfast. She was seriously ill and fully dependent on dialysis, so how could you bring her over to Spain. And the answer he told himself was money. Surely money could buy her whatever she needed for the trip? Spain and Ireland weren't that far apart. Two hours on a plane. How much would a medical flight, or plane, from Belfast to Spain cost? He had no idea, but he felt certain that the remaining three hundred thousand euros his dad had taken for himself would cover it.

In less than five minutes on google and he was a wealth of knowledge, what was it they said, "Every day is a school day." Well he definitely felt educated this morning. He also felt some admiration for his father. A respect that he had never had before. His dad's first time in prison had been a very honourable thing taking the rap for his brother, and now here he was fifty years later taking big risks in an effort to save his mother's life. Did a good cause out weigh a bad deed? No, probably not, but he still thought fair play to his dad.

The question now though was where was he? Ray flipped back to his home screen and selected the phone icon and then went to recent calls. He double tapped on the call log for his dad's mobile and the phone instantly began its cycle to make the call. Again, like the last attempts, the call went straight to the messaging service, but as his dad hadn't set up voicemail the call ended. The only thing that Ray could assume was that his dad was lying low for a few days. This fact, if it was indeed a fact, didn't help Ray now though. He only had a few hours before he had to meet Charlie. If he could in that time make contact with his dad maybe then his decision could change, but for now it was made up. He was going to follow in his father's footsteps and he was going to do it for the same reason. His problem for now was that he couldn't do it on his own.

He got up and retraced his steps to the sink, washing his face with cold water and then headed back to the kitchen, more slowly and carefully than he had left it.

"Were you on the phone on the loo you mingger?" Trace asked.

"It was a shit call anyway," Ray answered quickly.

"Ah you're disgusting," said Tracey.

"I'm only joking," replied Ray, "I was on with my mum and heard someone coming down and thought it might be Joe so just wanted to finish up in there, you know." He lied, which was starting to become a habit.

"How is she?"

"Shattered, but at least she answered this time, so it was good to get talking to her. No sign of a donor yet, so it's just a waiting game." To change the subject he asked, "any coffee left, I'd made a pot?"

"Maybe a small one," said Trace, "and we're out of water, along with everything else."

"I know, I need Joe to go shopping today, you gonna go with him?"

"Did Hard Rock pay you?"

"No, Pepe's had to go for a PCR test, so I can't go see him until he gets the result."

"So are me and Joe going shop lifting?" Tracey jibed.

"No, we'll have to use my credit card."

"Look Ray, Jess and I have savings for the wedding, you can borrow until we get things set up out here."

"No," said Ray quickly, "Thanks Trace but no not your wedding fund. We're supposed to be out here to help you add to it not spend it We'll be OK, I'll get it sorted." He found his mug of coffee, which was now cold so he threw the remains down the sink, poured out the dregs from the pot and set the mug back on the table. Before sitting down he retrieved his glass from the window sill and drank down the lot, which had now melted in to welcomingly cold water. Sitting down he said, "Would you mind going shopping with Joe this morning as I'd like to have a chat with everyone at lunch time."

"A chat?" Trace asked, "like a team meeting?" Before Ray answered she added, "You've got me worried, when you have these let's chat moments it's usually something serious. You don't need to worry as Joe has already told me that Lizzy is coming out tomorrow."

Shit, he'd forgotten about Liz.

"It's not about Liz," he said.

"Oh Jesus, you mean it's worse than Lizzy? It must be bad."

He agreed, it must be bad if it was worse than Liz, or Lizzy as Trace called her.

If only Liz was all he had to worry about.

"I'll get these lazy sods up," he said and then headed upstairs. Before leaving he spoke over his shoulder, "Trace? Do you fancy making another pot of coffee? There's drinking water in the saucepan," then to explain he added, "I melted the ice."

"You boys think I'm your skivvy," Tracey bantered.

Ray thought to himself as he started to climb the stairs, "Christ, wait till you hear what I want you to help with next!"

Chapter Fifteen

Tenerife, Canary Islands
Saturday 23rd October 2021

The Jet Ski had been running for the best part of the last hour. They had started it, with some trouble at first, and then taken turns on it, shouting and laughing as they did and enjoying an early session at the beach before the crowds came later that morning. Holiday makers just having a good time. Dennis had heard all of this through the open bathroom window and his jealousy that he wasn't out there with them added to his woes.

He wasn't really a holiday maker on this trip and he certainly wasn't having a good time. For the last four hours his bowels had been running and unlike the Jet Ski crew, he had no trouble starting it. The trouble he was having was bloody stopping it. He swore he would never have another Chinese for as long as he lived. That was if he lived beyond this morning.

Many times he had thought surely there can't be anything left inside me, but no sooner had the thought entered his head when the cramps flared up again and entered deep in his bowels and stomach. His arse was numb from sitting on the toilet seat for so long. He had pins and needles in his legs. And he was shattered. The life had quite simply drained out of him and flowed down the toilet. Jeffrey had gone out to see if the shops had any Imodium, as it was doubtful that the pharmacy would be open yet. The only thing that Dennis could do was sit and wait.

Jeffrey was waiting also, but he was having a coffee as he did so. He had struck lucky on the Imodium at the local Spar but he didn't want to go back too soon. It suited him if Dennis was out of action today and so the longer he waited the better it would be. Or actually the worse it would be for Dennis. Jeffrey needed some time on his own to hopefully find Charlie Bassett and if at all possible catch up with Arnie to find out why he had bolted on them last night. He didn't understand it as he had seen the surprise and then fear in Arnie's eyes and if he didn't know any better, he too like Dennis would be convinced that Arnie was over here stealing their stash. But the truth was he did no better and he knew it was Charlie, so why did Arnie run. Run he did though, and fast he'd been as Dennis and Jeffrey didn't even get close to catching up. They had lost him in a matter of seconds, and had spent hours scouring streets in the hope of finding him. Dennis was determined to find him, fuelled on Jeffrey thought, by the anger of having his Rolex and wallet stolen as his mood was foul. Now it was his arse that was foul, and that was a mix of the whisky and eating a Chinese takeaway so late at night. Jeffrey had also advised against the prawns though, but Dennis didn't listen so tough shit. Or maybe not so tough shit, depending on whichever way you looked at it.

Jeffrey was sitting in what he thought was a good vantage point. The restaurant gave him a view of the largest Spar in the area and of the main walkway leading to and from the beach. Looking down this walkway he could also see anyone walking past the main path which ran along the beach front. And it was busy, even though it was still early. Busy with shoppers, beach goers and people just out for a morning stroll and he hoped if Charlie or Arnie fitted in to any of these groups then he had a good chance of spying them. He did also accept that Playa de Las Americas which pretty much joined now with Los Cristianos heading east and Costa Adeje heading west along the coast was quite a large area with many Spars and the like, hundreds of hotels and hundreds of pathways, but something told him that Arnie for one was based around here, and as for Charlie he had no idea, but he needed to start somewhere. His phone dinged with an incoming message.

"Where R U??"

It was from Dennis. Jeffrey smiled to himself. To be more accurate it was a sly smirk. He finished his coffee and signalled to the waiter. Once he reached Jeffrey's table he said, "One breakfast special please," he pointed to the picture on the menu as he knew from his previous attempt to order coffee that the guy didn't speak much English, which was OK as Jeffrey didn't speak any Spanish. The waiter nodded his acknowledgement and then asked something that Jeffrey didn't understand until the waiter copied Jeffrey and pointed to the menu.

"Oh, orange please," answered Jeffrey as he now realised the question was about what breakfast juice he wanted, which was part of the breakfast special. Another thing about a lot of the breakfast specials which amused Jeffrey was that they came with chips. Not his usual breakfast choice at home, but he did admit, when away, he did quite enjoy them. He tapped his coffee cup to signal a top up and the waiter nodded again.

Breakfast ordered, he typed a message back to Dennis, "Waiting on chemist opening," then hit send. He toyed with the idea of reading the paper he had bought but passed as he was worried he could miss his chance of spying his fellow countrymen out for their morning stroll.

Unknown to Jeffrey, he wasn't going to spy either Charlie or Arnie and he might as well have read his paper and even done the crossword. At that precise moment Charlie Bassett's phone had just began its flight path towards the apartment wall. One moment it was a lovely example of modern technology, the next it was a pile of broken debris waiting to be swept up and laid to rest in the bin. As a result, and in a funk, Charlie wouldn't be heading out for some hours yet.

As for Arnie, he was at that precise moment watching Jeffrey and had just witnessed him ordering something from the waiter, breakfast he suspected. From his elevated position on his fifth floor balcony and partly hidden behind the towels hanging over the balcony rail, he had seen Jeffrey exit the Spar and walk to the café where he was now sitting. He also noticed over the next twenty minutes that Jeffrey was keeping watch, and it wasn't just a nosey tourist type of watching, it was obvious that he was watching and looking for someone, and Arnie was convinced that that someone was him.

During these past twenty minutes Arnie had also made a couple of phone calls and he was still on his third now. He said, "I'm watching him now and he's been there for twenty minutes."

"Tell me again about last night?" said Bobby.

"I first saw them at Hard Rock Café. They pretended they hadn't seen me, but just seconds after I turned and headed back they followed me. I stopped in the crowd at the fountains, you know the ones in the Safari centre and then so did they. I shouldn't have stopped, I know that, but I wanted to try to see what they were up to. But then I saw Dennis looking for me and as soon as I made eye contact with him I saw the mistake in his face. He looked away quickly, hoping I didn't notice, but then I turned and walked away as quick as I could, but they were straight on me following. I think if it hadn't been for the fireworks, and then someone broke a window, I mightn't have got away."

"OK," said Bobby, "who is over there with you?"

"Ritchie and Kevin, I've just phoned them both and they're on the way over. We're going to put Kevin in to watch Jeffrey. Jeffrey doesn't know Kevin but Ritchie's done some work for them in the past and so Jeffrey would spot him a mile off."

OK, and what about Ivan the Russian, when are you supposed to meet him?"

"This morning, in just over two hours." Arnie was going to mention that the Russian didn't like being called Ivan and insisted it was Evonne, but he decided just to leave it just in case Bobby thought that he was correcting him, and Bobby didn't like to be corrected. All these men with egos!

There was silence for a few moments, and then Bobby spoke again. "You might have to push that back till we see what's going on here with our two friends." Then before Arnie said what Bobby knew he was going to say Bobby continued, "I think we both know what Dennis and Jeffrey are up to, I know that. I agree with you Arnie and I don't believe in coincidences either. But think about it, eh? Think about it? We must have a snitch and until we know who that is I think we need to be very careful."

A snitch! Arnie nodded in agreement with Bobby. How else could they know? How else could they be here? There was no coincidence.

"You sure you can vouch for your two lads there?" Bobby asked.

"Ritchie and Kevin?" Arnie asked, although it was obvious who Bobby was talking about, but he said their names more in an effort to give himself time to think, and time to ponder the question to himself, before he gave his answer to Bobby. If he was wrong and the leak came from his side he could be in trouble, but he'd be in even more trouble if he didn't spot it and stop it. He went with his gut, "I think they're sound Bobby."

"OK, but you better be sure, or make sure son, there's a lot riding on this."

Arnie knew only too well what was riding on it; the entire thing had been his idea to start with. He was the one that had done work for Dennis and Jeffrey for years and that had enabled him to not only see the play, guess the profits, but get to know the contacts. And here he was in Tenerife this weekend to meet with one of those contacts and it just happens that Dennis and Jeffrey show up.

"I'm going to have to call in a couple of favours," said Bobby, "but it's Saturday and they usually go fishing so not sure if I'll be able to reach them. You're just going to have to handle things over there Arnie in the meantime."

"What will I tell the Russian?"

Bobby thought for a few seconds, "give me an hour Arnie, and don't do anything just yet. The Russian is the main deal and I don't want to spook him, but let's see what I can find out."

"OK Bobby."

"What's the Digger doing now?"

"Digging in to his breakfast," answered Arnie.

"And still no sign of Dennis?"

"No, none this morning."

"OK," said Bobby, "give me an hour." Then he hung up.

Guessing that Jeffrey wouldn't be going far for the next five to ten minutes at least while he ate his breakfast, Arnie took relief from his lookout duties to have a piss. As he was finishing, the prostitute he had phoned in late last night, or early this morning to be more precise, paddled naked in to the bathroom behind him.

"Need to pee," she said, in an accent that Arnie wasn't sure was Polish or Russian or something European. He couldn't remember if she had told him, he couldn't remember if she had told him her name either, so he just finished up, moved away from the toilet and said, "no problem."

Back out in the apartment he sorted out the euros in his wallet and left her fee on the bedside table, with no tip this time. No tip this time because she had pissed him off. Pissed him off big time and dented his ego.

He'd come back to the apartment last night somewhat spooked from the chase by Dennis and Jeffrey. He'd almost decided to scrap his plans to call the agency that the barman in Harry's Bar had given to him, but after a couple of drinks and almost convincing himself that Dennis and

Jeffrey weren't about to come crashing through his door, he reverted back to his original plans. Although by the time he'd phoned the agency the earliest he could get a girl was three in the morning. In the mood by that stage he had agreed. Now though he wished he hadn't have bothered.

He didn't know if it was the additional drinks he'd had, three or four more than usual, or that his mind was still distracted by Dennis and Jeffrey, but he hadn't gotten in to the whole thing as full on as he usually did. She had obliged with his usual request and put on the Bunny Girl strapless bodysuit, rabbit ears and fluffy tail. It had been his thing ever since he'd seen the film, Bridget Jones Diary and had developed a fetish for Renee Zellweger who had acted as a Bunny Girl in the movie. But even the rabbit look hadn't settled his mood.

He then noticed that she wasn't in to the whole thing either and her screams and moans of pleasure were all fake. This had thrown him, put him off, and reduced his ability to continue, so he'd blamed the booze, rolled over in the bed and pretended to fall asleep.

Tatyana, who was from Belarus, lying there dressed up like a rabbit almost joked, "What's up Doc?" But then thought better of it as it was actually what was down and not up that was the problem, and you never knew how some of these men would take things. One minute they wanted to be your lover and the next they were giving you a beating bad enough to keep you out of the game for a month. So she said nothing, and tired from her pursuits so far that night, she too rolled over and went to sleep. In a few minutes she was snoring like a train. Arnie lay awake for some time deflated, his mind rolling back through the years asking the question, "had they all been faking?" He'd thought he was king of the bedroom, shagging all these girls for years in to the land of ecstasy and pleasure, when all the time they'd been bored stiff and watching the television over his shoulder, like the bimbo last night had been doing. So all that, "oh baby, baby you're the best, harder, harder, yes, yes, oh you're so good, the best the best, oh, oh, oh YES." Had been complete and utter bullshit. What the all should have said was more like, "Is that all you've got and what time is Coronation Street on as Arnold Cherry you're boring the fucking tits clean off me! Call yourself a rabbit?"

He was actually a bit embarrassed by the whole thing, and he was glad when she had come out of the bathroom, got dressed, collected up her euros and left.

Arnie had made himself a black coffee and went back out on to his balcony to catch up with Jeffrey, but Jeffrey was gone.

"Shit," he said to no one, then spilt his coffee when he banged his cup down on the balcony table. As the table wasn't level the coffee began to run towards where he was sitting. "Shit," he repeated, then went inside to find a cloth. With no cloth's to be found and no kitchen roll as he hadn't bought any, he removed the toilet roll from its holder and went back outside. By then several drips of coffee had made their way on to his seat so he wiped up here first and then mopped up the remains on the table. He finished by wiping the bottom of his cup and then sat back down, but as he did so he caught movement from where Jeffrey had been sitting and he jerked around to see. His knee bumped one of the legs of the table and once again the coffee in his cup splashed like a wave heading towards the beach and spilt coffee once again on the table.

"Ah for fuck sake," he said disgusted. He grabbed the bog roll again and repeated the clean up and then sat back down, carefully this time, and watched Jeffrey get stuck back in to his breakfast, guessing and relieved that he must just have been away to the toilet.

His phone rang, it was Ritchie, he answered it but waited for Ritchie to speak.

"Arnie?" he asked.

"Is Kevin in place?" Arnie just asked, no hello or how you doing. Arnie liked to be like that with Ritchie. He liked to act distant, more superior, even though they were at the same level. Firstly, Arnie didn't like that as he thought he was above Ritchie, and secondly he thought it made him tougher and commanded more respect. More accurately he hated Ritchie because he had discovered his Bunny Girl fetish and had nicknamed him, "Bugs" which really pissed him off, which Ritchie was only too aware off.

"He's where you told me to put him," said Ritchie, "he'll keep tabs on Jeffrey and keep in touch with you."

"Did you tell him texts only as I've important calls to make, Bobby and the Russian?"

Ritchie knew the text thing was bullshit and was just a way for Arnie to emphasise that it was him dealing with all the "important" calls and dropping in Bobby's name to say, look at me I'm dealing with the top man, not you.

"He knows," answered Ritchie, "I'm heading back to lie low, you need me call me." Then he cut the call.

Arnie continued to watch as Jeffrey seemed to finish his breakfast and it made him realise how hungry he was himself. With Kevin now in place he was thinking about getting dressed and getting something to eat when his phone rang again. Assuming it was Ritchie calling back with something he'd forgot to say, or Kevin calling instead of texting, which pissed him off, he was about to answer the call with a grump when at the last moment he noticed it was actually Bobby.

"Bobby, how are you?" he said.

"Any developments?" Bobby asked, ignoring the greeting.

"Jeffrey is still in the café but now Kevin is in place to watch him."

"Where's Ritchie?"

"Gone back to his apartment to lie low."

"OK," said Bobby. "The general SP over here is that there's no leak. Not at our end. Most likely we think it's with the Russian, which causes a problem." Before Arnie spoke Bobby continued, "Arnie, I didn't share this with the lads over here, but there could be another answer," he paused, "are you sure about those two there with you, like I mean really sure?"

Arnie was totally certain about Kevin, he didn't even know Jeffrey or Dennis and had never worked for either of them. Ritchie? He thought he was also sure about Ritchie. Unlike Kevin, he had done some work for the two lads in the past but it wasn't much, just bits here and there, so he was certain that there was no relationship. Even though him and Ritchie didn't get on that well he still thought he could trust him. However, if he did want a chance to get rid of Ritchie to help further his own career now was a perfect opportunity. One word to Bobby that he wasn't sure about Ritchie and he was history. And no more Bugs jibes. On the other hand it didn't fix the leak though or help them discover where the leak was and so if he offered up Ritchie and later it came out that he was wrong, then his balls would be on the block. So best to just play it straight for now and so he went with his gut feeling.

"I'm certain Bobby."

"Certain enough to vouch for them? I'm going to be asked that over here Arnold," Bobby using Arnie's proper name to subtly make the point that this was serious shit, "you know what I'm saying?"

He was in deep now and had already vouched for them so to retract this would be questioned, "Yes Bobby," he said, "I'll vouch for both of them." As he said it though a pang of doubt sprang up at the back of his mind. If he was wrong then he would be tainted and then be culpable also. He had just taken a big risk, and it was a risk that could cost him dearly.

After ending the call with Arnie, Ritchie found a quiet seat at a café of his own and made another call. The first went unanswered but when he tried it again for the second time his call was accepted.

The best part of Jeffrey's breakfast had been the chips and plum tomatoes. The bacon had been very fatty and undercooked, the toast wasn't toast but better described as warm bread, the sausage had been Spanish, say no more, and the egg was swimming in so much grease and fat that if consumed a heart attack would have followed immediately.

He was finishing his orange juice and thinking he should maybe head back to the apartment and put poor Dennis out of his misery when his phone rang. The number was displayed, a UK number, but he didn't recognise it so he let it go to voicemail to see if whoever it was would leave a message. The call ended and he waited to see if the message text notification would come through, but the phone rang again and he recognised that it was the same number as before, so he decided to answer it. He hit the answer button and put the phone to his ear but said nothing. A few seconds later a voice said, "Jeffrey, did you enjoy your breakfast?"

He had a slight notion that he had heard the voice before but he couldn't place it. The fact that he had asked about his breakfast alerted Jeffrey that someone was watching him and it made him feel uneasy. He had taken Dennis's advice and had brought the gun with him, but with the thin shirt and shorts he was wearing his only option was to bring it in his back pack, which was under his seat. He gripped the bag gently with both of his feet and dragged it out from beneath his chair so the zipped top was just below his legs. He then casually brought his other hand below the table and began to prize open the zip as he said in to the phone in his other hand, "I passed on the egg as I've only got bronze health insurance."

"Good choice," said Ritchie, "I take it you don't recognise my voice? Don't worry I'm friend not foe."

"Glad to hear that, it's always good to have friends, but friends usually join each other for breakfast, not spy on each other."

"I'm not the one spying on you," said Ritchie, "but I'm calling to help you out on that front, that is if I can join the payroll?"

Jeffrey's mind was racing as he clearly knew the voice but just couldn't place the face or name. "I'm on holiday," Jeffrey said as he was thinking, "so I'm not really here to recruit. Anyway interviews are usually done face to face."

"What if I told you that we'd already done that part?"

"I was thinking the voice was familiar, but you'll have to excuse me or give me some help," said Jeffrey, his right hand had now retrieved the gun and he was holding it while still in the backpack, but ready to pull out if needed.

"Roy Keane," said Ritchie.

Jeffrey sat quietly for a few moments as the cylinders in his mind began to fall in to place.

"The look-alike?" Jeffrey said.

"I'd like to think I've weathered the years a bit better, but yes."

Jeffrey relaxed slightly. He now knew it was Ritchie on the phone and he had liked him when he had done some work for Dennis some years back, but he was still aware that Ritchie had inferred that he was being watched by somebody.

"I'm not in a position to comment on that at the moment," Jeffrey said, "but I do believe that you are still on the payroll, well of sorts."

"I could be, although it's been a few years, but what I'm looking for isn't to be on the payroll per say, I'm more looking for a one off bonus."

"A bonus?" asked Jeffrey. "Correct me if I'm wrong but a bonus is normally paid for achieving something or an excellent performance and from where I'm sitting all you've done is tell me someone is interested in my diet."

"Good point," said Ritchie, "but it's not about what I've done, it's about what I'm about to do."

"And what's that exactly?" asked Jeffrey.

"Save your life," answered Ritchie, with a sort of swagger to his voice, "and for a double bonus I'll save Dennis's as well."

Chapter Sixteen

Tenerife, Canary Islands
Saturday 23rd October 2021

"Terry if you teach me to cook, I'll teach you how to play the drums," said Joe.

"You've just had your last breakfast from me, Ruddock Junior," replied Terry. "And I'm not listening to your round the clock bollucks any more."

Joe, as the only sighted one in the house, gave them directions as to where things where on their plates in relation to the numbers on a clock. Eggs at nine o'clock, tomatoes at six o'clock, like that. It helped for meals like breakfasts that had many components, but wasn't required for meals like curries for example. But the rascal in Joe, which did make many appearances, had began to mess them around and lie about what was actually where.

"Just kidding Terrence," responded Joe quickly, "your breakfasts are just the best." Then fawning innocence, "and sorry, I just got my times mixed up."

"You can still fuck off," said Terry, "you're still not getting another one, and less of the Terrence, that reminds me of an old girlfriend of mine as she used to call me that when she was looking for something. And that something was usually access to my bank balance."

"Most of your girlfriends were old Terry," joined in Ray.

"What is this?" pleaded Terry, "pick on Terry day, and I notice that all the banter comes after I've made you all breakfast."

Both Tracey and Aurimas flagged that it was the Ruddock's who were to blame for the banter.

"Don't worry," said Terry, "I know exactly who the shit stirrers are, but I also know who is on dish washing duty, and hey would you believe it, it's the same deadly duo. Ha, Ha!" He laughed.

"Hardly ample punishment," said Aurimas, "It was their shift on the dishwashing anyway."

"Whose shit stirring now," said Joe?

"Make sure you wear those Marigolds Joe as you know that Fairy Liquid goes for your soft hands," chuckled Aurimas.

Joe was about to tell him to fuck off, but remembered his dad was there, and so instead said, "My mother's coming tomorrow, Aurimas, and I'm going to tell her about your super duper exercise routine. She is going to love that."

"Oh yeah," added Ray, "Liz will have you out there by the pool all day." Both Ruddock's laughing now in unison. Trace even saw the funny side of this jibe as she knew only too well what Liz was like.

Terry even pitched in, "I can just imagine you Aurimas and Liz strutting your stuff out there in your leotards."

Trying his best to protest over the laughter Aurimas said, "how come the banter has made its way to me, it was Joe started it?"

"Do the dishes," asked Joe, "and I'll forget about telling my mum."

Not caring about Joe's dad being there Aurimas replied, "you can fuck right off, it's your turn."

As Joe either seemed to concede, or couldn't think of any comeback, Terry asked, "I'm going to have a beer, anyone else want anything?"

Ray replied, "considering now we actually have food and drink, yes I think I'll join you." Aurimas also accepted Terry's offer for a beer, but Tracey declined and Joe just grumbled that he supposed he'd better make a start with the dishes.

It was almost eleven thirty and Ray was conscious that he needed to contact Charlie. But before he could do that he needed to continue on the conversation he'd had with Terry and Aurimas while Tracey and Joe had been out shopping. It had been a conversation that had surprised him.

They had both known bits and pieces about what Charlie had said, and they both knew quite a lot about Ray's background, his Mum and her illness with her kidneys, his dads past as a bank robber and his prison life, but Ray had thought that he would have needed to do some convincing or selling, or even down right begging, to get them to buy in to his idea of how to rob the bank. In his sketchy plan he needed them both, and a lot more besides, but without Terry and Aurimas he wasn't sure it could be a runner.

The fact was he needn't have worried. It very quickly became almost like the Three Musketeers, "All for one and one for all," and they both practically told Ray that they would do anything for him, no matter what. This did leave him with a slight feeling of guilt and the expression came to him, "The blind leading the blind," but it came with a different meaning than the phrase actually portrayed. Was he taking advantage of their blind faith in him? He knew though, with absolute certainty, that if the shoe or need was on the other foot he would do whatever, no matter what, to support them. Knowing this made him feel better and they got on discussing plans.

They agreed on most of what Ray suggested. When Ray mentioned masks, Terry had suggested using fancy dress as it was close to Halloween and there were so many events, parties and just people wearing costumes that it would be a great cover. It was unanimous that Monty wasn't going along, no matter what Charlie Bassett said. It was also agreed that they needed a sighted person, and the most likely candidate was Colin. They disagreed when Terry said that they could use Joe. Ray was adamant that Joe could take no part.

They were also divided on whether or not they needed to tell Tracey their plans. Ray was for it, Terry was against stating vigorously that she would never sanction such a thing, especially as Jess who she was marrying in a few months was a solicitor, and any involvement in such a criminal act could scupper their relationship and marriage. Aurimas was neutral here, as he didn't really know what Tracey would think, or what she would think if they went ahead without telling her. Finally Ray decided that he owed it to Tracey and Joe for that matter, to inform them. Even though they wouldn't be taking part or be at any risk, they were here, they were a part of "the team" and they deserved to be told. Now that the moment had arrived though Ray was beginning to have second thoughts.

They went through their usual ritual of passing their plates and things down to the end of the table nearest to the sink. Once sorted and set for Joe to start washing, Ray was on drying and putting away duty so he stayed seated for now, Terry sorted out the drinks, remembering that Ray had said earlier that he wanted to talk about something and having a bad feeling about it, Tracey changed her mind and asked Terry if she could have a glass of wine, then she got up and opened the patio doors to let Bumper outside. "Busy, busy," she said as Bumper waltzed past her and headed out to take care of his constitutionals. Tracey felt the hot midday air rush in against the air conditioned room and she looked forward to an afternoon by the pool after Ray had finished his little chat.

Terry was thinking that he might have preferred to have been doing the dishes as by standing at the sink with his back to the table he might have been more detached to what he feared was coming. He still felt strongly that Ray was doing the wrong thing in discussing this bank thing with Tracey and with Joe as well for that matter. He didn't know if he sensed tension in the room, or if it was just himself. He felt more nervous about the next ten minutes than he did about the upcoming robbery. He knew that may change come Monday morning.

Aurimas, although on the fence between the whole debate with Ray and Terry about Tracey was feeling a bit anxious as well. He just felt like going upstairs to listen to some music, or maybe practice some in the music room, but he knew he had to sit here and be his part of the group, even though he didn't imagine he would be saying much either way.

Ray took a large pull on his bottle of Budweiser. It was cold and crisp on his throat, and it had been on offer in the supermarket, which was a great combination. He was searching for the words to open the conversation he wanted to have. Want being the key word. Terry had been quite right on the fact that he didn't need to have this talk with Tracey, but the truth was he wanted to. He disguised taking a deep breath as he pulled on his beer and then said, "I have a bit of a problem."

"You can buy tablets for that now Ray," Terry said quickly, which got a giggle around the room. He was about to go on and say "Liz is here tomorrow and I'm sure she'll have some, knowing Liz," but he remembered just in time that Joe was there and so just said nothing more, and was glad for it.

"You's all know about my dad," Ray continued, "my dad who the Clash wrote a song for, the Bank Robber."

Everyone stayed silent.

"Did you all know that the first time he was in prison that he'd taken the rap for his younger brother?" Ray did know that they all knew, apart from Aurimas, although he suspected that maybe Joe and Aurimas had maybe spoken about it, but he wanted to make the point that his dad had a good side.

Aurimas did know because as Ray suspected Joe had told him the story, in great detail in fact, as Joe thought it was one of the most selfless acts he had ever heard of in real life, and it was something that Joe was proud of. But he guessed that Ray wouldn't be sure of that and so he thought for good manners he should pretend he knew nothing.

"Gees your kidding, how come Ray?" Aurimas asked.

"It's a long story Aurimas, but basically my grandmother asked him to because she thought his brother Billy couldn't do the time."

"Fuck," Aurimas said, "I don't know if I'd do that for our Marcus."

"Well he took a bit of a risk," said Ray and before he continued Aurimas cut in.

"A bit of a risk OK if you ask me!"

"What I mean is that he thought if he pleaded he'd get reduced sentence and maybe only do a couple of years as a first offence, but just after he pleaded guilty a security guard died who had been injured in the robbery and so my dads sentence changed to the maximum twenty years."

"Fuck me," Aurimas said again.

Tracey was wondering were Ray was going with this as he rarely talked about his dad and she couldn't think what relevance it would have now. Joe too was washing the dishes wondering along a similar thought path as Tracey, although he did suspect that this conversation was leading to something to do with little and large who had spoken to his dad at Hard Rock.

"He ended up serving fourteen years, got out early for good behaviour," continued Ray, "and do you know that my mum visited him every two weeks for all that time. And before that, they hadn't even had a date. As soon as he was released in 1982 they got married, and it didn't take long until yours truly came along."

Bumper came back in and Tracey heard him at his water bowl and then flopping down on the floor for a nap.

"Some woman my mother," Ray went on, "she stuck by my dad no matter what. Even when he ended up back in prison she was there without fail. She didn't condone what he did, but she didn't condemn him either. In a strange way you know he made good in prison. He taught music that's why they called him Jimmy Jazz."

"I thought it was to do with the Clash song?" asked Aurimas.

"No, believe it or not that's just a coincidence, the Jazz referred to Jazz because that was what my dad played most."

The words of the Clash song ran through Ray's mind then because they were now quite apt coincidence or not.

"Who is it they're looking for?

Jimmy Jazz, Jazz, Jazz, Jazz eh."

Terry was also wondering why Ray was going back over his mum and dad, although he did think he was maybe focusing on his mum to lead up to what the money was about now for the kidney and all, but truthfully all the talk about prison was giving him the shits considering they had just talked about robbing a bank on Monday. When Ray continued, Terry felt he had to intervene.

"All those years that my dad was in prison, and my mother never failed," Ray repeated.

"Ray," said Terry, "you're putting the shits up me with all this talk about prison time." Terry hoped that Ray would realise he was making a mistake about all this past stuff and maybe even drop the entire thing and forget about telling Tracey.

Terry's words made Ray think and he did realise that he maybe had made a mistake. Jesus if Terry was spooked what about Aurimas. Tracey was wondering what Terry had meant as his comment sounded somewhat out of context, and she also felt a bit of tension creep in to the room and it made her feel uneasy. What was Ray here to talk about?

"All yours," said Joe triumphantly as he let the water out of the sink, rinsed down the soap suds, dried and declared, "That's my shift done. Does anyone want to split a beer for a shandy?"

Aurimas said, "I'll go a shandy. Is the lemonade in the fridge?"

Joe checked the fridge and confirmed it was then asked, "anybody want anything before I sit?"

Everyone declined and the room then went in to an uneasy silence. Ray knew that Terry's words had meant either get on with it or drop it, and he knew that he was right. He blew out his breath and said, "Sorry."

The only person in the room that got what he meant and what the apology was for was Terry. Everyone else was puzzled. Aurimas just wanted to leave, Joe didn't think it was his place to get involved and was quite happy to have finished the dishes and now enjoy a shandy. Tracy though was beginning to think that there was something coming that she wasn't going to like and she was starting to feel a little scared. She was just about to ask Ray what he was sorry for when he spoke again.

"I've been beating around the bush, waffling." He scratched his head and then finished his beer, now regretting he hadn't asked Joe for another.

"The two men that came to see me at Hard Rock on Friday night were looking for my dad," he spat out. "Charlie Bassett and his hench man are over here to rob illegal funds that are stashed in banks here from criminal gangs from Belfast. They know the deposit boxes the money is stashed in and they have inside help from the banks." Ray paused, which gave Tracey her chance to ask, "so why did they come to see you?"

Another deep breath and then after letting it out Ray said, "Jimmy Jazz."

"Your dad, or the song this time?" Tracey asked.

"My dad," answered Ray. "He had robbed a bank here for them on Thursday. Him and Monty, that's the henchman, but my dad cracked him over the head and then cleared off with the," he paused as he was looking for the word, but then just said, "the cash."

There was silence for a few seconds then Joe said.

"Granddad robbed a bank here on Thursday?"

Ray heard the disappointment in his voice and realised again that maybe Terry had been right about this.

"Yes son," said Ray softly and before he could go on Joe asked another question, "and where is he now?"

"Lying low. I think." Said Ray and then regretted not being more certain.

"Think?" asked Joe.

"Look, let me explain what I think. That's why I was waffling. I was trying to bring in my mum, your granny, you know she's sick, right, waiting on a kidney donor. I think your Granddad is over here trying to get the money to take her to Spain for a kidney transplant."

"Spain?"

"I googled it," said Ray, now sure that Terry had been right and he just should have said nothing, "Spain has an opt out system for donors and it means that most people in Spain donate their organs and so the wait time is really short. You can pay private, it's about one hundred grand or so, and then there's all the other stuff, travel, and all that."

"And did Gran tell you this?" asked Joe,

"No," Ray said, "you know her, she told me he was in Tenerife but she didn't tell me about the bank. You know why, I've been his biggest critic."

There was silence for a few moments as they all gathered their thoughts on what Ray had told them. Along with the silence there was an atmosphere of tension. It hung there like an unanswered question.

It was Joe who broke the silence first.

"So what are we going to do?" asked Joe.

Here it was. It had come to the point were he needed to shit or get off the pot.

"Charlie Bassett is putting the squeeze on me, on us."

"What to find granddad?"

"Yes," said Ray, "but there was supposed to be another job."

"Job?"

"Bank robbery, it was supposed to be on Friday, but it's now Monday."

There was silence again for some minutes.

Terry and Aurimas were waiting on the crunch.

Joe was thinking about his Granddad.

Tracey was confused. Her worry had subsided as she could now see this was more about Ray's dad rather than them. It wasn't as if they could find him, four blind people, a kid and a dog. And of course she hoped that Ray's dad was OK, and she did admire him taking that risk to get a kidney for his wife, but it was more like something you would read in a book rather than real life. She was starting to think about getting Bumper's harness to take him out for a walk before she spent some time at the pool when Ray's words stunned her.

"Charlie has threatened me, says he's got someone watching my mum and so either we find my dad or I, we, need to rob the bank for him on Monday."

"He threatened Gran," Joe said with concern obvious in his voice. "I think he's bluffing," said Ray, "don't worry."

Trace was thinking surely it's a matter of phoning the police. She knew that this could be seen as grassing on Ray's dad but surely his mum's safety came first. Her thoughts though went out the window when Ray continued.

"We're going ahead with it, I've worked it out."

"Ahead with what?" asked Tracey, thinking she knew the answer but then thinking that the answer was so ridiculous.

"The bank," Ray said with a slight pause to his voice, he couldn't even say robbery.

"The bank? The bank? You can't even say robbery. Are you some sort of moron? Ray what are you thinking?"

"Tracey, I know it sounds crazy."

"Crazy is mild," Tracey said, her voice raised now. "What about Joe?" She then thought about Liz coming over on Sunday. "What about Liz, we going to sit around the table tomorrow night when Lizzy is here and tell her all this. Hey Liz I brought your son out here and you know what we're going to do? Play guitar, sing? No fuck that. We're going to rob a fucking bank!"

"Tracey," said Ray.

"Does this Charlie eejit not know you're blind?" Tracey asked and then said, "Ah, of course not, you and you're fucking games Ray. Why can't you just be blind and be happy with it. You put on this pretence that oh no I don't mind being blind, and then you go around having Joe follow you like a fucking remote control? Fuck sake Ray what's going on with you?"

"Tracey," it was Terry this time, "you're out of order."

"I'm out of order, are you not listening to what he's saying? He's going to rob a fucking bank. What about all those years his dad spent in jail? Does that mean nothing?"

"He's not going to rob a bank," said Terry firmly, "we are."

"Who's we?" she said.

"Me and Aurimas too."

She stood up pushing her chair firmly back behind her, "ah for fuck sake, you're all nuts. I can't have any part of this, Jess is a solicitor for fucks sake, how can I be a part of this. I've got to get out of here." She went to walk away and stopped as Joe had spoke.

"Dad," he said, "is Terry right?"

"Yeah, we talked about it earlier."

"And what about me?"

"Joe you're only fourteen," said Ray.

"Dad, you can't do this without me, you need someone that can see. I'll do the earpiece, remote control as Tracey said." His voice was pleading.

"I don't believe this," Tracey spat, "and I thought that Lizzy was the bad parent, she's fucking nothing compared to you, fucking getting your son involved with a fucking caper like this. You should be ashamed Raymond Ruddock, fucking ashamed."

Tracey headed for the stairs, or in the direction she hoped was to the stairs. She was crying now and almost totally out of control. She needed to leave before she said anything else, some of what she said she already regretted, but once you had said something it was very hard to take back. Luckily she judged her direction almost perfectly and once she felt the handrail she ran upstairs to her room, slamming her door behind her.

"Want a Jameson's?" asked Terry.

"A double please," said Ray, "and Terry."

"Yeah," said Terry as he got up.

"The next time I don't take your advice you have my permission to give me a swift kick to the balls. Might be a bit less painful than that."

"It's that Irish accent too," said Terry, "she doesn't curse much, that Tracey, but Christ when she does she doesn't hold back, and it's the way she says fuck," Terry laughed. "Sometimes its fooker like it's has all o's and others its fack like with an a or e or something like that. They must teach them that in those Catholic schools or Sunday schools. Makes us English look like nancies."

"It doesn't take much to make you English look like nancies," said Aurimas, "but what exactly is a nancy?"

Terry shook his head, "it's someone who tries to banter someone but actually doesn't know what he's actually bantering about."

"What?" asked Aurimas,

"Never mind," said Terry, "never mind."

Joe got up from the table and spoke to Bumper, "Bumper, c'mon boy. Your mamma has gone and left you so uncle Joe gonna take you out." Bumper was immediately up on his feet, his paws dancing and tapping on the tiled floor and his tail swishing and wagging.

Sensing that Joe wasn't happy with him and what was going on Ray said, "You taking Bumper out for a walk? You mind if I tag along?"

Joe was petting Bumper, ruffling the fur around his neck and scrubbing his head. After a few seconds delay he said, "Whatever." Continuing the sulking act he waited a few seconds more before saying, "you want the harness or just walk him on the lead?"

"Tracey says I need to act more like a blind person so let's do the harness, after all, I do need to keep up on my mobility skills," Ray said sarcastically.

Joe said nothing and went to get Bumper's harness, Bumper following closely behind him ensuring that Joe was going to follow through on the promise of a walk. Joe was thinking, "Perfect! I'll get dad on his own now and can pressure him in to letting me help." The thought cheered him up, but he was careful not to let it show.

Chapter Seventeen

Tenerife, Canary Islands
Saturday 23rd October 2021

Arnie wasn't having any luck with women. First the bimbo last night wanted to watch telly or maybe do the crossword or whatever. She certainly wasn't interested in what she was supposed to be doing, or more importantly interested in what he was doing, as after all, he was the one who was paying.

Now this little thing, who he'd really liked when she had shown up, in fact really, really liked, had taken a nose bleed. And just when he was getting in to his stride.

He had decided to try the agency again as his morning had ended up in limbo. Kevin had watched Jeffrey and followed him back to where they assumed was his apartment block, which was part of the Park Santiago Three, which turned out to be a maze. But even though he had lost sight of Jeffrey they were sure enough where he was and had also checked that he couldn't come back out without passing the entrance Kevin was now still watching. Bobby had then decided that they were maybe best to push the meeting with the Russian back to give them a chance to hopefully find out what Dennis and Jeffrey were up to and also maybe try to work out where the leak was coming from.

So bored, and still unsatisfied from the previous nights liaison Arnie thought he'd pass an hour or so shagging the fluffy tail of a bunny girl, provided it wasn't the same bitch as before. He had emphasised this when he had called, and thankfully the agency hadn't disappointed. When the door rapped and he opened to reveal this little dark haired beauty, he was delighted and so glad with himself for having the foresight to look past the disappointment of last night and give the agency another chance. As a bonus when the little treasure spoke he realised that she was French, which just added to his delight.

The only thing that did cross his mind was how young she looked. Not from a point of view that he minded, no, no not at all. For Arnie young was good. His mind did register though was she the legal age, which if not could cause him a problem if he was caught? But no sooner had the warning flashed when it dimmed away as he thought, "Caught? By who? The door's locked!" The warning totally diminished into insignificance when she had agreed to slip on his little Bunny Girl suit. Heaven!

And it had all been going so well. The telly wasn't turned on, so there was no danger of her watching that, and she really seemed as engrossed as he was. He was even certain that she wasn't faking, which did help to reinstate his ego, and of course his manhood.

But then two strange things happened, almost simultaneously.

The little bunny took a nose bleed. He got up off the bed and she sat up, her hand to her face trying to stem the flow of blood. He was trying to think if he had hit her face accidentally when he heard a noise behind that sounded like the apartment door opening. Thinking it might be the maid here to clean he shouted, "I'm OK, can you come back later?"

But then a man's voice said, "No we fucking can't, you treacherous little bastard."

Recognising the voice Arnie spun around to see Jeffrey coming through the bedroom door at speed straight at him. Arnie moved in an effort to side step Jeffrey but all this done was spin him right in to Ritchie who had now also entered the room right on Jeffrey's shoulder. Because of his move to avoid Jeffrey, Arnie was off balance to resist Ritchie and when he dropped his shoulder and hit Arnie smack in the middle of his chest, blowing out his entire air supply and forcing him across the room until he hit the bedroom wall with a thud. Jeffrey had continued in to the room and now swung his fist back handed in to the side of Arnie's head connecting perfectly on his right temple, whipping his head to the left and causing his equilibrium to shudder. Stepping back from the charge, Ritchie then swung his right fist in to Arnie's left temple. The two hard blows would have floored most heavy weight boxers, and Arnie was no exception to this and began to sink to the floor, first on to his knees and then tipping forward towards Ritchie.

Jeffrey then noticed the little girl sitting up in the bed wearing fluffy rabbit ears and a Bunny Girl bodysuit, her face covered in blood.

"Fuck, look at this Ritchie," he said, "that fucking pervert."

Ritchie turned and looked at the girl in the bed. After taking in the rabbit costume and the blood, he then took in the girl's age. "Fuck Jeff, she looks about fourteen at best." He felt the rage begin to build. "I knew that fucker was in to rabbits, but kids, fuck he's a fucking peedo." He swung back around then, fast and furious, and swung a vicious kick which connected with Arnie's head almost beside where his punch had landed. Arnie's head snapped back with a sickening crack, and then his body slumped and rolled to the floor where he lay totally still.

Jeffrey heard the crack in Arnie's neck and then watched helpless as he had slumped lifeless to the floor. "Jesus Ritchie, I think you've broke his fucking neck." Then remembering the girl, Jeffrey said nothing further and turned his attention to the bed. "You speak English?" he said. She nodded and he could see the fear in her face, despite the blood. "It's OK," said Jeffrey, "no one's going to hurt you, and we're just here to speak with our friend here." He moved to put himself in between the girl and Arnie's body on the floor and waving towards the door he said, "c'mon let's go and get something to clean you up with." She hesitated for a second and then threw her feet off the bed and paddled in to the bathroom. Jeffrey noticed bright coloured clothes on the chair in the corner, which he assumed belonged to the girl, so he collected them up, picked up a pair of high heels that were below the seat and then headed to the bathroom. "Wait here," he commanded to Ritchie.

During the few minutes that Jeffrey was gone, Ritchie calmed himself, dropped to check Arnie for a pulse and failing to find one sat back down on the bed. He wasn't sure if Arnie was dead as he wasn't an expert on finding pulses, but from where he sat he could see that he certainly wasn't in good shape at best. Ritchie had never killed anyone before. Yes, he roughed up plenty, maimed a few, but no kills. He had no empathy at all for Arnie, it had been an accident. He hadn't planned to kill him. At that moment Ritchie's concern was that his bonus might now be a goner also. How could his fortunes come and go in such a short period of time.

It had only just been two hours ago when he had first phoned Jeffrey. They had worked out a strategy to shake off Kevin by losing him in an apartment block that Ritchie knew was a maze and a maze that he had lied to Kevin that actually had two entrances and exits, rather than just one. So Jeffrey had gone in then out and left Kevin behind. Ritchie planned to call Kevin later and take him off the stake out.

Jeffrey and Ritchie had then met and went back to finally give Dennis his

Imodium, much to his relief. He took four tablets at once, probably wouldn't shit again for a week. While waiting on Dennis to feel confident on leaving the bathroom, Jeffrey listened to Ritchie tell him how Arnie was over here to meet with the Russian in an effort to take over Dennis's business connections and supply chains. Ritchie also answered Jeffrey's questions on why Arnie had ran when he had seen himself and Dennis, and then how Bobby Mulhern had been certain they had a leak.

"Like how else could you and Dennis be over here on our tails so quickly?" asked Ritchie, convinced himself that Bobby and Arnie were correct.

Jeffrey said nothing, which was what he was good at. He didn't mention banks or safety deposit boxes. He just couldn't believe their luck. Here they were trying to save their savings and catch whoever had already robbed a part of that, and they run in to another of their fellow Belfast mob also trying to rip them off. Wait until Dennis heard all of this he was going to blow his top and want to kill some people.

But Dennis hadn't the energy to blow his nose at the moment. Yes he was mad, but he was also exhausted. He listened and then he instructed. And his instructions were simple.

"Go get that fucker Arnie and find out every name that's involved in this." And then he went to bed.

The good thing for Ritchie, well at least he hoped it would be, was that he knew who was involved. Yes it would have been better to have had Arnie tell Jeffrey, but it didn't look like Arnie would be doing much more telling, or shagging little girls dressed up as rabbits. He thought of something that made him smile, "Pornography to poor old Arnie was probably watching the film about rabbits, Watership down?"

When Jeffrey came back in to the room the smile was still on Ritchie's face. Jeffrey asked, "what the fuck are you smiling about?"

Ritchie nodded towards Arnie, "just thinking of something about that prick."

"Dead prick you mean," replied Jeffrey, bending down himself to check Arnie's pulse. He checked his neck, his wrist and then put his ear against Arnie's mouth. After a few minutes he rose and said, "you've some right foot on you Ritchie," he nodded to Arnie, "if his head had of been a rugby ball you would have kicked it out of the park."

"Is he dead?" Ritchie asked.

"Let's just say," answered Jeffrey, "we won't need to reserve a sun bed at the pool today for our Arnie. Or tomorrow either for that matter."

Ritchie almost said he was sorry, but then decided to say nothing.

Jeffrey said, "Here, help me lift him up on to the bed." Ritchie obliged and they both took Arnie by the feet and shoulders and lifted him over and on to the bed.

"Is the girl gone?" asked Ritchie.

"Yeah," said Jeffrey and then paused, "I asked her age and she showed me ID that said she was eighteen, but I think she was younger than that. She certainly looked it anyway." Then after another pause he added, "dirty bastard, my daughter's only fourteen."

Ritchie nodded. If he had read Jeffrey's words correctly, he was maybe still on for the bonus as it sounded as if he was saying that Arnie deserved what he'd got.

"Help me wrap him in these sheets," asked Jeffrey, "I think we're going to have to get rid of him tonight out at sea in our boat.

"Boat?" asked Ritchie.

"We have a boat in Los Cristianos's marina,"

Ritchie nodded again, then said, "Wait." He left the room and headed for the bathroom. Finding what he hoped was there on the bathroom floor, he picked it up and went back to the bedroom. Leaning over Arnie's body he laid out the bunny suit face down so that the fluffy tail sat up above Arnie's crotch and then finished it off by placing the fluffy rabbit ears over Arnie's head. "There," he said, "maybe you might meet a nice rabbit where you're going?"

"Did you not hear me," asked Jeffrey, "we're going to dump him in the ocean! Rabbits don't live there."

"I meant rabbit heaven," Ritchie explained.

Jeffrey shook his head, "Perverts don't go to heaven, or rabbit heaven for that matter." Now Jeffrey smiled, "now fuck up and give me a hand to wrap him up. And then we need to work out how the fuck we're going to get him out of here and to the boat."

"Why not just leave him here?"

Jeffrey laughed. "Yeah, that might seem like the easiest thing to do, but trust me." Turning to look at Ritchie he then asked, "Do you know what they call me? My nickname?"

Ritchie did, but hesitated for a second as he wasn't sure if he should say he did, then deciding just to be frank he answered, "The Digger."

"And do you know why?"

In for a penny, in for a pound, Ritchie answered, "You dig graves?"

"Well, not literally, well maybe sometimes," said Jeffrey with a smirk, "I get rid of people, mainly dead ones mind you."

"So you're an expert?"

"Definitely, and trust me you don't want to leave bodies lying around as it causes all sorts of problems. Now, not that getting rid of them doesn't have its own set of problems, but at least these can be under your own control. But once a dead body pops up, then all sorts of shit starts to hit the fan." Jeffrey was enjoying giving his lesson so he continued. "Take our friend here, the rabbit," nodding at Arnie's body, which was now fully wrapped in the bed sheets. "Let's say we leave him here? I can guarantee you that within two hours this place will be crawling with police and forensics and all that shit. Then all sorts of questions will be asked, like who was he with? You for one. Who did he know? Check his phone for another. Before you know it doors over here and back in Belfast are being knocked, maybe kicked. Then someone panics and talks and then the next time we all see each other is in the queue for lunch at her Majesties pleasure." He pointed at Arnie now, "but makes him disappear, clear out his stuff and the people asking questions are Bobby Mulhern for example, and he's asking, I wonder where Arnie is? But nobody knows, and if we do it right, nobody ever will know. That way, we get done here over the next few days and then head on home, saying, Arnie who?"

Ritchie was nodding, "Sometimes when you learn something it seems so simple you wonder why you didn't think like that all the time."

Proud of himself, Jeffrey nodded to.

"And do you know what else is so simple, now that I'm looking at it that is," said Ritchie pointing at Arnie wrapped in the bed sheets. "We passed one of those maid trolleys downstairs full of dirty bed sheets. We get our hands on one of those and we can put him in it to get him down to the basement, and once there it's only a matter of transferring him in to a car, or van or something, whatever."

"I like your thinking," said Jeffrey, "I might just get you put on the payroll as my apprentice. We'll have to wait and do all this at night though, daylight is a no, no." Then fully grinning at Ritchie, "and guess what apprentice? That means that you're going to have to stay here until then and baby-sit Bugs Bunny here, and make sure that the maid doesn't come in to clean, or change the bed sheets."

Not ecstatic about spending the day with a corpse, but still hoping his bonus was still on the table, Ritchie said, "No, Christ she'd get some shock if she went to change those sheets, although I bet I know what she would say."

"What," asked Jeffrey?

"What have we got ear, ear?"

"Ah that's fucking shit," said Jeffrey, shaking his head, "it's just not bunny at all!"

Chapter Eighteen

Tenerife, Canary Islands
Saturday 23rd October 2021

Crying really stung. Tracey didn't know if it was because of her Trachoma that had destroyed her eyes when she was a baby, or if tears just stung everyone. Or that they only stung her as she was a bad person and deserved it.

Tracey's temperament was like an elevator, it came down at the same speed that it went up and by the time she had reached her bedroom her rage had subsided and had came back down as regret. Who was she, Miss prim and proper to lecture anybody? If her Irish mother hadn't risked everything and broken rules and laws, where would she be today. Probably would have never seen it past the age of three as most of her fellow country boys and girls hadn't during their so called civil war. She knew that it didn't bear thinking about.

But on the other hand, how could she condone such reckless behaviour to consider robbing a bank. Like, this was just crazy. And what she had said about Jess was perfectly true. If Tracey partook in any such behaviour then their relationship would be over. But was that selfish or sensible?

On the other hand. She was running out of hands! How could she turn her back on Ray, his mother or his dad? If the shoe was on the other foot, would Ray risk all to help her? She had no doubt of the answer.

She loved Jess and couldn't wait until they got married and could spend the rest of their lives together. But stupid as it sounded, being here in Tenerife, living in this house and sharing it with Ray and Joe and Terry and Aurimas, not forgetting her darling Bumper, gigging and living like they did was one of the best times of her life. As it had been when they had done the same thing back in 2019. She felt like an important part of a family, the mother almost in a strange way as she was the only woman. And she felt happy, content and importantly for a child born in conflict, secure. How, and why would you risk all of that just to rob a bank?

Or was this her being selfish yet again. Hadn't she just admitted to herself, that no matter what the risk and the potential loss, Ray wouldn't hesitate.

Like a song on repeat, these thoughts, played over in a constant shuffle in her mind. Maybe slight variances on the wording, but the point or question was basically the same. To try to break the cycle she plugged her earphones in to her phone and shuffled her music in an effort to close out her thought with other words and melody. This didn't help, in fact it made it worse.

The songs themselves held meanings similar to her questions, or words that she translated to be about her questions. The first song was, "Train in Vain" by the Clash no less.

"Will you stand by me? No not at all!"

The second, "Go Your Own Way" by Fleetwood Mac, spoke for itself. Then Yellow by Coldplay hit her heart strings as it was a song that Jess had sang to her,

"Look at the stars,

Look how they shine for you,

In everything you do,

And they are all yellow."

Tracey who had been blind from birth didn't know what a star looked like or the colour yellow. Jess had struggled to answer, she was a Solicitor and dealt with facts, but Ray had captured her imagination when he had told her.

"Trace, you know the science of what a star is, but it's the light, the brightness that is the key, and that's yellow. If I was a colour, I'd want to be yellow because it is bright and bold and brightness lights the way and takes away the darkness, and that's why it's beautiful, and that's why you're beautiful. You are a guiding light, you are the yellow."

She had cried then, and the tears stung then also. She loved the sound of yellow and if it was something that took away the darkness then it must be good, better than good. It was beautiful.

She enjoyed the song and its meaning to her started to make her feel better, so much that she was almost about to repeat it when it ended but then "From Eden" started by Hozier, which was one of her favourite songs and she let it play. It was a song that Ray sang accompanied by just his guitar, and he played it almost better than the original. When it came to the chorus, it was Ray's voice that she heard.

"Honey you're familiar like my mirror years ago,

Idealism sits in prison, chivalry fell on his sword, innocence died screaming,

Honey ask me I should know,

I slithered here from Eden just to sit outside your door."

Again, as was the magic of music and its words, she saw meaning in the words that related to her mood and mindset of that moment, which was maybe sometimes close but maybe most times far away from the writer's sentiment. Like "Yellow" she loved the melody and rhythm of the song and she let it wash over her. And again when it ended she considered playing it once more. But before she had unlocked her phone and found the repeat button, "Bank Robber" by the Clash had started to play its opening chorus, "Ahh, ahh, ah ah ah ah, ahh, ahh, ah ah ah ah."

She turned off her phone.

With the music silenced now she lay and listened to the sounds of the house. It was quiet. She couldn't hear talking or movement or other sounds like a radio playing or a television, or the two boys shouting as they played their X Box. Instead she heard the clicking sounds a house makes as some parts of it heated in the sun and other parts cooled down in the shade. She heard the wind rustling through the trees and in the distance heard the sea and the noise of children playing. A car came closer to the house and got louder and then passed and took the sound with it until she couldn't hear it any more. A dog barked, a playful bark then stopped. She thought of Bumper and remembered that she needed to take him out for a walk. She dropped her hand down to the side of the bed and gently tapped the frame but the usual feeling of a wet nose pushing in to her palm didn't come. She called his name, "Bumper, Bumper." No response.

This told her that someone else had taken Bumper out for his walk, and also explained why the house was quiet. She got up and went downstairs.

She sensed without the need to ask or call someone's name that there was no one in the kitchen and dining area. She could also tell that the patio doors were closed. She felt her way to the sink, found the kettle and checked it for water and satisfied that it had enough she flicked it on to boil. She then felt along two wall cupboards to find the mugs and then felt the handles to find her own mug, which had a football on it. Joe had bought it for her, but had told her it had been a Liverpool mug as she was a mad Liverpool fan just like her dad, but she later found out that it was actually a Manchester United mug. Joe didn't know that she knew and so she allowed his joke on her to live on for a while yet. Setting the mug on the counter she remembered the fresh cookies that her and Joe had bought when shopping and she bent down to search for them in the lower cupboards under the counter. Finding them she stood up and hit her head on the underside of the open cupboard door that she had forgot to close after getting her mug. As she hit upwards the door had no where to go and so resisted and stayed put, her head then and her neck took the full knock and she was immediately dazed. Still bent down she raised her right hand to inspect her head, and raised her left hand, which was still holding the cookies, even higher and slammed the cupboard door shut. She stayed like that for some moments as the pain in her head throbbed, then as the worst subsided she straightened up, cursing herself for her stupidity. Cupboard doors were a real hazard for blind people; in fact Tracey had removed the cupboard doors in her own kitchen at home. To a sighted person this was an eyesore, to a blind person it was a health and safety must do. Bumping a door face on wasn't bad as all you did was push it closed or open, depending on whichever way you hit it, but bumping a door straight on or from below, as Tracey had done, then it stayed put and rigid and hard, and then it was you that took the hurt. Lapses in concentration don't help much either when you can't see.

She sat down at the table with her coffee and her cookie and felt her head again. It was grazed and already a bump was starting to raise itself under her dark hair. It was tender to touch so she left it alone and tried to use the sweet coffee and even sweeter cookie to forget about it. The room was cool, too cool and it told her that Terry had been at the air conditioning. He always set it like a fridge, but she didn't like it too cold, in fact she didn't mind it warm or even hot. The controls were on the wall beside the patio door, it had taken her over a week to find them and since then it was a constant battle between Terry and herself to control the temperature. She got up, walked over to the patio doors and while there she opened them to let in the warm air from outside before moving to the air con controls on the wall and shutting it off. It didn't take long for the strength of the midday heat to invade the room and she was glad of the warmth. As she sat back down a voice startled her.

"You Irish sure can swear." Terry said.

"Jesus," Tracey said, "where did you come from, you almost scared the shit out of me."

"Sorry," offered Terry, "I was listening to my book out here and heard the doors opening." He stepped inside, "you've knocked off my air con again."

"Too cold," said Tracey.

"Yes, that's the point, warm outside, cool inside."

"Yes, but there's cold and there's cold, I bet when we open the fridge there's steam comes out as it's warmer in there than out here when you set that bloody thing."

Terry raised his arms in submission, "OK, I'll leave it alone." Then in a lower voice he said, "For now." Only giving in because he was going back outside to sit anyway.

"What's your book?" Tracey asked, always interested and looking for a book recommendation.

"The new Harry Bosch, ah I think it's called the dark hour."

"Any good?"

"I've got it on audible but it's one of those multiple narrator jobs and I don't like that. Makes it sound more like a play than a book. I just want a good book read by a good narrator, you know just read the bloomin' thing, don't act it out. I think I'm going to listen to it on the Kindle." The Kindle had text to speech as a screenreader. "It's a Michael Connelly book so you know it's going to be good, but I just want to listen to it as a book."

Tracey knew exactly what Terry meant and she agreed. They were both long time book readers, and being blind, meant long time book listeners. It wasn't that long ago that audiobooks came in big boxes with lots of cassettes, and then CD's. Now with smart phones and Ipods and the like it was all digital. Tracey had over six hundred books in her audible library, all stored on her tiny phone, whereas not that many years ago you would have needed five or more book shelves to hold them in and a spare room to house them all in. It was a subject that Terry and herself often discussed and they both shared the opinion that as audiobooks were now listened to by a much wider audience than the visual impaired, that their production was becoming more trendy and populist rather than just being a book reading provider.

"Bring back Dick Hill," Tracey said. Dick Hill had been the original narrator of the Harry Bosch series on audiobooks, but that had long since changed, which was another point of annoyance and debate between Terry and Tracey. It was like watching Only Fools and Horses with a different actor playing Del Boy, it just didn't work.

"Now you're talking," agreed Terry, "even Len Cariou would do." Cariou had narrated many of the Harry Bosch books also. Terry had just got accustomed to Len's voice following on from Dick Hill and then it changed again. The narrator now was the actor who acted Bosch in the now successful TV series, and Terry didn't like that, or just didn't like the actor's voice. It might have been OK for TV but on audio only his voice sounded like he was smiling all the time and Bosch was supposed to be a hard boiled tough Los Angeles detective, who Terry was certain didn't do a lot of smiling.

"My Kindle is on charge there at the end of the counter, if you want it. I did pre order the new Bosch book so it should be there now if it's released."

"You don't mind," asked Terry, "are you not wanting to listen to it yourself?"

"It's OK," said Tracey, "I finished Reacher last night."

"Well?" asked Terry.

"Predictable," answered Tracey, "the same old same old. I almost wish he'd join the army again. Maybe start a war with Russia or something."

"Yeah," agreed Terry, "there can't be many more unknown towns for him to saunter in to." Then he thought to himself, it is America so there probably is.

Terry disconnected the Kindle from the charger and unplugged the adapter from the wall.

"I'll leave your charger here."

He then headed back along the wall to the patio door, "you not coming out to sit in the sun?" He was thinking if she comes outside then I can slip the air con on again.

"Where's Ray?" she asked.

"He took Bumper a walk with Joe." She didn't make any comment so before Terry stepped back outside he added, "You don't have to condone him, but you don't need to condemn him." He took one step through the door then turned back and said, "I owe him, you know that, I owe him big time." Not giving Tracey the chance to comment he stepped fully outside and slid the patio door closed.

Tracey didn't say anything for Terry to miss; she just thought to herself, "yes, we all do."

Terry carefully made his way back to his sun bed. He wasn't worried about falling in to the pool as the cover on it was closed, it was just his habit to be careful. Reaching the bed he sat down and felt the strong sun begin to burn and it felt great. He placed the Kindle on the end of the bed and felt for his side table and for his sun cream. Once he was generously coated in sun protector, he wiped his hands with a handy wipe then put his baseball cap back on to protect his head. He removed his ear buds from his phone and transferred them to the Kindle but before he turned it on he sat reflecting on the words he had just said to Tracey.

He did owe Ray. Owed him for quite a lot. The first was a financial debt that he had almost paid off and would have he hoped by the end of their season in Tenerife. Some years ago he'd got in to some trouble and ran up some fairly substantial gambling debts. Ray lent him the money to sort them out. As a condition of the loan Ray insisted to teach Terry how to gamble and enjoy it. And he had. He had shown him how to have fun as gambling was fun as long as you only lost what you could afford or had budgeted to lose. He showed him that it wasn't the amount that was important, it was the thrill of winning or losing and as in most cases, adding a further element to enjoying something like sport. It didn't matter if the stake was ten pence or ten pounds; the thrill was exactly the same. Now Terry still gambled, but he did it in a controlled way that he not only enjoyed but was proud of. He knew many secret gamblers who keep it a secret because they are not only ashamed of it, but are most likely losing money they can't afford to lose. Terry knew that if Ray had insisted that he gave up gambling after getting in to such debts, which was in fact the most natural thing to do. He would have just gone under ground and became a secret gambler himself. But now that he was educated and under control he had his monthly gambling budget and his limits and this way it removed the worry and increased the enjoyment.

Some time later Terry learned what Ray had done and it had made him cry.

Not having the means himself to help out his friend Ray had gone to his mother and pretended that it was him who had ran up the debts. His mother, who was anti gambling, and had heard many stories from her husband about his father and his life of gambling, womanising and constant debts, And so Ray had come under severe criticism and had been immediately sent to a gambling councilling course as a preliminary requisition before any money could be borrowed. Ray had agreed and this is where he had learned what he had taught Terry. Ray had also taken out a loan so that he could lend Terry the money and paid it off month by month until such times as his mother was satisfied that he had been cured as a gambler and had given it up for good. Six months later she remortgaged her house, which had been left to her by her parents, and gave her son the money he needed. But Ray had rules of his own. He refused to accept the money as a gift and only took it on the agreement that he would be responsible for paying it back. All agreed, he accepted the funds, paid of his loan and from that time had paid for the mortgage each month from the money paid back to him from Terry. The whole deal cost Ray as he wasn't charging interest to Terry, but he had paid interest on his loan, and he was paying interest on the remortgage. Ray wasn't concerned about this and that was just that, the cost of helping out a good friend. But it had all come out a couple of years ago as Terry and Joe had gotten to know each other better and one night Terry had told Joe what his father had done for him. Innocently Joe then told Terry that his dad had also had gambling problems but his gran Julie had helped him out. Knowing that Ray didn't, and had never really gambled, apart from the Grand National and stuff like that, Terry confronted Ray and so Ray had no choice but to tell him the truth on how and what he had done to help him.

The second thing that Terry had done after breaking down in tears, was to go to see Ray's mother Julie and put the record straight. His mother then chastised him for a second time about the same thing, although this time it wasn't gambling that she was criticising him for, but for not coming to her with the truth. "I would have helped out Terry as well you know."

"I know you would have mother," he had said, "but firstly you would have sent him to counselling, and I knew that that wouldn't have worked for Terry. I needed him to feel beholding to me so that he would listen to me, which he did and it worked. And secondly, I couldn't tell you something a mate had told me in confidence."

She still gave off, but that's what mother's do, but deep down she admired what he had done, and how he had done it.

As Terry sat in the sunshine in this beautiful villa in Tenerife, here to do what he loved to do best playing the drums, and here with the group of people that were not only his friends but his family, he felt good and happy and content with his life. He did indeed owe Ray for quite a lot.

He heard the patio doors slide open and then the flip of flip flops coming towards him.

"I assume you're on your usual spot?" Tracey asked.

"As always," answered Terry.

She came closer until she had reached the sun bed on the other side of his side table.

"Here," she said, "I brought you out a cold beer."

He heard her set the bottle on his table

"Thanks," he said, reaching forward, first to find the table and then feeling carefully for the bottle. After taking a swig and loving it he said.

"Did you turn my air con back on before you came out here?"

"Fuck off," Tracey answered.

"Did I ever tell you," said Terry chuckling, "there's nobody says fuck quite like you Irish."

Chapter Nineteen

Tenerife, Canary Islands
Saturday 23rd October 2021

He'd just literally turned the phone on when it rang. A ring tone like a fog horn scared the shit out of him and he almost dropped the bloody thing on to the concrete balcony floor.

"Fuck!" snapped Charlie, then grabbed the phone before it skated off his lap. He blew out his breath. It didn't help much to relieve any pressure as he was wound up tighter than his fucking SIM card had been stuck in to his old phone. He had almost needed to disintegrate the phone to get it out, and then he was worried that the card itself would be destroyed. Obviously it was working though as the new phone he had bought was now ringing in his hand. Well squawking actually with a mind blowing ring tone. He answered, but as he did it struck him that it might be Stefan calling him back and that made him nervous, so he listened a bit first.

"Hello?" said Ray as a question.

Charlie didn't recognise the voice at first, "Who's that?"

"Ray Ruddock." Ray almost said Mr Bassett, then changed his mind to say Charlie, but then not sure he just said nothing more than his name.

"Oh, Jazz Junior," said Charlie, very relieved it wasn't the mad Stefan back to call him names.

"My name's Ray," said Ray sternly. He had more confidence with this guy over the phone than he'd had face to face the night before. "Can you talk?"

Ray and Joe were sitting on a park bench enjoying the sun. Bumper was at their feet watching some children play with a ball on the other side of the grass way. Joe had assured his dad that there was nobody around and so it was safe to talk. Joe launched Bumper's ball once more in a high lob and even though he was sure that Bumper hadn't been watching him, he set off in a split second his eye trained on the flight path of the ball until he circled and overtook it as it came back down to earth where Bumper caught it in his mouth without dropping his stride and immediately continued his loop back to Joe and dropped the now wet ball at his feet.

Joe congratulated him by rubbing his ears and head, which Bumper loved almost as much as chasing balls.

"You hear from Jazz yet?" asked Charlie.

"Nothing."

"You better not be lying to me junior."

"Look," said Ray, he had told himself that he needed to be assertive with this man. "We're going to do the job tomorrow, but here's the deal. Ten grand up front like you said, another forty grand when done, and we do it on our own, no Monty."

Charlie listened. He was suspicious, did this prick just want the ten grand and then do a runner like his dad?

"You trying to fuck me over," he said, not being able to ignore his suspicions.

Ray wasn't sure were Charlie was coming from. He had only asked for exactly what Charlie had offered. Terry had told him to push for more, but Ray said no. If they could do it and get what they could get and get back to gigging, then they'd all be happy.

"Because we don't want Monty?"

"Monty?" Charlie thought. You'd be lucky if Monty could steal a Cornetto at the moment. He'd left him in bed sleeping only because Charlie couldn't get him to wake up. Charlie was worried that he maybe had concussion and maybe needed a doctor. But all that would have to wait.

"I'm only asking for what you offered," continued Ray, "look, if you don't want us to do this job then that's fine by me. You came to me remember."

Charlie also had a problem because he didn't actually have the ten grand. He almost did, just over nine in fact, but there was no way he was giving this prick all he had. It was typical Charlie, over promising and under delivering.

"Five up front," Charlie said.

"You said ten."

"I'm only giving you five; I'm not giving you ten for you just to fuck off."

"No one's going to fuck off, if I was going to do that I just wouldn't be phoning you in the first place. Maybe I just should have gone to the police. All that crap about the sins of the father and it was now my responsibility is just complete and utter bullshit."

"Police?" said Charlie alarmed, "If Jazz heard you threaten to grass to the law he'd be doing to you what he did to poor Monty."

"I'm not going to the police, I was just saying. Look Charlie, you came to me so are we doing this or not?"

Charlie really had no choice. He paused thinking how to get round the ten grand, remembering that he had offered it and silently scolding himself for talking himself in to trouble once more. Finally he said, feeling weak for admitting it, "I've only got five."

Wanting to get this over and get on with it Ray said, "Fine five it is, and then forty-five after, but still no Monty."

"OK, but you better not shit on me like your fucking dad," then remembering something he'd lied about the previous night, "remember we're watching your mother junior."

"You don't need the threats, we're doing what you wanted," said Ray tiring from dealing with this man. "We need to meet to get the money; I need some of it for the job."

"I can meet you at Hard Rock like we said," suggested Charlie.

"No, I'm not doing this there. You know I gig there."

"How about your villa?"

The question rocked Ray. How did he know they were in a villa? Had he told him? He couldn't remember, and then he heard a low snigger over the phone.

"Got you there junior," Charlie said, gloating clear in his voice. "Yeah, your villa," he repeated, "me and Monty followed your little bimbo and that drummer of yours last night. They got a taxi back to your villa."

Ray was worried now. He felt exposed or something and he didn't want this man around the villa. Charlie continued.

"What's wrong with that drummer of yours? Your little lady, you shagging her junior? Yeah she had to lead him by the hand like he was fucking blind or something." Charlie laughed finding something funny, Ray wasn't sure which part he found funny. And why did everybody assume he and Tracey was an item? He was about to answer Charlie and tell him that maybe Terry had been drunk, but then he sensed some commotion from the other end of the phone and paused.

Charlie heard shouting close to his apartment and as he was too small to see over the balcony when sitting down he stood up to see what was going on. Seeing Jeffrey the digger only several feet away from his first floor balcony Charlie almost had a fit. His entire body jumped back pushing his chair against the wall. It bounced back towards him, but at an angle and so as he started to throw himself back down in to the seat in an effort to hide he hit the chair's arm which knocked the phone out of his hand.

"Holy fuck," he spat.

Bumping the chair's arm he then started to correct his movement to try and direct his arse towards the seat but some inner brain instinct shot out his arm to try and snatch the phone. His mind then froze as he panicked that the Digger maybe heard him curse. The combination of events had the following effect.

To anyone who had witnessed this, and thankfully for Charlie there was no one, he would have looked like a drunken Pigmy break dancing on ice.

The phone's first trajectory would have seen it land safely on the table beside Charlie's chair, but his lunge to snatch it had flicked it on a flight path that sent it skidding off the edge of the table, and hitting the wall where it sustained it's first crack on the new screen, then ping from the wall to the balcony floor where a chunk of glass split from the corner of the screen and disappeared below the balcony and out on to the street below.

Charlie's arse too had a similar fate to the phone as it skidded of the edge of the chair and then having to give up to the forces of gravity pulled Charlie down crashing to the floor with a thud and then another curse, louder than the first.

"FUCK SAKE!"

But the space where Charlie had fallen wasn't big enough to accommodate his frame, small as it was, and so seconds after his arse had hit the floor his feet hit the balcony with nowhere to go and so the force then pushed him backwards against the chair which hit the wall and also stopped. Charlie then slid to the floor in a heap, his legs and body almost closed up as tight as his wallet, and his back and head scraping the edge of the plastic chair as he went. He cursed for the third time although it was more muffled now as he lay piled on the floor.

"Mary mother of fucking Jesus!"

He heard his phone squeak with a tiny sound he couldn't make out. He ignored it. As he tried to focus his mind. He quickly decided that the Digger was his first priority so as best as he could he pushed himself up to peep over his balcony. Jeffrey was now three steps on from where Charlie had first seen him, which put him just past his balcony. To Charlie's relief Jeffrey's attention was focused forward and unaware of Charlie. He then noticed what he assumed was the reason for the shouts, which had not only gotten Charlie's attention, but thankfully Jeffrey's as well, which caused him not to notice Charlie. A cyclist had hit a pedestrian and they were both in the process of getting up and assessing their injuries. "Fucking bikes," mumbled Charlie as he had often wandered on to the cycle path only to have the fuckers ring their bell when they were right up his arse, or whizzed past him with a millimetre to spare, both causing him to almost shit his kaki shorts.

Ducking back down behind his balcony, which he silently thanked the lord above was one of those which you couldn't see through, he paddled on his hands and knees to find his phone.

Ray heard distant shouting, then muffled scrapes and bangs.

"Charlie?" he said.

Several seconds later he heard Charlie say, "Holy fuck," which was then followed by further banging and scraping noises. Then a distorted crack followed by electronic static before a second crack. The static noise then stopped and was followed by a muffled and echoed "fuck sake," again from Charlie.

Ray wasn't sure what to say as he had no idea what was going on. He just held the phone to his ear and waited. He heard Charlie say something else but he couldn't make out this time what it was, then several seconds later Charlie came back on the phone.

"You still there junior?" he said, his voice seeming flustered.

"What's going on?" Ray asked.

"The fucking digger was almost on my balcony," Charlie rambled out but then as he realised what he had said thought, "Christ I can't let junior know that there are some mad Irish men over here trying to find out who's ripping them off." As Charlie had no doubt what Jeffrey was doing here in Tenerife. He cursed that fucker Jazz for fucking him over as they should have had both bank jobs done on Thursday and Friday as planned and then the digger and his boss Dennis, who yes was a fucking menace, would have been too late to react. Now seeing they were here already was a big fucking worry.

"A digger?" Ray asked amazed, thinking that Charlie had meant an actual digger. "A digger hit your balcony?"

Thinking fast and remembering the cyclist and pedestrian he lied, "fuck yeah, fucking thing swerved to miss a cyclist and almost came straight towards my balcony." Then to dress it up he continued, "I had to hit the deck in a hurry there. fucking dropped my phone and think I've cracked the screen." He was about to add that he had only just bought the fucking thing after smashing his other one against the apartment wall just a while ago, but decided to keep that to himself just in case junior thought he was some sort of lunatic.

"Jesus," offered Ray, picturing the scene in his mind, "your phone sounds funny; your voice is all tinny like a robot."

Charlie thought to himself, "I just paid three hundred euros for the bastard thing twenty minutes ago!"

Keen to get back to the reason for the call Ray said, "We need to get sorted Charlie so Where can we meet?"

Nervous now after seeing Jeffrey Charlie didn't really want to go out anywhere, especially as he couldn't wake that fucker Monty up. But he also wasn't sure about bringing junior here. He was thinking about what they had to discuss yet and what they needed to do when he thought about the third shotgun.

"I'll need to give you the shotgun," he said, "so we need to go somewhere for that."

"I don't need it," Ray answered quickly.

"You don't need it?" questioned Charlie puzzled thinking "how the fuck are you going to rob a bank without it!"

"I'm covered," offered Ray as an explanation, which Charlie still didn't fully understand.

"Covered?"

Assured that nobody was within hearing distance Ray added, "Yeah covered, we have guns. Ones of our own."

Charlie was stunned. He had maybe under estimated Jazz junior; he maybe needed to be a bit more careful here. Jazz senior had already screwed him, well for now he was going to sort that fucker out later.

Ray too was concerned. Having told the lie he was now hoping that Charlie wouldn't ask him what sort they were as he had no idea. And he thought that the truth that Joe hadn't bought them from the toy shop yet wouldn't inspire much confidence either.

Fortunately Charlie went passed it, and from his tone Ray surmised that he had concerns of his own.

"OK Junior," he said, "I've maybe under estimated you." Then his voice got darker, even with the tinny tone, "but I'm telling you now, you try to fuck with me like your dad has and you're a dead man." Then for good measure he added, "and that little cutie plays in your band, the one you're shagging, me and Monty will have some fun with her as well."

Ray closed his eyes. This guy was just a low life. What was he getting involved with and what was he getting his friends, he corrected himself, family in to. He heard Tracey's words again and he felt the pain of guilt. He blew out trying to relieve his tension and said. "No need for any more threats Charlie or this ends here and now." He was also considering a threat of his own to Charlie if he ever went near Tracey but before he got there Charlie spoke again.

"OK junior. OK, but you can't blame me considering what Jazz; your dad did on me?"

He couldn't he supposed in a way.

"I'm not going to do that Charlie so let's get this sorted and get on with it or we're just going to talk all day."

Charlie made his mind up then said, "you know the Compestella Beach?"

Ray had played gigs there. "Yes," he answered.

"I'm on the first floor at the front facing that shop Zara." He paused, but Ray stayed silent, so assuming Ray knew where he was talking about Charlie continued, "phone me back when you're there and I'll tell you where to come to meet me." Then checking he asked, "you only need the money right?"

Ray answered, "I need the money yes, but Charlie you haven't told me which bank yet and I want to know who your insider is."

"Oh yeah," said Charlie feeling stupid, and then asked before hanging up, "how long will you be?"

"Ten minutes," Ray answered.

"Give me twenty," said Charlie then killed the call. Still on his hands and knees he crawled back inside the apartment making double sure that Jeff the digger had no sight of him and deciding as he went that if that big shite Monty didn't wake up he was going to get a large pot of water in the bake, and he would drown the big shite if he had too.

Ray exhaled a deep sigh and questioned his own sanity.

"What's up?" asked Joe.

Not sure how much to say or how much Joe had heard Ray just shook his head in an effort to clear his mind. In one way he couldn't understand the internal motives driving him to actually go through with this and deal with a waste of space like Charlie. But in another way he knew these drivers well. But maybe knowing and understanding were two totally different things.

Joe was also thinking hard. While his dad had been on the phone and he had been playing with Bumper he'd had an idea that he hoped could get him on board and he was now pondering how and when to pitch it to his dad. Knowing also that Colin had refused point blank to get involved and that this was potentially a deal breaker for his dad's plans, he was hoping that his dad would maybe discuss this with him, or even tell him what his thoughts about it were. The call from Colin had came just before his dad had phoned the Gnome and so his dad hadn't had a chance to make any comment. But Joe had given it some thought and depending on where the bank was, without a driver Joe didn't see how his dad could now do without him, so as he still hadn't answered Joe decided he needed to take the lead.

"I've been thinking," he said, "and I have an idea. It sort of goes along with your thing." He chuckled.

Ray didn't speak but thought, "my thing?"

Joe went on and explained, "you know you acting you can see and me guiding you? Well what if I took Bumper and done the opposite? Pretended I'm blind? I could pose as a customer in the bank and that way I could tell you what to do over the blue tooth," he raced on to ensure he got it all out before his dad butted in, "nobody is going to suspect a poor blind boy who is just a customer there to exchange some sterling. I still have money Gran gave me, two hundred I could exchange for euros." Then he added his final and best part he thought, of his pitch, "and since Colin won't drive I could also guide you there."

Ray listened and couldn't help thinking that he agreed with Joe in that it was a good idea, but flooding every thread of thought were Tracy's words and in particular her criticism of him as a father. Her words about Liz his ex wife had stung deep.

But he had a plan but without a driver he didn't know if it would work. Also, he felt like a bit of a hypocrite. Here he was about to use Joe to direct him round to meet Charlie, doing his thing, as Joe had put it and pretending he could see. Then he was going to get Joe to buy the toy guns and fancy dress outfits, so he presumed that in any court of law he would already be considered an accomplish. He heard himself say, "but what about Tracey and your mother?"

But Joe snookered him here, "are you going to tell mum all about it when she arrives tomorrow?"

Jesus Christ of course he wasn't, but he just said, "no."

They both then sat in silence for some time until finally Ray said. "Joe son, I think I must be the worst father in the world."

Joe was delighted as he knew these words meant he was in.

"No dad," he said, "not the world, just Tenerife!" Then he called Bumper.

Bumper had given up on the ball and was having a lazy sniff around the grass. There were a few other dogs about, but mainly scruffy mongrels who he ignored, a couple of Poodles with fancy hair cuts that made them look like toys, and a lady Schnauzer who was meandering lazily also, but making her way over to him and trying to be discreet about it. He had a few sniffs and stood his ground and waited for her to arrive.

"Hi," she said.

Bumper nodded playing it cool, "hey," he said.

"You here on holiday?" she asked circling him.

"Holiday?" he said, "no, no, I'm a working dog. No holidays for us chaps."

She sniffed his arse, "Oh yeah," sniff, sniff, "what sort of work do you do?"

He turned his head to find that he was now face to face with her backside, so he had a quick sniff. "I'm a Guide Dog for the Blind," he said proudly.

"Sounds exciting," she said sniffing his balls now.

"Sure is," he said, thinking "you watch you don't handle anything there baby that you maybe can't afford."

"Bumper, Bumper," Joe shouted.

Bumper looked over and saw Joe and Ray were both on their feet. It was time to go.

"Gotta go baby," he said, "maybe another time." He sprinted towards Joe.

"Maybe," she said, "maybe big boy," and watched him go.

Chapter Twenty

Tenerife, Canary Islands
Saturday 23rd October 2021

The phone network was shit hot. Calls, mostly unanswered, were bouncing off mobile towers and back, and then back again with a message alerting a missed call and then back again to signal a voicemail message. It was unending and relentless and to some it was very frustrating.

Dennis was totally fucked off. He was still sick, in need of more medication or maybe even a doctor and that useless bastard Jeffrey wasn't answering or returning his calls.

Kevin had called both Arnie and Ritchie to find out what they wanted him to do next. He had then text, but no one had answered or got back to him. Aware and nervous of how pissed off these guys could get if you took the wrong move or made the wrong decision he decided the safest thing to do was stay put at his last point of instruction.

Bobby had put five calls in to Arnie and was now about to flip his lid, which in fairness Bobby didn't do too often. But he had told that prick Arnie before he had gone to Tenerife to send him the contact details of the lads he was taking with him. But had he? Had he fuck! Here he now was, on a Saturday afternoon when most respectable people were either fishing, playing golf, down at the Oval or Windsor Park, or in the pub following the day's horse racing. And as all were otherwise engaged they weren't answering their bloody phones either and so he'd had zero luck trying to find out who the fuck Ritchie and Kevin were. That Arnie boy better not be playing around with under age bunny girls and ignoring his calls or if Bobby found out he would ensure that Arnie himself was buried so far down a rabbit hole that the rabbits them selves would be setting up home in his arsehole.

The Russian had turned up to meet Arnie and had been waiting there now for more than thirty minutes. He had put a call in to Arnie just over ten minutes ago and as yet had heard nothing. He was beginning to wonder if he had not only wrote down the wrong location for the meeting, but if he had maybe even got the days mixed up. These Northern Ireland accents were a bitch sometimes to understand as they talked that quickly and didn't listen at all. He was going to give it another fifteen then split, which was just going to add to his bad mood.

Ivan who like to be called Evonne, and wasn't actually a Russian at all, was already in a bad mood. It was partly because Arnie hadn't called back, partly because his wife was a frigid bitch and partly because his whining old battleaxe of a mother Had phoned earlier to inform him that not only her, but her two sisters were coming out to Tenerife on Tuesday for a month's holiday. Did the stupid bitch not get it, as he had told her often enough, that one of the main reasons he had moved to Tenerife was to get away from her and her two ugly sisters. All three of them insisted on calling him by his real first name, Cecile and not the one he now used, Ivan, which he insisted was pronounced Evonne. He wanted to be a Russian, people out here thought he was a Russian and now the remains of his Lithuanian family were coming to squat for a month. And he knew that a month was bollucks as when these three came it was like a sexually transmitted disease, it not only stayed around for a long time longer than you had hoped, but it was as itchy and as annoying as fuck.

So Arnie might have been his ticket out. Some business, more money in the pipeline and then maybe a trip to Northern Ireland for a jolly and leave his frigid wife and grumpy, hormonal teenage daughter here to deal with the three whore bags. But Arnie wasn't answering his phone, and it didn't look like he was going to turn up either.

Ritchie had finished cleaning Arnie's apartment and packed up all his belongings as his new boss Jeffrey had instructed. He had also used his initiative and bribed the maid to turn a blind eye about borrowing one of the laundry trolleys, telling her that they were going to play a joke on a friend who was here for his stag. This was good as it meant he wouldn't have to sit it out in this apartment for the next twelve hours and he and Jeffrey could get on with taking Arnie's body out to sea. But his new boss wasn't answering his phone. He'd called him three times and thought any more calls might piss Jeffrey off so he was now just sitting waiting on a call back. He'd had a couple of false alarms, but it had only been Kevin and Jeffrey had told him not to make contact with him for now.

Liz was calling both Joe and Ray to make final arrangements to be collected at the airport in Tenerife on Sunday, but neither was answering. On the beach she thought as she knew that they didn't take their phones with them on beach days. All she could do was wait, or worst came to worst she could call Colin her self later.

Aurimas had phoned home and spoken to his mother. She was in great form and he got all the usual questions on what they were doing. He had to admit to himself when he'd come off the phone that he felt bad even though he hadn't actually lied. But he hadn't actually told her that they were planning to rob a bank come Monday either.

Ray had given Charlie his twenty minutes then called back once he was across the road from his apartment, outside Zara. Joe had the blue tooth hooked up and they were on remote control mode. When Charlie had told him where to meet, Ray had to ask him to repeat it and then once confirmed he felt quite concerned.

"The disabled toilet?" he had questioned for a second time.

Hearing the concern in Ray's voice, Charlie then said, "Don't worry, I'm not going to try and shag you or anything like that, it's just its private here." He didn't mention yet again that he didn't want to venture out with that Jeffrey milling around. And that shit Monty was still sleeping, even after two pots of cold water up his nose.

As strange as it was and feeling a bit awkward they had met at the disabled toilet, although Ray had refused to go inside with Charlie, partly because he knew then he would be outside Joe's view and so the remote control would be cut off, but mainly because he didn't want to be locked in the bog with Charlie. With the exchange done, the information and cash changed hands, Ray left. Unknown to Ray as he walked back to Joe by his remote control, he passed within a foot of Jeffrey who was making his way back after stopping for a couple of drinks and then to a chemist to get more medication for Dennis.

Ray and Joe headed to scope out the bank, whose address he'd just gotten from Charlie. Jeffrey eventually headed back to his apartment to see what was wrong now with the wimp, Dennis.

As Ray walked his phone rang, he answered it on his earpiece.

"OK Colin?" he said.

"Ray," Colin said, "Look I'm sorry about earlier."

Ray said nothing.

"Listen," Colin went on, "I'll do it, OK, but I'm just going to drop and go, then switch cars and pick you's back up, so you'll need to tell me how long you need and we'll need to work exactly to that. Does that sound OK?"

Ray thought, it sounded perfect. "Colin, don't feel you have to do this. It was no problem you saying no. I've just my dad mixed up in this and all." He had told Colin everything.

"Ray, you're a mate. A good mate. I can cover it I just needed to give it some thought. I've got two people carriers with smoked glass and I'm going to use false plates, so shouldn't be any risk." He was going to add unless the police are on top of us, but decided not to.

"OK Colin, if you're sure?"

"You just need to work out times," Collin added.

"Yes, I'll give it some thought," Ray answered, then thinking about something else, "sorry, Collin I've missed calls from Liz, you still OK to collect her from the airport tomorrow?"

Colin laughed, "Even though that's going to be worse than the Italian job."

Ray laughed too and he agreed.

"I'm working tonight Ray, so just call me when you sort the timings, or tomorrow whatever. Just if I don't answer cause someone's in the car, I'll call you back."

"OK, thanks Colin." The call ended.

Joe caught the gist of the conversation and was now worried that Colin's involvement would put him back on the subs bench.

Tentatively he asked, "Colin changed his mind?"

Sensing the unsaid from Joe's question Ray said, "Yes, which makes things a bit easier, but don't worry I still need you inside as we agreed." Then he added, "I don't know if Tracey is going to agree to let you use Bumper though."

"Well if not," said Joe, "maybe we could find a Labrador costume for mum and we could stick Bumper's harness on her?"

"Oh Joseph," Ray said, "you're on dangerous ground there my son."

"Nah," answered Joe, "I'll just tell her it was your idea!"

Chapter Twenty-One

Tenerife, Canary Islands
Saturday 23rd October 2021

Ray walked with Bumper on his left. Bumper was in working mode now and was concentrating, listening to Ray's encouragement and instructions and watching for oncoming obstacles to navigate his charge around.

"Good boy, good boy," said Ray, "straight on, straight on." Ray also waved his right hand in a forward sweep to add a visual aid to his instructions to Bumper. Ray's left hand was softly gripping Bumper's harness feeling the movement. Bumper's lead was also held loosely in Ray's left hand. Ray was also concentrating to follow Bumper's lead and also ensure that he kept his body positioned just slightly in front of the handle of the harness, which made his left hand sit almost behind him. He was also careful not to be too close to Bumper, were he could maybe stand on his toes, but at the same time ensure he wasn't too far away which would mean that the harness wasn't straight and therefore causing him to pull and lead Bumper rather than the other way around.

"Find the curb Bumper, find the curb," Ray commanded as he sensed that they were now approaching the junction. He repeated the command and then added, "good boy, good boy Bumper," as he felt Bumper veer to the left preparing to guide Ray to the oncoming curb, positioning to the left so as to avoid the curve on the corner and then line Ray so that he faced straight to the opposite curb across the road. Once there Bumper took Ray to the edge and when satisfied the position was correct he stopped and sat down to await his next command.

Ray provided more congratulations and petted Bumper's head. From here he had the option to go straight, which meant crossing the road, therefore they would need to find the crossing, or take a left turn down the cross street.

Wanting to go left Ray brought his right hand to his chest, took a step back to make room for Bumper to be able to move once he was instructed in which direction they were moving to and said, "Left,

Bumper left." As he spoke he also swept his right arm in a sweeping movement to the right, and then began tapping his right leg. Because at a curb and wanting to head left, the first move was to move and turn right. The dog would then walk around in a circle starting to the right until he eventually faced left and then continued walking straight along the new street.

Once instructed Bumper moved, first in front of Ray to the right, then once past Ray he turned to his right circling Ray until he was lined up straight along the desired street. As Bumper made his move Ray pirouetted in a three quarter turn also to the right and ended up facing to the left of his original position. Once both dog and master were facing the desired direction Ray said, "good boy, straight on straight on.

Bumper, as usual, did as instructed and headed on down the street, walking at their normal pace and watching out for potential obstacles. He received another pat on his head, which triggered another swish of his tail. He was happy being congratulated for doing what he had been trained to do, and what he loved to do. When he was working that was all he did. Any other distractions were ignored, unless they posed a threat to his master.

Onward they walked, several paces later Ray said, "good boy, Bumper, good boy. Keep straight."

Bumper knew the route and had a fair idea where they were going. But it was still up to him to listen, just in case he was wrong as it was up to his master where he went, it was only up to Bumper to guide him from one move to another. One curb to the next, one turn to the next turn. They walked and moved in a grid like pattern which was laid out and broken down to left, right, straight on or back. Apart from diversions across roads, in to shops or something like that, that was pretty much how they walked and got from point A to point B.

Ray was listening for the sign to give him his next prompt and on hearing the noise of the busy Spar and the opening and closing of the electronic entrance doors he said, "Find the bench, Bumper, and find the bench."

Bumper began to veer right away from the middle of the path and towards the two benches which sat facing the doors of the shop and divided by a rubbish bin. The first bench was taken so Bumper moved on to the second and once level he began to slow. Sensing they were arriving at his desired spot Ray said, "Good boy Bumper good boy, now find the bench find the bench." Bumper made his final move and walked to the bench his nose almost touching the seat, and then stopped. Ray stopped as well and used his right hand to firstly pat Bumper's head and then run his hand gently down his nose until he found the front of the bench. Once located, he swung himself around and sat down.

"Good boy Bumper, good boy." He petted Bumper's head and ears with both of his hands. Bumpers tail wagged again in appreciation.

Ray lowered the handle of the harness, gently so as not to slam it down on Bumper's back. He then let go of the handle, but kept hold of the lead. He then felt below Bumper's midriff to find the buckle and released the fastening on the harness and then pulled it carefully over Bumper's head and through the loop of the lead. He set the harness on the seat beside him and petted Bumper once again. Bumper gave himself a good shake, which released any tension he might have from the workload. Being a Guide Dog was a stressful job and you needed to manage that stress.

"Sit Bumper, sit," Ray said. Bumper sat.

Ray then slid off his back pack, found the top zip and opened the compartment. He found the folding water bowl and pushed it to pop it open, then he found the water bottle and filled the bowl with fresh cold water, which he placed on the ground just in front of Bumper. Bumper was thirsty, but still on the lead and partially in work mode he waited for his instruction.

"Go on Bumper, take a drink that's a good boy," Ray said, and then heard the slopping as Bumper gratefully lapped up the cold refreshment.

Ray sat waiting for Joe to catch them up; he was doing some final shopping for their challenge ahead. They had scoped out the bank and Joe had bought their costumes. Ray wasn't that happy with Joe's choices, but Joe pointed out that they were the only ones he could get that ticked all the boxes. He had stipulated what they had to have, and buy everything in separate shops.

So Joe had followed his instructions to the letter and found to his surprise that the range of costumes wasn't as great as he thought it would have been. The toy guns however were easy. Even knowing they were toys, Joe thought they looked real.

Ray took out his phone and opened up the phone AP to the recent calls menu and double tapped his dad's number again. On the first tap the voiceover informed him, "Dad Mobile outgoing nine calls." The second tap set the phone in motion to make his tenth call, but like all the others the call went straight to voicemail. Ray killed the call.

"OK," said Joe as he sat down beside him.

Ray smelt the smoke, but said nothing.

"Yes, are we good to go?" Ray was feeling a bit apprehensive on how things were going to be with Tracey when they got back. The weather had also changed as the temperature and humidity had both rose. It made the heat seem more oppressive and "soupy" like as Ray called it. He guessed that maybe a storm was heading there way, which tended to happen when the heat really soared. He wondered if he was also heading in to a storm with one of his closest friends. Once Bumper had finished his water they headed back to face the music.

Back at the villa they discovered that Terry had fallen asleep on his sun bed, the Kindle still talking away in his earphones. Stretching due to the stiffness lying on the bed, he felt the tang of pain from sensitive skin and realised that he'd had an amateur hour and had gotten sun burn while sleeping. Saying nothing, as he knew he'd only get told off for falling asleep in such strong sun, he turned off the Kindle and asked the lads how they'd got on. Ray not wanting to say too much for now until he had sussed out the lay of the land with Tracey, said, "I'll fill you in later. Where's Tracey?"

"She had been here," answered Terry, "but she must have gone inside."

"OK," said Ray, "I'll be back in a minute." As he headed for the patio doors, he said to Joe, "Put all that where we said Joe, please." Then finding the doors, he slid it open and went inside saying Tracey's name to establish if she was in the kitchen dining area. No response told him she wasn't there. Or at least he hoped she wasn't there and just still ignoring him. He went with his instinct and felt his way to the staircase, then went up one flight to the landing where Tracey's room was. Feeling past two doors, Aurimas's room and the upstairs bathroom, he came to Tracey's door and knocked gently.

"Yes," he heard her say so he answered, "it's me Ray." Then after a short hesitation when he had hoped she would have invited him in, but didn't, he said, "can I come in?"

But just as he asked the door opened.

"You don't usually need to be invited in," she said.

"We don't usually fall out," he countered, and then added, "so I wasn't sure if I was welcome."

"You don't usually rob banks," she shot back, and then almost regretted it immediately. Shaking her head and stepping back in to her room she said, "come in."

He did as instructed and then closed the door behind him. He had sort of worked out in his mind what he was going to say, but before he got a chance Tracey said.

"I'm sorry," there was a slight quiver to her voice. "I shouldn't have said the things I said," a sniffle now, "you didn't deserve that, and not with Joe there."

Feeling bad as he thought that he did actually deserve most, or at least some of it, he stepped forward, using the sound of her voice to tell him exactly where she was. Once close he reached out to touch her face, careful not to be clumsy and touch her anywhere he shouldn't have. He felt the tears on her cheek and started to wipe them away with his thumb.

"Oh Trace," he said, and she immediately stepped in to his arms. "Don't cry," he said gently, "I know crying hurts you, please don't do that because of me?"

She thumped him on his chest. "I've been doing it all day because of you you idiot."

He squeezed her in another effort to say he was sorry.

"I came up here," she said, "bloody mad." He had noticed that, but thought it better to say nothing about it for now. She went on, "put my music on, and what's it playing?"

He knew it was a rhetorical question and so he still said nothing.

"Train in bloody Vain," she said, "all those words, you didn't stand by me, didn't stand by your man, and I'm thinking it's you singing to me and in no time at all I'm the one feeling bad and guilty. Then, as if you set up my play list its Fleetwood Mac singing about me going my own way, and next thing I'm crying my eyes out."

Ray said, "songs are like that, you can see all sorts of meanings sometimes." Then trying to lift her mood he began to taunt her, knowing it was a theme they had explored before and joked about, "anyway, Train in Vain is a sort of love song."

"So?" she said.

"Well," he added, emphasising the obvious.

She thumped his chest again, "You know how I feel?"

"I know, your brother," he said.

"You know it's more than that," she said, almost offended.

"Does Jess know," he teased.

She thumped him again, this time there was more in it. Exaggerating it he said, "Umph!"

"You know if I wasn't gay I'd be with you," she said.

"But what if I rejected your charms," he replied.

She thumped him this time with both fists.

"I'm only joking," he submitted, "You know too that if I was a lesbian I'd have you too!" He squeezed her playfully, and then added, "although I think I might be a lesbian as I do quite fancy women."

Playing now herself she responded, "Hey tiger, I'm not just any woman, I'm ME."

"Don't I know it," he laughed. She laughed too and it released a lot of the tension in the room.

Ray had sincerely meant everything he had said to Tracey, but there was also some deeper, more painful truth behind his words. He did love her and at times he wasn't sure if it was like a brother sister thing, or if it was something more. And when he did feel this way he didn't know if it was just his loneliness confusing his emotions, which he admitted wouldn't be that hard to do.

After a few moments she said, "right big, much older brother, sit your arse down on that bed and tell me what you are going to do and how we're going to rob this bank."

When he had sat down she added, "Anything I don't like we're changing, and oh, if we get caught you're the one going to tell Jess, and face to face, as I've never seen her perform circumcision with a nail file before." Cringing, he sat down on the bed and began to talk, trying to get the image out of his mind of Jess coming at him with a rusty nail file. Then worrying to himself why he was now thinking that the file was rusty, and he hoped it wasn't a bad omen.

Chapter Twenty-Two

Tenerife, Canary Islands
Saturday 23rd October 2021

The boat cruised south-west and out in to the Atlantic Ocean. It was a beautiful night, although hot and sticky as if brewing up for a storm. Jeffrey thought that was what was needed as maybe some thunder and rain would clear the heavy air.

Ritchie was below fascinated with the boat, rabbitting on about always wanting a boat like this and how amazing it was. Jeffrey was at his post in his "Captain's" chair were he had preset the boat's state of the art navigating system to take him out to where he had been many times before. He called it the Dead Sea. There were several boats on the boats radar system, which was again state of the art, but they were mainly heading back to land. One such boat was just about to pass on his port side and Jeffrey was counting down the distance before giving the usual toot on his horn as a greeting. His fellow mariner responded, then passed just thirty feet to port and was behind Jeffrey in a matter of seconds.

Sasha Moreno passed Jeffrey and gave the usual greeting. He was heading back to the marina having changed his mind about staying out all night as he suspected a storm was coming in. He was tired after his day fishing in the heat of the canary sun, but despite this he was looking forward to reading a few more chapters of his latest book and maybe having a couple of drinks. He was wondering at his fellow mariner heading out to sea so late at night, and the suspicious police mind did consider cruising by closer so that he could read the name of the boat. But the thought had came too late and to have changed coarse so abruptly would have been too obvious, and after all it could just be a couple looking for a romantic encounter out at sea under the stars. The thought made him slightly jealous and so having returned the greeting he settled back down to the rest of the cruise to shore.

Jeffrey had been watching on the off chance that the oncoming boat had changed coarse to come closer, but was glad now it had passed and now forgotten he concentrated on what lay ahead. The cruise would take just over an hour and as long as the radar told him he was very much alone, apart from Ritchie below, then he would be satisfied to stop and get to work.

Like Sasha he was tired. The day had been a long one. Since leaving Ritchie at Arnie's apartment he had decided to take a walk in the opposite direction from earlier that morning on the off chance of spotting Charlie Bassett. Since they had seen Arnie the night before things had changed somewhat, but he needed to try and focus on what they had come here to do and it was vital that he got to Bassett before Dennis did. Discovering what Arnie and his boys had been up to had also been important, but in a way more for Dennis than for him. He had been thinking that if things worked out as he hoped, that he could maybe use this Arnie stuff as a cover to let Dennis think that they were the ones over here trying to steal their money. But since Ritchie's phone call while he was having breakfast, he hadn't achieved anything else today but mopping up that mess. Then once Ritchie had broke Arnie's neck, albeit accidentally, getting rid of the body had become the priority. His fear was that if Arnie's body was discovered then it wouldn't only be the police that would come out in force; he reckoned that there would be yet more people over here with Northern Irish accents. Christ, as if there wasn't enough already.

He felt the boat gently change direction as they came out of the main channel lines and headed out to deep sea. Ritchie shouted something from below but Jeffrey couldn't hear the prick and he wasn't leaving his "Captain's" seat to ask what he wanted. If Ritchie wanted to say something then he'd have to come up top. Truth was the lad worried Jeffrey. He seemed to do things off his own bat, which in their line of work, just wasn't how you done things. OK, they weren't the army, but there was a chain of command, yet only a couple of hours after coming under Jeffrey's wing, he had taken it on himself to bribe one of the maids in to letting him borrow one of the linen trolleys. The fact was that it hadn't given them any advantage at all. It might have allowed them to get out of Arnie's apartment sooner, which he suspected may have been Ritchie's motive. But to do what they were doing now and get the body from the car to the boat required darkness.

So to make the point, and hopefully learn the lesson, Jeffrey had still made Ritchie sit tight in Arnie's apartment all day and just ensured that he had the "do not disturb" on the door. Then they could make their move with less risk.

Jeffrey had taken a risk himself by letting the prostitute go. He wasn't sure if she suspected Arnie was just knocked out, or if she thought herself he was dead, and that was a risk. But he had considered what he thought was her age, he agreed with Ritchie as she only looked fourteen, and he had a daughter of exactly the same age. He had also considered, as it looked like Arnie had given her a beating that she most likely couldn't care what happened to the bastard. So he'd paid her, with Arnie's money so no skin of his arse, given her a tip and let her go. Provided they could get rid of Arnie's body, get finished their business in Tenerife and get out before any questions were asked, and god forbid, Arnie's picture ended up on the news as a missing person, then he was satisfied. The maid though was a totally different prospect. As soon as something came up about the man in apartment five, three six, she would remember the man who had bribed her to borrow the linen trolley to play a joke on his friend on his stag do. Then she could provide an accurate description of Ritchie, and who knows who had then seen him with Ritchie and could then provide an accurate description of him as well. It had been a stupid move on Ritchie's part and one that they hadn't gained any advantage from, only risk.

Ritchie then came up from below and asked, "Do you want a coffee?"

"Please," answered Jeffrey, "there's travel mugs in one of the cupboards, I like to use those up here around the cockpit instruments."

"Yeah, think I seen those," Ritchie said then disappeared back below.

"Nosey fucker must be looking in everything down there,"

Jeffrey thought. He then reached behind him and took his fleece which was hanging over the back of his chair. The sea breeze now was cooler so he pulled it on and zipped it up tight. He also reached below the seat for his back pack and took out his baseball cap and pulled it tight over his head. The cruiser glided effortless over the calm sea, which tonight was just a very mild swell. The engines of the powerful boat just purred gently as they cruised.

Ritchie returned with his coffee but didn't stay up top, which pleased Jeffrey as he didn't really want to chat. He was just glad to sip his hot coffee and enjoy the mild sea

As it glided past. He loved boats, and he adored this boat in particular. It was one thing in his relationship with Dennis that he could actually call his, even though it wasn't. But it was registered in his name, which had been some sort of tax avoidance thing he didn't really understand, but never the less, it was his name on the owner's documents and his name registered with the marina. So as far as he was concerned, it was his.

The next hour passed peacefully and with no other boats either in sight or on the radar. They were out here alone, which was perfect.

He cut the engines and allowed the boat to drift.

"Ritchie," he called. Several seconds later Ritchie came out from below and said, "that us?"

"Aye, Aye my lad," said Jeffrey in a mock sailors voice, then in his own voice he continued, "let's get our friend Arnie up here."

They both went below and retrieved his body from the port side bedroom, which was Dennis's. Ritchie took his head as he had been first in to the cabin, and Jeffrey took his feet. Together they went up the steps until they were both on the deck and then laid Arnie down flat between the bench seats. Ritchie then went below again and retrieved Arnie's suitcase and the rope. They had filled the suitcase with any of Arnie's belongings from the apartment that didn't have his name on. His passport, bank cards and stuff like that, Jeffrey had taken. Then they had added the Digger's special touch, as he had instructed Ritchie, and these were dumb bell weights that he had stowed down below for just such occasions and to ensure that the body went straight to the bottom of the sea.

Moving to the cabin door and asking Ritchie to move to the stern so that they could start moving Arnie up on to the sun deck on the rear. As soon as Ritchie was towards the stern Jeffrey pulled out the gun from the back of his shorts and aimed to shoot Ritchie in his chest, as it was the largest target and almost certain to do the job required. But Ritchie must have sensed something because he moved to come back towards Jeffrey and instead of the bullet going through his back and through his chest it entered his left eye and blew the left side of his skull off. The top of his head spun out of the boat and slipped silently below the surface while the body it left behind began to crumble backwards and on to the deck at the rear of the boat.

Jeffrey stepped to his Captain's chair and put the gun back in to his back pack. Then he stepped over Ritchie's slumped body and slid him on to the deck. He then retrieved the rope and wrapped it around Ritchie's chest and secured it with several knots. He then hefted Arnie's suitcase on top of Ritchie and threaded the rope through its two handles and then knotted it once more to the rope around Ritchie. To finish his human depth charge he trailed Arnie's body to the deck beside Ritchie. He needed to rest for a minute after this as Arnie was a big man and heavy and he almost wished he'd got Ritchie to help him with this part before he'd blown his head off. Once he had his breath back, he lifted Arnie on top of the suitcase and wrapped the rope around him and through the handles. The rope was long enough for him to do this six times and then he fed it back through one handle and tied it tightly and securely to the rope around Ritchie's chest.

He checked his work and once satisfied he began to slide the mass towards the edge of the deck. Considering the weight this wasn't easy. It was one time when travelling that he really needed excess baggage and it would also be the one time when he didn't have to pay extortionate rates for the privilege. For a moment he considered pulling out the hose and wetting the decking to make it slippery, but then thought that could be more hazardous for him rather than his soon to be departing guests. So he persevered, even though it was slow work. Eventually though he had it to the edge and so he then went behind it and began taking it end by end to push it towards the waiting water. It took him several moves from end to end but eventually he felt gravity take over and then with one final push at the opposite end the entire package, two men and a suitcase, splashed in to the Atlantic and sank. Hopefully, Jeffrey thought, never to be seen again.

He came down from the stern deck and sat for some minutes getting his puff back. He felt the tiredness of the day now begin to bite but it would be some time yet before he could call it a night and slip gratefully in to his bed.

For the second time in the last few minutes, he wished that Ritchie was there to make him another coffee, but as he was now on his own he went below and fended for himself. Once he had set the kettle to boil, which could take some minutes, he returned top side and turned on the rear deck lights to inspect for any mess from shooting Ritchie. Thankfully his only cause for concern was on the rear deck which was easily cleaned, and in two minutes the hose had washed the remains over board and in to the sea.

Once he had made his coffee, he returned to his Captain's chair and set the sat nav for the Los Cristianos marina and settled back in the comfortable seat while the boat made his wide arc to head back to shore, pretty much along the same route it had taken on the way out. On this journey though the boat was considerably lighter than it had been on the outbound sailing.

The journey back only took thirty five minutes as Jeffrey had opened up the throttles and had some fun in the knowledge that there were no other vessels around and more importantly, that he now didn't have a dead body on board. On the way he had spontaneously thrown Arnie's passport, bank and credit cards and mobile phone over board. He had taken some time earlier to go through the phone and note any useful contact numbers or other details that might come in useful. So now back at his birth with his cleaning up duties complete he secured the boat and headed up to the car park for the short drive to their apartment in Playa de Las Americas.

Sasha Moreno watched him as he went. He had decided to spend the night on board his boat as he couldn't be bothered with the drive home. He was only heading back to an empty flat anyway. He wasn't one hundred percent certain, but he did think he was pretty sure that the boat that had just docked had been the one he had signalled to just a couple of hours before. But if correct on this assumption, it meant that his guess about the romantic liaison out at sea was now wrong. Also, he was sure that he had seen a man at the pilot's chair and someone moving around below in the lights of the cabin. But this man had returned alone. The pieces didn't fit and that annoyed him.

As he sat sipping his hot whisky, the policeman part of his brain was itchy, and the only thing you could do with an itch was scratch it.

He decided that he would visit the marina office in the morning and look in to who owned the boat in question. He sat the whisky back down and went back to reading his book, the latest Jeffrey Archer novel, which was at fault for keeping him away from his bed.

Chapter Twenty-Three

Tenerife, Canary Islands
Sunday 24th October 2021

Liz hit the villa like an assault team on speed. Her first military manoeuvre was a full tirade on Joe. Leaving Colin behind her like a footman carrying her luggage she sprinted towards Joe, her arms spread wide and her voice loud in the previously quiet dining area.

"Joseph darling," she said, almost like she was singing, "give your mummy a big hug." Before Joe had time to react or make any sort of movement his mother had embraced him in a bear hug that most wrestlers would have been proud of. Then the kisses came, delivered as if fired from a Tommy gun, accompanied with the exaggerated kissing sound of a Bollywood actress, "Mwa, mwa, mwa, mwa." Joe blushed and tried to free himself. He could smell the stale wine of her breath, even through the powerful perfume.

"Why didn't you come to the airport to meet your mother? I was looking for you there. Colin was late as usual. mwa, mwa, mwa. Oh I've missed you so much."

"Mum." Joe said sternly, still trying his best to pull away. "I've only been away for a week."

"A day, a week, a month, what difference does it make I just hate being away from my little boy, Mwa, Mwa, Mwa." She squeezed tighter. Joe's blush deepened.

Ray and Tracey were also in the room. Tracey at the opposite side of the table from Joe and Ray on the two seater sofa beside the door. Colin eventually made it through the door wrestling a suitcase, handbag and several shopping bags containing duty free and other purchases Liz had made on the way over. He sat them all on the floor.

"Hi Ray," he said, "Trace, Joe, how's things?"

Ray got up and headed over to Colin.

"There's bags there Ray. Liz's bags. Sorry I'll move them." Colin slid them all across the floor to the other side of the doorway where they wouldn't be in the way. Ray heard the scrape of the bags and the clink of bottles. He didn't need to ask what they were as he knew Liz and therefore knew well what she had bought.

"Thanks Colin for getting Liz."

"Will I just stick that on the account Ray?" Colin asked quietly. Ray was about to answer by asking if Liz hadn't paid him herself, when Liz's second military manoeuvre began.

"Raymond," Liz sang, "Raymond," she repeated knowing he hated being called by his full name. "Thanks so much for letting me come over, Mwa, Mwa, Mwa, oh I so needed a holiday."

Ray was about to point out that he'd had no choice but Liz continued.

"Oh you've cut your hair short, oh I love it, Mwa, Mwa." Running her hands around the back of his head and then she pulled him in close. "Oh Raymond so sorry to hear about your mum being poorly," she hugged tighter, "Julie was always so good to me. She treated me as if I was her own daughter." In other words, Ray thought, not the way you treated me you prick as you left me.

Freeing himself, "Thanks Liz, I was talking to her yesterday she's hanging in there." Stepping back to avoid another onslaught Ray said, "Joe could you take your mums stuff up and show her which room?" Joe didn't answer but Ray heard him move across the room and start to gather up the bags. "I was just about to make Trace and me a coffee, would you like one Liz, you Colin?"

"Coffee?" laughed Liz, "I'll have wine lover and if you have none in the fridge there's some in my bags there. Be a sweety and give me some ice with it." Ignoring the mention of Tracey Liz looked around, "Which way Joseph, lead the way?"

"I'm good," said Colin, "I want to get on here I've more pick ups to do.

Liz then made her final military manoeuvre as she retreated through the door looking for the stairs. Trace said, "See you later Liz."

Liz heard Tracey but instead of answering she lifted her left hand and gave Tracey a little backward wave to signify yes, yes they would indeed catch up later. Much later. Liz knew rightly that Tracey wouldn't see the wave, but she could tell Joe that she had just forgot. She disappeared,

Colin left and Joe moved across the room carrying his mother's bags and already in a funk and depressed. She was only here less than two minutes and already he'd been embarrassed by her, been embarrassed for her, and then eventually pissed off. The next week was going to be shit. He trudged up the stairs, "It's the room at the top mum," he muttered, then continued to follow. He said nothing more, he'd say more when they were in her room, alone.

It was pointless to tell her to stop; number one, stop calling him Joseph. Number two, stop hugging and kissing him, he was fourteen for Christ sake. Number three, stop flirting with dad, you know he doesn't like it. Strike that, he'd leave the last one well alone, let his dad fight his own battles on that front. But he would have to pull her about Tracey, this one really pissed him off. No matter how many times he had told her, no matter how obvious it was, it just didn't matter. Liz had it in her head that Tracey and Ray were an item. Or had been at one time, or were from time to time on a casual basis. And as a result she snubbed Tracey and when they happened to be in the same room with Ray she would do the double. Be all over his dad, and ignore Tracey.

"Oh look at the view," Liz said once she had entered the room at the top of the villa, "you can see the sea, and awe beautiful isn't it?"

Joe closed the door. "Mum," he said, with a slight pleading to his voice, "you did it again."

"Did what sweetie?"

"Snubbed Tracey."

"Nonsense!"

"Mum!" Joe said again, raising his voice slightly, "it's embarrassing. There's nothing going on with dad and Tracey."

"Embarrassing?" replied Liz, an edge of little girl in her voice, "I embarrass you now?"

"It's the same thing every time." Said Joe. And it was. He also knew what she would say next.

"Your paranoid sweetie, I just didn't get the chance that's all."

Joe guessed correctly.

"That's what you say all the time. This is what we say all the time. Mum Tracey is getting married to Jess next year. Her and dad are just good friends."

"She could be Bi," Liz said cheekily.

"Mum!" Joe said again shaking his head.

"OK, OK, I gave her a wave between us girls, you know, to say we'll catch up later." Liz offered innocently.

"A wave? To Trace?" Joe paused, then said, "Did you wave to dad too?"

"What?"

"Did you wave to dad as well?" Joe repeated, although he not only knew his mother had heard him, he knew that she knew only too well what he was getting at.

Liz paused. Joe had trapped her. She didn't want to say the obvious about his dad, if she did Joe would just make her feel bad for it. She decided to retreat.

"When we go down I'll talk to her." Using her rather than her name. "OK?" Although she did hope that maybe when they did go downstairs that she might have gone already.

"OK," Joe sighed. Then sensing that his mum was psyching up for another hugging session, he said, "I'll leave you to get all your stuff sorted out and I'll see you when you come down." Then he turned to leave.

"Think I'll get changed and catch some sun for a couple of hours. Sort all this out later.

"Whatever," Joe said leaving.

"You not going to join me by the pool?" she asked.

"I think me and Aurimas are going to take Bumper to the beach." He knew his mistake as soon as he had said it.

"The beach? Oh, that might be nice. Is it far to walk?"

Joe was thinking hard. "Ah no, emh," he stuttered, "there's one real close, but that's not the one we take Bumper too. It's ages away." He waited hoping. After a painful few seconds she complied.

"Nah, it's OK, I'll stick with the pool."

Joe closed the door and left quickly.

My Daddy Was a Bank Robber

Liz sat on the edge of the bed. She felt the warmth of the sun through the open window and the noise of the birds and the sea mixed in with the other noises of a busy holiday resort. Mixed music, traffic and an aeroplane in the distance, either taking off or landing, she wasn't sure as she couldn't see it. She sighed. A deep sigh she hoped would release some of her tension. She was here now, even though she knew full well that she wasn't wanted. The last five minutes hadn't helped that, but she couldn't help it either. She was the way she was and she couldn't change. And oh she had tried. Tried and failed. Failed to change and failed to hold on to Ray. She did know that there was no way back for her and Ray, but that didn't stop her loving him and that didn't stop the worst of her coming out, as a sort of shield, to protect the vulnerable of her when she was in his company. She had had other relationships since they had split up. Jesus of course she did, their split had been over twelve years ago and she wasn't a bloody nun. She needed company and she needed to have someone. But they had all mainly been about loneliness and sex. Yes, she'd had a couple of possible glimpses of commitment, but like with Ray, she couldn't hold on to those either. And it wasn't easy always ending up alone. Besides the company, there was the finances. Running a home and bringing up a son on your own was tough. Ray did do his bit for Joe, but the household stuff was down to her. Plus she was needy, and needy in an expensive way. She liked things to be the best. Clothes, shoes, make up, perfume, the list goes on, and she was a marketeers dream. So running the house and running the finances was something that she didn't do too well with. Hence the debt. Hence the trip to Tenerife.

Her high street credit had ran out long ago. This then led to high interest credit which was basically unaffordable. This then led to loan sharks. Unlike high street credit they did show their sharp teeth when you didn't pay, and unlike high street credit they called to your house, unannounced and with company. Mean company. And so needing a break, or an escape, Liz had juggled what remaining credit she had to pay for the flights, and of course, pick up a few bits on the way. You couldn't go on holiday without buying a few treats. No, no, what sort of holiday would that be?

Remembering the treats, which reminded her of the wine, she gave herself a shake and got changed in to her swim wear for the pool. Hopefully Ray would maybe accompany her there for a couple of hours, which would be nice. She did need someone to help her rub on her suntan oil. And hopefully Tracey was going to the beach with Joe.

Her wish ended up reversed. Ray had gone out with Joe and Tracey was out by the pool alone. Liz only realised when it was too late and she had given herself away to Tracey by calling Ray's name when she was walking through the villa and trying to establish where he was. When she stepped through the patio doors beside the pool she immediately was aware of her mistake. Recovering and trying her best to hide her disappointment she said.

"Oh hi Tracey darling, Raymond not here?"

Tracey didn't answer. Then Liz noticed her second mistake. Tracey had her ear buds in and was listening to music and so hadn't heard her. Liz reversed her track back in to the house and headed to find the fridge, and hopefully the wine.

Tracey, hearing Liz head back in doors blew out a great sigh of relief. Only due to the gap in between songs she had heard Liz coming through the kitchen calling Ray's name, so she had bunkered down and pretended that she hadn't heard her. She hoped that Liz would be grateful for this as she knew that Liz, or Lizzy as she like to call her, didn't like her and that was fine as she really didn't like Lizzy. All Tracey wanted to do was to relax and listen to some music and maybe read her book later. The lads had gone to the beach with Bumper and poor Terry was staying out of the sun today as his stupidity yesterday had left him with pretty bad sun burn. So bad in fact that he was now lying up in his room covered in yoghurt. Strawberry as it was all they had. The two boys had give him some stick for that, but fair play to Terry he had taken it on the chin. She heard the fridge door close and then unfortunately she heard Lizzy's steps get louder as she came back towards the patio door. Tracey quickly hit the play button on her ear buds and lay back pretending to be asleep. With the music now loud in her ears she sensed rather than heard Lizzy come out from the kitchen and walk over to the sun beds. A few seconds later her worse fears came true when she felt a gentle tap on her shoulder which she knew she couldn't ignore. She had no choice but to pause her music yet again.

"Tracey darling," sang Liz, "could you be a real sweetie and put some sun cream on my back?" Not waiting for an answer, Liz lay face down on the bed beside Tracey.

"I put the cream on the table beside us honey, oh it's a glorious day, isn't it sweetie, absolutely glorious."

Tracey took out her ear buds and wrapped them around her phone. She then sat up and felt for the sun cream, while thinking, "It was absolutely glorious before you arrived," but then saying, "sure Lizzy no problem." Then she froze for a second realising she had said Lizzy instead of Liz, but as Liz didn't flinch or say anything, Tracey squeezed out the cream on her back and started rubbing. Roughly!

"So," said Liz, "you still shagging my ex?"

Tracey had heard this all before. Heard it, argued and fought about it, but nothing she said, or Ray for that matter could penetrate this woman's mind and overcome her paranoia, or jealousy, or whatever it was up her arse. So prepared this time, Tracey took a different approach.

"Yeah, not half!"

Continuing to rub in the sun cream, which was starting to ball up now as she had rubbed it in too much. "He's some shag isn't he?" Tracey went on; rubbing this insult in to Lizzy's mind with the same vigour she had rubbed the cream in to her back. "I bet you miss a shag like that Liz. I can't get enough of it; we're at it like rabbits. Night and day." She put the lid back on the cream, set it back on the table. "That OK for you honey?" Liz said nothing. "I'm going to put my music back on, maybe have a nap; I'm exhausted, totally shagged out." She exaggerated a yawn, "see you later. Sweetie."

Tracey put her music back on, loud, and lay back satisfied and trying her best to keep the smirk off her face. She knew by Lizzy's silence that she had hit a home run, and she could feel the rage burning through her as she lay on the sun bed beside her. She was beginning to generate more heat than the sun.

Ray had been right. Don't argue, that's what she wants. The song changed on Tracey's play list and shuffled to "Cold Heart" by Elton John and Dua Lipa, Tracey wished it had been "I Can't Get No Satisfaction," by the Stones as she might just have asked Lizzy Sweetie if she wanted to have a little listened in. Music is for sharing, "Bitch!"

Chapter Twenty-Four

Tenerife, Canary Islands
Sunday 24th October 2021

Charlie had eventually woken Monty up. With an unusual act of kindness he had actually asked how he was feeling. Thinking that Monty was brain dead because he had just stared at him and then realising that the look on Monty's face was one of puzzlement he said.

"I was asking how you were feeling you fucking unappreciative shite."

Monty still stared.

"While you've been sleeping their like sleeping beauty, or more like sleeping ugly bastard, I've been sorting out all our stuff with that Jazz junior and almost got ambushed by Jeffrey the digger. You know Jeffrey Byrne?"

"The Digger," answered Monty.

"Yes that's what I fucking said, the Digger. He's a mean fucker so I need you up and about instead of snoozing all day there."

In his second act of kindness in as many minutes, he asked, "you want anything to eat? You haven't been awake for a whole day." But before Monty answered, Charlie leaned forward and said, "Say Cornetto and I'm going to hit your sore head with that fucking pan." He pointed to the sauce pan on the set of drawers that he had used the day before to throw water over him in an effort to wake the fucker up.

Monty shook his head. As if speaking to a child, Charlie said, "use your words."

Not sure what words to use as he didn't know what he wanted to eat. He was hungry, and yes he would love a Cornetto, but he wasn't going to say that and then Charlie would get all mad again. He noticed Charlie's new phone in his hand and then he noticed the big chunk broken off the corner. He then found some words, but they weren't words that pleased Charlie, "your new phone is broke."

Charlie looked at the phone in his hand, then back at Monty. He held up his other hand to show Monty the plaster wrapped around his index finger.

"I know the fucking phone is broke, look I've got this to prove it as the fucking thing nearly sliced the top of my fucking finger off." He waved his plastered finger at Monty. "It says swipe up to answer then it nearly decapitates your finger. Fucking useless piece of shit."

"How did it brake," asked Monty innocently. But now pissed off talking about his broken phone Charlie snapped, "I hit you over the fucking head with it as I was trying to wake you up."

Monty raised his hand to his head and began to feel for more damage than what was there before.

"I'm only joking," said Charlie, "although you don't stop asking about my phone and I might just introduce it to your thick skull."

"A burger," said Monty.

"What?" asked Charlie, having forgotten about his question on food?

"A burger," repeated Monty, "and chips."

"Gone off Cornettos," said Charlie.

"Can we go to the place has the chocolate milk shakes?" asked Monty excitedly.

"We're staying in and going to the pool bar, so if they do milk shakes, which they most likely will as the place is fucking swarming with kids, or brats I should say, then you're good, but we're not going to Hard Rock." And then to explain he added, "I don't want to bump in to the digger I told you."

"Oh yeah," said Monty, "the digger." And after a pause continued, "he's called Jeffrey Byrne." He knew he'd said something wrong when Charlie's face turned angry.

"I fucking said that two minutes ago you fucking moron. It was better in here when you were fucking sleeping. I thought you were dead at one point, oh what a pity eh that you woke up."

Monty decided to shut up. After a few minutes Charlie said, "Right c'mon, let's go I'm starving." He got up and Monty followed. On the way to the door Charlie added, "ask for a Cornetto, a song by Cliff

Richard or any other fucking stupid thing and I'm going to drown you in the pool."

Monty wasn't a bit concerned as swimming was something he was good at. He'd done all his badges at school and his mum had sowed them to his swimming shorts. He wished he had the shorts now and he could show the badges to Charlie and he also decided that when he got home he was going to find his old shorts and sow the badges on to his new speedos.

He soon forgot all about swimming and badges when they reached the pool bar. Not only did they have chocolate milk shake, they also had one of the ice cream freezers. He had tried not to look at it, worried that Charlie might shout, but he had managed a sneaky peak on the way to their table and the first thing he had seen were Cornettos. Lots of them. He needed to be good, well behaved and not say anything to annoy Charlie and he might then be able to get one later.

So he'd been quiet. Quiet was the best way to make sure you didn't say something stupid that would upset Charlie. He had eaten up all of his burger and chips, quietly, well as quietly as he could. He had only slurped his milk shake twice. Oh, and burped once.

Charlie had also been quiet, which wasn't like him. Monty had risked a couple of peaks and noticed that Charlie was paying a lot of attention to some women at another table. At one point Monty was even sure the little man had smiled. A crooked, smirking sort of a smile. This worried Monty, it worried him quite a bit. Times with Charlie and women didn't usually end up well and mostly, correct that, every time the fall out headed Monty's way. He tried his best not to look too much and so he listened to the music and tried to force himself to look at the table, or his milk shake, or the pool, although not at the ice cream freezer beside it. And then a Cliff Richard song came on the pool bar's radio. Three beats in and Monty knew what it was and already he was swaying to the rhythm and getting ready to mouth the words.

"When I was young, my father said,

Son I have something to say. Umph. Charlie had kicked him under the table.

As Charlie had reached for a napkin as an onion and some tomato sauce from his burger had stuck to his chin, he caught the eye of a woman sitting just two tables away. She grinned at him. He was convinced he had seen warmth in her smile, but he looked away embarrassed. He had continued to eat his burger and chips, although much more slowly and carefully now that he was sure she was watching him. He stole another glance, and there was the smile again. He was sure there was a "come on" in there.

Monty slurped his milk shake loud enough that the people at the pool in the hotel next door heard it and Charlie almost leaned over and cracked him one, but then he thought his female liaison might not approve of that so he sat tight and tried to ignore the sound. But then Monty had burped and Charlie almost had a fit. The restraint he had been able to conjure up surprised him and he helped himself remain calm by promising to deliver justice to Monty later. He tried another casual look and again there was the smile and the eyes this time. He was elected and that was no lie. He felt his chin and regretted not shaving that morning. Then he tried to remember if he had used deodorant, or even brushed his teeth. He couldn't remember. Never mind if he got this chick back to his room he could have a quick spruce up in the bathroom before he got down to the shaggy mamma stuff. He was delighted now that he had bought those multi coloured condoms as they did a great job hiding his super glued mangled manhood.

Then as he stole another glance, getting more confident now, another one of the women also smiled at him.

"Holy mamma," he thought, "they both want it." Then thinking that there were three of them at the table, "Jesus maybe all three of them want a good old servicing?"

He smiled, his best sexiest smile, but just as he did Monty started singing. Stunned for a second and caught between his smile to the lonely housewife threesome, and the burning desire to beat Monty to death with the bottle of tomato ketchup, he froze, now staring at this huge lump of lard singing like a fucking choir boy. He swung one of his little legs and kicked Monty as hard as he could under the table. Drawing back for a second kick he swung again, but by this time Monty had moved back slightly and so Charlie's little leg propelled his foot onwards and upwards until it connected with the underside of the table.

As Cliff now sang, "Son you'll be a bachelor boy until your dying days," glasses, plates and cutlery along with the sauce bottles took flight. Monty managed to save his chocolate milk shake but that was it. As the table had flipped up on Monty's side it had tilted back towards Charlie and so the laws of gravity had delivered it all in Charlie's direction, some landing in his lap the rest scattered and smashing on the tiled ground.

"Meet a girl and fall in love," Cliff continued, as Charlie gripped a fork he had removed from his lap. He was on his way up and off his seat, the fork on a perfect trajectory to Monty's right eye when he remembered his pending female fan club. He calmed, sort of, forced a smile, one straight out of his sexy repertoire, and sat back in his seat.

Thankfully the waitress was quickly on the scene and picked up what she could, and brushed up the rest. When she was gone Charlie took stock of his table of desire and was delighted to see that the smiles were still there. Before that fucker Monty could attempt to balls up his triple matinee any more he got to his feet and sauntered over to the women's table.

"Afternoon ladies," he said, his voice smooth and confident to make the most of his Irish accent, which he knew the women loved. "Can I get you chicks a drink?"

Their smiles turned in to giggles, which Charlie supposed was all part of the foreplay. Then the woman who had smiled at him first said, "A Baby Guinness!"

Now the giggles turned in to outright laughter. Charlie waited, still smiling his sexy smile waiting for the other two chicks to tell him what they wanted. Then he realised that the laughing was a conspiratorial laughter. They were leaning in to each other across the table, enjoying the joke and it suddenly dawned on Charlie that the joke was him.

"Baby Guinness!" They were calling him baby Guinness. At that moment he wished he had joined the circus all those years ago.

He stood there all five foot tall, feeling small and shrinking by the second.

Cliff was now singing, "But until then I'll be a bachelor boy and that's the way I'll stay." Monty was singing along as well.

Even Charlie's most dangerous weapon, his mouth, was silent. Frozen too in the moment. He walked away heading inside and then upstairs and then to their room to close the door tightly shut behind him. Monty watched him go and just assumed he was heading to the toilet and as the waitress was close to their table he seized his opportunity to order a Cornetto. A strawberry one as that was his favourite, a fact that he shared with the waitress. She smiled and he smiled too.

Chapter Twenty-Five

Tenerife, Canary Islands
Sunday 24th October 2021

Sasha had slept late, which was unusual for him. The previous day fishing in the hot sunshine followed by several drinks and too many chapters of the new Jeffrey Archer novel, "Over My Dead Body," had exhausted him. Then to cap things off when he had eventually gone to bed the storm he suspected was coming did put in an appearance during the small hours making sleep difficult. Now, sleeping late mixed with the slight hangover left him drowsy and fatigued and so he ditched his plans to head out for a second days fishing. Instead he cleaned his boat and bedded it down for another week.

Once he was sorted he collected his cooler, which contained the fish he had caught and headed to the marina's office to give some of the fish to his friend there Alonso and enquire who owned the boat he had seen last night and now knew was called, "The Carrickfergus Princess."

Jeffrey had also slept late, but not just as late as Sasha. Tired from his own exploits from the previous day and having also polished off Dennis's Johnny Walker's Black Label, it was almost ten when he had awoke busting for the bog.

The first thing he had done was to look in on Dennis, which had left him slightly shocked and worried as the man looked grim. He was beginning to wonder if he had the Corona virus as he was so washed out, weak and wretched. He did seem to have a temperature, although the heat in their rooms was stifling as they had no air conditioning. The only thing he didn't seem to have was a cough.

He gave him some fresh water and some paracetomol and left him alone. He had asked him what he needed. A doctor? More medicine or tablets? Something to eat? But Dennis had refused them all. Concerned that he wouldn't be fit to go to their bank the following morning, Jeffrey forced him to take more tablets.

So Jeffrey had got showered and dressed and headed out for breakfast and another walk about to see if he could spy that little shit Charlie Bassett. And thankfully he wasn't the only person looking for him now.

He did need help, but Ritchie had turned himself in to a liability when he had bribed the maid and so Jeffrey had no choice but to sever his employment, short and all as it had been.

So Jeffrey then thought he could maybe utilise Ritchie side kick Kevin. He text Kevin from Ritchie's phone and informed him that they were no longer looking for Jeffrey the Digger as he was now on board with them. He also told him that Arnie had gone to Santa Cruz and wouldn't be back for a couple of days. Kevin's instructions were to work with Jeffrey to try and find Charlie Bassett. Jeffrey had air dropped a photo of Charlie from his phone to Ritchie's and sent it to Kevin. Then he had told Kevin to meet Jeffrey tomorrow at noon at the café where he'd been watching him the day before.

Finally, after some text tennis, he had told Kevin, again from Ritchie's phone, that he would be away himself for a couple of days doing another job for Arnie and Bobby.

Jeffrey had sunk Arnie's phone to the bottom of the sea where Nemo was now probably using it to take selfies, but he had decided to hold on to Ritchie's. Risky as it was to hold on to a dead mans phone, he thought that Ritchie's could be worth the risk and be useful over the next few days. Next trip out on his boat, and if all went to plan he would have another deep sea excursion to look forward to in the upcoming days, he could then sink Ritchie's phone and offer Nemo a free upgrade.

He walked beach front until he skirted Los Cristianos and then headed inland to come back in a loop along the main road and back to his favourite café for breakfast. There were plenty of people mingled about and still many in fancy dress, even though it was still mid morning. Holiday's made some people carry on and do crazy things. He had just passed someone dressed up as a bear and the heat, even though it was still early, must be just over thirty degrees. Stunts like that could give you heat stroke.

But once again there was no sign of Charlie Bassett. He wondered if maybe he was waltzing around dressed up and maybe he'd passed him a dozen times already without knowing. But unless Charlie used stilts, which would also make him stand out, the likely costumes he could dress up in would be as a Gnome, an Elf, a Leprechaun, an Umpa Lumpas or maybe even old Nemo himself, although it would need to be a more sardine version of Nemo as opposed to a full size one, and he hadn't seen anything like any of these on his travels. Looked like he was going to have to rely on Kevin scouting Charlie out, so he went on to the café, even though he was early for his meeting.

At the café he ordered breakfast, no egg or bacon this time, just extra toast. Once sorted he settled down to think about his plans.

Dennis was his key concern. But there was nothing he could do but to keep him hydrated and well enough to make it to the bank in the morning. After that he didn't really care.

He'd put Kevin on Charlie and that would free him up for the rest of the day to deal with the double crossing shite, the Russian.

He had never liked the Russian, or trusted him at all; it was Dennis who had the relationship. Jeffrey had suggested several times that there were other options either in the Canary Islands, in Europe or across the coast in Morocco or Africa, and he had contacts in all that could replace the Russian. So maybe that was the play? Let knowledge be king. He knew that he was trying to make moves behind Dennis's back, so why not just make moves behind his. He decided that this maybe needed some more thought, but he also did like that he could think these things through without Dennis's input. Having Dennis off the board was good. As he was thinking, his breakfast arrived. He let the waiter set it out and when he had gone, he went back to his thoughts on Dennis and the business. If he played his cards right over the next couple of day's maybe he could then afford to buy a Rolex like Dennis's. He had travelled here to assist Dennis, but now the way things had progressed he could be on his way to a successful takeover bid. That sounded like music to his ears.

He sat back in his seat to relax and wait for Kevin.

Ray was also trying to relax and he did this best when playing music. They had prepared all they could in terms of planning for tomorrow, and he had done it all without feeling really anything about what they were about to do. What he was about to get his friends and family involved in. But now he had Butterflies in his stomach, or maybe more accurate too much air in his head.

Was he mad? Had he lost his perspective? He just didn't know. He flitted between calling it off and then feeling weak and selfish. Then he told himself he had to go through with it and yet again he felt weak and selfish.

So he'd done what he had done many times before and turned to music to try and hide the demons and distract him from the thoughts in his own mind. The music was Coldplay and the song was Everglow. It was one of the songs he was using to practice and improve his piano skills, and practice he needed as in his opinion he was miles away, probably years, from coming close to Tracey. But practice was the key, it was as simple as that, and there were no short cuts when it came to mastering a musical instrument. The more you played, the better you got, but it could also be a slow process.

He loved the piano, but preferred to play the organ. This was just simply down to were his skill level was at, and a little to do with the songs he chose to play with the organ, but he felt the note transition on the organ was easier because you could hold it for a split second longer if you were hesitant. If you were hesitant on the piano it got noticed.

The song also suited his mood. It's slow, sultry melody and simple but beautiful words sang almost pleadingly by Chris Martin were a strong and fixating mix. He was trying to emulate both Martin's singing and piano playing. He did admit he was coming up short on both as Martin was a skilled pianist like Tracey, and he also had one of those voices you could pick out from a crowd. Regardless Ray was enjoying the music and the words and the place they both took his mind to. Some of the words came through more than others, just like they did with most songs because they meant something to him, or because their meaning was cryptic, or because they were just beautiful words written with skill.

"There's a light that you give me,

When I'm in shadow,

There's a feeling you give me, an everglow."

Ray played and sang on unaware that Liz had softly entered the room.

"But when I'm cold, cold,

In water rolled, salt."

Liz stood at the door. She wanted to approach Ray, put her arms around his neck as he sang, but she was worried he would stop playing and singing if he knew she was there. So she stood, closed her eyes and listened. Wishing he was singing it for her.

"Oh what I would give for just a moment to hold, Yeah I live for this feeling, its everglow,

So if you love someone,

You should let them know."

Ray sat silent after he had finished the song.

"Chris Martin wrote that song about the break up of his marriage," she said, and immediately saw that she had startled him. "You never wrote a song for me when we split up."

She had made him jump. He reached to his old cassette recorder, as he had been taping his playing so that he could listen back and catch the mistakes. But he didn't want to record their conversation. He thought, "no Cliff Richard had already recorded that one, he wasn't sure if he had written it, Congratulations!" But he didn't say this, he wouldn't dare. Instead he dodged it, "you startled me there," he said as he twisted round on the stool to face where her voice had came from.

"Sorry," she said, "I didn't mean to. Your piano playing has come on loads that was really good."

He knew it was OK at best, certainly not really good, "thanks," he said, and then made his first mistake, "Tracey has been a good teacher."

He felt the buzz of tension and the cold draft caused by the mention of Tracey.

If Liz had been a cat her fur would have rose and spiked as if by an electric shock. And maybe her back would have arched? She tried to push past it and said, "have you any other new songs I haven't heard you play before? Joe says your new guitar sounds great."

The piano had been dismissed. Ray read it, play the guitar now Ray not the shitty piano.

They had learned loads of new stuff before coming out to Tenerife and so he tried to think of something he knew she wouldn't like. "We've added a few Eagles," he said.

"Nah," she said, and then asked, "any Westlife?"

"Westlife don't have any songs," Ray said and knew he was just being a pratt.

"What?" Liz asked puzzled, "they've loads, I must have," she paused working out a number, "well over fifty anyway."

"But they're not Westlife songs," stated Ray, "they only sing other people's songs."

She said nothing, not certain what to answer. Ray then felt bad, he knew he was being a bit of a prick and you could argue all night on how many songs Westlife had or didn't have. Loads of people sang other peoples songs; he was making a living out of it, or at least trying to. So why get uppity about Westlife?

"We've a couple of nice Biffy Clyro." He said, trying to be nice.

"Who?"

He didn't answer as he was thinking who she would like.

"Did you never write some of your own," she asked, "you always said you were going to."

He had, but didn't want to sing them to Liz. He was hoping that Joe hadn't told her and so took a risk.

"No not yet, too busy with all this."

She nodded, then realised her mistake and spoke, "you should you know, you with the poetry and all."

He had written her poems, but that was years ago. He still wrote, but mainly funny ones for friend's birthdays and stuff.

"Yeah," he said. He yawned, "I think I should pack up and go to bed."

"Alone?" she said straight away.

He knew she was teasing, but suspected there was some hope also mixed in there, and he sensed her loneliness. Sensed it because he knew it so well, but even though he too wanted what he suspected Liz wanted he didn't want them to find it together. He had loved her but that was well in their past. He admitted that he did still love her, but it was only a part love and also partly because of Joe. His opinion was that Liz was a complicated woman. The complexity came from the various women that lived inside her, and there were a few, and there was only one of them he liked.

"Liz!" he said.

"Sorry," she said, or sang to be more accurately, "ah go on play something, even play that one again it was lovely. The Coldplay one?"

He sighed.

"Please?" she pleaded.

He needed the practice, and he did want to go to bed, tomorrow was going to be a challenging day.

"OK," he said, "just the one."

He turned back to the keyboard and got set to play, but then turned around again and set his machine to record, then twisted back to begin to play.

He made a couple of mistakes on the intro, so he stopped for a couple of seconds and then started again.

Liz leaned back against the door, listening and contemplating on things loved and things lost. She wanted to embrace Ray as he sang and played, but she resisted.

"Life was tough", she thought and then remembered something her father always said, "look forward not back, you can't change the past but you can fix the future." She smiled, enjoying the song and her thoughts. "Maybe tomorrow would be a better day?"

Ray finished the song and switched the keyboard off. As he was bending down to get the cover Liz said.

"Ray, I think I'm going to lose the house."

He sat back up on the stool; the keyboards cover in his hand and swivelled around to face Liz.

"Lose the house?" he asked, surprise in his voice.

Liz forced back the tears and said, "yes."

Ray waited for her to say more but she was silent. He thought he heard a faint sniffle.

"Tell me," he said gently, "everything," he added, with a little no nonsense to his tone as he knew only too well that Liz's pride would make this difficult for her. He waited patiently to give her space and time.

Eventually she said, "I'm behind on the mortgage."

After some time Ray needed to prompt, "How behind?" He waited for some time and then had to say, "Liz?"

"Almost a year."

Ray paid her half of the mortgage each month as Joe lived there, but he tried not to sound judgemental or angry.

"But how?" he asked, keeping his voice flat. He heard more sniffles, louder this time.

"I'm not giving you a hard time Liz, but if you don't tell me how and why how can I help you?"

The tears came then and she spoke through them, her voice tripping on some of the words.

"I know you pay me Ray, I know that I'm sorry, I'm sorry Ray."

"I'm not looking for an apology Liz," he said, thinking that he should go to her, but also knowing that to comfort her now might stop her telling him everything. He had been here before, so he stayed put, even though a part of him felt bad, cold for doing so.

"I know Ray, I know," she blubbered, "I'm sorry, sorry, oh I'm a mess."

"Liz," he said calmly, "please tell me, tell me and I can help."

She sniffled and took some deep breaths. "I'm going to lose the house Ray, the house, everything."

"Have the bank said that?"

She didn't answer.

"Liz, have the bank said they're going to repossess the house?"

"No," she said, "I don't know, I don't know."

He was confused. "What do you mean you don't know?"

After a few moments she said, "I haven't opened the last letter." Another pause. "The last few letters. Oh Ray, I'm sorry."

He wanted to ask her where the money had gone. What had she spent it on? He remembered her arrival that morning and the shopping bags. Why was she here, on holiday? He wanted to ask her lots of things, but he didn't. He thought it would all sound accusing, judging.

"I need to know everything Liz, everything."

After some time she told him. The story of her spiral in to debt. First credit cards, then loans then more of the same, until the loans were from quick money high interest and then finally from back street lenders that didn't lend money or recover it with conventional methods that were monitored by some financial body. It was a classic story like an old fairy tale, or more likely an old horror story, and unfortunately it was quite common place. When she had finished he said.

"First thing we need to do is contact the bank about the house. We'll do that tomorrow."

She nodded, then caught herself and said, "OK." Then almost in a child like voice she asked, "will you do it for me Ray?"

"On one condition," he said, "and I mean this."

"What?" she asked, worry in her voice.

"You write down every penny you owe, and who to," then he did stand up and go to her, embracing her, "and you be totally honest, OK."

She nodded in to his chest and this time even though he still couldn't see her, she knew he had felt her do so.

"Then we'll put the list away until you get home and we'll sort it out then. As long as we sort the house from here tomorrow, then the rest can wait." He squeezed her, "that a deal?"

She nodded again. "Ray?"

"Yeah?"

"Don't tell Joe, please?" she pleaded.

"Joe doesn't need to know," he said, then thought, "that is as long as we can save the house!"

As they stood there Ray was reflecting that this Liz was the Liz he had fell in love with all those years ago. The other Liz, the brash one with all the "darling" and "sweetie" and all that brass front was the one he had divorced. But divorce or no divorce, they both had a son together and that would always create a bond between them, and that bond meant that he would help her in any way that he could.

"Thanks Ray," she whispered in to his chest.

Chapter Twenty-Six

Tenerife, Canary Islands
Monday 25th October 2021

Ray had never seen Terry in such a rage. It seemed so stupid but he was asking himself was it because of the bad sun burn. Or the sheer pressure of the situation? Whatever the reason, he was losing it and he was in danger of fucking this up for them all.

"Terry, calm down," shouted Ray, "calm down." But Terry continued to prod the bank teller in the chest with the shot-gun. "Jesus Terry, take it easy."

Things were starting to unravel out of control and Terry's adrenalin was pushing him to breaking point. Ray was regretting giving him the only real gun they had, but he had never seen Terry like this before, he was usually so calm and so under control. But he had never robbed a bank with Terry before, so they were sailing on uncharted waters.

Pushing the gun now in to the bank tellers face Terry screamed, "go near that button again and I'll fucking blow your fucking head off."

The teller backed up, but Terry pushed forward with the same aggression. The two female tellers were in hysterics and they weren't helping. "Ladies," Ray shouted, "go out there with the customers," pointing now, "out there, and sit down on the floor." They didn't move. "It will be OK," said Ray, "we're only here for the money, and no one is going to get hurt."

"I fucking told you," Terry said shouting again, then reversed the angle of the shot-gun and brought the wooden stock crashing down on the bank tellers head. His head split with a wet thwack and the blood splattered everywhere. The two female tellers screamed louder, and one grabbed the other to hold on as if she was going to faint. Before Ray could react shouting came from the front of the bank. It was Aurimas. "No," he heard him shout, and then there was a crash of glass.

"What's happening?" screamed Ray, "Aurimas, what's going on?" There was no answer. More shouting from more voices this time. Voices Ray didn't recognise. "Aurimas," Ray shouted again, pleading for an answer.

Terry spun around now ignoring the male teller who was crumpled on the floor, blood pouring from his head. The two female tellers jumped back to get out of his way as if Terry had some sort of contagious disease. But maybe he had worse. He had a gun, a weapon he had shown he would not hesitate to use. Sensing what Terry was about to do, Ray shouted, "No, Terry, no." He pushed himself forward to try and intercept him, but the movement of the two female tellers had now blocked his path. Fear gripped Ray like terror he had never felt before, never thought it was possible to feel. He felt sick. He had caused this. It was his fault, he had to try and stop what was about to happen.

Boom, boom.

"No, no," shouted Ray, tears running down his face now, but the gun shot and the screaming drowned out his own voice.

Another boom.

"NO."

Glass shattered and screams filled the entire space. The smoke and smell of gun fire was sickening. Ray fell to his knees, the whole thing now a blur, sweat and tears blinding him. He crawled forward on the floor and stopped when his hands touched something. He felt it, it was a face. He moved closer, his hands still probing. Then he felt the blood, and at the same time realised that the body wasn't moving. He pulled himself closer, the smoke and noise choking out all of his senses. He inched closer, but it was like the world had slowed down and everything was happening in slow motion. He tried to force his hands to move quicker but they felt too heavy. Too heavy for him to move, he just didn't have the strength. His entire body felt heavy and awkward and alien to him. It was like he was being sucked down in to a dark abyss and he just didn't have the power to resist. Someone pushed passed him and stood on his leg twisting his knee, he winced with the pain, but the pain was like a shock that brought him back and jolted his mind to reboot. He touched the face once

more. The body now below him as if he was trying to protect it. It seemed familiar to him, which in that moment seemed strange. Then it spoke. The voice rasping and trying its best to cling to the little life it had left, and the sound was almost inaudible in the midst of all the other noise. But Ray heard it. Two words muffled and faint, but enough to change the path of his life forever.

"Dad, dad."

"Joe, no, no, Joe, Joe."

His strength totally failed him then and the black took him, pulled him down deep, deep to a place where he had no will, no want to ever return from.

With his head spinning and his entire body sweating, he woke up. For some moments there in the dark of the early morning before dawn he sat completely still, the images of the dream still etched there on his mind like a movie reel. It was weird, he could see in his dreams. Every image was sharp, in full colour and distinct. He saw people as he imagined them to look and even though it was totally unlike his real life which was full of shadows, it seemed so life like and real to him. So real it took him several minutes to calm. Did dreams mean something? Was there a warning here, or were his dreams just a mix of what was going through his mind? Unfortunately nobody knew the answer so it was up to each individual to take out or translate their dreams to mean whatever. Now calmer he was only thankful that it had been a dream. He hit the button on his phone on the bedside table to check the time and it said, "one o three." It was going to be a long night as he guessed that sleep might be impossible now. He thought of getting up and going downstairs, but he was concerned that Liz might either still be up or as she was in the room next door, hear him up and come down to join him, but he wanted to remain alone. He was nervous about tomorrow, nervous and worried. But he also felt that he needed to be both of these things as he needed to make sure that these feelings helped him ensure that he pulled it off and that the plans he had made, and could still make, would be good enough. So he lay and thought and listened to the breeze through the trees and the sound of the sea. He loved this place, both Tenerife and this villa and he felt privileged to be here. Privileged to be living a life here doing what he loved best, playing music. Or was that wrong? Was music his favourite thing, or was his favourite thing proving that he could do what sighted people could do. Regardless of the fact that he was blind? There in the dark, on his own, he was honest with himself when he said, "I love them both!"

Chapter Twenty-Seven

Tenerife, Canary Islands
Monday 25th October 2021

Colin had pulled over and was giving them time to put their costumes on. Knowing they couldn't see he reassured them that the people carrier had tinted windows. It wasn't that they were undressing, as they were putting the costumes on over their T shirts and shorts; it was so that they knew they could put their head wear on and not worry about being seen.

"This fucking thing is itching my sun burn," said Terry.

"Live with it," said Ray, "it's the only one that fits you. Anyway this wig is driving me mad as well; I don't know what it's bloody made off. But let's hope we don't have them on for long."

Aurimas was blowing in to an air valve.

"What's that?" asked Terry.

"Your shoulders," said Aurimas, "you can inflate them, it's cool."

"That reminded me of my last blow job," said Terry.

"Fair play," said Aurimas, "you can remember that far back."

"Piss off!"

"Move over," Aurimas said, "I need to do your other shoulder."

"Fuck sake," moaned Terry, "wait till I get that fucker Joe, I think he picked these suits for badness."

"It was all they had," said Ray, "We needed ones with head wear to hide the headsets."

"You're hairier than Bumper," Aurimas teased, "pity he's not here as he might take a fancy to you."

"Fuck you," said Terry, "I bet you look like a fucking knob too."

"No Terrence," Aurimas said, "A bowling pin, not a knob."

Ray was amazed how relaxed Aurimas was. He himself was a bundle of nerves and thought he could throw up, especially considering the heat in this costume. He also knew that Terry was nervous as he heard the tension in his voice.

"We can still back out," Ray offered, "We don't need to go ahead with this if anyone doesn't want to."

No one spoke.

"I mean it," stated Ray.

"I'm good," said Aurimas.

"I'm just fucking itchy," said Terry.

"So would I be," laughed Aurimas, "if I slept for four hours in the sun."

Terry decided that silence was the best answer in this instance.

Ray hit the button on the side of his watch, it said, "nine forty for A M." It was an old watch he didn't use any more but thought it would be useful today.

"How far is it Colin?"

"Less than five minutes," Colin answered.

"All dressed," he asked.

"No," said Aurimas, "I can't get this head piece over my head set. Could you give me a hand, if I hold the head set could you pull down the mask thing."

Ray did and they got it sorted, but then Aurimas said, "Sorry Ray, I forgot my face mask."

Aurimas's suit was the only one that left his face revealed as it poked through the front of the head piece so he was going to wear a virus face mask and sunglasses to hide his face. The face mask also hid his mike from the head set. Ray helped him take it off again and once Aurimas had his mask on this time he pulled the head piece in to place.

"Cheers," said Aurimas, "anybody wanna go bowling?"

"Don't have the guns out until we're inside the bank, not until I speak." Reminded Ray. He was running through things in his mind, thinking his way through each step.

After fixing his own head set, wig, beard and hat he said, "Let's test the head sets."

Terry spoke, then Aurimas then Ray.

"All good," asked Ray.

"Loud and clear," said Aurimas.

"OK," said Terry.

Ray checked the time again, his watch said, "nine forty eight A M."

The bank opened at nine thirty but they wanted to wait for thirty minutes and had set ten o'clock as their target entry time. They didn't want to be there and possibly have to queue outside; Ray didn't think that bank robbers bothered to queue.

"We should probably go Colin," said Ray, "and hook up with Joe."

Colin restarted the engine and pulled back out of the parking space. He took greater care than usual to avoid his fellow drivers, and pedestrians. He wasn't sure why, must be the nerves. As he drove out of the supermarket car park he spoke to Ray.

"Once I drop you Ray I'm heading on to switch vehicles, it's the same type just a different colour. I'll be exactly fifteen minutes."

Terry coughed, Aurimas laughed. Ray thought it best to say nothing. Colin knew what the jibe was.

"I won't be late," he said, his voice that of an innocent man saying, "as if I would!" Then he added for good measure and to provide reassurance, "I've timed this yesterday."

"Fifteen is good," confirmed Ray.

"I'll sit facing out, the same way I'm dropping you off. That is if no one else is parked there. If so I'll pump the horn, so if you hear the horn I'll be in the second parking bay which is over to your right coming out from the bank. That OK?"

"Yes, Joe and I walked it yesterday with Bumper," Ray said, his adrenalin starting to unsettle his stomach.

He heard the beep of Colin's fare meter to indicate the journey charge increasing. "You got this on the meter?" asked Ray.

"You fucking bet," said Colin, "you fuckers get caught and I'm pleading that I just picked you up as a fare, thought you were going to a fancy dress party."

"Have you the air con on?" asked Terry, "it's fucking roasting in here. And since we're paying for the fare surely we can be comfortable?"

"That's cause you're in a bloody furry suit," said Colin, "I'll turn it up." He turned it up to high for cooler air. A few seconds later he felt the cold air, which was really cold, too cold for him. He asked himself the same old question, "Why do people come to places like Tenerife then complain about the heat?" OK Terry had an excuse as he was wrapped up like a cuddly bear, but the amount of people he taxied that just complained about the heat. For him, when he came back to Tenerife from a trip back to the UK he looked forward to that moment when the plane's doors opened and you could not only feel, but smell the heat. Bring it on, that was why Colin lived in Tenerife.

They were all quiet for the next few minutes as Colin drove through streets he knew had no CCTV. This was something else he had checked out yesterday. Most of it he knew as he drove these streets and roads every day of his life, but he had taken care to double check and had mapped out his routes to avoid them all. The only one he couldn't avoid was the one in the bank which he was almost sure would provide an outside view. This was why he was using two vehicles, and both with false number plates. Like most people Colin had watched lots of movies and he had seen criminals switch number plates off vehicles in car parks and places like that. Luckily for Colin he had a stack of them that were obsolete as he scoured the scrap yards for parts for his fleet of passenger vehicles, and he had brought many cars and vans back to his garage that he had stripped for spares. Sometimes he had also came across the odd number plate that was worth money, either by it's mix of letters or numbers that were either obvious as a name, or one you could manipulate the type of numbering to resemble letters, which then made it read like a name. Personal number plates were a big thing now and he was always surprised that the original owner of the vehicle hadn't realised that the value of the registration number was worth more than the vehicle.

"There's Joe," Colin said as they turned the penultimate corner before the banks street, "Tracey's with him, I thought she wasn't coming?"

"So did I," said Ray, feeling a pang of fear as he was concerned she too had changed her mind and was here to stop them going through with it. "Pull over beside them," he said, "we need to sync our head sets with Joe."

Colin did as Ray had asked and several seconds after the car had stopped Ray heard a beep in his ear that signalled that another device had just joined.

"Dad," said Joe, "can you hear me?"

"Yes," answered Ray then added, "Terry, Aurimas you getting Joe?" Both confirmed. Ray then asked a question that he was worried what the answer would be. "Joe, why is Tracey here?"

Sensing his dads nervous question Joe said, "It's OK, she changed her mind, she said I shouldn't be going in alone."

"OK," Ray answered his nerves now beginning to fray as the gig got closer. He swallowed then asked, "We all good to go?"

They all confirmed.

"Good," he said, taking a breath, "let's go. Joe we'll meet you at the door. As we discussed, when we start getting out of the car, you go in. OK?"

Joe said, "Yes."

Ray could hear the nerves in his son's voice and it made him feel awful, and bad, and a lousy father. It made his own nerves bubble up in his throat like bile. He swallowed to try to force it down, but that almost made him sick. He gagged and had to bite deep to stop himself from being sick. His mind won the battle thinking how poor it would look to everyone else. His idea, his lead, his gig and he was the one that puked before they'd even gone in the door. He took a deep breath and forced himself to calm.

"You OK Ray," Terry asked.

The fact that Terry had noticed his distress made him feel embarrassed, but the embarrassment brought him round and he said, "All good Terry thanks, just roasting in this suit."

Several seconds later they felt the swing of the car as Colin manoeuvred the nose out so that he could reverse in to the space he had hoped was free, and it was. When he was in place Colin said, "OK boys, good luck. See you in fifteen."

Ray unlocked the left hand door and slid it back. He stepped out and used his finger to trace along the car until he reached the rear. Once there he felt for the curb with his toe then stepped up. Joe came over in his ear.

"That's you, you're in line."

Ray didn't answer, that was the arrangement. Then Joe spoke again, "it's busy in here."

Ray heard the door slide back shut and then he felt Aurimas's hand touch his back gently and then move to his left. Terry then came last, which again they had arranged, touched Ray to get his bearings and then moved to his right. Ray said, "Go." Then began to count quietly, "one, two, three," he kept his steps measured and the three of them moved in sync, "four, five, six," Sweat began to run down Ray's neck. He heard Terry blow out. Aurimas seemed calm. "Seven, eight, nine," Ray said a silent prayer, quickly. "Ten, eleven." They had reached the door, he said, "OK," to tell Terry and Aurimas they were at the door, and then he reached out for the handle and began to pull it open.

There was no going back now. The words of the Clash song, "Police and Thieves," popped in to his mind.

"Police and thieves in the street,

Oh yeah!"

"Oh no," he thought, that was the one thing could fuck them up.

Chapter Twenty-Eight

Tenerife, Canary Islands
Monday 25th October 2021

All the positives gained from the relaxing weekend spent on his boat had evaporated and as a result Sasha Moreno felt like he was carrying the baggage that usually dredged him down at the end of the working week, and it was still only early on Monday morning. Even before he had signed on for his shift he knew the day was doomed when he discovered that someone had stolen his police car, which he had left in a public car park when he had decided to go drinking on Friday afternoon. He had planned to collect it on Saturday morning and return it to the station, but his rush to go fishing had made him put that off until this morning. He knew he was going to face a disciplinary for that one.

Once the theft had been reported, his boss, the arrogant French prick, Claude Eno, had chewed his ass off on the phone for over twenty minutes, during which Sasha had counted how many times he had been able to get the mumbling twit to repeat himself as due to his thick French accent and the marbles in his mouth no one could hardly understand a word he was saying. The station record for repeats in one meeting or call was currently twenty six. Sasha only achieved a mere fifteen on this call. But the game had still kept him occupied as his idiot boss had rambled on and deflected away from some of what he was saying, which due to the fact that his assigned car had been stolen some of the abuse was probably well deserved. The loss of his mode of transport, reporting the theft, and the time lag for his bollocking, had placed Sasha's plans for the morning in disarray. He had hoped to interview the bank staff from the robbery on the previous Thursday and then spend the rest of the morning visiting other banks in the area to make them aware of the robbery and also check if the person who owned the safety deposit boxes that had been robbed, rented any boxes in any other bank.

While fishing over the weekend off the west coast of Tenerife he had concluded that he was almost certain that the robbery had inside help and involvement. Even thought some of the actions could be easily put down to incompetence, he thought the lack of CCTV and no raised alarm were far too serious to put down to chance. He also considered that the knowledge of what was inside the deposit boxes to make them worth stealing was something that only their owner and the bank would know. His hunch also told him that the owner of the deposit boxes likely did indeed own boxes in other banks as people wanting to "stash" valuables tended to spread them around. So he was now on his way to visit some of the other banks in the area, and he was on his way on foot.

Jeffrey and Dennis were standing in the queue. The bank was very busy; they assumed it was because it was Monday morning. Dennis was struggling and Jeffrey was standing close almost ready to prop him up should he begin to fall. The sweat was dripping off his face and you could easily see that his shirt was saturated. Jeffrey was hoping they wouldn't get thrown out if they thought that Dennis had the virus. Jeffrey thought he might. The bank was actually quite pleasant as the air conditioning was running and the high ceilings gave the sense of space. Jeffrey was trying to watch Dennis and at the same time watch the customers and who was coming and going. He had Kevin posted to watch their other bank where they planned to go after this one. But even though they were almost at the front of the queue he was worried that Dennis was even going to make it to this counter never mind another several streets away.

In an effort to get Dennis prepared to come here he had given him a cold shower. It was Dennis's request. He had placed one of the plastic chairs from the balcony in to the shower cubicle, which allowed him to sit there under a tirade of cold water. It had revived him, but he was now lagging again and could do with another session in the shower.

"You OK?" he asked.

Dennis just nodded. It had been a weak nod, but Jeffrey could see it had taken an effort. He checked the counter hoping things would hurry up but some guy seemed to be taking an age. He casually checked the people in the queue behind him, but it was difficult to see if anyone looked suspicious with all the masks and sunglasses. He heard a slight moan from Dennis and turned back to check on him. Jesus he looked shit.

"C'mon," he said, taking Dennis's arm, "there's a chair over there, you need to sit down before you fall down." Dennis didn't refuse or resist.

Jeffrey turned to the girl behind and said, "Could you please mind my place?" Thankfully she nodded as he wasn't sure if she was or spoke English, but she obviously did. He walked Dennis over to the chair and sat him down. He almost collapsed as he was so weak.

"I think I need a doctor," said Dennis weakly.

"Maybe," Jeffrey answered, but thought, "Not where you're going boss when we get our cash sorted." Then he said, "We'll get you sorted when we sort the money out. That's what we came over here for."

He thought Dennis sort of nodded, but he wasn't sure. "I'll be back when it's our turn." Jeffrey said then headed back to his place in the queue. His phone beeped. He checked already knowing it would be from Kevin sending his thirty minute update. Jeffrey didn't need to check the time as there was a large ornate clock on the wall of the bank, which showed it was exactly ten o'clock. Kevin's message reported, "all clear."

Liz was checking the time on her watch and wondering where everyone had gone. She had checked every room in the villa and outside and no one was there. She was trying to remember if they had told her last night that they had something on this morning, but she didn't recall anything. She thought, or assumed, that Ray was going to call her bank this morning about her mortgage, although as she went back over their conversation she remembered that he had said tomorrow, so maybe he meant later. The villa was quiet and the only sound was the hum of the air conditioning, which she wanted to turn off as it was quite cool. She looked around for the controls and noticed a panel over by the patio doors. She went over and hit several buttons until she heard it knock off, then she opened the patio doors. Even though it was still only ten in the morning she felt the heat rushing in the door and she welcomed it.

She went to the kettle and flicked it on again, then went back upstairs to change from her pyjamas to her bikini. She may as well take advantage of the sun and have her coffee by the pool. And she might as well top up her tan as she did so.

At that same time a big furry dog was standing by a lamp post, but he wasn't thinking about having a piss. He was watching the bank across the road in an effort to ensure that that Jazz Junior didn't screw him over.

Charlie Bassett had been sulking on his balcony the day before, following his encounter with the three witches of Tenerife, when he thought about all the fancy dress that was about. This gave him an idea that would enable him to get out of this apartment and check up on junior without worrying about the digger catching him. So he had sent Monty out to buy some costumes, but he might as well have phoned up the Euthanasia society and asked them if they had a buy one get one free offer going at the moment.

On the first trip, Monty came back, his shirt covered in ice cream stains and with two ballerina costumes, which were both the same size. For badness Charlie made him try one on. Fifteen minutes later he had the tights up as far as his knees, the little lacy skirty Tutu thing around his waist, which he had repaired with cellotape as it had ripped, and the top just over his head and through his arms, but stretched so tight that his arms were suspended in mid air unable to move. He looked like Widow Twanky's Frankenstein on speed. Charlie sent him out again.

Almost one hour later he returned with fresh ice cream stains on his shirt and cornetto wrappers sticking out from his pocket. He had though managed to purchase three costumes; a dolphin that you blew up then stood in the middle of, which Monty said was cute. Charlie pointed out that it did nothing to disguise him as his fucking entire upper body was sticking out for all to see, and then burst it with a fork. Monty nearly took off out the patio doors. The second outfit was a cowboy, consisting of a hat, a gun belt and wader sort of things that went over your trousers. When Charlie asked how no one would recognise him, Monty demonstrated that you could walk with your head down and the cowboy hat sort of tilted forward and down to hide your face. Charlie took the hat and beat Monty with it until the decorative band flew off.

The third costume had promise. It was a bowling pin. Charlie tried it on and almost died with an asthma attack. The suit was made of foam and designed to be worn with a full body suit and then a head piece that pulled over your head with your eyes and mouth poking out the front. Charlie put the body suit on but when he put his arms through their holes his head didn't reach over the top of the body, instead the foam hugged in around him making it difficult for him to breathe. As Charlie jumped around the room trying to force his head out from the suit, Monty chased him with the head piece thinking they were playing a game. It was the most fun Monty had enjoyed the entire holiday. Charlie had gone to lie down after this one, but an hour later he sent Monty out once more for another attempt. This time he tried to provide him with a few more pointers. And also an incentive. "Come back with any more shitty costumes and I'm going to blow your balls off with the shot gun," advised Charlie.

Twenty minutes later he returned with two outfits. The first was a dog with a full head and body set. Charlie was wary of this as he thought one more asthma attack today and he was fucked. The other was a pirate's costume. It did have face coverings, a hat, an eye patch and a beard, so Charlie tried it on. It wasn't bad, wasn't too bad at all. He added all the accessories, the bandana, the two swashbuckler swords, one on each hip. Yes, he really looked the part, and there was no way that the digger or anybody else would recognise him. He headed out of the bedroom to show Monty, but his low stature didn't allow the two swords to sit proudly by his sides, ready for him to grab in an instant and cut down anybody in his path. Instead they caught in the doorway, locked under his feet and the door jam, bent to they reached their full elasticity before breaking, but instead of snapping like twigs, they sprang back to their original shape and pole vaulted Charlie forward and straight in to Monty's arms. As he took flight across the room, Charlie shouted, "ship ahoy there shipmates, shiver me timbers."

Monty thinking that Charlie was being nice and wanting a hug squeezed him like an orange then gave him a big sloppy kiss. Charlie cursed and spat, ripped off the costume and threw it in the bin.

The dog it would have to be. And it wasn't bad, although he had to make a few adjustments. Anyone that looked would notice that he didn't have any lower paws as Charlie needed to cut these off as the legs were too long. But apart from that the only other thing was he was looking out his mouth and not his eyes, but it worked and nobody would recognise him.

Charlie did think he recognised someone though. A guy who was sitting at a café across the road, who seemed to be chatting up some hot chick and to Charlie's frustration, he looked like he was on to a winner. Charlie immediately disliked him. He couldn't place the name but he was certain he had seen him before and he was certain that that had been back in Belfast. OK there were hundreds, maybe thousands of people here on holiday from Belfast, but this guy was someone that moved in the circles that Charlie did, or at least tried to. He wasn't sure though if this guy worked for Dennis and the Digger, or maybe their key rival Bobby Mulhern, but one thing he was sure of was that he was watching the bank just like Charlie was and he was also sending messages to someone on his phone.

Monty was sitting at the table behind him wearing his own form of disguise. He was wearing a huge sombrero, sunglasses and a large droopy Mexican moustache. Even at some distance away Charlie could see that the moustache was already covered in ice cream. He just shook his head. Bonny had Clyde, Dick Dastardly had Mutley and he had Monty. Life just wasn't fair.

Monty though had the shot-gun, which was in part giving Charlie some confidence and cover. It was hidden and duck taped underneath his Mexican poncho, which was as big, if not bigger, than a blanket. Its size not only provided great cover but it gave Monty the flexibility to be able to swing the gun to aim it at someone without having to remove it from the poncho. Charlie bet that Clint Eastwood had one of these in those westerns.

So Monty could have as many Cornetto's as he wanted, just as long as if the shit hit the fan he was there to cover Charlie's arse.

Chapter Twenty-Nine

Tenerife, Canary Islands
Monday 25th October 2021

Ray went through the door, his heart pumping and his mouth now dry. He tried his best to concentrate and think through and follow what he had planned and what they all had discussed. He took measured steps, remembering that at that moment he posed no threat, he was just Santa Clause. A loving and much loved character. He hoped there were no kids in the bank as he could soon destroy their love for Christmas once he pulled out his gun, although it had probably been made back at the Elf toy production factory, but they might not notice that it was a toy. Although he was depending quite a bit that no one noticed that it was only a toy. He stepped forward quite softly on the marbled floor even though he appeared to be wearing heavy black boots, but under the booty costume covers he was wearing his adidas trainers. His lavish red suit was trimmed with white fur and centred with a wide black shiny belt. His long white beard, white curly wig and red hat finished off the look. They also hid his head set and mike, which was tucked in under his beard. The wig and beard also itched like crazy and made him sweat buckets. He was carrying a large black sack over his right shoulder; it too was trimmed with white fur to match in with the suit. All in all a great costume for any kids party, but not one you saw too often robbing banks.

He heard Joe speak softly in his ear, "Eleven o'clock, and four."

This told him to head in the direction of eleven o'clock and to take four steps.

Terry followed Ray through the door and in to the bank. He too was concentrating to take measured steps and to try his best to follow Ray even though he found his movement difficult to hear over the bustle of noise in the bank. His skin was also on fire, which he was doing his best to ignore and not making much of a go at it. He thought briefly to himself, "how come I ended up with the Yeti suit in this fucking heat?"

The costume which was designed around the elusive creature, the Abominable Snowman, otherwise known as the Yeti, was a full creamy white body suit and matching fur head mask. The inflatable shoulder pads, which Aurimas had given life to, made the body look larger and muscular, just like the savage beast itself. It was completely white apart from the PVC palms and toes. Sweat had glued the inner of the suit to his skin and Terry guessed that they would need to peel the fucking think off him later like a fucking banana skin. He heard Joe speak. He ignored the first instruction that was for Ray but the second told him where to go and how far.

"One o'clock and three." Joe said.

Terry did as instructed and took up his position on the right of the man who had taught him to only gamble with what you could afford to lose and here he was taking the biggest gamble of his life. "Ah well, in for a penny, in for a pound!" He could afford to lose a pound.

Aurimas brought up the rear. Before he closed the door he hung the sign that Joe had pinched from the front door of a pharmacy the day before. The sign read, "Closed. Back in 30 minutes."

Aurimas then followed Terry in to the bank. This was relatively easy as Terry was panting and puffing like an old bagpipe with holes in it. His outfit was also warm, but what wouldn't be in this heat. He squeezed through the door, his large foam body just about made it without opening the second of the two doors. Once inside he heard Joe come through his head set. He ignored both the first and the second instructions and listened for the third.

"Ten o'clock and six, I think, but I'll let you know."

Aurimas judged where ten o'clock would be and began to take measured steps, as Ray had showed him, rather than the usually long gangly strides he walked with. Ray explained that this was the only way that Joe could judge the steps to tell them, because if he was to compensate for their various walking steps then they would end up all over the place. "This is going to be a bank robbery, not strictly come dancing," Ray had said.

Counting down in his head, Aurimas got to five when Joe spoke again. "Five's OK."

Aurimas stopped and waited for other sounds or noises that would allow him to turn to face where he judged he should be facing, but for now he stayed still. As still as the ten pin bowling pin he resembled, although maybe a thousand times bigger.

Tracey was having trouble coping with the stress. She was visibly shaking. She had never been in trouble in her life, well apart from the time she got detention in school for pushing Sean Boyle who then tripped, fell over and cut his head. It was just a scratch but the blood made it look worse and so she had been marched to the Head Mistress's office and duly punished. Not used to being in the wrong she had been so upset that she'd forgot to tell her peers that Sean Boyle, the dirty little pervert, had groped her and tried to stick his lizard like tongue down her throat. Yuk! She had almost puked, and she was almost about to puke now. Her stomach was doing summersaults that could win an Olympic gold medal. Even though she could see nothing, the image in her mind from the detailed description Joe had given her of the three costumes was playing like a Looney Tunes cartoon. Any second now she expected Porky Pig to say, "That's all Folks." She actually wished that any second now someone, anyone would say, "That's all folks."

She was really sorry now that she had come. She wasn't cut out for this and she could turn out to be a liability. Joe seemed calm and he was doing his part without any sort of fuss or any sort of realisation of the danger. Was that just youth? Well she was far from fitting in to that category, and after today she guessed she might age some, or at least feel like she had put on some additional years. What on earth were they doing here? This entire thing was Looney.

Joe stood with Tracey and Bumper in the queue. They were last as they had hoped, so that was good. He was wearing his holiday costume, flip flops, shorts and a tee shirt, on which his sunglasses were hanging from the neck. He was also wearing a New York baseball cap and a face mask that everyone was wearing for the virus. Both were perfect to hide his head set and mike. He noticed that Bumper's tail was going mad as he recognised Ray, Terry and Aurimas, even though all three were totally unrecognisable. Obviously not to a dog. Joe estimated that there were maybe ten other people in front of them in the queue and three bank staff behind the counter. He also saw that the bank staff, two women and one man, were also lined up as Charlie had told his dad they would be. The man was on Joe's far left as he looked on to the counter and the two women sat to his right. One of the women had disappeared below the counter and he hoped that she hadn't already sussed out that something was wrong and was pushing buttons to alarm the police.

Then he heard his dad speak, loudly.

Ray transferred his Santa sack in to his other hand and shoulder and then pulled out his gun from his right hand coat pocket.

"Don't be alarmed everyone, we're just here to make an unauthorised withdrawal. No one is going to get hurt."

At this prompt Terry and Aurimas took out their guns. Aurimas also shifted slightly to his right to face the banks customers so that he was aiming the gun in the right direction. The sounds from them had given him a perspective to where they were.

Petra Alonso had felt guilty coming in to work this morning. Her four-year-old son Philippe had been sick all day Sunday and when he got sick he got clingy to his mummy. Quite a common thing. Petra had spent all day Sunday as Mummy Nursemaid and had watched more Disney movies than she had ever done before. At times she was more engrossed in them than Philippe had been. At one point during the Hunchback of Notre Dame she was so entranced that she had told Philippe to "shush" when he had been crying and then immediately felt bad for it, paused the film and saw to his needs.

This morning hadn't seen much improvement and Petra considered taking the day off work to look after him. Her husband was away on business and so it was her or the nursery. Monday's though were an issue. Her manager, that prick Fred, got really pissed when you took a Monday off sick. He always aired on suspicion that if off sick on a Monday that it was due to over indulgence at the weekend, which was just downright irresponsible. And Monday was one of their busiest days. So rather than face Fred's wrath she had taken poor sick Philippe to nursery. Coming away from the nursery she had felt doubly bad as she felt that the nursery had also been pissed at her for leaving them with a sick child. She supposed it was the virus that had everyone so uptight. You coughed in public nowadays and it was like you had leprosy.

So this Monday was more of a drag than the usual Monday, which was always a drag anyway. She did agree with that song, "I don't like Monday's," it was an oldie, and she had no idea who sang it, but it had a good tune, and great lyrics.

She was waiting on her current customer signing a form, but he was struggling to find his glasses, when she noticed Santa Clause coming through the front door. He was followed with a big white furry creature and something else she couldn't quite see at that moment. A second later as they came in she realised it was a ten pin bowling pin. She smiled, it was most likely some promotional thing, or just more whacky tourists. "Philippe would love this," she thought and bent to her handbag on the floor at her feet to get her phone and take some photos that she could show him later and maybe help cheer him up. As she was hunting through her bag to find her phone, "I really need to sort this bag out," she thought hearing her husband asking, "What on earth have you got in there?" Then she heard shouting. With her head under the counter she couldn't fully make it out, but then she sensed that the atmosphere seemed to change. There were other noises, muffled under here, but they were slightly easier to understand. There were some gasps, a shrill and then an airy silence. It sounded wrong. She straightened up on her seat and renewed her view of the waiting area and froze. The lovely Santa, the cuddly white furry thing and the bowling pin were now all holding guns. She lunged to her right to hit the alarm button but that prick Fred got in her way. "What the," she said, what was he doing. It looked like the cowardly little shit was taking a dive below the counter to the ground, but he was stopping her from getting to the alarm. "Fred," she shouted now, "Fred, hit the fucking alarm." She slapped his hand and thought she felt the button depress. She had no way of telling as the alarm was silent inside the bank but if she heard police sirens in a couple of minutes then she would be satisfied that she had carried out her required duties. As for Fred, the wimp seemed in bits. "What a Pussy!" she thought, then turned her attention to the picture in front of her which she couldn't help thinking looked like a scene from a pantomime rather than a bank robbery. She could hear the jokes already. "They robbed the bank. No they didn't. Yes they did. Look out he's behind you! Boo."

She cursed herself for not staying at home and pulling that sicky, but then smiled thinking that fawning stress from today might just get her the rest of the week on the sick. Full pay as well. Her and Philippe could go to the beach, providing the little darling got better.

She turned to see her other colleague, Grace who had only started in the job last week and immediately she felt guilty for focusing on Fred in her panic to press the alarm. Grace was as white as a ghost. "Jesus, another pantomime character," Petra thought. Tears were streaming down her cheeks and her eyes already burned red. She was shaking, her hands pulled up to her face in total terror. Petra slipped off her stool and went to her, putting her arms around and saying, "It's OK Grace, don't worry." She guessed that Grace had maybe never seen a gun before, or maybe that it was pointed at her, which was fair enough. "These morons won't shoot anybody," she said, squeezing her hand now, "they just want the money. So we're going to get their withdrawal slip filled in and get them cashed up and shipped out. OK?"

Grace's nod was a weak one. Petra tried a joke, "or should we tell the Yeti that there's SNOW money?"

Grace didn't get it.

Chapter Thirty

Tenerife, Canary Islands
Monday 25th October 2021

Charlie watched as three people in fancy dress entered the bank. One was Santa, the second he wasn't sure but looked like a white dog, maybe it was Snoopy and the third looked like a big dildo. It made him nervous as he worried it might be some promotional event that could get in the way and make junior's job even harder. All they needed now was a troop of photographers or media wankers arriving to take lots of pictures or video. He looked back to Monty just in time to witness a large chocolate milk shake being set in front of him by the waiter. Charlie just shook his head, but then everything went black as the furry dog's head swivelled around until he was looking in to the inside of one of its ears. He felt his own hot breath on his face. It began to shorten his breathing and he started to panic that he was going to have an asthma attack. He tried to put it right but the large furry paws on his hands made him clumsy. He had to pull out his hand from the inside of the paw and just let it fall to the ground and then he brought his hand up inside to find the opening of the mouth and pulled it back so that he could see again. Then he had to bend down and feel around to find the paw. Eventually he retrieved it and pulled it back on, with some difficulty. During all this manoeuvring he swore eight times. Anyone passing might have changed their mind about being a dog lover and just concluded that they were nasty little shits.

Now that he had regained his sight he looked back to Monty, but instead the guy sitting in front caught his eye, or to be more accurate, the hot chick who by the look of things was almost ready to take her fucking knickers off. Even from distance he could see that she was leaning forward, her tits nearly escaping her skinny bikini top, and her face close to the guy, what the fuck was his name? Her mouth was open, her tongue licking her lips, and her eyes saying, "Hurry up and take me to bed."

Life just wasn't fucking fair! He didn't know this prick, well actually he thought he did but he couldn't remember his name, but it didn't matter as now hated the bastard to the extent that he felt like telling Monty he could have a life's supply of Cornettos and chocolate milk shake if he blew the fuckers head off.

Life just wasn't fair. Why couldn't he have been born tall and handsome? Why couldn't he have those steely blue eyes that pulled the women in like those mysterious questions that everyone wanted to know the answers to? Just one look and it was knickers off and on you go. But no, Charlie's sex and love life wasn't like something out of a Mills and Boon romantic novel. His script was more like something from the Beano. Deep down and late at night when he lay alone in the dark, he told himself that there was someone out there for him. Someone who looked past his littleness, his comic features and his mangled penis, thanks to that mad fucking Nun. Someone who would care for him and be his friend and companion. Someone more caring than the mad Monty and someone whose outlook on life went past strawberry Cornettos and chocolate milk shakes.

Jesus he was sweating and stressed to fuck in this outfit. And where was that fucking Jazz junior? And more importantly, why couldn't he pull a chick as hot as that?

He wondered if plastic surgery could do leg extensions. It was something he could explore whenever he got his hands on this money he had come to this melting pot to steal. Well force others to steal for him. Money was surely the answer to all his problems. He thought about Sting. He was fucking loaded, I mean fucking minted. And he had seen him on TV just before he'd come over to Tenerife and he looked twenty years younger than he had done twenty fucking years ago. Don't tell me that wasn't down to money? OK, he knew he did yoga and all that shit, but that didn't make you age like Peter fucking Pan. He had also heard that Sting had made love to his wife for a solid non stop fourteen hours. Fuck! It had been fourteen years since he'd last had sex and that had only lasted fourteen fucking seconds. And ten of those were spent getting his Y fronts off. He thought of fourteen hours with the hot chick across the road and almost had another asthma attack. He told himself to calm down and concentrate on the job at hand. Once he had the money, the chicks would come.

He looked back at the bank and noticed something hanging on the front door. He couldn't make out what it was, or what it said. He assumed it was an advert maybe to do with whatever the event was that was going on inside the bank. A charity thing or something. "Fucking charity," he spat, "The Charlie Bassett Benevolent Fund was the only charity he was worried about, and if that junior shit didn't get a move on he was going to be pissed off. If the fucker had fucked off with his five grand then he would never play the guitar again. And sing in a much higher key.

He took another peep at Monty, or more accurately the sex show going on in front of him. Holy fucking Jesus, she almost had her head in his mouth! "Hussie," he hissed, jealously, and went back to watching the bank.

Just over fifty feet away Kevin was finding it difficult to concentrate. His focus on the bank, the time, everything besides this girl was fading away. He had first met her on a night out with Ritchie a few nights ago, and things then had got heated, but then had been cut short as Ritchie made him leave the bar. Kevin loved women and women loved Kevin and that's the way it had always been for him. He was nearly thirty years of age, just over six foot tall and had an athletic build mainly thanks to playing tennis three or four times per week for his local club. He was pretty good and his mum had the trophies on display to prove it. But apart from the girls and women and the tennis, there wasn't much else in Kevin's life. Sport had pulled him through school but at the expense of every other subject. Jobs also came and went, because that's all they were just jobs, and if he got fed up he gave them up. He still lived with his mother and so bills weren't the highest priority of his life. And so he had drifted in with Ritchie and then Arnie because it wasn't a job and it was sort of casual and adhoc, but it paid well and didn't interfere with his tennis. But unlike Arnie and Ritchie he wasn't in to the whole thing either like they were. To them it was almost like a cult. An organisation, a gang, whatever it was, but they treated it like the army or something like that. And they backed it all up with the troubles and religion, which Kevin just didn't get. This guy Jeffrey also gave him the shits. His mum had always told him that you could tell what people were like by their eyes and Jeffrey had ferret like eyes that were always looking and searching around almost nervously. But Ritchie had given him his instructions and he didn't know what else to do. But for now he knew what he wanted to do and it didn't include banks, or thugs or sitting in cafes watching people. The sun was shining and there was a girl, a gorgeous girl at that, who was practically sitting on his lap. He blew out his cheeks, in two minds what to do.

"You OK baby," she said, stroking his face.

He didn't know how to answer her. He was OK, more than OK, but then he wasn't OK. He couldn't just abandon his post. There you go, it sounded like the army thing again. But he was only human. And he was only a man, and this girl was driving him crazy. By the way she was acting; he was driving her crazy too. You didn't need to know much more about the birds and the bees to work out what the solution was for both of them. And it could be a mutual solution and a very enjoyable one at that. Whereas this watching lark was as boring as his school work had been. However there was a huge risk. Fucking that Jeffrey boy around could have costly consequences, very costly indeed.

He checked his watch. It was only a couple of minutes after ten. Could he get this girl back to his room and be back in time for his next report in just under thirty minutes? He wasn't sure, but it was worth a chance.

"Let's go," he said, getting up.

"Where?" she asked.

"Heaven hopefully," he thought.

As Kevin headed to heaven, Jeffrey was considering raising hell. The queue just wasn't moving and Dennis was fading fast. If he didn't get Dennis past the initial security check and identity confirmation soon then the whole thing might go to shit. They needed to get their stash out of these safety deposit boxes and they needed to do it quickly. They had the second bank to get to after this one, which thankfully was only around the corner. He didn't really care if Dennis dropped dead after that, in fact if he did then that would be another problem solved.

Finally the customer that had caused most of the hold up seemed to be finishing up. But then a flash of red at the front door caught Jeffrey's eye and he wondered to himself, "What the fuck is this now?"

Chapter Thirty-One

Tenerife, Canary Islands
Monday 25th October 2021

Ray heard the gasps and nervous mumbles from the crowd in the bank and so he repeated himself, "don't worry, no one is going to get hurt."

The noises from the customers were a good thing as it let him know where they were and it also gave him a sense of roughly how many there were. He guessed around ten, or maybe just slightly less. They needed to control the noise so that they could continue to know where they were, but that was up to Terry to sort that out in a minute. His first task was to get the bank staff out from behind their counter and out here with the crowd, so that everyone was in the same place.

He took one step forward, which was the signal to Joe to prompt him for the next stage, and Joe didn't let him down.

"Three and a quarter turn left," he heard through his head set. He turned as instructed and then took three more measured steps. He had guessed himself that he needed to move to his left as he had turned to the sound of the crowd when he was speaking to them, and they were on his right. Now though he needed to be facing the bank staff. Happy about his position he raised his gun and said, "Step back from the counter and then come out here." Being able to make eye contact with each individual would have helped to be more assertive, but he just wasn't capable of doing that. He wasn't even certain if he was looking directly at any of the three staff he knew were there. In an effort to overcome his inability to make eye contact and to help emphasise his request, he nodded his head and waved the gun in the direction of the customers to hopefully show the staff exactly where he wanted them to go.

He waited.

The arrangement with Joe was to only let him know if they didn't do as he had asked, but as Joe was silent he assumed the staff were doing as instructed. That was good as he was worried how they would react as there was a possibility that one, or maybe two of them could have tried to thwart the robbery and go in to lock down.

Then Joe said, "They're coming out."

Relieved Ray said, "Move over there," he motioned to his right again using the gun as a pointer, "stand with the customers."

Again he assumed that they had complied as Joe was silent.

A few seconds later Joe then said, "As if you were at twelve, move to two, the name badge says Fred."

Ray adjusted his position, pointed were Joe had told him and said, "You Fred, you are going to come with me. I need you to take me to where the safety deposit boxes are kept."

Fred stayed still.

"No," Joe said, so Ray assumed that Fred hadn't moved.

"Fred, come on," Ray insisted, pushing the gun forward slightly to underline his instruction. "There's nothing to worry about if you just do what I ask."

Ray heard Fred move closer to him, which again was confirmed by Joe's silence.

"The deposit boxes," Ray said again, "let's go. You lead the way."

The next part was going to be very difficult for Ray as he needed to go solo. He would be relying on Joe to get him started and lined up so that he could go through the door without walking in to the wall. But once through the door he was on his own. He would need to use Fred as a guide by either following his sound, provided he made one, or by getting him talking then following the sound of his voice. He also had a rough layout of where they were heading provided by Charlie, which Ray assumed had been provided to him by Fred.

Fred had started walking and so Ray began to follow. Very nervous now as he knew he'd be working blind. Joe said, "Edge right."

Ray veered to his right.

A couple of seconds later Joe said, thinking his dad had moved too far right, "slightly left again." Then a second later. "OK."

Finished with his dad for now, Joe checked on Aurimas and Terry.

Aurimas's position and direction was fine. He was acting as their cover man standing furthest away. Terry now had a job to do and so Joe's next communication was for him.

"Forward two then a quarter turn left."

Terry complied then said, "OK folks, as my friend said, no one is going to get hurt." He paused, "as we are waiting we are going to sing some songs."

Terry heard the muffled murmurs of questions. They were almost as confused as when they had witnessed Santa turned bank robber, and with a Yeti and a bowling pin as his back up.

"It'll pass the time and help the nerves," he lied. They were using this so that they could tell where everyone was by sound.

"OK," Terry went on, "here's a song that you all should know." They had googled this and debated it for some time, actually argued about it, but they had agreed a list of a few songs that they guessed everyone would know. Surprisingly the lists on google for the best songs ever were quite abstract, even for music lovers like themselves.

"We're going to sing Love me Tender by Elvis," Terry said, "I'm sure you all know that?" Ray had pulled rank and insisted this was their first choice. His actual comment had been, "you would have needed to be living in a cave not to know this song!"

A few murmurs came from the queue of people.

He was about to count them in when a woman's voice said, "Excuse me, but I don't know that one." Claire looked around at the other customers as she said it to see if anyone else was in agreement with her.

A young mans voice then added, "no me either." Michael then nodded to Claire in thanks for her raising what he had been thinking, but hadn't wanted to say.

If Ray had still been there he would now be insisting they were both cave dwellers.

Terry who had argued against Ray's first choice was inwardly pleased and so quickly moved on to what was his first choice. He said, "Love me do, by the Beatles?"

Another woman's voice, it was Sandra this time, said, "Oh I love the Beatles. Wasn't it awful when they shot John Lennon?"

A mans voice answered, "Terrible," he said sadly, "My wife and I cried that day." Adrian then continued, "That's one of those days when you always remember where you were when it happened."

"Like Princess Diana," Claire said.

"Yes," Oswaldo agreed, "we sat up all night that night watching sky news."

"And George Michael," a man said, "he died at Christmas, it was really sad. He wrote the best Christmas song ever too, isn't that a coincidence, him dying at Christmas and all." A devoted George Michael fan he was shaking his head still in disbelief and a tear forming in his eye.

"George Michael and Princess Diana were close friends," said Oswaldo.

"Were they," said Sandra, surprise in her voice, "I didn't know that." Then with a giggle she added, "You learn something every day don't you?"

Terry didn't know what to say. It was turning out more like a coffee morning rather than a bank robbery. He ditched the Beatles and tried to remember what the next song on their list had been. Then he thought, "Last Christmas?"

"Do you all know Last Christmas?" he asked.

More murmurs, and a few, "oh yes."

"I might know the chorus," Felicity, who was known as Fliss said, then started singing, "Last Christmas I gave you my heart, on boxing day you gave it away."

"That's not the words," the man who was the George Michael fan said, "it's not Boxing Day."

Fliss responded, "What's the next day after Christmas day?" she asked.

Several responded that it was indeed Boxing Day.

Then Brinie who was Irish said, "we call it St. Stephen's Day."

"Do you, I never knew that before." Said Sandra, "You see I told you, every day is a school day!"

"Oh yes, I think it's some religious thing, cause I've no idea who St. Stephen is," answered Brinie, "or was I should say."

Terry said, "Can we try singing the song."

The George Michael fan said, "Only if we sing the right words. I'm not singing a George Michael song with the wrong fucking words."

"There's no need to swear about it," said Fliss, who had been the only one who had sang the few words of the day, and was obviously annoyed with Georges number one fan for swearing.

Terry said, "We'll try something else. Do you all know tie a Yellow Ribbon Round the Old Oak Tree?"

"Oak or Oat tree?" Petra from the bank asked.

"Oak," confirmed Terry, "I've never heard of an Oat tree."

"No, I just thought you said Oat, that's all," added Petra apologetically, "it was maybe your accent."

"Was it not a blue ribbon?" Kane asked. Terry hadn't heard this voice before.

"Yes, blue," said George's fan, "I saw it in a film."

"Forget that one," Terry said, beginning to get exasperated. He began to list out songs, "Bohemian Rhapsody?"

"Too complicated," said Sandra.

"Sweet Caroline?"

"Who sang that?" Oswaldo asked.

"Dancing Queen by Abba," Terry said, prepared to bet money that they all knew it.

"Oh I loved the blonde one," Pierre said, who had a French accent.

"Was that the one with the beard?" questioned George Michael's number one fan, chuckling to himself, having a ball now.

Terry was sorry now that they had brought toy guns as he wanted to shoot George Michael's number one fan six times. The first shot was to kill him; the other five were to make sure.

Joe wanted to join in, but wanted to suggest the Clash song, "Bank Robber," but then thought better of it. This crowd might not thank him for his mischievous sense of humour.

Wrecking his brain now Terry offered, "Theme from the Monkey's?"

"Was that from one of those wildlife programmes?" Fliss asked.

"Anything from Grease?"

"You're the one that I want." Petra suggested.

"Do you all know the words to that?" Terry asked, hope in his voice.

"What?" Brinie asked.

"You're the one that I want?" Terry repeated.

"No." both Clair and Fliss said.

"Mary, Jesus and Joseph," Terry mumbled to himself then threw out another suggestion, "Sandy?"

"Sandy who?" asked Kane.

The Grease movie was abandoned.

"Yellow by Coldplay?"

"Their songs are so dreary," said Claire, "my husband calls it suicide music."

"Sounds like an idea," said Terry, "will we do it all together? Here? Now? Please?" Sounding as if he was almost crying he added, "Shoot me now, Please?"

Aurimas tried to help, "Valerie by Amy Whinehouse?"

"She's dead too," George Michael's number one fan pointed out.

Fliss really didn't like George's fan. He swore, thought he was funny when he clearly wasn't, and the selfish pig was the only one not wearing a mask. She jibed, "you seem to know an awful lot about dead people!"

Oswaldo, Kane and Sandra all laughed. George's fan didn't.

Purple Rain?" Aurimas continued in hope.

A lot of,"Mmm's."

Aurimas was wrecking his brain trying to think of songs they would all know, partly sorry now he'd got involved. He took one last chance, inspired by his native country, "Walk like an Egyptian?" he said, and to help prompt his audience he began, as best as he could dressed up all in foam as a ten pin bowling pin, to do the actions of the dance that went with the song.

He got a couple of laughs, but he guessed that was only because he looked like a total tool, so he gave up and went back to standing guard.

"Annie's Song by John Denver?" Terry said.

Brinie said, proudly, "Oh James Galway's version of that song was the best."

Terry asked, "Does anybody have a flute?"

"What?" Brinie asked.

"A flute," answered Terry, then said "Never mind," and thought, "if I had one I'd beat myself to death with the fucking thing."

Tracey hearing Terry's despair said, "I've got a suggestion."

Everyone stopped talking to listen.

"Jingle Bells," Tracey said and then started to sing it confident that they all should know it, and not caring if there were a few bluffers.

"Jingle bells, jingle bells," she sang, still solo.

"Jingle all the way," a few joined in now.

"Oh what fun it is to ride," the choir was building. Petra and Grace from the bank joined in. Grace had stopped crying now.

"In a one horse open sleigh," they were going full pelt now.

"Jingle bells, jingle bells

Jingle all the way,"

Joe was even giving it some now, not wanting to be left out. For one tiny second Aurimas even considered joining in, but then remembered how he had crashed and burned walking like an Egyptian, so he just tapped his foot, slightly, in time to the music.

"Oh what fun it is to ride,

In a one horse open sleigh."

When the chorus had finished they failed miserably once Tracey, and in fairness Petra who sang along, started in to the main verse. A few did their best but the words were all wrong. A few hummed, the rest just gave up. By the time the duet of Tracey and Petra got to the "through the fields" they were on their own and so they stopped.

Grace now feeling a lot better and getting in to the singing, but miffed she couldn't remember all the words to Jingle Bells, tried to make amends and support Petra by launching in to a rendition of "Away in a

Manger."

"Away in a manger,

No crib for a bed,"

No one joined in and so being on her own she felt silly and stopped. But the Christmas songs had inspired thought amongst the others and continuing to fly the flag for Ireland Brinie said, "What about, do they know it's Christmas?"

"The Band Aid song," Petra asked.

"Oh yes, I preferred the original one," added Brinie.

"Do you know," piped up George Michael's number one fan, "that the original Band Aid song stopped Last Christmas getting to number one in 1984?"

"Did it?" asked Fliss, mostly uninterested.

"Yeah, a real shame as Last Christmas is the best Christmas song ever and it never got to number one." He was nodding now reflecting, "a real shame," he confirmed, just so that everyone was sure.

Brinie said proudly, "Bob Geldof, wrote that. He's Irish."

"Was he," Grace said, "I thought he was Scottish."

Brinie crossed herself and said three hail Mary's, "Sir Bob Geldof Scottish," she said, "I've never heard such nonsense in me life." Fliss shook her head in agreement with Brinie who continued, with a slight laugh, "the next thing you'll be telling me is that the Pope himself is a protestant."

Fliss and Sandra both laughed and were also soon joined by Oswaldo, who as a devout Catholic found the suggestion of the Pope being a Prod the funniest thing he had heard today.

"I don't like Monday's" is a good song, Petra suggested, inspired by the mention of Bob Geldof.

That perked Brinie up and she was about to agree when the smart arse George Michael's number one fan said, "It was the Boomtown Rats sang that song, not Bob Geldof."

"Would you ever listen to that eejit," Brinie said, "sure it was Bob Geldof who was in the Boomtown Rats."

"No it was Fergal Sharkey," protested George's fan.

Brinie's Irish blood was starting to boil now. "Fergal Sharkey was in the Undertones and Bob Geldof was in the Rats, you facking twat."

George's number one fan said nothing.

Fliss said, "We were better at the Christmas songs." But she didn't chastise Brinie for swearing as she didn't mind as she had swore to the pig who liked Wham.

"Santa Clause is coming to town," is a good song said Grace, picking up on the Christmas suggestion.

"Not for us," George Michaels number one fan pointed out, solemn now, "Santa Clause came to town to rob us today!"

That flattened the mood as they'd all pretty much forgotten about the robbery.

Terry in an effort to gain control suggested they sing the national anthem, but then soon realised his mistake as there were several nationalities in the room. A debate ensued.

"No, the Queen God damn it!" he corrected. He silently wished that the Abominable Snowman would maybe melt and flow away down some drain somewhere. Anywhere but here!

"I've got it," shouted Tracey in an effort to help as she thought that Terry might leave, and having inspiration from her Sunday school days she started to sing.

> "Jesus loves me,
> This I know,
> For the bible tells me so,"

"C'mon everybody," she said encouragingly, and then continued singing,

"Little ones to Him belong," A few had joined in, then Petra and Grace waded in.

"They are weak, but he is strong." They were still only running at about sixty percent, but then the chorus sealed the deal as they became a complete choir, and a gospel one at that.

> "Yes Jesus loves me,
> Yes Jesus loves me,
> Yes Jesus loves me,

Cause the bible tells me so."

During the third rendition the original enthusiasm was waning and so Tracey changed it up.

"We'll do this one," she announced.

> "Jesus love is very wonderful,
> Jesus love is very wonderful,
> Jesus love is very wonderful,
> Oh wonderful love."

She had lead with a solo, but once again the chorus lit the match and not only did they all join in, but they did the actions as well.

"So high you can't get over it," George Michael's number one fan almost pulled his back out.

"So low you can't get under it," Brinie needed some assistance getting back up again.

"And so wide you can't get around it," two of them punched their neighbours in the process. But they apologised and hugged each other apologetically.

Bumper hadn't seen anything like it before in his life and career as a guide dog. Trips to the bank were usually solemn and boring, all business like events. Fancy dress costumes, guns, singing and now dancing and jumping, arms flying everywhere, had they all gone mad? He shook his head in disbelief. He had heard an expression these humans used, "Mad dogs and Englishmen." He shook his head harder, disgusted now, "It should be, Mad People and fucking foreigners." And Bumper didn't swear lightly.

As he thought it they were all jumping skyward once again, their hands held aloft and motioning as if they were climbing over something. Terry too, dressed up in a white furry costume, was jumping like something out of Sesame Street.

No sooner were they all jumping skyward but then they all dropped to the floor in mass. He looked to see thinking that someone had dropped a fiver! But then they were on their feet once more, arms spread wide as if they were about to hug Humpty Dumpty.

His stomach started to rumble again. This entire thing was giving him the shits. He was trying his best not to fart when his sensitive ears heard the sirens. Now he knew that he couldn't risk a fart or he might just get more than he bargained for.

The police were on their way and he was about to go down in history as the first guide dog arrested for bank robbery. His family and his entire guide dog profession would be ashamed. He hung his head low and thought, "I wonder what prison food is like for dogs?"

Then he farted.

Chapter Thirty-Two

Tenerife, Canary Islands
Monday 25th October 2021

Joe's guidance had been slightly off and Ray's shoulder clipped the corner edge of the doorway as he was following Fred. He stifled an "Umph," and walked on hoping that no one had noticed. He took the empty sack in the same hand that was holding his gun and used his left hand to trace the wall and use it as a guide. He considered putting the gun back in his jacket pocket, but worried then if they were captured on the banks CCTV that this would look bad on Fred. After several steps his hand felt the door frame and he was able to position himself through it with ease.

According to Charlie there was now one flight of stairs going down, which was located to the right of the door. To be sure of the direction he asked Fred.

"Which way?"

"Down these stairs," Fred answered and his voice gave Ray a bearing on where he was. It also confirmed Charlie's information. Ray walked on slowly, hoping to pick up the sound of Fred hitting the stairs. He focused his hearing, trying to hear past the noise of the main lobby that he had just left behind him. He couldn't hear Fred's footsteps and it forced him to pause. He needed to know where the stairs started down as the last thing he wanted to do was to fall head over tit down the staircase. If he did, then that was that and they were all fucked.

He still heard nothing; Fred must be wearing soft soled shoes. He purposely dropped the sack, then bent to pick it up and at the same time he felt the ground in the hope of feeling the beginning of the stairs going down. He then realised his mistake.

Fred was on him. Ray was crouching and off balance and so had no resistance and went sprawling backwards, banging his head hard on the concrete floor. The gun flew from his hand and skidded across the floor, bouncing off the wall. Ray was stunned by the bang to his head and winded by the force of Fred landing on top of him. He was sure he heard, and felt a rib crack.

"What the fuck was going on?" Ray thought, "This man was supposed to be greased, or had Charlie fucked up."

Fear gripped Ray as he lay almost helpless with the weight of Fred's body pinning him down to the floor. Fred was heavier than him and he couldn't move. If he didn't get control of this they could all be heading to jail. He wondered if Aurimas or Terry had heard and would maybe come in here to help him.

Fred was pushing hard trying to pin Ray down. He gripped Ray's arms and rocked right, then left. He moved his hands down to Ray's wrists and tried to pull them up, but Ray tried his best to resist. Fred rocked left, Ray thought he was going to roll off, then he rocked right again. Ray didn't know what was going on. Then Fred seemed to try to rock backwards, which Ray just didn't understand. Had Terry heard? Was he trying to pull him off? Ray didn't know if he was actually helping or hindering by holding on to Fred, or if he should let go so that Terry or Aurimas could pull him back. But then Fred pitched forward again and pushed down, coming in close to Ray. Fred whispered, "Make it look good, we're on camera out here."

Suddenly Ray understood. Fred released his left wrist which enabled Ray to pull it out from between them and use it to grab Fred's neck. He pulled and Fred rolled to the left almost like Ray had the strength of Hercules. Ray thought he knew what he was doing and so dramatically rolled over to be on top of Fred. They were now almost against the far wall and he felt something digging in to his right knee. He didn't want to release his hands to see what it was.

Whatever it was it had rhythm. It wasn't digging in to his leg, it was knocking against it. He felt down with his right hand and Fred then stopped the knocking and pushed the gun in to Ray's hand.

With the gun now back in his possession, Ray stood up and took two steps backwards away from Fred. He pointed the gun at Fred, or at least he hoped he was. He couldn't believe how out of breath he was and thought it must be to do with the heat, the Santa suit and the stress.

"Good try, but we don't want any heroes today," said Ray.

Fred got up, blowing out his breath as well. The noise helped Ray locate him so he made a slight correction with his aim and said.

"Let's go and this time no messing around."

He also made Fred pick up the sack, which saved him groping round the floor. Fred did so and coughed and spluttered as he went, which again also helped Ray to track him. But now that his back was against the far wall to the door, this also helped him to find the top of the stairs and the stair rail. Thankfully he gripped the rail and made his way downstairs.

Charlie had been wrong though as it was two flights down to the vaults where the deposit boxes were housed. Halfway down his head set beeped and the sound in his ears disappeared. He now heard the singing from upstairs in the distance coming through the door and down the stair well. They were singing Jingle Bells, which he wondered how as it hadn't been on the song list that they had spent hours debating.

His nerves had settled, although now he was sure he had a bruise on his left shoulder, his head was aching from hitting the floor and his ribs were sore from Fred jumping on top of him. If he made it back to the villa he was going to have a soothing dip in the pool. He reached the bottom of the stairs and paused. Charlie had said that there were a couple of rooms here and Ray didn't know which one they were going to. He was hoping that Fred would speak to orientate him. He didn't.

Ray needed a bearing so he said, "Here's the numbers of the boxes," and extended his hand out holding a slip of paper.

"Call them out," Fred said, his voice coming from a ten o'clock position. Ray stepped in that direction, his hand still extended with the piece of paper. Joe had told him the numbers, but he couldn't remember them. He remembered the name.

"Will the name do?"

"No," answered Fred, "not unless I go back upstairs and look it up on the computer."

"Shit," thought Ray, thinking fast and trying to come up with a way of getting Fred to read the numbers himself, without having to say, "oh by the way I'm blind and can't read this!" Then he heard it. The same sound that Bumper had heard. Police sirens and Ray could tell that they were heading in their direction.

"Hurry up," he said to Fred.

"Tell me the numbers," answered Fred, his voice showing more nerves than Ray's.

Ray paused, and then opened the paper in his hand. He stared at it, and then said, "I can't make out the writing," pushing it towards Fred he added, "can you?"

Fred took the paper, reviewed it and said, "The first are letters, that's maybe what confused you," then headed to find the deposit boxes.

Ray's nerves weren't settled any more, in fact the opposite. As he waited for Fred he put his hands behind his back and squeezed his palms together in an effort to ring out the stress. While his arms were tensed the shaking stopped, but as soon as he relaxed again the shaking came back. Standing waiting wasn't helping so he walked forward a couple of steps and then spoke to Fred to help get his Barings.

"Have you found them?"

"Just one," Fred said, his voice coming from the opposite end of the room.

"Can I help you hold the sack?" Ray asked.

Fred nodded and held the sack out towards Ray, but said nothing assuming the gesture answered his question. They stood there like that for several seconds until Fred said, "here, you gonna hold it?"

Realising what had likely just happened, Ray said, "sorry," then walked forward with his hands out trying to look natural and relaxed hoping he would make contact with the sack.

Fred was watching Ray and thinking he looked awkward and odd. He put it down to the stress and nerves, his own heart was thumping in his chest. As Ray came towards him Fred raised the sack in to his hands and asked, "You got it?"

Ray grasped the sack, which already had some weight, and answered Fred, "got it." He heard Fred transfer the contents of the box in to the sack and felt the sack get heavier.

Fred said, "That's that one," then he opened the second one and repeated the transfer of the bundles of money in to Ray's sack. They both could hear the sirens getting closer.

Ray was thinking if they should cut there losses and go now when Fred said, "over here," which meant they'd emptied box two. Ray judged the weight of the sack and was now hoping that they would have room for it all. And that he could carry it. Fred must have read his mind as when he was close and putting more bundles in to the sack he whispered, "You should have brought two bags."

Ray whispered back, "do you have anything else I can use?"

"My gym bag," Fred said, "but that's going to be really awkward to get. It's upstairs."

Thinking of time Ray said, "No, forget it we go with what we have."

The sirens were getting louder by the minute. Fred said, "That's the third one," dropping another bundle in to the sack.

Ray estimated the weight was close on twenty kilos as it felt almost as heavy as a suitcase when going on your holidays.

"Right, let's go," he said.

"You don't want the last one?" asked Fred.

"No time," Ray said swinging the sack over his shoulder with some difficulty. Fred said, "No, just drag it behind you."

Ray dropped the sack to the ground and told Fred to lead the way. He had pretty good Barings on where he needed to go to get back upstairs. He found the door, then the stair rail. Out now in the open stairwell he heard the singing upstairs, it sounded like Sunday school. He also heard the sirens and was beginning to think they were fucked. He began to trail the sack up the stairs, but it was awkward and wouldn't pull as easy as it had on the flat surface of the floor. "Fuck it," he said, and put the gun in his jacket pocket and lifted the sack with both hands. With both hands now being used he had no way to hold the hand rail and guide himself upwards. So he used and relied on his feet. He slid each one over the steps instead of lifting them fully. This way it kept him steady and safe from tripping and falling. It was slower but more reliable. When he came to the top of each staircase his foot slid on to indicate that the stairs had finished, so he turned and walked until his foot slid and found the bottom step, then he repeated his movement upwards. At the top of each stairway he repeated his shuffle until he was at the top and beside the door which would take him back out behind the counter. He turned right and used his shoulder this time to guide him along the wall, dragging the sack behind him. He was sweating and beginning to pant for breath. He expected to hear Joe in his ear but heard nothing. Then he heard a low beep that he knew signalled that his blue tooth was trying to sync again with the others, but was failing.

The sound of singing and sirens filled his ears and without any guidance from Joe the only thing he could do was chance it, so he walked on in the direction he thought would take him to the front door, which at this stage would probably lead them all, straight in to the arms of the police.

Chapter Thirty-Three

Tenerife, Canary Islands
Monday 25th October 2021

Charlie heard the sirens and cursed, several times. He promised himself that he was never coming back to Tenerife again for as long as he lived. Cross his heart and hope to die. Nothing had gone right from the moment he'd arrived and everyone was out to fuck him over. Jazz senior and now Jazz junior had screwed him and taken him for a fool. But they would pay. He would make them pay, and he was starting with junior and his girlfriend.

Giving up on watching the bank and wanting to get the fuck out of there before the police came, he was heading back to Monty and they were going to head to junior's villa. The two love birds had disappeared from the café and he didn't want to think about where they had gone, or what they might actually be doing at that precise moment in time. He would maybe think more about that later.

He stayed outside the café and circled the rail until he was beside Monty's table. The table was covered in empty Cornetto wrappers and four empty milk shake glasses. He shook his head in disgust.

"You do know that you're paying your own bill?" he said to Monty, "my income isn't exactly on track since we came over to this shit whole."

Monty shrugged, "OK."

"Well hurry up," said Charlie, "I don't want to hang around here."

He waited as Monty signalled for the waitress and as he waited he looked over again at the bank.

"Fuck," he said, "that's a closed sign."

The waitress had arrived at Monty's table and Monty said, "Could I have my bill please?"

Charlie's mouth dropped. He was looking at Monty but hearing a voice like little Lord Fauntleroy.

The waitress smiled warmly, "Cash or card?" she asked.

"Card," answered Monty, "do you take American Express?"

Charlie was speechless.

"Oh yes sir," she said, "back in a mo."

Finding his voice again Charlie said, "American Express?" Total surprise in his voice. "We've been over here almost a week and you haven't paid for as much as a fucking cup of tea. And now all of a sudden you're a member of the fucking Amex diner's club!"

"You don't like tea," said Monty, back to his usual voice now.

"Fuck if I like tea, that's not the point."

Monty pulled out his wallet and produced a Platinum American Express card.

Charlie stared, his entire tiny head now sticking out from the furry dog's mouth. It looked like the dog had swallowed him feet first.

Looking around to make sure no one could hear he asked, "You steal that?"

Seeming offended by the suggestion, "No," Monty answered, sulking.

"whose is it then?"

"Mine," answered Monty, a bit sheepish now as he recognised the look in Charlie's face. It was that nasty look that Charlie got just before he would hit Monty. He didn't like it and in an effort to pacify Charlie he added, "Look after your money and your money will look after you."

Charlie rolled his eyes, "what is this," he tried to remember the guys name from the telly that gave everybody financial advice, but couldn't get it so he just said, "what is this, financial advice from a man who lives on Cornettos and fucking chocolate milk shakes?" Charlie's face was getting redder now, Monty was on edge. "Who filled your head with that shite?"

"My uncle Wilbur," said Monty, his head lowered and his face passive and innocent like a little boy.

"Your uncle Wilbur?" asked Charlie, almost choking on the words. "Your uncle Wilbur that used to beat the shit out of you, and then get you to play with his fucking willy?"

"Yeah," said Monty, "but he knew a lot about money."

"I know what a tenner and a fiver look like," said Charlie, "but I don't get little boys to stick their fucking hands down my Y-fronts." "Well those accusations were never proven anyway," he thought to himself.

The waitress came back with the bill and the card machine. "There you go," she said, presenting Monty with the receipt and then asking for his card.

"Oh," she said in a high pitch voice, "American Express Platinum, lovely Sir, that'll do nicely."

Charlie stared at Monty's poncho. He pictured the shot-gun underneath, almost within his reach, and wondered if he pulled it out and pointed at this bitch would she still be saying, "that'll do nicely Sir," in a fucking squeaky whiney voice.

Life was really starting to disappoint him. Correct that. Life had always disappointed him. Now it just totally sucked.

"Where had he gone wrong," he pondered. This was his gig, his plan, he was the boss, and here he was standing out in the street dressed up as a fucking dog looking like he was out there to have a shit, while the fucking mad Mexican with a sombrero bigger than Donald Trumps ego, and with more milk stains down his front than a new born baby. But here was this waitress, "yes Sir, no Sir, do you want a fucking blow job Sir," just because the prick had a bit of fucking plastic that went as fast as you like.

He had actually applied for one himself, but the eligibility checker had come back laughing.

"Fuck Tenerife and fuck life," Charlie mumbled as he walked away.

As he walked, or waddled to be more accurate as the bulky furry dog suit sagged down and made his short legs look even shorter, he got a different view inside the bank. He stopped dead and stared. It was junior's girlfriend, he was sure of it. And she was jumping up and down and waving her hands in the air, "had the world gone mad?" he thought.

Then he saw that they were all doing it. All the customers in the bank were dancing or something. He was certain now that there was some sort of promotional event going on there, but the coincidence that junior's girlfriend was there as well niggled at him. He stood watching as he waited for Monty. The sirens were louder now, very close and if Monty didn't hurry his fat Mexican arse up, he could walk back on his own.

Sasha Moreno turned the corner and headed to the next bank on his list, which was now just a few blocks up the street. He could hear the sirens and knew they were close, but he didn't know yet where they were heading to, his police radio was in his car. Well at least it had been before it had been stolen.

He walked on quickly. He was wondering if he should stop at a shop or something and use their phone to call headquarters to see what was going on, but then he decided that the bank was closer and he could put a call in from there. As he got nearer he noticed someone dressed as a tiny dog standing across the road from the bank. He seemed to be staring straight at the bank. In Sasha's judgement this person looked suspicious whoever they were and he decided that he may well speak to them before heading in to the bank. Then a tall man dressed in a huge sombrero and a Mexican poncho came and stood beside the tiny dog. The large man made the dog look smaller, or maybe it was the other way around. All this fancy dress was boring him now and he couldn't wait until Halloween was over and done with. He walked on. Two blocks away a bright yellow people carrier swung in and reversed to park in front of the bank. Some moments later the bank's doors burst open and Santa Clause ran out carrying a heavy sack that somehow Sasha didn't think was full of parcels for Christmas. Sasha began to run and as he did he fumbled with the release button on his holster so that he could pull out his gun.

He began to shout.

Chapter Thirty-Four

Tenerife, Canary Islands
Monday 25th October 2021

"Hey, Chingedy ching, hee haw, hee haw,

It's Dominick, the donkey

Hey, Chingedy ching, hee haw, hee haw."

Brinie and Petra were adlibbing on the hee haws and really getting in to this now, "hee haw, hee haw, hee haw, hee haw." Brinie was bent over pretending to be a donkey.

George Michael's number one fan was staring at her arse.

Fliss was thinking it was the best fun she'd had on this holiday so far.

"The Italian Christmas donkey," Petra, Brinie, Fliss and Tracey sang on. The rest danced. Some sang backing with the odd, "Hee haw, hee haw," in a different key.

"La, la, la, la, la, la, la, la, la,

La, la, la, la, la, la, ladioda."

Adlibbing again, "Hee haw, hee haw, hee haw, hee haw."

Thinking he was now singing like George Michael, his number one fan adlibbed as well, "ladioda," then in a high pitched voice and added, "ole!"

The rest preferred the donkey's part,

"Hee haw, hee haw, hee haw, hee haw."

Joe was thinking that they had maybe missed their calling and were in the wrong career. Forget the gigging and robbing banks, they should become either Cheerleaders or a party warm up act. These people were having a ball. Two of them had just high fived each other after their last rendition of donkey noises. He too had almost got caught up in the whole thing and had very nearly rapped out a few hee haw's, hee haws.

247

Tracey was fully in the groove and was conducting this choir with ease. Even George Michael's number one fan was fully taking part and had forgotten all about his references to his idol and other dead people. The singing had drowned out the sirens for a while but as they were obviously much closer now Joe could hear them. He also heard the beep beep in his ear as the blue tooth tried to connect back to his dad's head set, but it was failing to sync. His dad was coming through the door now, trailing the sack behind him, but he was heading straight for Terry and Joe had no way to communicate this to him. His dad had also told him not to use names just in case the banks CCTV picked them up, but he needed to say something to Terry otherwise both of them could end up on the floor, and he guessed they didn't have much time left, and this could really slow them down. Plus giveaway the fact that they couldn't see. He was almost about to tell Terry that he needed to move back, when his brain engaged once more.

"Yeti," he said, "3 back quick." Then as an after thought he added, "Santa's offline."

He watched as Terry moved back immediately. The singing and animal impersonations tailed off as Santa Clause came back in to the room. His presence along with the heavy sack now full of money seemed to bring everyone back to the reality that this was actually a bank robbery and not a fun day out. Joe also noticed that Santa's wig and beard were now crooked giving the impression that his head was twisted to one side. His floppy red Santa hat was gone. He saw his dad tap the side of his wig again and the beep beep in his ear told him that he was trying once more to get the blue tooth to sync, but the double beep indicated that it had failed again. Obviously realising this himself, Joe saw that his dad was now abandoning the head set and was starting to push on, guessing his line to take for the front door. Joe was satisfied now that Terry was out of the way of any collision with his dad but he tracked his trajectory and guessed that he was heading too far to his left and therefore going to miss the door and hit the wall to the left.

Terry stood now trying to track if Ray passed in front of him and if so he would then follow him to the front door. He did think that Joe would give him guidance but he couldn't remember now in what order the instructions would come. Was he next, or was it Aurimas? He waited, his heart thumping as he too could hear the approaching sirens. The customers and the songs were now forgotten. That gig was over and there would be no encore. All he wanted to do now was to get out of there. He was desperate now that they had come this close. Everything had gone to Ray's plan but the dread in his gut told him that they were going to run out of time and get caught. He felt bad for Aurimas and Ray if they did. They were younger, especially Aurimas and had more to lose. He had come in to this with open eyes, even though they weren't much bloody use to him, but he had done as his dear friend Ray had taught him to do and he had only gambled with what he could afford to lose. A few years in prison were a fair price to pay for him if it meant he could help a friend who had done so much to help him. He also hoped that Joe and Tracey would be OK. He did think they would be, provided they stuck to what Ray had told them to do. Play the blind card and for Joe to use his mother's surname so that they didn't connect him to his dad. Terry couldn't help but see the irony in that here they were, Aurimas, Ray and himself, pretending they weren't blind, and yet Joe was pretending he was blind so that he would be overlooked and dismissed as an innocent bystander.

Aurimas, who up to now had been a vision of calm, was now sweating, mainly due to the foam suit, but underneath the foam exterior he was now shaking and feeling sick. He could hear the sirens and he was thinking that they should maybe now give it up. Set down the toy guns and surrender. To go outside, with the police either about to arrive or already waiting, could be very dangerous, and he really didn't want to get shot. He saw a picture in his mind from when he could see and had gone ten pin bowling and he saw the bowling pins part and fall when hit by the heavy ball. He saw his face and hands and feet sticking out from one of those pins as it fell to the ground after being hit by a bullet rather than a bowling ball. He thought of his mum and wondered what she would say to him, and he knew it wouldn't be good. He could see the shame on her face, and it hurt. He realised then that he had gone in to this whole thing blind. Blinder than he had ever been in the last five years as he hadn't seen the obvious danger that lay ahead. He bent down, as best as he could in his bulky foam bodysuit, and set the toy gun on the floor and he was about to remove his head piece to help him to breathe and cool down when he heard Joe speak over his head set.

Ray cursed to himself. The head set wouldn't reconnect and it left him momentarily paralysed not knowing what direction to go in. The sirens were loud now and effecting his thinking. He had to think. He had to move. He couldn't just freeze up and let them all down. He had to get them all out of here and he knew he only had seconds, if even that, to do it. He gripped the sack and headed forward in what he thought would take him to the front doors. He could feel the tension in the room. The singing had stopped and the crowd of people were silent. It was even as if they were all holding their breath. He felt all the eyes staring at him, eyes that worked perfectly unlike his own, but he tried his best to shut out all the attention and he focused as best he could to keep pushing towards the door. He didn't know where Terry and Aurimas where and he didn't have the time to stop and check. This was a sprint to the finish and one he was making in the dark, despite the fact that he felt as if the spotlights were shining brightly on him. A few steps later he also realised that he had forgot to count his steps and so now not only was his direction unsure but the distance was also a mystery. The sack was awkward and in hindsight maybe wasn't the best choice but it had seemed so clever at the time as it blended in to the whole Santa thing. He let go of the sack with his right hand so that he could use this as a guide in front of him to hopefully stop him walking head first in to the doors or the wall. It made walking more difficult and made him walk almost sideways as he trailed the heavy sack behind him with his left hand, his right stretched out in front of him searching for the door. He walked on, the sirens now filling his ears. Then he heard something else. A cough and he thought it sounded like Tracey. Not really sure though why he thought that and he wondered if it was more in hope rather than fact. Nevertheless he took a chance that he was correct and he took a baring from the sound and from where he thought Tracey and Joe were standing as they had been last in, he corrected his direction and took a quarter turn to the right and then walked on.

Joe watched as Aurimas set his gun on the floor and thought he knew what he was doing, preparing to give up. He also saw that his judgement had been correct and his dad was heading closer to him and Tracey than he was to the front door. He noticed his dad let go of the sack with his right hand and begin to walk almost sideways with his right hand now out in front of him acting as a buffer and searching for the door. It looked like a natural thing to do from Joe's perspective as he knew his father couldn't see, but he was sure it looked odd to the rest of the customers in the bank. He looked back to Aurimas, thinking fast. He looked to the door, then back to Aurimas.

"Pin," he said through his mike, which was still tucked under his mask, "a quarter left then four to the door."

He saw Aurimas hesitate, but then move as he had instructed. He looked back to his dad who was almost heading straight for him and was thinking how to signal to him to turn right when Tracey coughed. It was a fake sort of cough and Joe wondered if anyone else would pick that up. Then he got a sort of an answer as his dad changed direction, now heading for the door. He had obviously picked up Tracey's signal.

Aurimas was at the door now and pulled it open. The sirens got louder as the noise flooded in along with the warm air.

Ray heard the rush of the sirens and the feel of the warm air and it too gave him a baring that he was heading in the right direction. He walked on, speeding up slightly as fast as he could, trailing the sack behind him. In a few seconds he was there. He bumped his left shoulder on the doorway again as he went through, but he didn't care. Outside he took care this time to start counting and used the doorway as a guide to line himself up to where he hoped Colin would be parked as arranged.

He paused and spoke quietly over his shoulder, "Terry, Aurimas you both there?"

"Yes," said Aurimas, Ray could hear the nerves in his voice.

"Almost there," said Ray in an effort to help. But the sirens were squealing now although he got the sense that they weren't in the street yet as the sound, although loud as sirens were, felt like it still had buildings between them.

"One, two, three," he counted, trying his best to focus on taking measured steps.

"Four, five, six, seven, eight," he heard someone shout "stop, stop police," but whoever it was also sounded some distance away.

"Nine, ten," he slowed and pushed his right foot forward keeping it to the ground trying to feel for the curb. His toe felt the edge and told him where the curb was. He reached forward and was grateful to feel the back of a vehicle. He used his hand to trace along its rear door and then up the side. He found the side door and pulled it open, sliding it back for Aurimas and Terry to get in. He then moved forward to the front door, pulled it open and got ready to jump in. He heard someone get in, wasn't sure if it was Terry or Aurimas and so asked, "All OK?"

Terry's voice came back at him, almost right there beside him, "I wouldn't go as far as that," he said, then jumped in to the back and slid the door closed.

Ray stepped in to the front seat and dragged the sack in to the footwell. As he reached to close the door he said, "Go, go go."

Chapter Thirty-Five

Tenerife, Canary Islands
Monday 25th October 2021

"Stop, stop, police," Sasha shouted. He was running fast now and as he ran he brought his gun up. His mind was running through his options and his training. He watched as a man dressed as Santa headed towards the back of the yellow people carrier he had seen pull up and park only moments ago. What puzzled him was that the guy was walking, not running, and he was walking taking slow deliberate steps. Following behind him was a tall bowling pin and some sort of white furry animal. He was wondering if his first suspicions were wrong and this was something harmless. A stunt of some sort. Or a promotional event. His uncertainty made him pause. The last thing he wanted to do was to start shooting to find out later that it had all been innocent. Wrong decisions like that cost lives and ended careers. He lowered his gun so that it was no longer pointing at anyone or anything.

He continued to think, considering the situation as he close down the distance. No matter what was going on here they still needed to stop as he had ordered them to do exactly that. And they could clearly see that he was a policeman. On the off chance that they hadn't heard him over the sirens, which were loud now and very close, he shouted again.

"Stop, stop police."

They ignored him.

By now Santa was making his way around the side of the vehicle and the bowling pin was at the back. The white furry thing then raised his arm to touch the back of the car and that's when Sasha noticed that he had something in his hand. Because of the costumes big furry paws, he couldn't fully make out what it was, but it did seem at first glance to be a gun.

"What the hell was this?" he thought. "Was this a robbery or some stupid stunt?" He shouted again.

"Police, stop, this is the police, stop now."

They ignored him again. His patience was running out, but he relied on his training to keep calm and not make any rash decisions.

The white furry thing was now around at the other side of the car and it didn't look like they were going to heed him and stop. He could shoot out the tyres. He surveyed both sides of the street and saw that there were other people about. Walking and sitting in street side cafes and bars. If he shot the tyres out he would have no control about what would happen to the car and the resulting accident and casualties, if any, would be all on him.

The car pulled off and headed away as the whine of the sirens increased considerably.

He tried to run faster, but by the time he reached the bank the car was turning at the end of the street and in a few seconds it was gone. Sasha would now just need to establish what exactly had went down here. He placed his gun back in its holster and headed for the door of the bank. Remembering the dog and the Mexican, he turned and shouted across the road, "Please wait there, I'll be back to talk to you both in a couple of minutes. Don't go anywhere." Then he opened the door and went in to the bank, but as he turned his back he didn't see Charlie giving him the two fingers and then shouting to Monty to hurry the fuck up!

After his dad had left the bank, Joe detached his mike from his head set and slipped it in to his pocket. He then took off his baseball cap; careful to keep the head set inside it and then put both in his back pack. Nobody was paying him any attention as they had all started to talk between themselves as the relief that this was now over sunk in. The three bank staff went back to behind the counter and Joe noticed that one of the girls was giving Fred a hard time about something. Joe could still hear the sirens and he was surprised that they hadn't arrived by now as for a few minutes there he thought sure his dad, Terry and Aurimas weren't going to make it out in time. He now just hoped that the police hadn't stopped them as they tried to get away.

"You OK," he asked Tracey. She blew out her cheeks, "just about," she didn't want to say too much as she didn't know who was close and could hear them. For now they still needed to play their roles as just two innocent bank customers.

The door to the bank opened and a policeman entered. "Good morning folks," he said, "firstly is everyone OK? And can someone please tell me what has just gone on here."

There was an explosion of voices in answer to his question.

George Michael's number one fan stepped forward and said, "Santa and his crew have just robbed the fucking bank."

Fliss tutted about the foul language.

Brinie said, "Oh by Jesus are we glad to see you," she crossed herself, "thank the lord the guards are here."

Oswaldo said, "Yes officer, three armed men have just robbed the bank."

"They made us sing songs," said Claire.

"Christmas songs," offered Sandra.

"And ones about Jesus?" said Pierre.

"Do you think we'll be able to claim for compensation," asked Michael.

"Look," said Fliss pointing, "One of them has left their gun there."

Amongst all the wall of words, Sasha had picked up what Fliss had said and followed her direction to the floor over near the far wall and yes indeed there was a gun lying there. Sasha walked over to look at it. He didn't want to lift it as he had no snap on gloves with him and no evidence bags. But he also didn't want to just leave it lying there in case it was loaded it posed a serious health and safety threat, and if he didn't sort it and neutralise it then he would be liable for the consequences. He removed a handkerchief from his pocket, shook it out to unfold it and used it to pick up the gun. He looked at it closer and a slow puzzled look came over his face.

Joe witnessed this and he almost laughed. He could see that the policeman had recognised that the gun was a toy.

Petra had now come out from behind the counter and was speaking to the policeman, "Excuse me Sir, my name is Petra and I'm the supervisor on duty here at the bank." So in other words, you need to be talking to me.

Joe's phone beeped and he removed it from his pocket to read the message. It said, "Where's your dad?" The text was from Colin. Joe looked outside and saw that there was now another people carrier parked there. This one was silver and it had tinted windows, which stopped him from seeing inside. He checked the time on his phone and saw it was now twenty two minutes past ten. Joe sent a quick text back, "I thought he was with you?"

Several seconds later his phone beeped again, "No. I'm waiting here."

Joe looked up and checked what was happening now inside the bank. He didn't want to say too much on his phone as with more detail these messages could be somewhat incriminating. He text back trying his best to be as vague as possible. "Left here five mins ago. Got a lift."

A text came back almost instantly, "Oh shit, I was late,

Got held up."

In normal circumstances Joe would be looking for Terry to start the banter to Colin for being, yet again, late. But on this occasion thinking about Terry, or any kind of banter, didn't register in Joe's mind.

"What's wrong?" whispered Tracey.

Joe bent over so that he was close to Tracey's ear and said quietly, "I think they've just got in to the wrong get away car."

Tracey closed her eyes and swore, just the way that Terry liked it, and just the way the Irish do, "Oh holy fewk!"

> "Get away, get away, get away, get away, get away, get away, get away,
> My daddy was a bank robber,
> But he never hurt nobody,
> He just loved to live that way,
> And he loved to steal your money,
> Hey,
> Run, rabbit run,
> Brrp, strike out boys, for the hills."
>
> *The Clash*

The End (For Now)

To Be Continued

Available worldwide online and from all good bookstores

www.facebook.com/mtp.agency

@mtp_agency

www.ingramcontent.com/pod-product-compliance
Lightning Source LLC
LaVergne TN
LVHW041625060526
838200LV00040B/1444